The Summer After

A NOVEL

CHANDRA HOFFMAN

Author of *Chosen* and *What Pretty Gets You*

FIFTH
GENERATION

This book is a work of fiction. Names, characters, places, and incidents are either the product of the author's imagination or are used fictitiously. Any resemblance to actual persons living or dead, business establishments, events, or locales, is entirely coincidental.

CONTENT WARNING: This book contains mature language, scenes and themes which may be disturbing to some readers.

All rights reserved. In accordance with the US Copyright. No part of this book may be reproduced in any manner whatsoever without written permission, except in the case of brief quotations in critical articles or reviews. For information, address Fifth Generation Publishing, PO Box 801, Bryn Athyn, PA 19009 or info@5genpress.com.

First Edition

The Summer After
1st Edition © 2021 by Chandra Hoffman
Fifth Generation Publishing
Edited by Romy Sommer
Cover Design: Asya Blue Design
Author photo: Robin Trautmann

e-ISBN 978-1-7367258-2-5
ISBN 978-1-7367258-3-2

DEDICATION

---

for J
because once we have slept on an island

PRELUDE

The night their phone call was cut short by Jack's death, Juliet cooked breakfast for dinner. She poured pancakes and fried sizzling, thick-cut butcher's bacon in her grandmother's cast iron pan for their children. After, she read three chapters of *Pippi Longstocking* aloud before letting them fall asleep on either side of her in the master bed. If Jack cared to sleep alone with her, if he intended to slide his hands under her T-shirt and use his trademark back-of-the-neck kisses to start something, he could make the effort to move them when he came home.

He called her just before midnight on his long commute with the usual command: "Talk to me, Jules, keep me awake."

Later, she would think that she should have asked where he was. But would his answer have meant anything? Lately, 'client meetings' translated into everything from Seven Rivers Links to the craps table at Ballys. If she had known his location, would they have been able to find him soon enough to save him?

Instead, they argued about their daughter's chickens, two black Australorps and six silkie bantams, that were proving to be excellent escape artists with a penchant for roosting on the arms of Juliet's grandmother's wooden rocking chair.

"I agreed to a gentlemen's farm, not chickens crapping all over the front porch!"

"What does it matter when you're not here?" she threw the next jab, but he dodged, ducking out with a sweeping, somber statement in what she called his, 'for the public radio news audience' voice:

"I'm trapped in the conundrum of the American dream, Jules. There's no way for me to be with you and the kids and make the money to support you at the same time."

"We can't get rid of the chickens!" Juliet steered Jack back to the topic at hand. "The kids will be devastated!" Without realizing those might be the last words she ever spoke to her husband—apt, true, because Simon and Sonnet had been devastated,

i

but not because they lost their chickens.

"I don't want to fight tonight," Jack sighed, his voice unusually heavy and sad. There was a pause, and she knew before he said it what he would say next, what he always said before hanging up, "Tell the kids I—"

Interrupted by the screech of rubber on road, the horrible crunching of metal and shattering glass. Jack's voice, a strangely high-pitched scream of terror. And, too quickly, a whooshing sound, impossible to discern whether it was wind or water at the time—later, she would know it was the brackish ocean rushing in—and a hissing, the seconds ticking in time to the popping of the dying engine.

"Jack!" she screamed his name three more times before the phone went dead.

Juliet clutched her cell phone in one hand and ran, her bare feet slapping the cold, scuffed wooden stairs of their farmhouse, to the kitchen phone, the original rotary one they had decided to keep for folly, her fingers jerking around the circle, dialing 9-1-1.

She had very little information for the dispatcher. She told him the only thing she knew to be true: somewhere between New York, New Jersey and Pennsylvania, her husband was in trouble.

BOOK ONE

June-July

CHAPTER 1

Dean

When Dean first steps out of the 737's door at Owen Roberts Airport on Grand Cayman, he briefly mistakes the humidity for exhaust blasting from another plane's jets. This worries him. On this small island, do airplanes just taxi around the stunted runway haphazard? He wonders if what is left of his fragmented family might be in danger—they cannot afford more tragedy.

"I've never exited a plane by stairs before." Dean tries to make a joke out of it to his daughter and the passengers around them, but he is thinking: How primitive is an island that doesn't have a jetway? What do they do when it rains? He hefts Owen to his hip for his safety, though he is already overloaded, their carry-on bags draped over his shoulders—the family's lone pack mule.

"Dad, come on." Behind him, Holly is nudging, anxious to get going. She thinks they have come here for a vacation. Unfortunately, this is not a trip for umbrella drinks and snorkeling and sandcastles. This is Dean answering last Sunday's heart-stopping, crackling international phone call at four in the morning, blinking, bleary-eyed, and scrambling for his glasses and a pen to scribble down the facts:

accident
Luc, emerg. room, Cayman Islands, Hospital!
Luc vitals = good, poss concussion, stitches? but ok
Girl, (kiwi?) coma?
Blood alcohol test pending
police invest. driver of vehicle???
need: passports, call Cayman Airways, flight thru NC or PHL Fri/Sat?

This trip is about a father coming to rescue his oldest son.

The airport's pitched pole-and-thatch roof looks unnervingly antiquated. By the runway, chickens scratch in the dirt and a green iguana sunbathes on the rocks. Dean follows the string of people exiting the plane, thinking what a sad, small trio his family makes now. A year ago, there were five of them.

He shepherds Holly and Owen through the lines inside the airport, pausing over the question from the cat-faced woman perched on her stool at Immigration.

"I'm sorry?" he says, missing the question in her thick accent.

"You left ah blank. Ree-son for ya stay."

"Oh," Dean scrambles, sweat running down his side where Owen is clamped on, refusing to get down—why hadn't he brought a stroller like a sensible parent? Why hadn't Holly reminded him?

"Um, well, last October, my wife died—she'd had cancer so it wasn't unexpected, but hard, still," Dean can feel Holly's pleading eyes on his face but does not look down to meet them, "and I thought the children would be better off with a change of scenery. A friend of mine, Tony, from college, he lives down here, and he suggested we come to the Cayman Islands."

He does not mention that his oldest, his teenage son, Luc came here six months before, that he was on a work permit for Tony in the dive shop at Rum Point, up until what happened last Saturday night. He wonders if she sees their last name, if it means anything to her, if Luc Alder is flagged on a Do Not Fly list somewhere. Tony has told him that the police are holding Luc's American passport; he is not allowed to leave the island while the investigation is pending.

Dean plows on, his eyes scanning the posters for tourist activities on the walls behind the woman, "So we thought, what a nice place for a vacation. We're renting a cottage in Cayman Kai and I'm hoping—"

"Lee-shuh?" she cuts him off.

"What?" Dean shifts Owen to his other side.

"Re-CREE-ay-SHUN?"

"Yes," Dean answers, and she stamps their passports for thirty days, waving for the next person in line.

Holly pushes past him to the luggage carousel. She is like an adolescent swan, all neck and legs, with a little braided rope belt woven through her white denim pants, barely holding them up on her nonexistent hips, and her bulging Hello Kitty backpack. What she has stuffed in there, he has no idea. Holly does so many things for herself, brushing and braiding her straight blonde hair, packing her own carry-on and the diaper bag. To his chagrin, she does lots of other things for Owen too. Back home, friends have been calling her "the little mother" for years, even before Amélie was gone. Though they mean it as a compliment of how responsible and nurturing his daughter is, it irks Dean. He wants Holly to be a girl, and at twelve, time is running out. These are not the luxuries of a child whose mother was diagnosed with cancer when she was sixteen months old, whose father later rashly decided in a giddy period of remission that they should conceive a "celebration of life", tossing caution and birth control literally to the wind.

This celebration is Owen, who hasn't slept once in the ten hours since they left Michigan, when Dean lifted him sweaty and sleep-heavy out of the master bed in the starry pre-dawn. Owen didn't close his eyes on the drive from Saline to Detroit International, or the first flight to Philadelphia, or the final one to Grand Cayman. Dean knows he still needs naps, but Owen's reluctance to give in to sleep, a constant fear of missing something, is legendary. The downside: he is frequently overtired and grouchy, perceived as more difficult than he really is. Worse, Owen often falls asleep for the night during dinner, mid-chew, and wakes up starving at 4 am.

Before, Luc used to take videos of this on his phone, Owen's head lolling around with chicken nugget bits in his mouth, eyes slow-blinking, until his forehead came down to the kitchen table with a thump. That was last summer, when they still laughed, when they all told each other Amélie was only out of remission, that she would beat it again. The night before the first gamma knife treatment, Luc and Holly showed these videos to Amélie at the hospital, and they laughed about how one of the sleeping-chewing-baby-brother-clips might win them a spot on America's Funniest Home Videos. Luc and Holly liked to fantasize about what to do with the twenty-five thousand dollar prize, but Amélie insisted it would go into college funds, or educational travel. What would she think now, if she knew her oldest son were living abroad, but as a high school dropout?

Customs is their last stop in the airport, and then they are done. Owen lets his sister carry him, Holly's hip jutting out at a 45-degree angle to hold him up while Dean maneuvers the luggage cart out into the blinding sunshine.

There it is again, that slap of wet furnace air. Good thing he'd taken Tony's emailed advice and packed nothing but bathing suits and short sleeves. He wishes for a moment that this trip is what he told the woman at Immigration—fun in the sun, to help his children get over the death of their mother. His teeth grit into their grooves as a flash of anger at Luc, at circumstances, at himself, washes over him.

We cannot afford more tragedy.

"You made it, man." Tony gets up from where he was leaning against an over-sized cement planter, loping over to pull Dean into a hug with lots of hard shoulder slapping. The last time they had all been together was their ten-year college reunion, after the mastectomy, when Amélie was in remission, and wore a slinky black dress over her chemo-skinny frame and drank three glasses of wine and danced with her arms over her head for the cover band's fast songs. She'd surprised Dean by pulling him away from chatting at the bar, looping her arms around his neck like a lover's for "Wild Horses."

Since then, Tony has shaved his tan head to disguise a receding hairline and grown a silver-flecked goatee. In surf shorts and mirrored sunglasses, he looks younger than they are. Dean glances down; noting Tony is actually barefoot, that he has come to the airport to pick them up without any shoes at all.

"Truck's running," Tony says, tugging the luggage cart out of Dean's hands. "Look at these little ankle biters. Not so little anymore, eh? How old are you, eighteen? Twenty-one?" He winks at Holly. "Just throw everything in the back."

Surreptitiously, Dean glances at the white pick-up. It is a Ford, older, salt-burnt and rusted on the bottom, the White Beaches Dive Shop logo in red on the door. On the premise of walking around to the other side, Dean checks the front for damage. The left fender is dented and hangs crooked, like a dead tree branch not yet fallen, but it is difficult to tell if this is recent. How many vehicles does the dive shop have? Dean wonders. Would the Royal Cayman Islands Police be keeping the truck for evidence, like on CSI? Or is this the one his son may or may not have been driving late last Saturday night?

"Hop in. Little guy can ride on your lap," Tony calls from the other side of the truck. "Cops don't care here. It's safe, man, just one main road." He seems to have no sense of the irony of this statement.

Against his judgment, feeling miles outside his comfort zone (but when had he been there at all recently?) Dean gets in up front, Holly wedged between them, Owen on his lap. His car seat is like an overturned turtle, useless, in the truck bed with their bags. Dean is aching to ask about Luc, about the details of the accident, but not in front of the littles.

"No change," Tony says quietly as he starts the engine, the truck's air conditioner roaring to life, and Dean knows exactly what he means: the victim from the accident, the girl who was in the truck when Luc may or may not have been driving, is alive six days later, but still unconscious. Medically-sedated, he tells himself, since coma sounds like a soap opera. No change.

"You and Luc ever get a chance to talk?" Dean asks, as direct as he can be in front of Holly and Owen.

"Nah," Tony reddens under his tan. "Time's not been right, man."

Dean thinks, but does not say, Luc has been here for six months.

"It's so beautiful here," Holly says, hands folded carefully between her narrow knees.

"This is nothing," Tony assures them. "Bad government planning put the worst shit out by the airport, the industrial park, the dump, so it's the first thing folks see when they land. Wait 'til we get out to the other side of the island. You're going to love it—dead quiet." Tony stops, his last words hanging awkwardly in the air.

"It's good to be here," Dean rescues Tony. No need for people to worry about what they can say in front of them. They've had months of that back in Michigan. "Thanks for coming to get us."

"Yeah, I just wish the circumstances were better."

Dean nods.

It had been Tony's idea. After Amélie died in October, Dean was touched and surprised at how often his old roommate checked in on him. They had been close, when they were twenty, but not since. Those days last fall when darkness came at four thirty and the cold settled over Michigan and ruby-colored glasses of wine and History channel documentaries were all that passed the long nights, Dean was grateful for the hopeful ping of WhatsApp, an electronic connection, Tony checking in at one, two, three in the morning.

When Dean wrote to him about Luc, how Dean could not physically get him out of bed for his last semester of high school, about the parade of girls sneaking into the house, shaking Luc's metal bedframe and waking up Owen, Tony didn't hesitate to offer.

TonytheDeepDiver: Send him down here. I'll get him certified— he can work for me at the dive shop. Get his mind off things. I'll drag his ass out of bed, run him ragged, good hard physical work. Nothing like being on the ocean.

Dean Alder, Prof: What about school? Shouldn't I make him graduate?

TonytheDeepDiver: He can get his GED any time. You got to get him out of that house. Away from the memories. Hell, you all should come.

It was a regular offer: Come to the islands, get away from it all.

Dean Alder, Prof: Maybe when the semester is over. June?
Well, Dean thinks wryly, they're here now.

⟋

"So, are there any kids at Rum Point?" Holly asks.

"You know, an American lady just came to the cottages a few weeks ago, two kids, the boy's around your age. Actually," Tony turns to Dean and smirks, "she's a bit of a fox."

Dean tries not to sigh, his molars fitting into their grooves. This is not what he is here for. Is there a specific time frame, an email thread he's not on, where all his friends and family decided when they should start setting him up with women? Because in the last two months, it's been an onslaught.

Dean looks out the window, about to ask how much longer the drive is. Luc was discharged from the hospital on Sunday afternoon, scratches and scrapes, concussion, Tony had said. Out of everyone in the accident, the two other White Beaches workers in the truck and the poor girl from New Zealand, Luc made out the best.

"But," Tony continues, "This chick is baggage city. A mess. Trust me. You don't want to go there, man." He drops his voice as though the kids won't be able to hear and raises his eyebrows for effect. "Tragedy, just like you: a widow."

CHAPTER 2

Dean

The first time Dean sees Juliet, he assumes she is a bikini-clad waitress, walking between the outdoor tables at Rum Point with what looks like a shiny tray held high over her head, spinning in a slow circle. If The Wreck Bar and surrounding beach weren't deserted, Dean is sure every eye would be on her; this arrow-thin, tan, dainty music box ballerina pirouetting in the sun.

Dean steps out of Tony's truck in the clothes he'd put on in the dark, cool dawn of late spring in Michigan, baggy khakis and a rumpled dress shirt he has to pull away from his body. It sucks back to his chest like a starfish, damp with sweat and humidity. Dean's knees ache from a morning of flying and nearly an hour crammed in the truck cab with Owen on his lap. He squints and notes that Tony wears sunglasses constantly. They are watching the same woman on the beach. Tony's gaze passes coolly over her and then he slams the truck door and claps Dean on the shoulder.

"Luc's out on the water. I told you I'd work him hard." Tony looks like he's expecting a compliment. "He'll be back around sunset."

But this is the difference between him and Tony: a father doesn't get woken up by a phone call that his son has been in a bad accident, doesn't drive to Detroit and stand in line for expedited passports, throw together suitcases, make phone calls to lawyers, and fly two thousand miles five days later to find the son in question is out on a boat in the middle of the ocean, taking tourists snorkeling. A father wants to see him, get his hands on him, even if it is to shake his skinny shoulders and scream,

"What in the hell were you thinking?"

"We'll stop at the bar for drinks before we head to the cottages." Tony leads the way into the dimly-lit, open-air thatch roof bar. "Leo likes to get folks hooked early, gives you something strong and complimentary now, then waters that shit down and charges a fortune for it. Come on, fruit punch for the kiddies!"

Dean stands in the doorway for a minute, taking in the view: the sun sparkling on the turquoise ocean, the pristine white beach, the brightly-painted picnic tables, the coconut palms and canopy of casuarinas. Two dark-haired children swing each other in a hammock strung between the trees. Dean has looked up the native birds in some of his mother's books and can easily identify the ching-chings and vireos hopping in the sand. A volleyball net waits for players and inviting ivory lawn chairs stretch the length of the beach. It is like stepping into a postcard from paradise.

Somewhere out there on the aqua water between him and the horizon is his son. Dean feels a flutter at being physically closer to Luc than he has been in six months, followed by the flood of anxiety over what he has flown here to deal with. In person, he believes, Luc will tell him what happened, the truth. Dean swallows his panic and thinks, *And then they can go from there.*

The woman with her arms over her head swirls in a circle, her sun-brown limbs doing a strange, staggering dance, like a drunken sea bird. Dean realizes what she is holding is not an empty bar tray, but a glinting silver Mac laptop. She is twisting with the keyboard held over her head.

"Juliet!" the bartender calls from inside. "Come plug in here—I've got a direct line to Cable and Worthless! Only thing you'll get out there is a fried motherboard and funky tan lines."

Dean turns and blinks in the comparable darkness of the bar, a headache starting behind his eyes, a grating dryness in his throat. A cool drink would be nice. He can't help but notice that the woman has followed him in and is plugging her laptop into the bartender's connection cable nearby, pulling up a wooden stool painted like a tangerine starfish. She leans forward and props her elbows on the heavily-lacquered bar. Her bare feet arch on the stool's crossbar.

"Who's hungry?" Tony asks.

"Just the drinks," Dean says quickly. He is still stinging from not having packed food for traveling—eighteen dollars of McMuffins and hash browns and chocolate milk for breakfast in the Detroit airport terminal and then, when everyone was hungry again, mid-flight, eight dollars apiece for sandwiches off the snack tray; only two meals under his belt and he's already spent almost fifty bucks.

"Dad?" Holly peers up at him in Amélie's Jackie O shades. "You're making the Face. Relax. We're here."

Dean pretends to be reading the chalkboard littered with Stupid Tourist Questions—*Can you swim under the island? Is there shopping at Stingray City?*—but really he is gawking at the drink prices. Sixteen dollars for a piña colada?

"Hey," Tony calls to the woman on her computer. "The kid speaks the truth. Relax." He points to one of the many hand-painted wooden signs—NO FROWNING ALLOWED, YOU'RE IN DA ISLANDS, MON!

She ignores Tony, typing away on her laptop with frequent looks over her shoulder out the doorway to where the children are swinging each other raucously high.

"Hot," Owen whimpers, sweat beading his upper lip, likely stinging the anxiety sores he's picked into his face the last few months. These deep red craters, along with his difficulty napping, have made him unpopular at the university day care.

"Yeah, that's the one bummer about the summer here. Hot as a Swedish porno." Tony glances to see if the woman is listening. "Still, too. Around the end of May, the wind just dies—I mean, disappears—and the temps go up around the nineties, hundred in the day. 'Ninety-six degree—ees, in da shade,'" Tony breaks into song before adding soberly. "Let's hope you folks got one of the cottages with working AC."

"Listen to this," the woman says to the bartender, reading aloud from her computer. "I've started getting these quotes—they're called Daily Inspirations, but they come from a Gmail account, and they don't have any ads, so I'm pretty sure it's my brother or his passive-aggressive wife sending them."

"Oh yeah?" Leo says and Dean can tell he is a seasoned bartender, good at making people feel interesting while he continues to fill orders. He's even mastered the eyebrow arch, which he tosses Tony's way when she's not looking.

"They're the type who believe whatever they're doing is the best: Anusara yoga, gluten-free, colon cleansing. Now it looks like they found literary inspiration, or some hokey spiritualism. Typical older brother, thinks he knows what's best. Listen to this one: What we call the beginning is often the end. And to make an end is to make a beginning. The end is where we start from."

"T.S. Eliot," Dean says, and for the first time, she looks right at him. Her eyes are the pale amber of a Hefeweizen and freckles dot her nose like those painted on Holly's American Girl doll. Dean can feel Tony watching them.

"Yes," she says, smiling at Dean; white, straight teeth. "Well done."

"I think you got to hang it up, Julie. Put the laptop away," the bartender says. "Remember, no worries." He slides the fruit punches to Holly and Owen. There is a sign behind him that says: It's five o'clock somewhere, complete with fluorescent pink flip flops, a Scarlett Macaw and a flamingo, though Dean knows from his books that neither of these species are native to the Cayman Islands.

"You guys think I'm a cliché, right? High-strung American, can't relax? I was fine with giving up my cell phone, but I need to be able to read my emails! The cottages are supposed to come with free Internet! I have a hundred-year-old farmhouse halfway through renovations, with the roof practically off the kitchen, and my house sitter complaining the toilets and appliances are turning orange, that there's some kind of metal in the well water, and she wants to bill me for her flats of Evian and her ruined clothes…"

Leo pours her a diet Coke. His back to Juliet, Leo winks at Dean while passing him a Corona with a wedge of lime.

Dean clears his throat, wonders if he should tell her that adding salt, a softener system, can help with iron in the water, if that's the problem. Her eyes pass over him and she continues.

"And now this! After barely speaking to me for nine years, my brother is sending me some new daily inspirational quote du jour. This is yesterday's," she scrolls back and reads, *"It is human nature to want to go back and fix things or change things that we regret."*

Her eyes slide to Dean, and there is a pause while everyone waits for him to provide the source. When he doesn't, she turns to Leo.

"So if these are from my brother, does that sound like an apology?"

"I don't get paid enough to interpret foreign emails or get in the middle of family dramas." Leo laughs. "You sure you don't want some Cap'n Morgan in that diet Coke?"

It would be an absurd question in the middle of the day, anywhere but here: Rum Point. She shakes her head, reads the Eliot quote again, and wonders aloud if it is literal or existential.

Tony snorts. "My opinion, not that anyone asked, is I'd love to have your rich-lady problems. I should introduce you properly to Dean, my buddy from college here." Tony whacks him on the shoulder. "He's a shrink from the Midwest. Maybe you should schedule an appointment, talk about last weekend? He'll have a line out the door a mile long. Folks go a little crazy here in hurricane season."

Juliet does not answer Tony. She stands up and closes the laptop with a loud snap and picks up her straw hat.

"Thanks." She nods coolly to Leo, jerking the cord out of the back of her computer. Like seasoned tennis spectators, Holly and Owen's heads swivel to Tony, to see how he will respond, but he is bent over his beer, peeling the shimmery Red Stripe label. Dean wonders if he is thinking of the girl from New Zealand in the hospital, of the pending police investigation.

Juliet walks to the doorway, her computer under her arm, the slim curves of her body silhouetted by the sun on the ocean. At the picnic table behind her, the two children are feeding their leftovers to the striped cats weaving under the bench.

"Sonny, Simon, siesta! Let's get out of the sun!"

Leo slides a bill in front of Dean. He exhales when he sees the words "Welcome to paradise!" scrawled across the mint green paper in place of numbers.

On the stereo, Bob Marley is singing how every little thing is going to be alright.

Tony leans over the bar and cranks it, making Juliet whirl around.

"Island time, Jules!" Tony booms.

"Is that all you guys have got? Your answer for everything? Rasta-wisdom?" She turns to leave. Dean feels a prickle of resentment at being lumped in with them. He's certainly not convinced that travel industry taglines and Jah-inspired sentiment are any kind of words to live by. Look where it has gotten Luc.

"Nice to meet you," Juliet adds over her shoulder to Dean.

Dean watches through the open doorway as she collects her children and walks them across the sandy road to where Tony had pointed out the cluster of rental cottages. He recognizes two things about Juliet—the way her eyes scan, swivel, head bobbing. He knows just what she is doing, the mark of a good parent: counting heads, surveying the area, making sure everyone is safe and accounted for.

But there is something else: an otherness that clings to her like an early morning Michigan fog. Perhaps it is the way her shoulders rest on her body, a cocktail of tension and exhaustion, sadness. Like him, she is wearing a cape of grief. Dean sits up straighter on the bar stool, hoping his can't be seen, or if it is, it will be mistaken for a mantle of responsibility.

He looks past her to the glittering ocean. He needs to speak to his son.

CHAPTER 3

Dean

It was Amélie who believed in superstitious things like fate. She was the staunch pusher of reincarnation and parallel lives, insisting that no spider or centipede in the bathtub could be crushed, that everything, even metastatic cancer, happened for a reason.

So why, Dean wonders as Tony drives them across the sandy road to the rental cottages, does he keep thinking about the American woman in the wide-brimmed hat and black bikini? Why does he keep picturing her hands on the shoulders of her children as she shepherded them across the street? Why does he keep replaying the moment Juliet looked right at him and said, "Well done," because he recognized the T.S. Eliot quote from a poster in the faculty lounge?

"Those are the kids I was telling you about," Tony says to Holly, nodding to where Juliet and a skinny boy and little girl just a year or two older than Owen had crossed the empty, sand road that separates the cottages from the Rum Point resort and White Beaches Watersports. The truck bumps over a rut and the maraschino cherry bobs in Holly's sweating plastic glass of punch. Tony turns into a nearly empty parking lot, utility lines snaking among the palm trees from the lone pole on the street to the roofs of the four white cottages. "That's her, the wealthy widow."

Not interested, Dean thinks. He knows a few women like Juliet back home— high-maintenance, Pilates addicts, let their babies cry it out while they watch *Real Housewives*, pay their husband's money to a Mercedes-SUV-driving interior decorator to tell them how their McMansion should look and short-tip the women from Vietnam at their weekly pedicures. Women like Sherry Sanders, the mom who comes to Holly's field hockey games in her LL Bean folding chair and instead of watching their daughters and cheering, scrolls through her phone, sipping off a Starbucks.

"They look like nice kids," Holly says gamely. "I can tell we'll be good friends."

This worries Dean — Holly's quickness to fall hard in friendships, how vulnerable she makes herself. These kids, vacationers, won't be Holly's friends. And Dean's not staying on the island longer than it takes to get Luc sorted out. Back home, Dean should have signed Holly up for summer camp, something more stable, but he'd panicked at the prices and missed the deadlines, another thing to heap on the regret pile.

Luc is the opposite of Holly. He already shows the signs of an early womanizer, the careful detachment of a beautiful boy grieving the loss of his first love: his mother. In the weeks after Amélie's death, there had been no shortage of girls with questionable self-esteem willing to help Luc through the loss with horizontal therapy. And loud—what was with the moaning and yipping? How come teenage girls all sounded like seasoned porn stars these days? Dean sighs. He had been so sure he was doing the right thing by sending Luc down here to Tony.

At least for Owen, he can be everything, pour his deep well of love and nurture into their last-chance-that-never-really-was.

At Amélie's first ultrasound with Owen, the OB used a pen to point out spots, several big enough to be considered masses on her uterus, evidence of breast cancer's insidious spread.

"I would advise terminating the pregnancy, getting on an aggressive treatment plan of dual chemo and radiation." Amélie's obstetrician said, while paging Dr. J. It was a testimony to their long relationship with him that he had come right down from the oncology floor to consult. Amélie's OB had given up her desk to him and was clicking her pen anxiously over by the door. In her world, an ultrasound was supposed to reveal potential, the unfurling aqua-baby of life. These beginnings were not supposed to be buffered by malignant masses that indicated an inevitable end.

Amélie, who had taken the news that she was out of remission again with a thinning of her already pencil-drawn lips, shook her head sharply. Her short hair had grown back in curlier than ever, threaded with silver, like a lacy *mantilla*.

"You're saying stage four. Uterine cancer, now. And you think it might be other places."

"We're always suspicious of the lymph system," Dr. J had said. "When the origin is the breast…" he stopped, started again. "We took as much lymphatic tissue as we could when we did the mastectomy, but we all knew there were margins. The skin cancer that developed at the incision sites was not a good sign."

Amélie snorted peevishly.

"You've already gotten my breasts," she said, her French accent thicker than ever. This was a sign, Dean knew, of barely-contained emotion. He placed his hand over hers on the vinyl armrest of the chair. It was supposed to have been such a happy day—they had just seen images of their unborn son, rolling and swimming in his obsidian maternal sea. "You won't take the baby. We'll wait. What's four more months, no?"

Could he love her more? Dean had wondered then, flooded with relief that she wouldn't terminate. It had been his idea, his hand that tossed the birth control out the bedroom window that night. Maybe it was his Catholic roots, or maybe it was that the baby represented another precious human tether for their relationship.

But his relief was immediately replaced by the sensation of the floor beneath their feet opening up—he found himself staring, terrified, into a black abyss: the prospect of losing Amélie, of being a single father to three children.

⌒

"Dad?" Holly nudges him. The truck has stopped outside a cluster of four white cottages, their shutters and trim painted colors that Amélie would have derisively called '80s Miami'. He still does this—less than he used to—imagining Amélie's reactions to everything from the kitchen knife infomercial helping him pass the night to Luc's latest girl's lower-back dolphin tattoo peeking out from under his rumpled sheets.

On Dean's shoulder, Owen is asleep at last, a damp circle of drool on his one nice shirt. Dean shifts Owen to his left arm so he can use his right for carrying suitcases. Months of toting a thirty-pound toddler have made the bicep of his non-dominant arm stronger, something Dean means to balance out whenever he can hit the gym again. It's been too long, too many comfort casseroles from the freezer, cakes in the faculty room at work, breakfasts from a drive-thru on the way to the university.

Dean and Holly take quick stock of the grounds while Tony unlocks the cottage. Through the palm trees, there's a skinny finger of water that qualifies the cottages as "waterfront," and on cement footings, a blue-tiled oval pool. From the cottage two doors down, the one with the towels over the railing and an abundance of potted plants, he hears the sounds of children. He instinctively straightens under the weight of bags and toddler. When he double checks the jauntiness to his heartbeat, a tentative thumping under his son's head, he realizes it is because this means Juliet, the woman from the bar, lives right there.

Inside the cottage, the air is sour and wet. Dean fiddles with the air conditioners and there is a blast of wheezy, lukewarm air that reeks of old water.

"I warned you," Tony says with a chuckle, as though Dean chose the cottage with faulty HVAC on purpose. Together, they open all the louvers and windows, and turn the three ceiling fans on high.

"Will Luc stay with us?" Holly wonders—there are two ground floor bedrooms, one with a king size bed and the other with two twins. Since December, Luc has been living in a studio apartment, down the beach near Tony's with five other White Beaches employees. Dean has a mental image of this situation from the infrequent phone calls with few details: a lottery system for real beds and shower time, sheets hung from the ceiling for privacy, a fridge that holds more beer than food.

Dean doesn't answer. Holly has unzipped their suitcases and she and Owen are flinging the contents around the living room in search of bathing suits.

"Hey, before I get back, a word?" Tony nods his head to the narrow kitchen, and everything in Dean tenses—this is not a conversation he is sure he's ready to have. The cottage owners have picked a white-on-white theme for the kitchen. White tile, white pressed board cabinets and counter, white appliances—only the plastic spatula sticking out of a white ceramic pot has yellowed to beige. The size and color scheme reminds Dean of the family kitchen on the hospice floor.

"Listen, I have to warn you, when you talk to Luc," Tony says, "we just got some bad news this morning. Looks like there's more than just a girlfriend in a coma."

"Girlfriend?" Never, in the eight months since Amélie, has Luc had an actual girlfriend.

"It's a song. Remember, The Smiths?"

Dean stands there, feeling the blood pool in the hands that hang by his sides.

"Anyway, there are new allegations, after the investigation. The police suspect there is another victim, that whoever was driving also might have hit someone."

"What? How do they know?"

"It's not for sure," Tony holds up both hands and waves the air down with them, as though Dean is getting riled, when instead he feels completely drained. "Cops out here are a three-ring circus with no ringleader. Someone probably saw too many episodes of *Law and Order*. No formal charges have actually been filed."

A steady line of tiny ants stream in through the window over the sink, zigzagging along the counter.

"They say there was blood on the hood, and some, uh, matter on the outside of the windshield. It doesn't jive with the report of one driver and three passengers, where at least two if not three of them were likely riding in the bed of the truck."

Owen has come to stand in the doorway of the kitchen, naked from the waist down.

"Who do they think it is?"

"Well, that's the problem—there's no sign of another victim. And nobody has reported anyone missing. It's not helping that all the kids are claiming amnesia. Police are suspicious that whoever was driving the truck knew enough to," Tony glances at Owen, swallows and drops his voice even lower, "take care of the body."

Dean sags against the bright white counter where the galley kitchen walls are shifting like a funhouse, closing in on him.

CHAPTER 4

Dean

After Tony leaves, Dean is still numb. He lets Holly and Owen tug him out through their screen porch to the pool deck, where Juliet is spread out on a beach chair and her children are splashing in the shady, shallow end. The only other lounge chair is next to hers. Dean lowers himself into it, trying not to moan. His body feels like he hiked and swam all the way from Michigan, with two children and their belongings strapped to his back. A tension headache is twisting its way up his neck and tightening the muscles in his forehead.

"Long trip?" Juliet asks and Dean can only sigh.

"Really, help yourself, you can use any of these!" Holly offers grandly to Juliet's dark-haired younger girl, across the pool, showing off the basket of water toys she found in the cottage owner's storage closet. He could take this as a good sign, that she is not permanently damaged by the early loss of her mother, but he has to worry —is this more than just social? Is Holly attachment-deficient? Does she feel like she has to use extreme kindness to ingratiate herself to others?

"I see yours actually came with the things they're supposed to," Juliet says, and for a minute he thinks she's talking about children: generosity, compassion, and dimples, check-check-check.

But then he realizes she means the rental cottage: the beach toys.

"It looks like it," Dean mumbles, because he is noticing her legs. He tries not to, but they're naked, smooth and tan and lightly muscled, stretched out in front of her, crossed at the ankle.

It has been a long time since he has seen this much of any woman's body. Back at EMU, spring had been slow in coming, with students layered in jeans and hoodies and the ubiquitous UGG boots. The one date he had been on with Erika from the English department, she wore a turtleneck and high-waisted, swishy-sounding black pants that Dean's sister would have called "slacks."

On the round table beside Juliet's beach chair is a glass of ice water and three bottles of nail polish—her toenails are painted pale pink with crimson polka dots and when he checks over by the basket of beach toys, he sees her daughter's are the same. Okay, he thinks, not a weekly pedicure with underpaid immigrants, but polished. Amélie's toenails were unashamedly plain, knobbed and ridged, two of them permanently black from her years as a dancer, before Luc.

"Does your place have good Internet?" Juliet asks him.

"I don't know. I just got here, and I'm trying to escape all that."

This past week, he spent his sleepless nights searching for decent airfares and digging around the Internet:

—how long can a person stay in a coma?

—difference between real coma and medically induced coma?

—laws of Cayman Islands?

—DUI sentencing, British West Indies

—death penalty rulings in British protectorates?

When Tony left to go back to the resort, he promised he'd send Luc to the cottages as soon as the boat came in from their last trip. Sunset, he'd said. Dean checks the sun's position, just at the crest of the Norfolk pines on the finger of sand by the inlet. The air here feels oppressively heavy; Dean struggles for a deep breath.

Another victim? A missing person? When can we all go home?

The woman fills the air between them with small talk—her name is Juliet Wilde and her children are Simon and Sonnet, ages nine and five, almost six. They live in an old family farmhouse north of Philadelphia; she does not mention a job or a husband.

"And Tony said you're a therapist?"

"Um, no. I mean, I could be, I used to have a practice, but I'm a professor at Eastern Michigan University. Psychology."

"That must be nice, to have the summers off to spend with your family," she says and her eyes dart to the screened porch of his cottage, as though she is waiting for his wife to come out with trays of sandwiches and chips, a sarong wrapped around her waist.

So he tells her. Blurts it out really. When will it get easier, and why does he keep saying it to everyone he meets? "My wife died in October. Last October. Brain cancer."

"I'm so sorry," she murmurs, and then, "Simon! Get off her! You cannot climb on Sonny when she's in the water!"

"But we're in the shallow end," her son calls back.

"Off!"

Dean glances down. For the first time, he is glad that Owen is clingy. It makes him cautious, content to squat in the sand and stack up pieces of coral by the wheels of Dean's beach chair.

"Yes," he continues, because his story has a script and it is like an itch, a compulsion to make sure he does the whole thing. "She was diagnosed with breast cancer when she was only thirty-one. She had a double mastectomy and did everything right, chemo, radiation, diet. The doctors gave us decent odds, because she was young and relatively healthy. So we decided to have this little guy,"—*we*, he says, as though Amélie might have thought of the idea, might have done more than lay submissively beneath him that night— "And at our ultrasound, they found masses in her uterus." He can see across the pool that Holly is listening. Soon, she will create a distraction, but Dean has noticed women, especially ones around Juliet's age, like to hear this story. They nod along, mouth corners creasing in a show of sympathy, but it's a mask for their relief over someone else taking up the statistical margin for early-onset, aggressive, terminal breast cancer.

"Dad, watch!" Holly calls on cue and dives under, sticking her legs out in a perfect, toes-pointed handstand. And why shouldn't she? Among other things, her mother had been an accomplished dancer. Amélie always said she could have gone far with it if she hadn't gotten pregnant with Luc.

"Great!" he calls to Holly and wraps the story up. It's a funny thing, the hierarchy of tragedy—this story feels lighter, easier today, now that Luc's problems loom large.

"So, we're here on our own. I thought the kids could use a change of scenery, and Tony is a friend from college, got us a summertime rate on the cottage, so here we are."

He does not mention Luc, whose blood alcohol results are not back, who he spoke to briefly on the phone Tuesday night, short answers, "fine" and "I don't know." Like the rest of the White Beaches workers, he claims to have no memory of who was driving or any of what happened before the accident last Saturday night.

"How long are you here?" she asks.

"Um, undecided, at this point," Dean says, mentally ticking through the facts he knows. There were three others besides Luc in the truck when it wrecked. Dusty, the

Canadian supervisor who's worked for Tony for eight years; Darvin, a Jamaican who has been there a year; and the girl from New Zealand who has a nasty cut on her leg, who has turned her head once, but otherwise remains unconscious. Medically-sedated, due to swelling in her brain. Tony told him that all of the bodies were found scattered on the ground when the EMTs and police arrived on the scene, approximately fourteen minutes after the crash. And now the latest: another possible victim? Couldn't the blood on the windshield have been from the inside? Dean is grasping, he knows it. Sweat runs down his back like ticklish spider legs.

The heat is so overpowering Dean leans forward and reluctantly takes off his shirt, holding his abdominal muscles taut, hoping it's not obvious that the only rigorous exercise he has had in the past year was a short sprint after Owen in the Detroit airport this morning.

Juliet is looking at him expectantly; had she asked another question? Hadn't he answered?

"They're staying all summer!" Holly yells from where she and Juliet's son are doing handstands. "Can we?"

"All summer?" Dean asks Juliet instead of answering Holly.

"Probably," she says carefully. "Change of scenery as well. Last minute. My family sort of…insisted."

He waits, imagines she will tell him her story now, what Tony told him in the truck. This is the woman with the dead husband? But she doesn't say anything more. She turns her head out to the inlet of water.

"I miss running the most," she says. "My legs, at night, run circles in my sleep. Sometimes, when the kids sleep in my bed, I accidentally kick them."

"She does!" Simon yells from the shallow end. "You have to build a pillow wall or she nails you!"

This is how it's going to be, an understood that she is here alone, but the specifics won't be shared today. She plays it closer to the vest, and he wants to ask her how she does that, but he isn't supposed to know she has a story to tell.

"I haven't worked out since…" he trails off, thinks woefully of the softness of his midsection. It's not a paunch, but that's not far away. After the freezer casseroles ran out, it was easier to drive the kids through Burger King than actually make dinner. Before, years ago, he used to cook; a delicate *osso bucco* with risotto, and on weekends, when they were first together, he and Amélie and three-year-old Luc rolled their own sushi—his mother remarked on the sophisticated palate of her new grandson. Dean looks to the tree line; the sun is shining through the hash marks of the palm fronds now, sliding orange down the sky.

"Running's a great stress reliever, that time to myself," Juliet is saying.

"Hey! You can't pick those! Those are my mom's!" It is Simon, pointing at Owen who has wandered away from the pool and is denuding the pots outside Juliet's screen porch, hoarding fistfuls of tiny green tomatoes. "Mom! He's picking our Sweet One Hundreds!"

Though they both run, Dean gets there ahead of her, grabbing Owen as he bends the stems, stripping them away from the stalk so the yellow fiber frays out at the tear. Dean pries open Owen's balled up fist and sheepishly passes a handful of unripe tomatoes the size of wasabi peas into Juliet's palm.

"I'm so sorry," he says.

"It's alright. I'll see if they ripen."

But he can see that it's not. She lines them up carefully on her railing, steadies one that threatens to roll off.

"You planted these?" he says, holding a wriggling Owen. "How long have you been here?"

"Almost a month. We didn't start them from seeds. I cheated, went last week and got the plants. I noticed the Vigoro nursery on my way from the airport." She bends over, inspecting the damage. "It's an addiction, really."

"My mom can spot a plant store like a fatty can find a bakery," Simon calls from the pool.

"I can't help it," Juliet continues, abandoning the drooping stalks of her plants and nimble-stepping back over the prickly grass to the pool deck and the other children. "When I was first married, we moved all the time, every few months, for my husband's job. We followed his projects around—Jackson Hole, Aspen, Tahoe, and everywhere I started gardens. My grandparents were farmers; it's in my blood. It drove my husband crazy. I'd plant things and leave them behind like Hansel and Gretel's breadcrumbs. Asparagus was the tipping point; it takes three years before it's ready to harvest."

"Three years?" Dean shakes his head. "I didn't know that."

But he is thinking, gardening? Farmer grandparents? If Amélie were here, she might twist her thin lips into a *so perhaps our first impression of her as Sherry-Sanders-type was wrong, hmm?* smirk.

"Hazel, have you met her? The realtor who manages the cottages? She's not too happy about the tomatoes. She says the owners might not like to have a whole vegetable garden out here when they come for the winter. I promised not to put anything into the ground, and I bought them a lot of nice ceramic pots. I figured, pots you can put flowers in, there's no deep roots," she trails off. "Growing things, nurturing them, I can't help it. It's what I do."

"Luc!" Owen spots his brother before any of them and wriggles out of Dean's arms. He tears across the sand to him. Luc's skin is so dark that the White Beaches polo shirt practically glows in contrast. He looks like a mini-Tony, wearing the same red surf shorts and mirrored sunglasses, earbuds dangling around his neck. His hair has gone even blonder and longer; it swoops off his forehead in the same way that made girls back in Michigan belly crawl through dead leaves and earwigs in the window well to lower themselves into Dean's basement and straddle his son.

He can see it from here—the practiced casual walk of teenage bravado, the defensive tilt to the stubborn, French peasant jaw Luc inherited from his mother. Owen stops short of his big brother, suddenly shy, and Luc bends down to scoop Owen into a hug. Dean's throat constricts. As they come closer, he sees the signs of raspberry-colored scabbing on Luc's cheek and left forearm. Road rash, he hopes, because it means his son was likely not the one behind the wheel.

Holly runs, dripping, past Dean and then slows to stand awkwardly in front of Luc. Dean has handled the calls to Tony and the brief phone consult with Spencer, the British lawyer he recommended, privately, whispering from the back porch back in Saline. He has told Holly only that they have come to the island to visit their brother.

"What happened to your face?" Holly blurts. Beside him, Dean senses Juliet pretending not to witness all of this.

Luc shoves her in the shoulder. "What happened to _yours?_"

And then it is Dean's turn. Ahh, all of his children together for the first time in six months. The trio reaches him.

"Hey," Luc says.

Dean is surprised that after imagining this moment for the past six days, thinking of hugging his son, of crushing him in his arms because he isn't the one in a coma, of turning him around and examining him to be sure he is really okay, of all the things he would say to him, that now the moment is here, his arms hang heavy at his sides, and the words catch, unspoken in his throat, a stuck elevator. Beside him, Juliet turns away and shakes out a beach towel. She takes her time and folds it carefully into a perfect square.

Owen is still in his brother's arms and he reaches out with reverence to softly brush Luc's scabbed face with his chubby palm.

"Ouch?"

24

"Yes! Ow! That hurts. Here," Luc passes Owen back to Dean. "Which place is ours?"

Holly points to the cottage with the rip in the screen door.

"Great, I'm going to lie down. My head's killing me."

Luc pushes past them and Dean watches him walk away, stuffing in his earbuds as he goes.

Juliet turns to Dean with a question in her eyes as she places the folded towel in her beach bag. It is almost sunset. A mosquito sings past Dean's ear and he slaps it, too hard.

"Well," he says carefully, "now you've met the whole Alder family. That was Luc," he adds, "my son."

CHAPTER 5

Juliet

When the sun sets, you warn Dean that the bugs will swarm. Your children, veterans of this, dash ahead of you into your cottage, calling "See you tomorrow!" to their new friends. You wave, feeling him watch you walk away.

So, you think, this is Luc's father?

You send Si upstairs for a shower and run Sonny a tub in the downstairs bath. You tilt your forehead against the tile wall; it cools your sun-warmed cheek. This is the hardest part of the day, as the air conditioner rattles, the homestretch before darkness.

Sonny chatters away, wrapping the coconut-scented soap in a washcloth.

"Here you go, baby, nice and cozy," she says in a rumbly voice and then, "Oh thank you, Daddy." Suddenly, she looks right at you. "I haven't seen Daddy."

Your stomach clutches and your heart thuds.

"No, honey," you say evenly. "You won't."

It started shortly after your arrival, Sonnet's insistence that she could "see" Jack, a chill making the hairs on your arms stand up in the midday heat.

"Hi, Daddy!" she'd call, waving to nothing. This turned into her insisting on a fourth chair at dinner, making both parts of two-sided conversations. You asked her to stop; it upset Simon.

Then again, last Saturday: "I see Daddy!" She pointed at the sea grape bushes as you crossed the road in search of the source of the festive music. You'd seen flyers for the outdoor concert.

"Where, honey?" You imagined it was best to pretend along, keep your strangled voice calm.

"There." She pointed to the dark thatch across from the parking lot, what she and Simon called the jungle. Darvin had warned them not to chase the baby chicks or curlytail lizards into the brush, about the burning maidenplum.

"You didn't see Dad!" Simon accused her. It was Si's idea to go to the party across the street, the thrum of live music calling to him.

"I did! Right there!" Sonnet pointed into the thicket where beams of the harsh overhead sunlight fell in sharp, dust-flecked lines.

You put your hands on their shoulders and shushed them, hurried them across the sandy street. When they were in line for limbo and Tony had offered you a shot of tequila, you took two, unable to shake the feeling that you were being watched.

In the bathroom, you squeeze out a washcloth over Sonny's dark hair and reassure your daughter that she won't see her father again.

She squeezes her eyes closed. "I can see him right now."

You push yourself to your feet, every muscle in your quads tensed.

"It's okay," you whisper, tilting your head to the ceiling in case Jack's spirit is hanging around, watching you leave Sonny alone in the bath. You feel ridiculous, but you add in your head, *She can swim now! She's older now, old enough to leave alone for a bath while I make dinner.*

The truth? You are afraid to be alone with her when she talks like this. Why here? Why now?

A clatter outside your screen porch startles you so badly you drop the box of pasta. There is someone in the bushes. Your heart pounds. You step back into the darkness of the kitchen, reach for the phone. Last week, when the workers from White Beaches wrecked, Hazel told you it took almost fifteen minutes for the police and ambulance to reach Rum Point.

A man's head pokes up above the sill of the living room window. It's him, from the pool, Tony's friend, crouching in the periwinkle light of evening outside your cottage, the little boy clamped to his side. You step out of the shadows, closer, relief flooding to your fingertips. Everything about him reminds you of a Labrador Retriever, open-hearted and honest. He is slapping at mosquitoes as he struggles to tie up your broken tomato plants with what looks like green dental floss.

He catches you watching, but because your windows are closed for air conditioning, he mouths the word, "Sorry," before struggling to his feet. He calls to his daughter who is picking plumeria blooms off the sparse tree by the pool. Though she is on the verge of developing the angles of a woman's face, Holly's hands are still those of a child, all peeling purple nail polish and ragged fingernails. She scatters the creamy petals on the stoop of your screen porch. You lift your hand and Holly smiles. They step carefully through your potted plants and he turns once more, waving over his shoulder, before he walks them to the restaurant across the street.

CHAPTER 6

Dean

Dean's second day on the island, there are two problems:

The first is food. The night before, after trying to fix Juliet's tomato plants, they had eaten a hasty, overpriced dinner of fried food at Rum Point's painted outdoor tables while the mosquitoes feasted on their tender skin. Seventeen bites welted up on Owen's already sore-raw cheeks, and when the bill came, Dean's full stomach heaved. He had spent $140, their usual entire week's grocery allowance, for one day of poorly planned eating. And now, in the morning, there is nothing in the cottage kitchen except for a brick of ground coffee in the back of the freezer and some packets of Sweet'n Low in the cupboard. There are fresh black droppings along the bright white countertop—mouse or roach, he can't be sure.

The second problem is Luc. When Dean followed him into the cottage the night before, he found his son sprawled on the couch with an ice pack over his eyes. Luc has his mother's legs, like a stork's, slightly bowed. His surprisingly delicate ankles were crossed on one of the throw pillows shaped like an angelfish.

"My head's killing me," he said from under the dripping bag of ice. Dean walked past. Dean let himself be swept up in the familiar care of the younger two, getting Owen bathed, rifling through the strewn contents of the suitcases to find clothes and shoes for dinner.

"Are you coming?" Dean asked Luc's horizontal form, the ice bag now a plastic puddle, like the breast implant samples Dr. J had plopped on his desk for Amélie to frown and poke at and decline before the mastectomy.

No reply. Dean was angry with himself for posing it as a question.

He tried again. "You're coming to dinner."

Luc mumbled that he didn't feel well. Dean left with the dental floss tucked into his pocket. When they came home, Luc had moved to the other twin bed across from Holly's, his body an S under the thin cotton blanket, the pillow over his face. There was something else, a gaping duffel bag on the nightstand, with another work polo and the handle of a toothbrush.

"So, he *is* staying here," Holly whispered, and Dean could tell from the twitching smile that she was glad.

Now it is morning, though, and Luc is gone again. Tony said they started early, at 6:30. It will be sunset before he sees his son again. Dean cannot deny his relief, that this means his biggest problem now is the younger children, and breakfast. Holly raids the bottom of her Hello Kitty backpack for stray pieces of Trix cereal. Dean fills a saucepan with water to boil and is folding a paper towel to manufacture a coffee filter when they hear voices outside the screen porch. Holly and Owen scramble to their feet and run out, Dean following them to where Juliet's family is eating a breakfast of bagels, sliced mango, strawberries and grapes out by the pool. He tries to keep his children from hovering like birds, the black ching-chings and thick-beaked Old Arnolds that hop and skulk and beg food under the tables at the resort.

"What's the closest grocery store?" he asks Juliet, watching her de-stem and split a strawberry with a short paring knife against the pad of her thumb, one-handed, a mother's trick.

"Hurley's-by-the-Bay is about twenty-five minutes back toward the airport, but it won't be open today. It's Sunday. Christian island, so nothing happens here on Sunday."

Though technically, this is not true, because it was very early last Sunday morning, after an all-day Saturday party, a music fest at Rum Point with limbo and bucket specials of Stingray Beer and a band called The Barefoot Man—Dean has seen the faded flyer tacked to the palm tree by the parking lot—that Luc and three other White Beaches workers decided to pile into Tony's truck.

"What about the car rental places?"

"I don't know. Tony didn't take you for groceries on your way out yesterday?" When he shakes his head, she makes a small, snorting exhalation of judgment.

"Not the kind of thing you think about when you're a bachelor dive master. Here," she puts the plate of strawberries down in front of his kids. He tries not to stare after her bikini body as she disappears up the boardwalk ramp to her screened porch and returns with a tray—Rice Krispies and milk, bowls, a battalion of plastic-wrapped cheese sticks, and a teetering pineapple.

Dean is mortified when Owen strips and shoves four cheese sticks into his mouth, one after another, like logs into a chipper.

"Hey-hey, at least let me get the wrapper off," Dean jokes. "The peacocks at the zoo have better manners than my guy."

"It's fine," she assures him. "I have to go for my weekly provisions tomorrow anyway." She nods to her repaired plants with a smile, "I think your graft work might take. Thank you."

The families spend most of their first full day together. Sonnet and Simon lead the way, miniature tour guides. They hide from the strong mid-morning sun at their shady, narrow inlet just outside the cottages, in the deep, U-shaped bucket of still, green water where the ocean is shallow and flecked with turtle grass. The older three don beach shoes and borrow Dean's watch, timing each other to see how quickly they can run splashing across the crescent.

"How do you do it?" Juliet asks him once, when the kids are occupied.

"Do what?"

"Be their everything?"

"Oh, I don't. I could write a list as long as my grocery receipt of all the ways I'm screwing up." Of course, right now, he means Luc.

In the afternoon, Juliet packs clean towels and a bag of plastic shovels and goggles and leads the way across the road to the prettier, expansive beach at the Rum Point resort where the casuarinas bow to the sea. Before lunch, they spot Luc in his White Beaches uniform polo and red surf shorts, beaching the dive boat and carrying two SCUBA tanks, one on each shoulder, to the shack where the compressor rattles. Behind his mirrored shades, Luc pretends not to know them. Dean tries once to give him a two-finger salute, their old first grade code for *I love you* when kids at the playground were watching. Radio silence.

"I didn't realize that was your son, who works at White Beaches," Juliet says, patting the sides of the castle her daughter is making in the shallows. This is a strange remark, considering Luc was in his uniform polo the day before. "I hope he wasn't one of the kids involved in the accident last weekend."

"What accident?" Holly asks.

Dean glances up, a quick shake of his head.

"Wow, look at this," Juliet says, holding up a hermit crab the size of a freckle.

31

"Is this the littlest one you've ever seen?" And the conversation moves on, one meaningful look passing between Dean and Juliet. He hopes she can read his gratitude, for understanding, in the arc of his eyebrows.

Later, as they rinse their feet off at the outdoor showers by the bar, she apologizes softly to Dean under the hiss of the spray. "I'm sorry for bringing that up, earlier. It's none of my business about last week, and I don't know any details really, just gossip I heard," she trails off when he doesn't answer. "This island is really just a small town. You'll see."

Lunch is another expensive round of conch fritters and fish and chips and virgin piña coladas with maraschino cherries from Leo over at the resort, followed by Juliet suggesting quiet time in their own cottages.

"And then maybe, after, the pool, when the heat subsides," she adds, "we could take turns watching each other's kids, go for a run?"

Dean hasn't run seriously in years, not since the long miles under the inky night sky in Africa, when they were on a service semester abroad in college and Amélie was breaking his twenty-year-old heart. Running along the red dirt roads of the Ashanti region, in a land of famously predatory animals and poisonous snakes that worried the locals less than the spirits, seemed safer than aching in the *atakpame* near her, generator-lights flickering, watching Amélie smoke her clove cigarettes and write letters to Robert, her lover back home.

Still, he pictures making slow progress in the soft white sand of the beach here, the necessary shedding of the cocoon of his grief, time away from the demands of Holly and Owen. He could clear his head; compose the right conversation with Luc.

"Great idea," he tells Juliet.

Just before sunset, they spray each other with Deep Woods Off. Juliet double knots her running shoes and passes the poolside care of the four children to him like a relay baton. She goes first, iPod in hand, prancing like a racehorse at the start gate, and returns almost an hour later from the direction she had come, the long road back toward the airport and civilization, drenched and beaming. There is a droplet of sweat hanging from the tip of her pointed nose. Dean has to stop himself from brushing it off. He barely knows her, but being dressed in the equivalent of underwear all day, the isolation and quiet of the island has accelerated a sense of intimacy.

"Thank you so much," she gushes, accepting a thigh hug from her daughter. "You have no idea! I feel incredible, like myself again. It's been too long. Thank you!"

But now it is his turn. When he gets up from the beach chair, his legs feel filled with sand. He has to peel Owen off him like a baby koala and is not surprised when he refuses to go to Juliet. Dean notes with a sliver of disappointment that she doesn't push it, doesn't try harder to coax him into her arms. In the end, it's Holly who collects her little brother, who hauls him down to the sand where they are digging for mole crabs.

"Here." Juliet offers Dean her iPod. "Do you want music? I have to have it. If I hear myself breathe, I can totally convince myself I'm dying." He notes that she uses the phrase without any of Tony's self-consciousness about death, because she owns a history of tragedy too. All day together and no mention of her husband; he wonders when she will tell him the story.

"We're bordered by water on all sides; there's no such thing as a circular route out here," she says. "You have to be careful about pacing yourself, or you'll end up burning out, or turning back too early." She points down the road that flanks the resort's parking lot. "If you want a shorter run, you can go this way, to Kaibo and back; it's about two miles."

She can tell, he realizes, probably from the fact that his running shoes are practically as old as Holly, creased and splitting at the soles, that he is not a regular.

"You just go down this road, you'll pass the Kaibo restaurant, and then there are these huge cement pillars at the end, iron gates that open out to an empty lot with nothing but a lot of truffula trees and some great shell specimens."

"Truffula trees?" he asks.

"I asked the guys at Vigoro—they're called petticoat palms, but with all their underskirts, they look like the truffula trees in 'The Lorax.' It used to be Si's favorite Dr. Seuss book."

"Yeah, until my mom cried every time she got to the last page!" Simon yells from the beach where he is digging, always listening. "So embarrassing!"

Juliet presses her iPod into Dean's hand, their fingers brushing. Under bug spray, detergent and sunscreen, a pharmacy of scents, he can smell the sweet tang of her sweat. "Anyway, you'll see you're at the end of the road, you'll come to the ocean, and then it's straight back. Two miles, maybe less."

He fits the ear buds in, still squishy and damp from her, and tries to adopt a normal but fast pace to the road, feeling everyone watching. Fifteen years ago, when they were first together and things were actually good, Amélie would occasionally praise or lovingly pat his ass when he walked to the shower—God, he hopes it doesn't jiggle now.

Juliet's playlist is terrible, nothing but jangly pop music and audio books, most of them for children. After a few agonizing minutes of 'Where the Wild Things Are' read by the author, he turns it off and runs to the chug-and-huff of his own breathing and slap of his sneaker soles on the scorching pavement. He tries to find the Zen in this sound, in the rhythm of running, as he had in Ghana all those years ago, but his mind keeps wiggling back to Luc.

He had stopped Tony outside the dive shop this morning—"still no change"—and he had asked if he should call the lawyer, set up a meeting for this week.

"Tomorrow, man," Tony said. "Nothing happens here on Sunday." This made Dean smile, he realized, because it was an echo of Juliet. "Come Monday," Tony crooned as he hefted two dive tanks to his shoulders.

Tonight, he vows, he will sit down with his son. He will not let Luc hide under ice packs and pillows. Somewhere inside him, in Luc's newly muscled and battered body, there is the truth. The fact that it hasn't found its way out yet means it may be bad.

⌒⟶

As he huffs past the vacation houses, Dean's mind drifts back to Juliet. Specifically, her hands: a curious mix of capable and feminine, brown from the sun, lightly freckled and corded with tendons and veins, ending in perfect, natural nails with their sliver of white quarter moons. He has been watching them all day, dancing protectively over her children's shoulders whenever they cross the road to Rum Point, though whole minutes pass between any cars. Those hands reached across the picnic table at lunch to break Owen's steaming fries in half so they would cool more quickly—never mind, he tells himself, that she didn't try harder to hold him tonight.

Her hands are not the erotic, candy-pink acrylic-tipped ones of the women who cup their own breasts on the covers of the *Sports Illustrated* swimsuit issue at the airport newsstand. They're not mauve and rounded like the sensible ones on Erika, the divorced English professor of the one disastrous date.

The allure of Juliet's hands is as simple as the solitary platinum band that circles her left ring finger: Her hands are the natural, nurturing hands of a mother. The hands holding open a sun-warmed beach towel, smoothing Sonnet's salt-sticky hair back into a ponytail and out of the way of lunch's ketchup and tartar sauce, rubbing a second application of sunscreen onto the shoulders of her squirming children, then offering the bottle to him.

Thinking about Juliet's hands gets him all the way to Kaibo, past the vacation houses with their cutesy names, conch-lined pathways and covered sport boats, past the two-story open-air restaurant and marina, to the promised arches and gates to nowhere, and the trees that really do look like nature's inspiration for the wild and silk-tufted truffula trees in Dr. Seuss' story.

He puzzles over this all the way back: what had made Juliet cry every time she read that book? He knows they have it back in Michigan, crammed in the overflowing bookcases on the second floor, somewhere up there with all the other increasingly political, more recent Seuss—*Butter Side Up, Star Belly Sneetches...* Dean remembers reading *The Lorax* to Holly and finding it void of Seuss' earlier whimsy and imagination, saturated with over-the-top environmental dogma—he can't remember if he ever even read it to Owen. What in this had resonated with this woman whose hands he can't stop thinking about? And what is so mesmerizing about hands that are capable and generous, that automatically reach across the table to tear his son's French fries in half?

Though he hasn't run this far since Africa, since before the children, somewhere in the homestretch, Dean finds his winter-heavy legs are lighter, pumping faster. He decides to sprint the sandy road on the last spans of the telephone poles, come in at an impressive pace. But when he rounds the turn to Rum Point, lungs on fire, expecting to see the children and Juliet waiting, instead there are two blunt-nosed Royal Cayman Islands Police cars, and his son is in the backseat of the first one.

CHAPTER 7

Dean

"What's going on here?" Dean gasps as he slows his pace, gulping air that is thick and heavy as corn syrup. There is a small cluster over by the dive shack: two officers, Tony and two other White Beaches workers. Dean assumes from their various medical accoutrements that these were the other occupants of the truck. Dusty, a guy with hair so yellow it is tinged green, has one arm in a sling and the other in a cast. The bruises around his eyes have spread beyond the rims of his mirrored sunglasses, purplish blue like opals. Beside him, Darvin, a lanky, dark-skinned young man, rocks back and forth on a pair of crutches.

Dean bends in half at the waist in the simulation of a stretch, but really, he might pass out if he can't get blood to his head. Inside the police car, Luc is staring straight ahead. He looks all of eight years old. One of the officers is in the back beside him, a clipboard in hand, and the engine is running.

"What's going on?" Dean repeats, and Tony takes him by the elbow, tugs him away from the others, who shuffle like cattle in a corral, eyes on the branding chute.

"They're interviewing them again, one at a time. I get the feeling nobody's talking."

Tony snaps his cinnamon gum and continues. "Dusty's folks are getting in tomorrow. His stepdad's got a lawyer lined up to get him cleared and released for medical reasons. He's had a doctor look at his X-rays, worried about infections. I trust Dusty; he's been with me forever, but he was out of his gourd Saturday. We all were. I told you everybody goes a little crazy in hurricane season. And Darvin, he's Jamaican."

"What does that mean?" Dean asks.

Tony shrugs. "Inter-island prejudice. He'll be the one they're after. I think whoever was driving was smart or sober enough to get out of the truck and lie down in the grass with everyone else who got thrown out of the bed."

Dean wonders, is that accusation in Tony's voice? Does he really think Luc has told him something, confessed that he was the driver, and Dean is protecting him?

"Luc doesn't remember anything."

Tony slams a palm against the side of the dive shack, causing two of the officers to glance over. "God, I had a feeling something bad was going to happen when Luc left."

Later, Dean will think back on this, wonder why he didn't ask Tony exactly where he was the night the staff piled in and took his truck to town.

The squad car door opens and Luc gets out. He passes his finger and thumb over his eyes before he puts his sunglasses back on. He shakes his head lightly at Dusty, who goes in next.

Dean crosses to his son in three strides, grips him around the upper arm and drags him down the beach to where the large rental equipment is stored under the casaurinas.

"What the hell was that?"

"What was what?" Luc asks. They stop by the three oversized aqua trikes with their huge orange plastic wheels. Summer is a slow rental season; everything is covered in a dusting of sand and pine needles from the overhanging trees.

"You shook your head at him. What does that mean? Some secret code? Is this a game?"

"It means I still couldn't remember anything," Luc says quietly. "I don't remember, Dad."

"What about the girl? Was something going on? With you two?"

Luc looks away.

"Tony says the police think you hit someone. Or whoever was driving hit someone. Is that true?"

"So you think it was me?"

It is Dean's turn to be silent.

"What do you want me to say? I don't remember! You don't believe me?"

Luc storms back to the group and Dean has no choice but to follow. Darvin, is in the back of the car now; the interviews are going quickly.

Dean stands next to Tony.

"Have they made any formal charges? About the other person?"

Tony shakes his head.

"That guy, Ebanks," he nods at one of the officers, "he's got a hard-on about it. Says there is no possible way they didn't hit someone."

"What about whoever was in the truck bed? If they slammed on the brakes, could it have been their blood?"

"Who did you cheat off of to pass physics?" Tony snorts.

"Okay, well, but nobody's reported anyone missing, right? That's good?"

The way Tony looks at him reminds Dean that they're talking about life here, a person.

"You're right. It could have been a Cuban refugee who showed up on a rubber raft, or a Jamaican on an expired work permit, overstaying his welcome. Maybe he's crawled off into the bush and is being eaten alive by fire ants. We should be grateful it wasn't an American tourist with a relative who works at CNN, or Cayman royalty—a Bodden or a Kirkconnell."

"I'm just saying," Dean clarifies, "it could have been anybody, or it could have been nobody. Speculation."

"You weren't there," Tony says flatly.

"How's the girl today? Bridget?"

Tony's eyebrows shoot up. "Luc didn't tell you?"

Dean shakes his head. Over by the thick trunk of the largest casuarina tree, where a hand-painted sign prohibits any outside music or food, Luc is looking like he would like to evaporate.

"Her brain function tests came back positive, and the swelling is down so they can start to lower the sedation levels soon."

"Good, good," Dean says, smiling at Tony.

"Sort of," Tony's face looks odd, pained. "The cut on her calf went septic. They amputated this morning, just below the knee."

Back at the pool by the cottages, Juliet is doing the now-familiar Internet connection dance with the computer high over her head.

"You're back! What do you think about this one?" she calls to Dean and reads aloud from her laptop. "It's my newest daily inspiration, Alan Alda," and she tries to form her eyebrow into an arch like Leo's before she continues. "'You have to leave the city of your comfort and go into the wilderness of your intuition. What you'll discover will be wonderful. What you'll discover is yourself.'"

"Nice." The greasy lunch bucks in his stomach, jostled by thirty minutes of jogging, and now somewhere on this island there is a girl, somebody's daughter, who may or may not wake up, look down, and see nothing but white sheet where the rest of her leg should be.

"I like it better than this morning's: 'It took me less than half a lifetime to realize that regret is one of the few guaranteed certainties. Sooner or later, everything is touched by it, despite our naive and senseless hope that just this time we will be spared its cold hand on our heart.' That one," she says, closing her computer, "was definitely my brother."

He knows this is female fishing—Amélie used to do it too—he is supposed to ask her about her brother, about his regrets. She's waiting, but Dean has a lot on his mind.

Finally, Dean sighs, "Who doesn't have regrets?" He hands her iPod back. Down by the water, Holly and Owen haven't noticed his return. They are digging a deep hole. Owen spots him and comes running up the beach and Juliet smiles at their reunion. "I know I have enough to fill a shipping container."

"I kind of like the Alda one." Juliet gestures around them. "It goes with the setting out here at this end of the island, the wilderness of our intuition, the wilds of the beaches and the sea grape and the pines. That sounds like a good place to find yourself."

"If you're lost." Dean sinks into a lawn chair and lets Owen fidget with the laces of his running shoes. At home, Owen liked everyone to be barefoot—it meant nobody was leaving.

"Not lost," she says softly. "Maybe just a little off track."

Dean looks up.

"Last week," Juliet does not meet his eyes, "Saturday, something happened. I hit an anniversary. It was harder than I thought. I'm not quite sure where I'm supposed to be on the Kubler-Ross grief scale, but I'm pretty sure it doesn't include blind drunk by dinner time." She turns her back to him under the premise of collecting stray beach toys.

She was there, at the Rum Point party, the night of the accident?

He is wondering how to respond when she continues.

"I've got a stack of self-help books as high as my waist I'm meant to be reading.

39

Monday, tomorrow, I'm going to start using them, and the quiet wilderness of this island, and running, to plow through this. I'm going to pull myself up by my bootstraps. Move on. My goal is to be better by the middle of the summer, maybe before."

"You can't tick grieving off your to-do list," Dean says, as close as he comes to asking outright what happened.

"Why not?" She laughs. "Here, sweetheart." She uses a corner of her towel to dust the sand from Owen's outstretched palms. "I've always revved at a decent, productive RPM. Why can't I use that to my advantage here?"

Because that's now how grief works. He should tell her that it moves in like an unwelcome houseguest, silent as termites, and colonizes in the rafters. Unaddressed, it can do irreparable damage.

In a moment, the sun will dip beyond the horizon, and the mosquitoes will swarm with their high-pitched warning whines. Their children run up from the beach complaining they are hungry.

"What's that restaurant out there like?" he asks.

"Kaibo? They claim to have the best burgers on the island, but I'd hate to try some of the restaurants on the west side if that's true. And, like everything around here, overpriced. Surly waitresses too."

"Wow." Dean smiles for the first time in hours. "You should write that up for Michelin."

"We have cheese dogs," Simon says. "Right, Mom? And popsicles."

There is a long pause before Juliet says, "It's my last day before grocery shopping. It's like Mother Hubbard in there, but I do have the cheese dogs, and one or two boxes of macaroni, and maybe the makings for some kind of a salad, if you're interested."

There is a delicate moment while they are both considering this, the precedent it might set, the boundaries that should be established. They have already spent most of the day together. Dean looks through the palms at the edge of the cottages, to where the sand road divides them from the White Beaches parking lot. At some point, Luc will come back to his cottage. He should be waiting.

"My mom makes the best mac and cheese," Simon brags to Holly, running ahead to open the screen door. Dean knows he should go home and wait for his son, sit him down and figure out a game plan.

But when Juliet laughs and says, "Mac and cheese, yes, my strong suit," and turns her body in an angle of invitation, Dean does not hesitate to follow her.

CHAPTER 8

Juliet

In the cottage kitchen, you put on water for pasta and think how what you just told him about last Saturday, "I got a little off track" is the woolly mammoth of understatements. That was the day when Sonny insisted Jack was here, watching you, and Simon looked like you had pointed out Disney World as you callously drove past, so brokenhearted, and how you took them across the street to the festive lanterns and limbo and steel drums, where the Barefoot Man sang, and you let a man pour you two fast shots of Leo's tequila and pull you close on the dance floor.

When he handed you a third shot, he whispered, his goatee scraping your sunburned cheek, "I'm sorry about your husband."

He'd laughed that you'd thought he wouldn't have known, telling you the island is just one big small town. "I'm sorry about your late husband," he'd whispered again into your ear, "and I'm not."

How when Luc and Bridget had your kids engaged in a limbo contest on the dance floor, you let him pull you behind the dive shack, pressed up against the rumble of the compressor wall. You had puzzled at the differences, having only kissed Jack for so many years, this strange stubble burning your skin raw. But how his hand at the waistband of your skirt had a black diver's watch with arms pointing up and down, six o'clock, and the mother in you had recognized through the bleary haze that these meant something significant, that you needed to push away from this man, take your children home and feed them dinner.

Where back in the cottage you shrieked at your children—"That's enough! You never know when to stop!"— for laughing over the sputtering, farting end of the nearly empty ketchup bottle. Devastation on Simon's face, those huge brown eyes that first met yours over surgical tape and plastic tubing, the expression that led Jack to call Simon an "old soul."

"The moment I first met my son," Jack loved to tell the story, "he opened his eyes and glanced around the NICU, and I swear those eyes said, 'aw shit, here we go again.'"

You don't remember if you apologized to Si and Sonny right then or if you were righteously indignant as well as drunk. You told them to go upstairs to bed, and you remember they went, though you had never in nine years known your children to put themselves to sleep without at least one story.

He'd said he would come, "when your kids are asleep." You hoped he would hurry up, before you got sober, or maybe better, not come at all, before you created more regret. You undressed right in the living room, stripping off your white skirt and shirt, stretching yourself out on the couch in a pose of invitation, one foot balanced against the floor so you didn't fall. Then, nothing.

The final flashes in the long dark space of this night:

The distinctive click of the cottage door opening—he came. In his face you recognized hunger, strangely pale skin around his sun-wrinkled eyes as he approached. How he looked older, less attractive, without his sunglasses.

Then someone else, by the door – a white knight in a white polo.

Outside, yelling.

"You know she's not thinking clearly! It's not right!"

Where were your children? You tried to move, open your eyes, but your limbs felt as heavy as waterlogged driftwood, the room spinning like rough seas.

You remember later—a dream, you hope—lips grazing yours, sunburned, with petal pink tenderness. The familiar rawness of a man, inside you, your legs wrapped around his narrow back and a moan, coming from somewhere deep in your chest.

"Mama? Mama" Your daughter, hands on your shoulder. "There's a ghost!"

Outside, the screech of tires, the scream of a girl—not Sonny, you could tell—the crash of metal, shattering glass. Then, the silence, the horrible absence of noise. The distant wail of sirens.

"Mom? Here, Mom." Simon, a blanket being spread over your body, warm where it had been

artificially chilled. Your children curled up on the couch opposite you, as the golden light of dawn seared through your eyelids.

Now, you set a table for six, and smile shakily at the pleasant chaos of the four children in this same room, a week later. The kids mean instant playmates for yours, and in him, an inspiring audience. Of course, you notice the way he watches you. His easygoing honesty, his steadiness, is a comforting wall.

You twist the ring on your finger. Jack, typically impulsive, proposed the first day you met. You glance up at the corner of the ceiling, just in case he's here, watching. Nothing. Sonny still talks to him in the bath, presses her face against the screen of the cottage, staring at the dark tangle of sea grape where she insists she sees him.

Left to your own devices, drowning your grief and anxiety in tequila, you skidded off track last week, your spinning tires meeting the loose gravel at road's edge. You carry a steaming bowl of mac and cheese to the table, thinking, you could use a guardrail like Dean.

CHAPTER 9

Dean

There are new sounds to the night here—the wonk and clack of the ceiling fan, the shush of Holly turning a page in the *Warriors* series she is reading across the hall and the trill of the tree frogs outside the screens. Farther in the distance, past the cottage where he had said a polite good night and thanks for dinner to Juliet, Dean hears the twang of Leo's rockabilly playlist. Beyond it all, there is the rise and fall of the waves. A quiet fury builds in Dean as he waits, molars grinding, for Luc.

We cannot afford more tragedy.

He dipped into Amélie's slim life insurance policy to buy the plane tickets and rent the cottage. What if Luc needs a lawyer? At Tony's urging, he had called David Spencer of Watler, Spencer and McGhee from Saline last week. Spencer recommended waiting until formal charges were filed to retain his services. He quoted, in a chipper British accent, a staggering retainer and hourly fee.

When Dean hears the screen door open, ten minutes after eleven, he leaps from the bed, propelled by rage. He catches Luc in the living room, where the light from Holly's bedroom makes the reef fish throw pillows look half-alive.

"Where have you been?"

Luc stinks of yeasty beer and tangy smoke; he tries to pass. Dean slams his palm against the wall to stop him from walking away. Though there is nothing in modern psychology to support its use, Dean always felt like spanking was his ace in the hole, a last resort if he ever really needed it. Technically, he and Amélie had agreed they did not believe in corporal punishment, though Dean had seen Amélie occasionally slap Luc's toddler wrist, and once she threw a cup of lukewarm coffee over Luc and Holly when they squabbled at the breakfast table.

"Where were you?"

He regards his son, just eighteen years old, staring defiantly back at him in the half-light from Holly's open door. Could he force the truth out of him, physically extract it?

He drops his arm and Luc flinches and ducks like a tattered-ear junkyard dog.

"What happened?" Dean asks again, quietly.

"I don't remember."

When had it become impossible to tell if Luc was lying? There were years when he couldn't pull it off, a twitchy grin giving him away into his early teens.

"You were drunk," he tries again, leading the witness.

"People started early, midday. There was a concert. Our last boat trip was back at one. Everyone was at the Barefoot Man, drinking, dancing. I remember I was fooling around with a girl on the beach before it got dark." Luc scowls. "I remember a few things from earlier that night."

"Where were you going in the truck?"

"I don't know, probably somewhere on the West Side, Royal Palms or Lone Star. What can I say, Dad?" Luc tilts forward like the seven-year-old boy who used to head-butt Dean's stomach in a hint for a hug. When Dean steps toward him, though, Luc backs away. "I wish we never got in."

They stand in the hallway between the two bedrooms.

"Tony tells me they amputated her leg this morning."

Luc's expression contorts, like Dean has intentionally punched a charley horse.

"I just want to know the truth, Luc." Dean's voice feels diamond tipped.

"If that's the only reason you're here, you came a long way for nothing."

Luc starts to walk away, and then he turns. "Will it come back?"

Dean softens; it has been a long time since he deferred to his father's knowledge on any subject. "What?"

Luc crosses to the couch, tosses an angelfish pillow aside. "Will I ever remember what happened?"

Dean shifts his weight. In what Holly calls his professor voice, he explains the different alcohol-related blackouts. "Well, with excessive amounts of drinking, there are two types. You can experience an *en bloc* blackout, which means you remember nothing of the entire time you were drinking, even when triggered for recall. Or you can have what people in the medical profession call fragmentary blackouts, bits and pieces."

"Dusty calls those a brownout," Luc offers with a twist of a smile. "I said I remember some stuff."

"Was she your girlfriend? The girl in the truck?"

"Please." A look passes over Luc's face.

It reminds Dean of a snippet of conversation he'd overheard back in Michigan just after Amélie died, passing by Luc's infrequently open bedroom door: Luc, lounging on the bed, giving a sexual play-by-play to his friend Matt. He heard the phrase, "tits all up to here" and then Luc, sensing his presence, stopped.

"So is she, like, your girlfriend now?" Matt had asked.

"Dude, they're *all* my girlfriends. And none of them are." Luc's laugh was horrible and hollow, a brittle version of his mother's. Dean had called Tony and booked Luc's ticket to Grand Cayman the next day.

"What are other kinds of memory loss?" Luc prompts. "Not alcohol related."

"Well," Dean sags into a chair across from him, "there is a medical phenomenon where people develop amnesia following a traumatic brain injury. You did hit your head, somewhere." Dean pauses, praying again that the abrasion on his cheek is from the hard earth of this fossilized coral island and not the truck's dashboard.

"What else?"

Dean thinks how to phrase this. "The last one is called dissociative amnesia. It's common in PTSD; you see it with victims of abuse or trauma. That's more of a psychological issue, a self-protective mechanism."

"For when the truth hurts," Luc says simply. He looks very small, folded into the cushions of the couch, bunching the starfish pillow between his palms.

"Yes." Dean sighs and stands. He turns for his bedroom. "So, the short answer is, whatever the reason you can't remember what happened that night, I don't know that your memory is coming back."

In the early morning, Luc is gone again, and out by the pool, Juliet is laying out breakfast. She is wearing a new bikini, navy and white striped, strapless. With her freckles and perfect teeth, she looks like she belongs on the cover of the Martha Stewart LIVING magazine the women fought over in the faculty lounge, like she should be in a New England beachfront town, setting out a fourth of July table with lobster napkin rings. She is setting out six plates and calls to Owen.

"Here, my little fruit monster." She offers him a squat banana the size of a gorilla's finger.

Holly and Simon are planning their day; they call it their camp schedule. Lizard catching is next on the agenda. Dean keeps all four kids while Juliet drives her tiny blue rental car to the Hurley's in Grand Harbour and picks up a freezer full of kid-friendly food: chicken nuggets, waffle fries and frozen Go-Gurt tubes, bulging bags of tropical fruit.

"Try this," she hands Dean a fresh coconut water. "From the farm stand. And look!" She displays beads and embroidery thread for the girls and fabric paint from the craft store. "We can decorate camp T-shirts!"

They do the same things they had on Sunday, the beginnings of a routine: late morning together at their shallow beach and pool, and then across the road to the Rum Point beach. They snorkel around the rock jetties, where Sonnet and Holly squeal at the barracuda lurking under the dock. In the mid-afternoon there is quiet time in their separate cottages, then one more late afternoon swim, and their second respective tag-team runs. The day ends with dinner at Juliet's.

This continues for the next four days. Holly formalizes it, paints the words Camp Sunshine and a smiling sun wearing shades on six T-shirts, for everyone but Luc. Dean and Juliet shadow the children. They reapply sunscreen and adjust swim goggles, but mostly they talk. The two things they do not discuss: Juliet's husband, and what is happening with Luc.

It is okay; they have so many other things to say, and interruptions are frequent—*I'm thirsty! Saltwater in my eyes! Tell Simon to quit throwing sand!* It took a whole morning of start-stop conversation for Juliet to relay the story of her grandmother's transition from high society Philadelphia to a Bucks County dairy farmer's wife.

She tells Dean more about their life in the farmhouse on Furlong Rd. "When I got pregnant with Si, we were living in Aspen for one of Jack's projects. My Nana broke her hip, and the project closed phase three, so it made sense to go home."

"What were you doing in Aspen?" Dean asks.

"Jack worked for a sales team, selling timeshares for a luxury developer. We lived all over, Lake Tahoe, Park City, Vail, all the resort towns."

"Where did you plant the asparagus?"

She looks surprised that he remembered. "That was Aspen."

"What did you do, other than grow plants you had to leave behind?"

"I took hourly jobs, restaurants, daycare centers, bookstores, whatever. It drove my father crazy; he was like, I paid for Wake Forest so you could be a waitress?"

"I bet." Dean laughs. "That school is not cheap."

"It was a fun life, for a while. Jack loved it because he got paid to ski on his lunch break, wearing jackets that advertised the project. We had friends on the sales team. I suppose it's sort of like the military: you become a family, quickly. This was before we had kids—we'd go out late, hit the bars wearing all the gear, chat up the tourists. It was understood that we, the girlfriends and wives, were to dress up and make sure every casual conversation mentioned the project's name. There was a script with three talking points and redirects. Everything was product placement. Jack's job was to always be selling."

"But then you got pregnant?"

"Right, with Si." They look out at their four on the beach, creating a chain to move buckets of water from the shoreline to their castle fortress, little Owen staggering under the weight.

"And my grandma broke her hip, so we went home to care for her. Jack insisted this was temporary. He started hyperventilating about the lack of topography when we drove into Kansas."

"But you stayed?"

"All our friends went to the next two projects, Whistler and La Jolla. Jack wasn't happy, but Nana wasn't doing well. It probably might have been best if he went on without me, but," she shrugs. "I loved my grandma. She'd tell me stories while I washed her hair in the sink, about them bottle-feeding orphaned calves right on the kitchen table, about how my grandpa laid the cobbles in the courtyard by hand while she trained the wisteria and honeysuckle over the arch. She said even when they were working, they never liked to be more than shouting distance from each other. She wasn't afraid of dying; she was excited to see him again." Juliet smiles, reaching down to sift sand through her fingers between their chairs in the shade.

"When did she pass?"

"The summer before Si was born. We'd set her up a bed in the front room. She wanted the windows open so she could smell the earth after a summer thunderstorm. She told me she wanted me to have the farm. I remember she put her hand over my belly, and said she wanted me and my 'handsome salesman to fill the house with babies and chickens and laughter.' She died peacefully that night, in her sleep."

"That's as much as any of us can ask for."

"Exactly—the wisdom of Kenny Rogers and the gambler," Juliet laughs. "Anyway, it turned out to be lucky that we were living there, so when Si was born blue, he could be airlifted to CHOP. It's one of the best hospitals in the world."

Ahh, Dean thinks. Now they will talk about the pale scars Dean has noticed but not known how to ask about, criss-crossing the boy's narrow chest.

"Simon was born with a congenital heart defect. He likes to tell everyone he got to take his first helicopter ride before he was one day old. It was—" their eyes both travel to him, where he darts back and forth down the beach, buckets of water sloshing, "—probably the hardest, or right up there with the hardest, time of my life. He spent two and a half months in the NICU. Two open heart surgeries, infection after infection. But mothers can't stay overnight when your baby is in NICU, so I was like a zombie, back and forth to the city. Most of that time, I couldn't hold him. All I could do was sit by his isolette and let him hold my finger or go in the pumping closet and cry."

Dean wonders where Jack was in all of this, but their conversation is interrupted, when the patient in question dumps a bucket of water over his little sister's head, and Juliet jumps up to intervene.

CHAPTER 10

Juliet

You bring Simon up the beach, away from the altercation, to put more zinc sunscreen on his scars. The bright-white oxide illuminates them against his sun-brown skin, like a small, shirtless warrior. When you let go of his arm, he wriggles free, whooping away.

"Si, come on! We need to make a moat for the dragon!" Holly yells. She is already using the short version of your son's name.

You feel Dean watching the entire interaction, the quick kiss you place on your son's curls before setting him free.

"And what do you farm now, on your family's land?" Dean asks.

Resentment, you think, but do not say.

Back when Simon was born, with his heart conditions, you rarely left the hospital. It was Jack who went with Lear and your sisters to the reading of Nana's will, who called your cell phone at the hospital with the startling news that Nana had left everything, the farmhouse and its vast surrounding acres "of potential!" Jack said, to you.

While you watched the rise and fall of Simon's recently-sutured breast, Jack and Marty, a new business partner he had met at a New Jersey job fair, were sitting at your Nana's wooden kitchen table where the calves suckled bottles, writing the business plan for the project he called 'their baby' with no hint of irony.

They formed a corporation called Compass and named their first project Poet's Promise—a three phase luxury home development. Jack breathed life into it while you trusted ventilators to do the same for Simon, your fingertips tracing the networks of veins on his twiggy thigh. Bleary-eyed, you co-signed paperwork—bank loans and incorporation documents. You tried to make sense of blueprints and schematic drawings Jack unrolled on the scuffed farmhouse table late at night when you came home from the hospital for a shower and fresh clothes. You shuttled each day's tiny, cream-colored bottles of breast milk into the basement freezer, optimistic Simon would one day come home and drink them.

"The potential in Bucks County is more in real estate than any agricultural crop," you tell Dean now. "We still have some gardens, up at the house. Kitchen gardens, and berry patches."

"But these look really close to us!" you had said to Jack, pointing to hulking, 5,000 square foot McMansions, triple the size of the farmhouse on the drawings—they seemed to be right in the backyard. "Remember, we're going to save some land close to the house in case any of my brother or sisters wants to build here."

"That's just a later phase, drawn in so we can get zoning approval now while the iron is hot and the county is on board. The first phase is out here, the far pasture." Jack tapped an area of the property that bordered a county road, whole fields away from the house. "We're projected to make so much money on this, Jules, on Phase One, we probably won't even do Phase Two or Three."

"Okay, we'll save some lots for my family?"

"I have something special in mind for them..." Jack said breezily. He kissed you hard on the mouth and crowed, "This is going to be huge! Epic, Jules. Set for life."

In the years that follow, you will wish a thousand times that you had paid better attention that night, read things more closely before putting your name on any documents.

"Does most of your family live nearby then?" Dean asks, refilling their iced teas.

"All five of my siblings and their families are within a weekend drive."

"That's enviable! I have one sister, Amy. She's eight years older, a research librarian, in Iowa. She has," Dean laughs, "probably too many cats. All named after Brontë characters, if you're into that sort of thing. No kids. It must be nice, for Simon and Sonnet, to have all those cousins so close."

You nod, your lips pinched between your teeth.

"It's going to be the best Christmas ever, Jules!" Another of Jack's promises.

It was supposed to be their first of many years hosting Christmas at Nana's farmhouse. Simon was out of the hospital, four months old and almost eight pounds, the feet of his reindeer-print pajamas cut off to feed the wire apnea and oxygen monitor leads through. You invited everyone out to the farm to meet him, to come see Julie and Jack setting up house in Nana's old place. Your five siblings and spouses, nieces and nephews, your mother, all nineteen of them crammed like mice under the nooks and eaves of the attic bedrooms. In the mornings, a long line snaked outside the one working bathroom and despite your protests, Jack and Lear and your nephews all peed on the snowplow bank out by the withered stalks of the kitchen garden, staining the snow yellow.

The grown-ups stayed up late around the old pine table, drinking off the case of California red that Percy brought, playing endless hands of Hearts, chocolate chip cookies cut off a dough log browning in the oven at midnight. Impossibly, more snow fell on December twenty-fourth and you all marveled at it—a rare Pennsylvania white Christmas.

Christmas morning, Jack was giddy, dancing wobbly-necked Simon around in his arms, waving his little fist to dole out paper-thin gifts to all of your siblings: envelopes with $15,000 checks for each of them, profits from the sale of the family's land.

"And then Jules and I are going to remodel this old place into something fabulous, a huge homestead where everyone will be welcome to come, any time, every holiday, and celebrate with us."

Silence. Bing Crosby crooning on the stereo until Lear said quietly, "So how much property is left for anyone else? How much isn't in your McMansion project, Jack?"

"You're sitting in it," Jack had said. "We have an acre and a half here. But the house will be bigger, better, a place for everyone, once we make some sales and start the renovation."

Lear and his pointy-chinned wife Jenna left abruptly, zipping the twins into their snowsuits, not even staying for the pie made from blackberries you had picked and frozen the summer before. That night, in bed Jack hissed to you that he had wanted to snatch the $15,000 right out of your brother's claws.

"None of them had any vision to see that this was the value of the land for this family! I had the vision, Jules. I had the vision, for us."

"Mama!" Sonny calls. "Come see the castle! It's the best, most beautiful castle ever!"

Dean's friend Tony is coming down the beach from the restaurant, ubiquitous sunglasses covering his eyes.

So you stand up, dusting the sand off your backside and head down the beach, explaining to Dean,

"I don't see how I can resist that!"

CHAPTER 11

Dean

When Juliet is down the beach with the kids, Tony stops by to give the latest news: The girl, Bridget, has been transferred out of ICU. The doctors feel confident they stopped the spread of the sepsis.

"She turned her head to one side when her mom and sister got here from Auckland, but she hasn't opened her eyes yet."

Tony says the police are frustrated; in lieu of a confirmed driver, when the blood alcohol labs come back from Miami, they threaten to file DUI charges against everyone over the legal limit in the truck.

"But, can they do that?" Dean sputters. "Probable cause, no evidence, no witnesses?"

"This ain't the motherland." Tony laughs. "This is the Cayman cowboys of East End. They can do whatever they want."

Luc never comes home before eleven, one of the nights not at all. He complains of headaches, goes through all the Advil in Dean's travel kit. They see each other on the beach in the day but continue their dance of avoidance. Dean tells himself he is waiting his son out. In sales, this is called the Take Away. In modern psychology, it is called withholding, or less flattering, manipulation.

To Juliet, Dean is constantly apologetic about not having gone to town, to get a car or groceries from the store yet. He keeps trying to give her money but she waves him off.

"Next week it's your turn."

Next week? he thinks.

Dean's favorite part of the day is evening, after their runs and shower, after the kids are all serviced and fed. In Juliet's kitchen, they do the dishes, together.

"This is nice." She smiles at him. "Company. One of the hazards of becoming a career housewife is that doing the same things over and over, the monotony of the job wears on you. You're doing things with and for those you love most, but the hundreds of times you do it can erase the meaning. I can read them stories, prepare their food, say 'what?' and not listen to their answers... I want to bring back intention to my life. I want to do things from love, be present again."

"Maybe it's just the grief," Dean suggests. In the close quarters of her kitchen, their shoulders brush. Once. Twice. "It can suck the joy right out of things you really used to enjoy."

"Well," Juliet laughs, "I'm pretty sure I never enjoyed washing the dishes!"

"One of the hard things about having a terminally-ill partner," Dean says, "is if there were ever clean sheets on the bed, it's because I put them there. If the dishwasher was unstacked, it was because I stayed up late to do it. Not that I expected her to. But the lack of partnership..."

He remembers back in Michigan, startling at his vacant reflection in the window over the sink, horrified at how old he looked, the way his eyebrows frowned when he wasn't thinking of anything sad.

She nods and hands him a plate to dry. Their fingers touch in its passing, and again, with the silverware.

Juliet sighs, "The lone captains of the ship."

A ship captain, Dean reminds himself as he resolutely turns off the faucet, who is there to throw a life ring to his floundering son.

On the fifth day, Dean rides with Tony into town and rents his own cobalt blue clown car—the cheapest thing Andy's Autos had, and it wasn't even—and follows the map back to the grocery store. He fills the impossibly small trunk with food and four clinking bottles of red and white wine from the Red Rabbit Liquor Store. Three hundred and twenty-nine US dollars. He tries not to think about this on the drive back to Rum Point, assembling a menu instead. He is already planning to invite Juliet, a thank you for feeding them all these days, for watching the kids, for helping out. For everything.

Maybe also because the idea of an evening without her feels as hollow as a coconut husk.

She shows up ten minutes early, freshly showered, Simon and Sonnet in pajamas, her daughter's palms like a teacup filled with creamy, pink-tinged plumeria blooms, the same flowers Holly had scattered on her doorstep after the tomato plant incident. Juliet is wearing a gauzy white dress, her wet hair twisted into a messy bun. For the first time, he can see she has put on mascara and a peachy lipstick. She looks better without both.

"We brought these for Holly." Sonnet dumps the flowers on his table. "We ladies can wear them in our hair."

The tang of vinegar and earthy thyme and garlic smells swirl in the sticky, fan-spun air. Dean pulls a Pyrex from the oven where fresh fish and onions and peppers are crackling from a quick broiling.

"What stinks?" Simon makes a gagging noise as he grabs the jumbo BB-Q chip bag Owen is dragging around.

"Wahoo *escovitch*," Dean says.

"Simon! Sorry. What is *escovitch*?" Juliet asks.

"Not sure. I found a recipe in one of the Caribbean cookbooks here, and the guy at the store said this fish is so fresh it was swimming this morning. The sauce tastes a little spicy. It's got some local pepper called Scotch bonnet in it, so I kept it on the side, for the kids."

The broiling oven has made his cottage even hotter than outside, the ceiling fan stirring the heavy air. Sweat runs in a little rivulet down Juliet's neck and disappears between her breasts. He watches her blot it with the fabric of her dress.

"Sorry about the temperature," he says. "We got one of the cottages without good AC. Tony warned me there were a few." He doesn't add that it does not matter; that they will be leaving as soon as things with Luc are resolved. Soon.

On the floor in the corner of Dean's living room is a tiny TV, the local channel showing snowy old Tom and Jerry cartoons. The cottages don't have cable, only DVD players and a pile of movies. Simon fiddles with the antenna until the cartoon comes in color, and the kids line up to it on their stomachs like little piglets at an electronic teat, hands fishing blindly in the bag of potato chips.

"It smells amazing," Juliet tells him, pulling open his sliding door to let what little breeze there is flit in off the North Sound.

"I've got garlic mashed potatoes, and I'm sautéing some asparagus and a cold beet salad and," he looks around the kitchen, "I think that's it. Luc hasn't come back yet, so I guess it's just us." He counts heads, noting everyone's shower damp hair and jokes, "The Not-So-Dirty-Half-Dozen."

Juliet tilts a pile of books she has brought from her cottage so he can read the titles before she places them on his coffee table—*I Wasn't Ready to Say Goodbye, The Tender Scar, Getting to the Other Side of Grief.*

"Just in case. Road maps for the wilderness of our intuition or whatever." She laughs, nervous. "You probably co-authored half of these. You're probably way farther along in the Kubler-Ross grief scale than me."

"Why do you say that?"

"Because," Juliet flushes, "I mean, didn't you know, all along, Amélie was going to die?"

"Actually," Dean draws on his years as a clinical psychologist to keep the calm in his voice, "we were sure she wasn't. Why else would we have had Owen?"

They watch him now, shoving great handfuls of chip crumbs into his mouth, giggling at the cartoon, his curls bouncing as his whole body rocks with joy.

"That baby's delicious laugh," Juliet smiles as all the kids appreciate his enjoyment; they are watching him more than the movie, "is better than any antidepressant on the market."

"Anyway…" Dean clears his throat. "Would you like a glass of wine? Everything has about ten more minutes."

There is a bottle of Santa Margherita, what had been Amélie's favorite splurge white, lolling in a bath of ice water in the kitchen sink.

"Oh, well, just one," she says.

"You're welcome to have as many as you like! You've fed my family for the past week."

"No, I meant, that was a note to self."

"Ah." He nods. "Okay." He remembers what she said, about the anniversary— blind drunk by dinner. There is not much Juliet says that Dean doesn't file away.

He pours the glass, the liquid so cold droplets form on the rim and race down the sides when he sets it down beside her.

"Before all this, I promise, I never really used to drink. Jack and I had a system, after what happened at my sister's wedding."

While they sip from their glasses, she tells Dean the story. "Simon was three. He'd come down with some virus. Sky-high fever and the most violent vomiting, and he couldn't keep anything down. I had to do those Tylenol suppositories, poor baby."

Dean nods; they went through that with Luc once.

"Our whole family was supposed to be in Percy's wedding—I was her matron of honor, Jack was an usher, Simon was meant to be the adorable ring-bearer. Instead, I took Simon to an Urgent Care while Jack stood up for my sister in the ceremony."

"Wait, but this is *your* sister's wedding?" Dean asks, sipping. "Her name is Percy?"

"Persephone, yes."

"But why didn't your husband take Si to the clinic?"

She shakes her head, a wry laugh. "That wasn't how things worked with us, the division of labor. Jack was money, I was kids."

Dean grabs at the first piece of unflattering intel on Juliet's husband.

"They gave us the fever suppositories, and afterward, I drove to the hotel where they were having the reception. By then, the Tylenol kicked in, and Si was resting. Jack wanted me to come down to the reception, so he charmed my stepmom, my dad's third wife, who never really liked to do stuff with the original family anyway, into sitting with Si up in the hotel room. Jack was always good at that, a successful salesman." Juliet sips from her wine and Dean tucks this too away in his slim file on Juliet's husband—*charming, successful.*

But he made his wife miss her own sister's wedding?

"Jack and I convinced each other Simon would be fine. We walked into the ballroom just as the bandleader was announcing my matron of honor speech. I was nervous. I drank a half glass of champagne too fast, on an empty stomach, and as I was toasting my sister, I saw Jack across the room doing shots of Jager with her husband, and then two minutes later, there was my stepmother, hobbling across the dance floor with Si limp in her arms, his legs dangling, this horrible foam coming out of his mouth."

"Febrile seizure?" Dean guesses.

"Yes!" Her expression is the same one from that first day at The Wreck bar, when he correctly sourced her email quote. "With his heart history, nobody took anything lightly. We needed to go to the ER, but we'd both had too much to drink. So my stepmother, who has macular degeneration, had to drive my father's big boat of a Cadillac." Juliet mimics the pose, hunched over, squinting and laughing. "She hit every parking pylon in the hotel lot!" The freckles by her eyes wink into the tiny sun lines as she laughs. "My father was furious."

"I bet." Dean chuckles. He loves listening to her stories.

"So, after that night," she says, "Jack and I had an agreement, that one of us always needed to stay on duty. If friends came out to the farmhouse for dinner with a few bottles of wine, we'd have a glass, but when Jack had another, I wouldn't. I never drank, really, until..." she trails off.

"It has its place in the grief process," Dean says, pouring them each a second glass. They clink—a somber cheers. "It's only a problem when it becomes a source of grief itself."

She draws the cold wine into her mouth, holding it there, before she swallows.

"So. How long then, for you?" he asks her, and he can see she knows exactly what he means.

"Six months, on June first."

"Eight months and one day, on June first." They toast again, and he appreciates the music of their glasses and the gentle nod of recognition; shell-shocked soldiers newly home from the same war zone, different platoons.

"After timeshare sales, and moving all the time, after losing my Nana, and then Si in CHOP, we decided to stay in Bucks County. Jack became a real estate developer."

Ahh, a developer. Amélie would have called Juliet's husband a *tueuses d'arbres* — tree killer.

"He'd met his business partner, Marty, and they started Compass with the land around the property. Compass had projects going all over the tri-state area and he worked a lot, late. It was almost midnight, the first of December. There was black ice on the bridge—we were talking on our phones when it happened. I heard it happen. I heard him hit the guardrail, and the water, and I heard his voice, and then the phone went dead." Her sun-brown fingers twirl the stem of the wineglass so fast that the liquid sloshes up the sides.

"I'm sorry," he murmurs.

"Anyway..." She drains her glass. "That's the sad story. That's the wilderness of grief I'm working through. Cheers." They do not clink glasses this time.

Their eyes drift over to the children, their connection, a diversion from the intimacy. Owen has his head on the small of Holly's back, his eyes closing in long slow blinks.

"It's easier, better here," Dean says. He means not being in their old house anymore, not having Amélie's closet of clothes and silky chemo scarves to bury his face in, her cello case perched in the corner of their bedroom like Dracula's coffin.

"My wife was a cellist, and a dancer, and a lot of things. Afterward, I knew I should give her instrument to someone at the University, one of her students," he says. "But I can't do it yet."

They are quiet.

"Some things are worse here," she blurts suddenly. "I feel like…this sounds crazy, but I feel like Jack's ghost is haunting us. Some nights I can't fall asleep. I," she ducks her head, "I know, crazy, but I feel like he's watching us. Sonny says she sees him. And I think, why now?"

"What do you mean?"

"I mean it's still difficult, even almost seven months later, for me to believe Jack is dead. I tried to talk to people about it, back home. They told me I had to move on. I remember my friend Helen, from book club, sitting at my kitchen table, shelling pistachios, not eating them, just licking the salt off the shells, because she's dieting, you know, for match-dot-com. She told me I had to move on, that just because we hadn't buried him didn't mean Jack wasn't dead. She said, 'It's like me finally admitting my marriage to Roman was six feet under and crawling with worms.' She said I had to do it, for the kids' sake. I'm trying."

Dean nods. They hadn't buried Amélie either. Her ashes sit in a Folgers can in the top of the hall closet, because he hasn't figured out what to do with them.

"Do you sleep?" Juliet asks.

"I didn't, at home. But that's better here too," Dean says. "I lie down with my little guy," he nods at Owen, "and we turn the bedroom fan on high, and I tuck O in my crook here, and I don't wake up until we hear the Cayman parrots and the whistling ducks and the coots—" He trails off and sips at his wine. He doesn't tell her that the past few mornings, he has heard Luc get up, and has waited for him to leave, because part of him dreads what Luc might confess to him, alone, in the first light of dawn.

"I worry, here, too. What if Simon gets really sick? You can't imagine what it's like to look at someone you love like a ticking time bomb, to wait their whole life for things to go wrong again, to wonder if every little thing, every little fever, is his heart—"

Luckily, he sees she realizes what she's just said, and she stops, her hand cupped over her mouth. Otherwise, tearing Owen's French fries in half or not, he might have walked her to the door and never looked back.

Her cheeks are slack, flaming red. "Oh, my god, Dean," she says. "I'm so sorry. What a self-absorbed, idiotic thing for me to say."

Dean looks around, for something that needs his attention, the asparagus on the stove, a child, or a line of sugar ants to squash, anything, but it is just them.

"That is exactly what it was like, isn't it?" Juliet whispers. "With Amélie?"

He can barely breathe. Why is it hardest when someone acknowledges his pain, the hardship of those years of watching Amélie die in increments, like the slivering of an apple, each slice so thin the light shines through? He swallows.

"And she was diagnosed when Holly was still a baby, the same year Simon was born?"

Dean doesn't remember telling her this, which means it was Holly. His daughter is confiding in Juliet, stories of their past, when he is out on his run—this makes his throat throb.

"Nine years. This means, you went through nine years, as long as Simon has been alive, worrying and wondering if her cancer would come back—"

Dean nods. *Not if,* he thinks. *When.*

"The thing about loving someone while they're in the hospital," he begins, glad his voice sounds stronger than he worried it might, "is that no matter where you are—"

"It feels like the wrong place to be," Juliet interrupts, perfectly finishing his thought.

"Yes, exactly! I'd look forward to visiting Amélie at the end of every day, count down the minutes, try to leave work early. I'd drive too fast, on the way over, but then as soon as I was there, I'd hate it so much, the machines and the smells and the sounds, and watching her struggle, fighting with the nurses over her rescue doses of morphine, and I'd think, 'Oh my God, I can't wait to get out of here.'"

"I know. But then as soon as you're in the parking garage, the minute you're pulling out and driving toward all the things you've been fantasizing about, the hot shower to wash the germs and stink off you, you immediately want to be right back with them again."

"It makes you feel completely schizophrenic," Dean says.

"Sometimes, I'd call and tell Jack I was on my way home, and I'd have that parking garage regret, and I'd shove my eight dollars at the attendant, and then flip a U-turn and drive right back in the entrance."

"It's the most timeless place in the world. Hours flew by, when I knew I should be home, letting the sitter go, or tackling the laundry, but then minutes could be excruciating, waiting for her meds to kick in, as she begged me to end it all, to make the pain go away. I've never been so exhausted in all my life from doing nothing."

Juliet touches his hand once, lightly.

"I used to hover over Si, I'd watch his heart beat and his monitors and the clock, and I'd time my day in little increments of escape—in ten minutes, I'll get up and wash my hands at the nurse's station. At noon, I'll go buy a milkshake."

"You make a lot of deals with yourself in that time," Dean says.

"Yes. Promises to God, if there is a God," Juliet's voice is soft.

"I think we can agree," Dean finishes his wine, "there's no competition in grief."

Juliet starts to fill her glass and stops, lowers the bottle to the table.

"I said just one, didn't I? And that's two."

He tells her about the flasks he saw slipping out of pockets to spike the punch at the one grief support group he'd tried, how many wine and cheese nights they seemed to have on their calendar.

"I'm on the other side of it," he says. "Or the worst of it, anyway. I can be your sponsor, like a twelve-step program."

"I hope you understand," she says carefully, her voice low because of the children, Simon always listening, "I am not an alcoholic."

"I'm sorry. That was me, trying to make a joke, that I would be your sponsor in moderation, not abstinence. I mean, I certainly don't think you need to abstain."

She smiles, twirling the stem of the wine glass again as she waits for him to realize the double entendre of his words. He stares at her fingers dancing over the shaft of glass.

"Anyway..." He looks away. "We'll share custody. The wine will live at my place, but you're welcome to visit it any time."

He is aware that while their children are physically present, they're electronically occupied. They are a man and a woman having a drink together—everyone knows how this story can end.

He jumps up, suddenly. "Let me, um, check on the fish."

CHAPTER 12

Juliet

Y ou watch as he puts the wine back in the refrigerator. There is something
so different, attractive, in the solidness of him, the breadth of his shoulders.
Dean looks like a man. Last year, when a Jehovah's Witness surprised Jack
mowing the front lawn at the farmhouse on a Saturday, shirtless and wearing jeans,
they'd assumed he was a teenager, asked if his parents were home.

Dean pauses in the doorway of the kitchen, his eyes on the children on the floor.
He takes a breath and consciously straightens his shoulders before coming back into the
room, like he is shrugging something off. A therapist must have to do that, you realize,
or they end up toting everyone's sad stories with them like an overburdened Sherpa.

Finally, you think, and exhale a shaky breath. You've told him, your first stranger,
the whole story. Most of it, anyway, and your voice didn't break once. It's getting
easier; everyone said it would with time.

⌒

"He's been in an accident!" You can still hear your strangled gasp to the 911 dispatcher,
clutching the receiver of the black rotary phone, your eyes on the congealing bacon
grease in Nana's heavy cast iron pan. "I don't know where—he was in his car. A silver
Mercedes." No, you didn't know the model or his license number by heart. "I think
he was coming back from one of his New Jersey projects."

You had been unable to retrieve the exact information from the morning's exchange of daily minutiae over your shared toothbrush, your intended plans for the day. You had reluctantly admitted that maybe the dispatcher should call Jack's business partner, Marty, that he might know more about Jack's schedule than his own wife.

You didn't sleep. Two hours before sunrise, a patrolman found the fresh gap in the metal guardrail of the Route 71 bridge in Belmar, New Jersey, no sign of skid marks.

"There were reports of black ice on area bridges last night," one officer told you. "He wouldn't have seen it coming."

You remember riding to the scene in the periwinkle pre-dawn with Marty and your brother, Lear, cradled in the tiny backseat of Marty's red Porsche, the stench of oiled seat leather so strong you had to breathe through your mouth. Lear's wife stayed with the kids. Your brother had grabbed a rag quilt from the farmhouse and wrapped it around your shoulders—threadbare and antique, it did nothing to keep you warm.

As the sun rose, rescue divers located Jack's Mercedes in the deep black water just beyond the marina.

"Front airbag deployed," they told you. "Some cobwebbing and signs of head trauma on the driver's window at the point of impact."

"Driver's side door closed—a sign that he was unconscious at the moment the car went under."

"The body has only so long that it can survive in temperatures like this, maybe ten, twelve minutes at the most, uninjured."

The recovery divers went out in short shifts in dry suits. At noon, the search for Jack's body was called off as an early snowstorm dusted the East Coast and whipped the ocean beyond the bay into frothy whitecaps.

On the dock, you stood far away from Marty, who spent the entire morning on his cell phone. You caught snippets of information, the same spare handful of facts you considered yours alone, being scattered by the barking, over-eager voice of Jack's business partner.

"Yeah, his car's been found, black ice on the bridge, no sign of the body, winter storm watch…"

You remember delighting in the slow ruin of Marty's expensive, pointy-toed shoes as he paced the salty grit and gravel of the marina. You didn't mind it from the emergency professionals, but how dare Marty call your husband, 'the body'?

Lear gave you his jacket and you stood shoulder to shoulder, as though the past nine years, the bitterness over Jack and the family farmland and the money had never happened. You watched in silence as the Mercedes was loaded onto a flatbed, bleeding dirty grey water and debris from its underbelly. The passenger door was crumpled from where it must have hit the post of the bridge, hanging ajar like a fractured limb.

The hapless deputy, hands jammed deep in the pockets of his parka mentioned the difficulty of ever recovering a body in waters where large predators came to feed at night.

"It's not called Shark River for nothing," he said.

A week later, as sleet replaced the snow and stung the faces of the mourners who forgot umbrellas, or those like Jack's mother who craved physical misery to complement their anguish, you buried all that had been recovered from the Mercedes and the ocean debris that cluttered slips in the nearby marina: one of Jack's black Cole Haans, a shred of his French blue shirt the size and shape of piece of toast, and though some family members thought it wasn't appropriate, his waterlogged laptop and Blackberry, found floating on the passenger seat of the Mercedes.

Now you squint through the night dark windows of Dean's cottage to the wild tangle of the sea grape bushes. A surprising shiver of wind shakes their dried leaves like a rattlesnake. You look away, back to the big-hearted man with the dish towel over his shoulder, a flaming pan of asparagus, and feel a stab of worry that you haven't really told him everything about last weekend, and the weeks before that, and his son. If you're not careful, it will be too late.

CHAPTER 13

Dean

Dinner itself does not go the way he planned. Chaotic; loud. Dean notices Juliet barely sits down, jumping up to fill kids' water glasses, running back to her own kitchen to get Simon some mac and cheese after he gagged over the tender wahoo. She compliments the food but barely eats. During coconut ice cream with hot fudge, Luc comes home.

He drops his backpack and glares around the room. In the dome light over the table, the scab on his cheek looks like stage make-up, drag queen blush. All six chairs at the table are taken.

"Here," Dean pulls Owen to his lap, "have a seat."

When Luc doesn't move, when he rakes his eyes over the filled chairs, Dean makes a quick introduction.

"This is Juliet, from Pennsylvania, and her children, Simon and Son—"

"Yeah, I've seen them around," Luc interrupts. Juliet stands.

"It's late. We should get going anyway," she says.

"I'll walk you back, then." Dean jumps up, puts Owen down in his empty chair.

"I'm starving." Luc voice has an edge of accusation.

"Here." Dean pushes Simon's plate at him, the corner of the fish hacked off and pocked by the tines of Simon's finicky fork.

"That's what I get? Some kid's leftovers?"

"Si, let's go." Juliet nudges him from the slurping of the melted ice cream at the bottom of his bowl.

"I would've made you a plate, but I had no idea when to expect you home."

Luc pokes at the food on Simon's plate.

Juliet passes Dean on her way to the door, the wake of her powdery female smells, deodorant and shampoo wafting past create a surge of longing.

"Thank you for a lovely dinner. The fish was delicious, and the conversation meant a lot to me."

"Wait, hold on. I'll walk you home."

"What—all fifteen yards?" Luc mutters without looking up.

"We're fine. We'll see you all in the morning, bright and early."

"For the daily camp routine!" Holly chimes.

Dean sinks into his chair. After Juliet is gone, he listens to the scrape of Luc's fork against Simon's plate and the wonk of the unbalanced living room fan, the chatter and zigzagging music of the cartoons Holly and Owen are watching. He carries their two empty wineglasses to the sink, and uses the pads of his fingers to gently rub lipstick from the rim of her glass.

Luc stands in the doorway of the dark kitchen. "What are those people doing here?"

"They're our neighbors. I invited her, them, to dinner, as a thank you for..." he trails off. He doesn't have to justify it.

"Here." Luc hands him Simon's plate to wash, much of the expensive fish, $12.99 CI/lb, uneaten. "It was cold."

Dean scrapes it into the trash.

As Luc turns to leave, he adds, "She woke up."

Like an aside, an oh by the way.

"What?" Dean says, but he knows, relief flooding, filling him like liquid gold, pooling in the soles of his feet. *She woke up.*

"Bridget. Twelve days. She opened her eyes. They say she asked for a jerk chicken patty." Luc half-smiles. "They think she's maybe going to be okay."

In the morning, Dean wakes to Caribbean birdsong and the sounds of Luc. This time, Dean slides out from under Owen and brews coffee. Luc is waiting on the screened porch, ear buds in, sunglasses dangling under his chin. Dean stirs in plenty of whole milk and sugar, the way Amélie had been making Luc's *café au lait* since Dean first met him, age three. It must be a myth about caffeine stunting growth, or Luc's father had some dominant height genes.

When he sets their steaming coffees down, Luc pulls out his ear buds and Dean is surprised to hear violin and somber cello—*is that Mahler?*—before he flips it off.

"Thanks. What's that one?" Luc gestures with his mug to a little gray-capped bird with a chartreuse breast carrying strands of coconut husk fibers to a nest in the cottage's accordioned hurricane shutters.

"Bananaquit, I think. I'd have to look it up. I don't know a lot of them here yet."

It rained in the night, a shushing downpour that woke Owen briefly and now everything is washed new, the green of the succulents sparkling, the bromeliads a gaudy fuchsia and ruby, like barmaid lipstick.

Dean sits next to Luc in comfortable silence, remembering a thousand morning-afters with Luc's mother. The fights, her temper, her baiting Dean until he fought back, Amélie's irritations like the snapping pack of dogs set on the English bear, until he roared, or more often, retreated. And then somehow, if they worked through it, the morning after, there was a newness, a relief. Fresh, polite conversation, coffee, the comfort of having made it through a storm together.

"It's making a nest," Luc nods at the bird. "That'll be nice for the littles to see, when they hatch."

Dean is so grateful to have this quiet moment with Luc that he does not point out they will be long gone before the birds hatch.

She woke up!

There is the same pang of relief he has been experiencing all night, every time his mind flits back to this fact. Just like Leo whistles, every little thing is going to be all right.

"Your Mom, Nana, she's why you love birds so much?" Luc asks, sipping his milky-sweet coffee.

Dean can see them, him and his late mother in her dented Oldsmobile with the faded, handmade window sticker that read: *BIRDWATCHER-beware of frequent stops.* Long after her mind had slipped completely, when she would call Dean by the name of any man she had ever known or sometimes even their long-dead family dog, she could still identify all the most viable breeding places of the rare Michigan Prairie Warbler. Though it took them almost an hour to get down the trail, Dean and his mother had passed many afternoons watching the swans at Ford Lake by the highway, a painfully slow sojourn on the boardwalk above the marshes to the nests of the giant, majestic creatures. It was no surprise that Dean ended up back at Ford Lake, hurling stones at the swans, that clear day last October, after he had done the unthinkable.

Does he actually love birds? Dean wonders now. He is more the dog-and-kid type, drawn to the cuddly, the loyal and physically affectionate. But naming, pointing birds out to his children, feels grounding, tethering them to the souls of generations past.

Nana's window sticker is on his Honda now, not because he might whip out his binoculars for a blue jay, but he hoped it would keep them from being rear-ended if he accidentally fell asleep at a red light or had to brake suddenly to retrieve an object Owen hurled from the backseat.

He imagines Luc is thinking about his biological father, who he doesn't think he knows at all.

At some point, Dean thinks, soon, they will have to talk.

Or maybe he's wondering about Amélie—what ties do they share? It had been so hard, her swift decline, the plummets out of remission, first spots in the uterus, then the lung, finally the brain, just as Luc was thrust into the sea of puberty, her patience, her presence waning. Their mother adored them, but he's afraid that all Luc and Holly will remember is that before, before she got sick, Amélie was rabid about her work.

"You should rehearse, see students at home," Dean told her more than once. "It would be good for the kids to hear music coming down from the third floor," he said, imagining the haunting cello strains of Saint-Saens› *The Carnival of the Animals*.

She'd tried, flying down the stairs in a furious thunder of ballet flats on the wooden stairs after Luc accidentally shut Holly's finger in a Matchbox garage.

"How are we supposed to practice when it sounds like a nursery school down here?!" Her French accent was so thick her R's trilled. "It's not professional!"

After that, she left for the university studio each morning, sometimes not coming home from rehearsals until after Dean put the kids to bed. And then that summer at the lake, only eight candles on Luc's birthday cake, Dean's palms prickled with sweat as they glided over the unfamiliar lump under her bathing suit top.

⌒⟩

"Hey." There's a rap on the screen door.

Tony sticks his head around the doorjamb; it's the first time Dean has seen him without his sunglasses on since he got here. He looks strangely naked, blinking like a mole, the skin around his eyes a peachy Michigan-pale, wrinkled. It shows their age.

"Sorry to bug you so early, man, but we've got to go."

Luc stands up and checks his watch. He carries his mug to the dishwasher, showing off for his boss, Dean notes.

"So, she woke up." Dean likes just saying it aloud. He takes a deep breath; it feels like the first stone has been lifted off his chest.

"Yeah, she's surprisingly with it. Good. Her ma wants to take her home as soon as she can."

There is a moment when they are obviously both thinking about Bridget, and her missing leg.

"Police want everyone from the truck down at the hospital this morning. See if we can get to the bottom of this. Might be about time to call that lawyer," he says and yells into the cottage, "Come on, man! Truck's running!"

"Wait." Dean stops Luc at the door. "If I make dinner tonight, you think you could be here, hang out with the family?"

"Coconut chicken?" Luc asks. "And green beans and buttered rice?"

"I can do that," Dean says, though he is missing a few key ingredients, Juliet might have them.

"Just us? Not Juliet and her kids?"

"Of course," he says, though he had been planning to ask them again, for Holly and Owen's sake. "Why? You don't like them?"

"Enh, it's just…" Luc trails off.

"Just what?" Dean asks. Outside, the truck honks.

"Just, if they're here, it's a little awkward, you know, if they're here all the time."

"All the time? I had her, them, to dinner once!"

"But you all went to her place the nights before. I saw you in there. Hanging out. It's awkward. What if we want to talk about Mom?"

Dean pictures Luc standing in the night outside Juliet's cottage, the heavy, wet-velvet air, watching them like a hungry waif in a Dickens' story. He is aware of the fast-approaching end to this moment, Luc's hand on the cottage's front door where Tony's truck idles in the parking lot.

"Why would it be awkward to talk about your mom?"

"Because of Juliet. And you."

"What do you mean, Juliet and me?" Dean can feel his own heart, an accelerated thumping against the back of his ribs.

Luc gives his father the same look Dean uses to coax out the truth—that Luc hadn't actually done his homework, that there really hadn't been any parents home at the party, had there?

"Come on, Dad."

"She just lost her husband! I'm helping her process her grief!"

"Is that what they're calling it these days?" Luc turns the door handle. Outside, Tony honks the truck horn, longer and louder.

"Okay, well." Dean swallows. "It's just you and me here. Do you want to talk about your mom now?"

"Nope." Luc opens the front door. "You're not coming?"

Dean starts to shake his head; they have a plan. Juliet wants to build out three raised garden beds for lettuce, herbs and peppers, and her Brandywine tomatoes need staking. Before all this, he planned to enjoy the quiet, sit alone on the porch with a second cup of coffee, watching the bananaquit dipping into the wild brush for strands of pine and coconut fiber, feathering her nest.

Luc looks down. Fourteen years of making it to every soccer game, every parent-teacher conference, every stage performance from Luc's first grade debut as Garlic in the Nutrition Mission to his most recent hilarious Deadeye Dick in *Pirates of Penzance*, none of it means anything if he doesn't do this now.

"Let me see if Juliet can keep the littles."

And his heart surges when Luc leans out to the parking lot, waves Tony on and yells, "Go on, I'll ride in with my dad."

CHAPTER 14

Dean

Though they're together, Luc is quiet most of the drive into town. His right leg jiggles like a sewing machine. They listen to calypso on a staticky station. Finally, as they pass an elementary school playground where children in uniforms—teal and white checkered shirts and khaki shorts—dart in a game of tag, oblivious to the sapping heat, Luc turns to him.

"When are you guys going home?"

Dean pretends to be intent on not turning on the windshield wipers when he means to signal for a turn; everything is backwards in the clown car. It buys him time.

"I don't know. I guess it depends. Our plane tickets and passports are stamped for the end of the month." This is something new—a strange, gripping clutch of anxiety whenever he thinks about leaving the island. "We'll see."

When Luc doesn't comment, Dean adds, "The littles seem happy here."

At the Cayman Islands Hospital parking lot, Dean parks under the sentry of respectable-sized palm trees and cuts the engine.

"I don't want to go to prison, Dad."

Dean claps his hand over Luc's bouncing knee and squeezes hard. His head tips forward until his chin touches his chest. *Please*, he prays silently as he has been at night, a paraphrase of a childhood Bible school passage, let this cup pass from Luc.

"But I'm not sure I can go home either." Luc's voice is as tight as Amelie's tuned cello strings. "She's everywhere, in the house."

Dean thinks about what Juliet said, feeling like her husband is watching them, with them all the time.

"I don't know what to do."

A police car pulls up beside theirs, and Ebanks, from that day at Rum Point, gets out. He nods at Luc, and past their car, at Tony's truck, where Darvin and Dusty hobble out.

"It might not be our choice, buddy."

Outside Bridget's room, they all wash their hands at a sink that is no cleaner than his at the cottage after a morning of dishes. The nurse at the main station seems more interested in the contents of her styrofoam to-go container, stabbing at red beans with a plastic fork as they pass.

In the room, the sound of COPS: *Houston* blares from the corner mount TV. Ebanks' eyes go right to it as they all shuffle and file to fill the small room. On the screen, a shirtless man with a blurred out face is being forced to the pavement. In the sun-filled yard beyond the hospital window, wild chickens peck in the sandy patches between the shocks of dry grass.

Dean notices her mother first; he makes a point to look her in the eye, nod hello. She and her younger daughter have flown from Auckland. Tony says she hasn't left Bridget's bedside more than once in the last five days; she looks it.

Tony surprises him, crosses right to the girl and stands by her head, while the rest of the boys hang back. She tilts her face up to him.

"Bridge," Tony says softly. He nudges her shoulder. "Glad to see those pretty green eyes open again."

Her mother blows her nose into a crumpled tissue, a honking sound.

"You understand, though, I'm going to have to count this time here while you were napping as unpaid vacation, right? Dock your pay?"

Dusty and Darvin make obligatory exhalations of humor, and the girl struggles to smile. She turns to look past them all to Luc. He bobs his head once, like the curly-tail lizards around the pool back at the cottages.

There is a long, uncomfortable silence. By this point, Dean is sure everyone has stolen a glimpse at the sheet-covered spot on the bed where her left leg ends.

"Alright," Ebanks says, in a strangely high-pitched voice for such a big man.

"We're here to talk about the accident, see what anyone remembers."

The mother nudges the girl, Bridget's little sister, sitting beside her. She is about Holly's age, thick, in a bright yellow T-shirt that reads *Too Hot 2 Handle*. "Evangeline. Go on and get a soft drink."

"I'll take her," Tony offers.

The mother makes no move to turn off the television and everyone's heads swivel in its direction whenever the pauses in the room go too long. Ebanks seems caught up in the plot.

"What do you mean," Bridget asks, long spaces between each word. "See what we remember?"

She is puffy with IV fluids, but she has cherry lips and her smile is wide, a charming gap between her front teeth. There is a natural upswing to her eyes, which are sea green against the white pillowcase.

"We're trying to get to the bottom of a few things."

"What?" Bridget blinks. "Why?"

"Well, everyone, the boys here, are claiming total blackout, nobody willing to confess to where they were at the moment of the accident."

"Oh." She looks right at Luc. His face is unreadable, flat. Dean imagines he would still be wearing his sunglasses if Dean hadn't insisted he take them off.

"We know you all had been drinking. But can you say who was driving, or who—" Ebanks stops and starts, "or what you might have hit?"

"Well," Bridget draws the word out in her accent. She looks from Luc to the police officer. "I'll say I know where two of us were."

Luc turns to the television screen, a commercial for lunchmeat.

Dean has never felt such relief, because Bridget's expression is the one of dozens of girls back in Saline, girls who called a familiar "hi" to Luc back in the Briarwood Mall, girls who looked after Luc expectantly when Dean came to pick him up from school. It was a look that faded quickly to shock and embarrassment when Luc stared straight ahead. It was a look that said: *how can you act like you don't know me, after what went on between us, the places we put our mouths, who I thought I was to you?*

Ebanks is still talking.

"But you can't say who was driving?"

"No." Bridget looks down at her leg. They all do. She adds softly, "I was in the back, in the truck bed. Lying down."

Luc was with her, Bridget, in the bed of the truck, at the time of the accident, which means he wasn't driving—his son is innocent! Dean wants to run screaming this down the halls of the hospital, wants to dance Luc around the parking lot. He wants to tell someone, his throat aches to crow it out. He has to stop himself from slapping Luc on the back in congrats, throwing victory fists in the air. Dean looks at everyone else, but nobody seems to have seen it. Surely her mother, Dean thinks, but she is leaning forward anxiously, her hand clamped over Bridget's forearm.

Bridget looks up at the semicircle of men. Two tears run down her face.

"I'm sorry, can I, can we..." She sniffs. "I'm afraid I'm a little tired, just now."

"I'm done here. You've been through a lot." Ebanks backs away, scowling at the three other workers, like this whole thing wasn't his idea. "Get out of here! Let the poor girl rest."

The relief in the room, that this is ending, fills it like a balloon, pushing them toward the open door. They shuffle, Darvin's crutches squeaking, on a hasty retreat, mumbling, "We'll come see you again" and "Get better, Bridge."

Only Luc pauses in the hallway. "Dad."

Out here it is dim, and the walls are a graying green that shimmers under the few fluorescent tubes.

"What?"

"I'm just going to... for a sec..." He doesn't finish. "Hey." He sticks his head back around the door. Bridget looks up hopefully. Luc makes his way to her bedside. He is an old veteran of this, Dean knows, hospital vigil. He likes his chair on the side without the IV, not positioned up at the head like most visitors, but about midway down. He used to put his feet up beside Amélie's bare ones on the end of her bed, big Nike sneakers on the sheets that drove the nurses nuts, and sling his arm over the rail, in case Amélie woke up and wanted to hold his hand.

Dean lifts a finger, signals to Bridget's mother.

"Can I get you a coffee?" She smiles, relief smoothing every worry crease, and crosses to him. When she passes Luc, she pats his arm, familiar. She is a small woman who barely comes up to his chest. In the back, her hair is a nest of tangles.

They both stand in the doorway and watch as Luc pulls up the chair Bridget's mother vacated. He puts a hand easily, lightly, on her thigh, the one with the truncated end, high enough not to hurt her, low enough to be appropriate. She plucks at the skin over his knuckles, once, twice.

"Hi."

"Hey, yourself."

They smile at each other, commiserative. It reminds Dean of him and Juliet, telling each other their war stories of loss and grief the night before.

"You okay then?" she asks Luc. Her eyes are on his scab, pale pink where the maroon skin is flaking off. Luc hasn't been careful about putting sunscreen on it; Juliet warned Dean it will scar.

"This is your son?" Bridget's mother asks. Dean nods, not sure if he should feel proud Luc stayed, or apologetic for everything that has happened.

"I'm okay. I hit my head. I was out," Luc is saying.

"Yah, me too. Zonked!"

They laugh.

"I see you'll do anything to get out of filling tanks or pulling your turn on the couch." It's the same gallows humor Tony had tried, but for Luc, she beams.

"It's not that bad," she says bravely, and Luc tilts his forehead down toward her. "Got me drugged to the gills, so it doesn't hurt, really." She makes a curious little laugh, puts her hand on the crown of Luc's bowed white-blonde hair. "Really. Could be worse. Could've been me head."

"He's a good boy," Bridget's mother says, tugging Dean's elbow, pulling him to the hallway. "Been keeping me company in the evenings, plays cards with my Evie."

"Luc's been here?"

She nods. If she is surprised he doesn't know this, she keeps it hidden. "And he stayed with her the one night, so I could go back to the Sunshine Suites and wash up, close my eyes for a bit."

They walk the long corridor to the Pink Hibsicus Café together.

"He told me about your wife. I'm so sorry."

Dean is stunned into silence.

"I doubt your boy was the one driving," she continues.

"Really?" Dean can't keep the eager out of his voice. Has Bridget told her mother something she didn't share with Ebanks?

"He says he doesn't remember a thing, but my senses tell me that your boy was in the truck bed," she smiles wryly. "Fooling about. With my Bridge."

Later, on the drive back to Rum Point, Dean can't stop smiling. The adrenaline of the past two weeks bleeds out of him, like gas from a rusted-out engine, and it leaves effervescent joy in its place.

They stop for a beer at Paradise Bar on the waterfront, just the two of them, and Luc tells him about an encounter with a manta ray on a night dive.

"She was huge, Dad, like thirteen feet, wingtip to wingtip, stayed right with me. It sounds crazy, but I felt like, somehow, she was meant to be with me, like a message. Like she was trying to say, in spite of all this shit, everything's going to be okay. It was something, Dad."

When they turn at Pedro's Castle, Dean steps on the gas so the rental motor whines. He can't wait to tell all of this to Juliet. When the time comes for their sunset runs, Dean is sure he could sprint to the end of the island and back, twice! After running, dinner is next. He pictures them on her screened porch, wine and conversation, a citronella candle flickering between them. He cannot wait. The tickle under his sternum is so faint and foreign, it is unrecognizable—but it feels like anticipation

But then Luc reminds him he promised coconut chicken and just their family, and when he arrives back at Juliet's cottage, it is quiet time and there is a burnt popcorn smell hanging in the over-air-conditioned air. Owen runs to him, and leaps into his arms.

"What's going on?"

Holly and Simon are on their feet in front of Juliet's laptop giving their loudest he did it/she did it arguments and good lord, there's water pooling around Juliet's computer, and the screen flickers before there is a sickening sci-fi sound. Then it goes blank.

"What happened here?" he explodes, not caring how loud he is shouting right in Owen's ear, horrified, embarrassed—how will they ever replace this?

"It's not my fault, it was Simon's drink!" Holly says, her face blotchy red.

"*You* knocked it over!"

"Only because you weren't letting me have my turn! You hog it all the time, Si!"

Juliet scoops the laptop into her arms like a wronged toddler and tilts it sideways so the water pours out.

"Nobody should have a drink around my computer, Si. You know the rules," is all she says. She hasn't met Dean's eyes.

"It's not my fault!" Holly wails; her legs are in straddle, like she wants to run to her father, but is afraid she won't find the usual shelter.

"You know better too! You kids shouldn't be horsing around with water near a computer!" *Horsing around?* Did he really just say that? When did he start channeling his father?

"Mom, we can fix it, can't we? Take it to Uncle Adam—" Simon trails off.

"No, hon, we can't fix it. Uncle Adam is in New Jersey." Juliet snatches a beach towel off the back of a chair and drapes it on the dining room table. She flips the computer open like a tent, water still dripping.

Sonnet glances at Holly, openly sobbing, and her lips tremble, and she joins in too, hysterical wails.

Behind him, Luc says, "God, Holl, you're such an idiot!" and the mature young man from the hospital morphs back into an obnoxious teenage brother.

"Let's call it for today," Juliet says tightly, her hand on Holly's shoulder, pointing her toward Dean and the screen door. *What's done is done.*

"What?" Dean says.

"Nothing. It's Macbeth, today's Daily Inspiration," she adds flatly.

"How is that inspirational?" he sputters. He wants to evaporate, for all of them to be back home in Michigan, where at least he had a semblance of control over his children. What's done is done?

The planes of Juliet's bare, freckled shoulders draw the line in sharp focus where before, it had been blurring. She passes Holly off to him—this is yours. Meeting Dean's eyes she adds, "Maybe everyone needs to take a break, for the rest of the day."

CHAPTER 15

Juliet

After dinner, you lock the cottage doors, front and back, and slip between the sheets of your bed. Your legs are restless, scissoring the sheets. You missed your run today.

"Mom?" It is Si, in the doorway. He is wearing his red Phillies pajama bottoms and no shirt. The white lines crisscrossing his chest glow against his tan—you have been religious about applying SPF 50 to them since you got here. You told Dean he should do the same for Owen's cheek sores, and really Luc's face as well. Raw skin can scar, permanently.

Simon slides into bed next to you and puts his head on your heart, a bare arm slung over your waist. "I'm sorry, about your computer."

You sift your fingers through his dark hair, silky like Jack's.

"Dean was really mad. And Luc."

You murmur that it will be okay. Poor Holly, you think. Poor all of them.

You think Si has fallen asleep when he lifts his head.

"Holly says she sees her mom in her dreams, all the time," he blurts, eyes wide.

You kiss his forehead; settle it back on your chest. "Shh."

"Do you dream about Dad?"

"Sometimes. Not really." You don't tell him about your nightmares.

"And Sonny says she sees Dad everywhere! What's wrong with me? I don't see him. I don't dream about him. I don't even remember what he sounds like anymore."

You think about Jack and Simon, how his parenting interactions were inconsistent, all or nothing. Consumed by work for weeks, and then in short bursts, Jack would fix his son with the white-hot tractor beams of his attention—let's build a pillow fort! Let's ditch school, drive down to the stadium to watch training day! Let's go see the new Transformers movie at midnight! These tended to leave Si more paralyzed than connected.

"I have some movie clips," you say, kissing his head. You rub his warm shoulders with your hand. "You can hear him on those."

"But they were on your computer." Simon's voice is miserable.

"Oh well. When we go home, then," you say. Whenever that will be.

"I'm sorry," he whispers again, his voice near sleep.

"Shh," you say. You do not tell him how relieved you were when it happened. You're not sorry it means the end of Luc coming over, and with what you have been reading—emails from your brother and your Daily Inspirations—you think it might not be the worst thing in the world that you lost your connection to the United States.

CHAPTER 16

Dean

Unprompted, Holly writes an apology letter to Juliet that is three pages long, pages two and three entirely composed of her dark, curly-cursive "reallys" and "verys," ending with a simple "sorry," underlined.

She shows it to Dean when the morning sun is streaming in the through the dusty screens on the side of the cottage that faces the parking lot. The pop and hiss of the coffee maker fills the narrow kitchen with its roasted chicory scent. The dishes from last night's uninspired chicken (no coconut or green beans) and rice are piled in the sink, peppered with sugar ants.

"Very nice," he says but he is thinking, *that's more than I would have done.* He's still bristling over the night before while he makes their breakfast, furiously whipping the scrambled eggs. Has he been wrong about Juliet? He pictures her capable hands escorting his sobbing daughter to the door.

Kids spill things! Can't you see how awful she feels? Two of the many phrases that he's turned over in his head all night, things he should have said, ways he wished he'd come to his daughter's defense. He thinks of Luc—is there some horrible Murphy's Law of parenting that dictates it is only possible to do well with one of your children at a time?

He makes a resolution: today, they'll spend time without Juliet and her kids. Boundaries! The irony is that he teaches an entire section on this topic in the fall semester Psych 204—Love, Marriage and Family Relationships. He uses the Cloud & Johnson tomes as textbooks, lectures his students on the importance of healthy boundaries, "especially when one is experiencing a significant life-changing event." It doesn't get much more significant than the loss of a parent and partner. Amélie's absence still aches like an arthritic joint. For Luc, this is compounded by the trauma of the accident.

Dean is surprised when his son saunters into the kitchen in his boxer shorts; his walk, slightly bow-legged, is the epitome of his mother's. It is enough to make Dean's breath catch at the collar of his T-shirt. He swallows hard, and it passes.

"Tony give you the day off or are you late?"

"I'm off — first time in three months. He said we all need to spend some time thinking about if we still want to work here." The way Luc mimics Tony, it comes out like a threat. To Dean, it sounds hopeful—Tony will fire him, the government will revoke his work permit, give him back his passport, and they can all go home. The only problem is that thought makes Dean's empty stomach heave a little. He reaches for the coffee.

"Okay, then, so let's do something different today," he says, smiling at Owen and Holly as he slices bananas. "Something new."

But then there are Simon and Sonnet at the screen door, and Owen scrambling down from his chair to open it for them. Despite Dean's noises that they finish eating, they're off, Holly clutching the letter. Dean swipes the line of sugar ants marching along the kitchen backsplash before chasing after his children, catching up in time to see Holly hand the letter to Juliet at the pool with a handful of hibiscus plucked from the bush.

Juliet folds Holly in her arms, meeting Dean's eyes as she says, "Now, let's forget about all that. I've been thinking we need to shake up our camp routine." She keeps an arm slung around Holly's shoulders, and she wiggles his daughter lightly, leaning in to watch her reaction until she is sure there is a smile. "I was thinking we should take a day trip to the Turtle Farm, on the other side of the island. Si's been asking about it ever since we saw the posters in the airport."

They let out a collective cheer, Owen's chubby fists in the air, though he has no idea why.

"Okay," Dean says slowly. "I'll go get my wallet."

He is surprised when Luc volunteers to join them, slouching in the front seat with the map from the cottage's coffee table. They travel caravan-style, and it takes more than an hour, following the lone road around the perimeter of the island, keeping the turquoise sea on their left. They pass through the bustle of George Town, Owen fascinated by the cargo ships, forklifts and cranes at the shipyard. Traffic slows to a crawl as sunburned tourists file off the tender boats from the all-you-can-eat cruise ships, waddling straight into the Señor Frogs and Margaritaville restaurants on the waterfront.

When they pass the turn off for the hospital, Dean notices Luc looks down the long road into town. He claps a hand over his son's knee and is rewarded with a look of quiet understanding. They're going to get through this.

Seven Mile Beach is a stretch of beige condos and endless white lounge chairs and Dean is relieved that they are staying out at their cove at Cayman Kai. For one, he is sure it is cheaper, and he appreciates the quieter, more remote side of the island. He notices he hasn't seen an interesting bird since they left Bodden Town.

⁓

The Turtle Farm, situated in a local district called West Bay can be smelled long before they reach the entrance. Stagnant water and the curious stench of wet dog food, Dean has to shush Holly's dramatic protests, the pulling of her tank top up above the lower half of her face and exaggerated mouth breathing. Although she has the most sensitive nose of all his children, so delicate she once threw up in the cheese aisle at Whole Foods and blamed the Saga Bleu, he doesn't want their trip to start out on a bad note, not when Juliet is being such a good sport about her ruined computer.

"Are you kidding? She did me a favor," she says when he apologizes on the way to the entrance, a hushed offer to replace it somehow. "It was completely liberating to get up this morning and not go right to the computer for the daily drama back home. I'd gotten a little obsessed with those obscure daily inspirations about regret and risk. I don't want to dredge up old stuff, not when I'm making such good progress wading through the wilderness of my grief. This, right now, is the most relaxed I've been since I got here."

"I have an ancient Dell from work and decent wireless at my place. You're welcome to come over any time," he adds. It was the computer that he had used late into the night, trying to get an accurate price on the gut-dropping replacement value of her ruined platinum MacBook Pro.

"You brought your computer here?" Luc is eavesdropping.

"Yes, why?" Dean asks.

"No reason," Luc mumbles.

"One of my brothers-in-law in New Jersey is a Mac guru. When we go home, whatever he can salvage, great. I backed up all my photos before I left, and Holly's been taking more than I have here. You can email them to me sometime. It's no big deal. A computer is totally replaceable."

He feels a pang as she says this. Somewhere at the end of all this looms their return to Michigan. He pictures them exchanging email addresses so they can share photos, and for a few years, maybe even holiday cards. He imagines a teenage Owen squinting at a photo stuck to their fridge with an EMU magnet, murmuring, "Wait, who were those guys again?"

His eyes drift to where Juliet has Owen and Sonnet's hands clutched in hers, dropping them only to dig out her wallet at the entrance. She offers to pay for Dean's admission as well, saying something about dinner, but he insists.

Boundaries, he thinks again. They have only known each other for a week, he reminds himself as he counts out the colorful Cayman Island dollars.

The first half of the tour is an underwhelming trek through a tacky gift shop and some local birds in cages. He has seen better specimens just paying quiet attention outside his screened porch at dawn and on his sunset runs.

But then they come to the tanks of the ancient turtles, 850-pound prehistoric beasts. Their eyes carry the wisdom of the ages as they pass the thick Plexiglas viewing windows in the murky green water. Owen's somber "Ohhh," his toddler hand starfished against the viewing glass alone is well worth the price of admission.

"Pretty awesome," Juliet says, and her eyes rest on Owen's face, drinking in his reaction.

"This was a great idea," Dean says, and together they take stock of their five children, all mesmerized in a rare moment of silent wonder. They share a smile.

But then the tour takes them across the road to the more utilitarian part of the farm; where turtles swim in crowded tanks, a hopeless clockwise circle three deep, scrambling to push their fins through their tank mates to the surface for an audible gasp of air.

The turtles in this tank are one year old—a sign reads, and they stare soberly at dinner-plate size turtles swimming in their swill.

The turtles in this tank are two years old—reads the second one, and there is more of the same, with a slightly larger, platter-sized group of turtles.

Turtles are harvested for meat at three years old—is the final sign, and then there are no more tanks.

"Jesus, this place is great," Luc mutters. "Auschwitz for turtles. Great idea! I'm so glad we came!"

Simon and Holly read more slowly, and then turn a slow circle, eyes narrowing when they find no more turtles, only low-slung cement buildings with rusted, corrugated roofs.

"Harvest?" Holly looks at Dean, trying to reconcile a word that to her means pumpkins and auburn leaves and kettle corn with turtles swimming in desperate circles under the glare of the Caribbean sun. She reads it again, her lips moving over the words, her eyes back on the buildings by the chain-link fence.

"Oh, no," Holly hiccups on a sob, "do you think that's where they—"

Simon turns his face up to Juliet.

"Mom? They aren't going to…" he pauses, distress turning his eyebrows into dark squiggles. "Are they?"

"Nice idea, adults," Luc says. "As if we haven't been dealing with enough of this shit already."

"Where are the rest of the turtles?" Sonnet asks.

Owen takes up the cry, "I want da turtles!"

"Wow," Juliet looks around. "Well. I guess that's it." They have arrived at a chain link gate with the word EXIT, and an arrow guiding them back to the gift shop. Simon tilts his head into Juliet's ribcage and she cups his bony shoulder.

"What, are you guys going to start crying?" Luc hip checks Holly into Dean. A quick clutch of her elbow keeps Holly from stumbling onto the marl crunching under their feet. "Seriously? You're crying for turtles? What did you expect? It's a freaking *farm*. I bet you can have really fresh turtle soup at the restaurant up the road."

"How about a little sensitivity, Luc?" Juliet snaps. "And watch your language, hmm?"

Dean knows Luc only acts cruel when he is forced into uncomfortable emotion. He wants to point out to Juliet, privately, that Luc has been staring down his mother's expiration date for the past three years, swimming in gasping, helpless circles.

But then something passes between Juliet and Luc, a look, a moment that speaks of some history. Dean turns away, but he cannot unsee it.

"That's enough," Dean says; he means both of them.

Luc kicks a smattering of shells and sand and broken coral from the side of the road before they cross back to their cars; it pings against a van shuttling tourists back to George Town.

Dean wills Juliet to meet his eyes, but she is avoiding them, hunched over slightly, her arms curling over her children's backs like a sentry.

"Who's hungry?" Juliet straightens up, and they make miserable, slow progress up the road into the midday heat of the open-air Cracked Conch Restaurant.

CHAPTER 17

Dean

"**Y**our son had better not say anything about the turtle schnitzel entree," Juliet whispers after reading aloud the few items from the kids' menu and then jerking it out of Simon's hands before he can browse any farther. "Is it just me or is it really hot in here?" She makes a fan out of the menu.

"Why don't you see if it's cooler out on the deck?" Dean offers. "I'll manage the ordering, help the kids." Luc doesn't look up from his menu until she is gone, but then Dean notices him watch Juliet walk to the shaded dock at the northwest point of the island.

Is Luc watching her, Dean worries, like Bridget, and all the others, watch him?

When the waitress has snapped her pad closed with their orders, Dean follows Juliet out to the dock, stopping at the bar for a quick drink.

"Hey." Dean stands next to Juliet at the railing, facing the sea. He is trying to think of how to begin. To Luc, the turtles trapped in the tanks might be images of his mother, or fear that the police will make good on their threat to charge everyone from Saturday night. He needs to explain that Luc might be imagining himself here, gasping for breath in a crowded, sweltering prison. Or perhaps he should address the tension between Luc and her. Instead, Dean offers Juliet a sip of an unnaturally green drink.

"What is that?"

"It's supposed to be a margarita on the rocks. Smells a little like a urinal puck." He's relieved to see her smile, but she shakes her head.

"Oh, no thanks. Tequila and me… "

They stand in commiserative misery.

"I ordered, and Luc's watching the kids." He tries again, "Seven turtle soups, right?"

She laughs, finally.

They stare into the clear water below where silver-finned fish as big as Owen cruise the shallows.

"He's going through a lot. I'm not saying it excuses him, but Luc is under a terrific amount of stress right now."

There is a long silence.

Finally, she sighs, "I'm sorry I was short with him. And I'm sorry I didn't look into this more. That wasn't exactly what anyone needed today."

"It's not your fault."

"I've been thinking that it's Jack's, actually," she says. "For dying. Jack would never have let the kids end up in a foul-smelling death camp for slow-swimming turtles."

Dean thinks but does not say that if Jack and Amélie had not died, it might not have been so upsetting. But if that had not happened, none of them might be here right now. That he feels panicked about this surprises him. It is the second time today that the thought of leaving here and returning to Michigan makes his gut lurch.

"Whenever we moved or traveled, Jack bought all those skinny, alternative guidebooks, scoured the travel blogs. He prided himself on discovering the real gems of a new location."

See? Dean wants to say to Luc, to point to this conversation as proof that there is no "Juliet and you". They're just processing grief!

"I remember on our honeymoon in Italy," she continues, "I wanted to try gelato. We were in the Piazza del Campo and I suggested GROM, the touristy place on Banchi di Sopra. But Jack insisted we find one called Kopa Kabana. It was off a little side street by the university and their *ricotta e fichi*? It was like clouds of heaven. The whole time, Jack was so proud, pointing out that nobody around us spoke a word of English."

Right now, while he is noticing that it might not just be leaving the island that bothers him, that by the way, even Juliet's earlobes are perfect, she is waxing poetic about her honeymoon.

"I suppose," Juliet continues, "I'm actually angry at myself for putting the kids in another situation that forces them to face death. Luc was right, it's in the name: turtle farm!"

"He does this sort of thing whenever he feels threatened. He was a handful the first few months, the first year I met him. Abandonment issues. It's common, textbook. He's not the best at processing emotion. Out of the three of them, I think Luc's got the worst of it. I mean, the littles," Dean continues, "they've still got me for their primary parent. Owen will never remember anything different. So long as I'm constant, that might be enough. And Holly, she takes care of herself, and the rest of us, probably too much. But with Luc, sometimes I feel like I'm back where we were when Amélie and I were first together, trying to convince him I'm not going anywhere, that I'm in his life for good."

Juliet straightens up off the railing, flecks of its peeling paint sticking to her arms in the humidity, but she doesn't seem surprised when he adds, "Luc is not my biological son."

Other than height and the same hair color, they look nothing alike—Luc is lanky, darker skinned and bow-legged, while Dean is more square and fair. He waits for her to process this.

"Do you, does he, have any relationship, with his father?"

"I'm his father," Dean says quickly. He thinks of the last few days of Amélie's life, how Robert's reappearance in their marriage drove him to do something so horrible, unforgivable, the regret sometimes threatens to swallow him.

"But the way Luc holds his arms, the expression he makes when he's listening… they're one hundred percent you. You're so good, so natural with him."

They are quiet for a moment. Below them, the waves slap against the concrete pylons of the deck. It is his turn to tell his love story, just so they're clear, because from a distance, a man and a woman standing so close their shoulders are touching on a dock at the Northwest point of a sunlit Caribbean island might look, might *feel*, like something else.

"I fell in love with Amélie the moment I laid eyes on her, in college, on a service trip abroad. She had a red bandana on her head, covered in sweat and dirt, hoeing a teaching garden in Ghana. But for several years, for a long time, for her, there was someone else."

"But…" A frown creases between Juliet's eyes. One day, he thinks, these will be part of the permanent pattern that graces her beautiful face. "West Africa? I thought Holly said she was French. Do French women even wear bandanas? And gardening? I've been picturing her exotic, like some film star, smoking, definitely big dark glasses, like Holly's…" She trails off; an embarrassed laugh.

So she has been picturing, talking about, wondering about Amélie too, Dean notes.

"Those glasses were Amélie's. Holly was always obsessed with them. I wasn't surprised when they disappeared off the dresser, afterward. And she did smoke, Djarums, when we first met."

Juliet doesn't say anything; he can see she is still putting this all together. How to describe Amélie, the unabashedly Bohemian edge to her, the smell of her clove-scented breath, the beauty in the slight crookedness of her bottom teeth, the stunning ugliness of her dancer's feet, the erotic bulge of her knotted calves, the wildness of her dark curls and impassioned speech. She derided everything American, threw out all the mail-order toy catalogs that arrived the month before Christmas, but splurged at an art supply store, buying six-year-old Holly three hundred dollars of real sable brushes and oil paints and canvasses.

How to explain that what kept Amélie at work for twelve-hour days was not the drive for more money for the family, but her hunger to create, to shape her students into something worthy, to produce performances that had reviewers scratching their heads and scrambling for their thesauruses.

"I'm telling you all this," he says to Juliet, "to explain Luc's behavior today. I think it makes this harder for him, losing Amélie. And then the accident." Dean pauses to sip from his citrusy drink. "Do you think they actually put any tequila in this, or did I just pay fifteen dollars CI for some nuclear Drano and rock salt?" He looks into the glass, sniffs.

"So Luc was in the truck that night? When the girl got hurt?"

Dean nods. "We're not really here on vacation." What is there to say about the dented fender, the blood on the windshield, the potential missing victim? "I'm more here... in case."

"In case?"

"In case he needs me."

"Hazel, when she stopped by the other day, she told me the girl lost her leg."

Dean nods.

"Was he driving?" One of Juliet's hands rests lightly on Dean's forearm like the lorikeets in the Detroit Zoo.

"None of them can seem to remember who was at the wheel. We're still waiting on the blood alcohol labs from Miami. Blackout, post-traumatic amnesia, or they're lying. I don't know. At this point, the police are threatening to arrest them all. Tony's threatening to fire them."

"I'm so sorry. You certainly didn't need this."

We cannot afford more tragedy.

"No," Dean sighs. "The kicker is, I sent him here, to Tony. I was so sure I was doing the right thing, getting him away from the house, and the memories."

"Do *you* think he was the driver?"

Dean swallows before he answers. "No, I don't think so."

He pictures Luc and Bridget in the hospital, her hand resting on the crown of his head.

"Bridget's awake; we were there yesterday. But I don't know what that means, legally. There are some other pending charges. Whatever happens, I assume they are going to want some resolution. I mean, someone was driving the truck."

"I'm so sorry." Juliet's hand is on his back now. "I never wanted to raise damaged children," she blurts. "Before. It's why no matter how rocky things were with Jack, I made him promise never to divorce. Everyone around us, all the problematic kids, the ones who tortured stray cats or stole the school computers, it seemed to be the common denominator."

Dean nods, but he catches himself clutching at the first thing she said, thinking, *so things weren't good before, with your husband?*

And then he wonders at what she is saying? Does she see Luc as damaged? A problem child? What exactly is her history, that long look in the parking lot, with his son?

Back home, before he sent Luc to Tony, the principal called to say there were rumors about Luc and the assistant tennis coach, a mother of twins the same age as Owen.

But then he thinks of Luc, hitching the long ride each night to George Town and back, to sit with a girl who nobody was sure would wake up.

Juliet glances over his shoulder, frowning. "Simon!"

He ducks sheepishly behind a pole, his cheeks red.

"Go sit down!"

"I'm hungry," he whines.

"Then go back to the table and sit down! See if the food arrived. We'll be right there."

She makes an exasperated, affectionate noise in her throat. Simon slinks back, throwing looks over his shoulder.

"Anyway, I feel like, now," Juliet continues when Si is gone, "now I have to be enough, to be larger than life, better than me and Jack even, so they never feel the loss, or feel sad, or get upset because I stupidly dragged them to 'Auschwitz for turtles' six and a half months after their father drowned."

Like Holly had outside the turtle tanks, Juliet tips her forehead into Dean's sun-warmed shoulder. He can feel her surreptitiously wiping her tears on the fabric of his shirt. He rests his drink on the railing so he can wrap his arms around her, surprised at how fragile she feels, how well they fit. They are both broken, but together, there is a wholeness.

"Is this what happens?" she whispers. He can feel her lips moving against his biceps. "When you are a psychologist, does everyone, strangers on the airplane, do they just blurt out their problems?"

"You're hardly a stranger anymore." He takes a deep breath—can she feel his heart thudding?—inhaling her herbal shampoo, and beyond that, the earthy warmth of her scalp.

"We should go back," she whispers, but it takes them a long time to separate.

At the table, the middle three are drawing on the paper tablecloth, macabre cartoons of turtles being dragged by a machete-wielding, angry eye-browed executioner.

"Hey now," Dean says, and he can feel Juliet watching him as he scribbles over Holly's shoulder, turning the machete into a rose and putting skateboards under the turtles' fins, making them laugh.

When the soup arrives, Holly has ordered vichyssoise.

"Doesn't it sound French?' she asks.

"It is French, duh," Luc says, and Dean is irritated at him, thinking, *show her who you are! Show her you're not damaged!* After her first bite, Holly raves and passes it around, makes everyone try a bite.

"It tastes like cold potato soup," Luc huffs. Dean wants to kick him under the table.

"That *is* delicious," Juliet tells her. "I'm going to order a bowl myself."

"And one for me!" Sonnet tells the waitress.

"I'll have two more," Holly says confidently. "You can cancel my chicken fingers."

"Now, wait a minute, Hol," Dean says, reaching for the menu.

"It's fine," Juliet interrupts. "She's right. It's the best vichyssoise I've ever had. We don't have room or time to put potatoes in the garden, and I certainly won't go to the trouble to make this for the rest of the summer. Let them enjoy it, order as much as they want. Please. Lunch is my treat."

"I can take care of my own," Luc says, his eyes on his plate. "Tony just paid us all yesterday."

"Not at all," she tells him, and Dean watches as she waits for Luc to look up. The smile she gives him now, he notes with relief, definitely looks more maternal. "It's my treat. Besides, it's only money."

"We'll make more of it!" Simon and Sonny chime in unison.

At Rum Point, behind her back, Dean has heard Tony and Leo call Juliet the Wealthy Widow, Tony making predatory spidery claws out of his hands when he says it. "Hazel said her dead husband was a mega-millionaire."

Afterward, they walk out to their separate clown cars for the long drive back to Cayman Kai. Their shoulders bump and he smells it again, under her shampoo, sunscreen and bug spray, the intoxicating scent of her essence. It is like the stretching and breaking of a magnetic field to move away from her.

"Do you know you're both left-handed?" she says quietly, and he knows she means Luc. He has felt her watching them all through lunch. "And you both hold your forks in the same, unique way, like a stylus?"

"Nurture vs. nature," he says. "It's fascinating stuff; keeps psych grad students busy for years."

"I wish Luc had his international license," she says, unlocking her car. "Or we had cell phones."

"Why?" he asks, lowering Owen into his car seat.

"There's just," she pauses. "I wish we could ride together. I have so many things I want to talk about. You're such a natural father, to all of them. How you turned it around, like that, at the table, with the cartoons, and coming here, in case. I wish… I want to keep talking."

Dean clips Owen's car seat, his back to her, aware of Luc in the front.

"I've been thinking," she continues, "if you stay, if you have to stay—I don't want to wish for bad circumstances, but I hope you'll all stay—we should trade in our two rental cars and split a van. It makes more sense, financially, and I could fit the lumber for the raised beds in, and if we wanted to go back to Vigoro for your herbs… "

"I have a conference, in July, in Ypsilanti. Owen is signed up for swim lessons at the YMCA."

"Swim lessons? Ha!" she laughs. "A couple more weeks here and he'll be diving to bring up conch with Darvin!"

In the front seat, Dean notices Luc is staring out at the ocean with the careful expression of the disinterested on his face as he listens.

"Today was really nice, and I'm going to have dinner with just my family tonight," Dean says, closing Owen's door. "With Luc, since it's his one night off."

"Oh, of course." Her chin bobs down, a quick nod. She tucks her sleek brown hair back behind her ear, resettles her sunglasses on her nose. "Great idea."

Boundaries, he thinks. On the drive back, he is hyper-aware of her in the car behind him. He can feel her eyes on the corner of his face in the rearview mirror, and while Luc talks about spotted eagle rays and spinner dolphins, Dean takes extra care to keep both hands on the wheel.

CHAPTER 18

Juliet

After dinner, you go outside with your daughter under the premise of picking hibiscus and plumeria. There is a rare ruffle of a breeze on the inlet, and the wet sand shifts under your bare feet. It reminds you of your grandmother, how her idea of a good exfoliating pedicure was to put on old sneakers and take you and Lear and your sisters to hike upriver in Neshaminy Creek, the grit and pebbles filling your shoes and leaving the soles of your feet newborn pink.

Illuminated by the screen porch light, you see them. Dean with his arm wrapped around Owen on his lap, laughter and friendly trash talk as the cards are slapped down on the table, the golden light under the fan casting a perfect circle around them.

You want to tell him what Simon just told you back in the chilled air of your cottage, how you were braiding Sonny's wet hair and he looked up from *Harry Potter* and said, "I know who was driving the truck."

"What?" You looked down at your hands, a tremble, and you dropped a section of slippery hair.

"After the limbo party. That night."

Sonnet jerked her head, and you dropped another section.

"Hold still!" Your heart pounding, you pull tight.

"It wasn't Luc," Simon said, tilting his face back between the covers of the book.

"But how would you know who was driving the truck?"

Sonnet turned her head so sharply to Simon that the braid fell apart in your hands.

"Because, when you were inside, sleeping, Sonny went out there." Simon said softly, and he raised the story of wizards and fantasy to obscure his red face.

———

You want to be in Dean's circle of porch light, away from your cottage and their stories, Sonnet's insistence that Jack is with you. You want to whisper to Dean what Simon said, to watch as you gift him the one thing he is waiting to hear, relief, to watch his shoulders unfurl. But you know the truth of where you were that night, where you believe his son was and what that means he knows, before, and so you cannot tell him.

———

Dean catches you watching, creeping around in the bushes outside, and he calls you in to the screen porch. You pretend you were coming by to use his computer. Sonnet is folded seamlessly into their card game, wedged on a chair with Holly, an easy invitation to form a team, their skinny, bare thighs mashed together. She absentmindedly hooks her fingers through the embroidered friendship bracelet on Holly's wrist and you swallow a pang—you always dreamed of giving her a sister.

"No teams!" Luc protests. "You two are going to cheat!"

None of Dean is an act—the good father—nothing changes because you are there. Dean is who he is, with or without an audience. So different from Jack, whose public parenting persona was boisterous, tossing Sonny high over his head with one eye on the crowd, tickling Simon until his eyes watered. His private parenting, at the farmhouse, always included a Blackberry or a closed office door.

Dean smooths over Luc's protests and slides a pile of Cayman pennies to Sonnet; the card game continues.

A week after Jack's funeral, Helen from Classics-Only Book Club had come by with an uncovered steaming tuna casserole, its cat food stench filling the farmhouse kitchen.

"The worst of this whole thing with Jack isn't your loss, you know," Helen said, her painted mouth turned down like a clown's frown. A recent divorcée, she was starving herself thin. She had come by under the guise of delivering food, but it was really to ask if she could have her online dating profile photo snapped among the white birches outside your kitchen window.

"Look at you! You're young and beautiful; you'll love again," Helen said, her bony hand gripping your wrist. "But your children will never have another father. I've been in it and let me tell you, there is not a single man out there who can love another's children like his own."

You turn away from Dean and open his laptop to two new emails.

To: **Juliet B. Wilde <jbwilde@gmail.com>**
From: **Daily Inspirations**
Date: **June 18, 2007**

You only have roughly thirty thousand days on this planet, and then you die.

To: **Juliet B. Wilde <jbwilde@gmail.com>**
From: **Lear Burke <ljb@hotmail.com>**
Date: **June 18, 2007**
Subject: **Business**

J—
Hope you're well.
The twins won their hockey championship this weekend, and on the way back from the tournament I passed by the Compass project in Cherry Hill. Nothing happening. I asked across the street and they said no one's been there in a month.

Our friend Marty hasn't returned my calls, and when I went by the office, Alice says he hasn't been in. I'll keep trying to track him down.

I hope you and the kids are having a nice time. I'm sure you would enjoy some duty-free shopping. Jenna reminded me about Kirk Freeport, a store worth checking out in George Town—the Cayman Islands are known for their jewelry.

I imagine you are having such a great time that you might never want to come back to reality, so check out this link:

http://www.sothebysrealestatecaymanislands.com/database/propertydetails.id324
There are some real gems in the Cayman Islands!

I was by the farmhouse last weekend—your house sitter is certainly making herself at home. I cleaned up, including Jack's office, and picked up some files I'd like to go over with you.

Call me at your earliest convenience?

-L

*Delete the contents of this email and erase it from your hard drive

You close Dean's laptop carefully and put your shaking hand on your daughter's shoulder, tell her it's time to go. It is becoming very clear to you: There is a reason you are here, in the Cayman Islands, of all the tropical paradises that dot the earth's blue oceans.

CHAPTER 19

Dean

Dean's eyes snap open to the trill of the night-singing tree frogs, interrupted by the crunch of car tires on gravel, just outside. Though there are no sirens, the lightbars make patterns of red and white across his ceiling. Careful not to wake Owen, he stumbles in the dark, looking for something to put on over his boxers. He worries they are coming for Luc; how do you dress to meet the police who will handcuff your son, who will put a hand on the crown of his head where Bridget's rested, where Amélie laid hers when he collapsed, weeping into her arms at the hospital that final month, so that he doesn't hit it on the metal of the patrol car doorway?

Dean grabs a T-shirt and wrinkled khakis; they gap at the waist without a belt and he holds them up as he hobbles across the hallway. Luc and Holly are sleeping in the twin beds, the *Warriors* book splayed open on her chest, a pillow clutched in Luc's arms. The moonlight streams through the louvers and casts black bars of shadow over his son's peaceful face.

He'll let him sleep a few minutes more, go out and meet them in the parking lot. He pats his pocket for something, anything, a notebook to write down the charges, and finds his cell phone from the United States. He hasn't touched it since he arrived, the battery dead.

Shit, Dean curses, thinking he should have paid for an international SIM, paid the retainer, met with Spencer already, so he had his cell phone number, his permission to call him at any hour—Dean checks his watch, surprised to notice it's only eleven-fifteen; they'd gone to bed early, exhausted from the day at the Turtle Farm.

Outside, their flashes of ruby light up the arching canopy of island pines.

Juliet's front door opens and she stumbles out. "What's happening?"

She is wearing a thin tank top and no bra, a pair of black men's boxer briefs that hug her legs tightly. *If these were her husband's,* Dean thinks, *he must have been small.*

She wraps her arms around her waist like she is cold, though he knows it is hotter outside than it ever is in her icebox of a cottage. If this were a romantic movie, he would drape a jacket over her rounded shoulders, only he doesn't have one, and it is sweltering.

"I thought..." she stops, and lets out an exhale that sounds like relief.

"Were you asleep?" he asks.

"Sort of. Bad dream."

They watch together as the officers get out.

"I'm afraid they're coming for Luc," Dean says. He has closed the cottage door behind him and he backs up against it. What is he going to do, block their entry?

"Why? I thought you said the girl was okay?"

"They're making claims about another victim, that they might have hit some-one. If that's the case, where's the body?" He thinks again that he should have called Spencer, gotten him to look at the accident report. Were there any photos from that night? What has he been doing all this time, making *escovitch*, getting in shape and comforting the beautiful woman next door?

The officers get out. It is Ebanks and a woman with a walk like a bulldog.

"But Luc wasn't driving!" Juliet exclaims, her eyes wide under the streetlight.

Dean is grateful for her faith in his son, but none of it seems to matter. They watch as the officers glance across the street at them, and then turn and head for The Wreck. They have turned off their lightbars but left their engines running. Dean can hear Leo's music playing, Marley singing about freedom and redemption.

The door opens behind him: Luc, rubbing his eyes like Owen.

"What's going on?" Luc asks, his voice scratchy from sleep.

There is no time to explain—the police are back, one of each of their hands under Dusty's broken arms, his head down, Tony following. They open the back door of Ebank's car and load him in, gently. A panic flutters in Dean's chest. What about Darvin? Why did they bring two cars?

But they pull quick U-turns and leave, one whoop of their sirens, before they disappear back down the road in the direction they came. Tony is left standing under the only streetlight. He crosses the sand road to them slowly. In spite of his surf shorts and bare feet, the way the light shines on the dome of his shaved hand and the broken posture, nobody would mistake him for one of the boys.

Tony takes curious stock of the three of them, Luc and Juliet in boxer shorts and clearly straight from bed, Dean clutching at the waist of his sagging pants.

"The lights woke me," Juliet volunteers, gesturing to the window of her cottage. "Dusty confessed."

"What?" they chorus.

"It was eating him, I guess. He called me tonight, asked me to come meet him here. We had a few drinks and he told me to call Ebanks. Said his time here was done."

"What will happen to him?" Juliet asks.

"They'll charge him with the DUI, aggravated assault with a vehicle, because of Bridge. He'll likely get sent back to Canada for sentencing."

"What about..." Dean trails off. He is so relieved; he does not want to buy trouble by mentioning the earlier allegations. Tony understands perfectly.

"Dusty told Ebanks he tried to swerve, there was something in the road. He said it was a potcake, maybe."

"Potcake?" Juliet asks.

"The island dogs." Luc speaks for the first time. "Car chasers. It can be hard not to hit them, sometimes. At night."

"He says he may have hit it, he's not sure. And then, everyone in the back—" Tony draws an arc in the air with his hand, like the trajectory of a catapult.

"So that's it?" Dean's hands shake a little, a side effect of the adrenaline. A smile jerks at the corner of his mouth, but then he remembers Bridget, and her mother in the Pink Hibiscus Café at the hospital, her hands wrapped around the cup and the creases around her mouth as she said, "I just want this over. I just want to take me girl home."

"That's it," Tony sighs. "He was a good one, Dusty. It's a shame."

Luc nods soberly.

"How about you, kid? I'm going to need some help out here."

"Of course," Luc says.

Juliet glances back at her cottage door, like she might go in.

"How about you, Papa Bear?" Tony looks up at Dean. "When are you heading back to the motherland?"

"I don't know. Our tickets are for the end of the month, but..." Dean trails off. He still can't believe it. He looks at Luc—he wants to hug him, to whoop in celebration—but his shoulders are slumped over Dusty, and Bridget.

"You should stay!" Juliet blurts. "For the rest of Camp Sunshine! At least until the end of the month, until we get the raised beds built, and the herbs in. The kids are having a great time..."

There is a moment while he weighs his options, but not for very long.

Dean does not appreciate the look that passes between Luc and Tony when he says, "Why not? We'll stay."

But the smile on Juliet's face makes up for it.

CHAPTER 20

DEAN

Ten days pass. When they don't think it can get any hotter, the wind disappears. The air outside is like the open door on a preheating oven, tolerable only when submersed up to their shoulders in the tepid ocean or pool.

As Tony predicted, Dusty is sent back to Canada where he is sentenced to thirty days in a minimum-security facility. The doctors clear Bridget for medical transport a week later. Tony drives Luc into town, and he rides with Bridget and her mother and little sister to the airport. Tony reports that Luc held her hand and walked beside the wheelchair to the metal steps, then he scooped her up and carried her up them on to the plane.

Tony takes Dean aside, while Juliet has the others at the pool. He tells him what Luc needs is good, hard work. "I'm promoting him in Dusty's place. Got to just keep him moving."

"Are you going to tell him?"

"Yeah," Tony runs his hand over his goatee.

"Before we leave," Dean says, frustrated that he has to be the grown up, again.

"Yeah, it's just about to get really busy." Tony doesn't meet Dean's eyes.

A high school group arrives from Washington for a three-week marine biology course—they are expected to do several dives a day and have chalk talks and quizzes on ocean life in the evenings. With his windows open at night to catch any breeze off the water, Dean can smell their beach bonfires, hear their music and laughter and the gentle clink of glass bottles, like wind chimes.

He makes a point to have coffee with Luc every morning. They talk about the bananaquit nest or things Luc sees on his dives. Curiously, his blood alcohol report from the accident comes back at .04, or the equivalent of two beers. When Dean tries to bring this up, Luc shrugs it off, asks if he can practice his marine biology chalk talk on cnidarians on Dean one more time. Dean lets it go, for now.

At the cottages, Juliet orders a truckload of lumber from Cox. She fills the backs of their clown cars with four hundred and twenty dollars of heat-hardy vegetable plants. The area outside her screen porch is starting to resemble the learning garden in Ghana. She surprises him with her ability to use a radial saw and a miter box. She hefts forty pound bags of topsoil, what Darvin calls "black gold" to her shoulder and mixes it with peat moss and sand, the sweat running down her body in skinny brown streams before she wades into the green inlet to rinse off. Sonny and Owen spread zigzagging seed tapes of carrots and radishes; they sprout overnight and threaten to wither under the strong sun.

Dean puts in herbs and pepper plants and Juliet tapes pieces of paper together to make a garden map and a chore chart. She requires the four children to "Weed, Water or Pick" in the garden for fifteen minutes each day, with Holly and Simon rotating as Dean's dinner sous chef and everyone helping with dishes. Dean teases Juliet about being equal parts cruise-director and drill sergeant, threatens to buy her a whistle on a neck-string. Only Luc doesn't play along.

"So," she says, in a long, leading way. It's Wednesday afternoon, before his last day on the island. Their plane tickets are set for Friday, the two twenty-five flight to Charlotte, connecting to Detroit.

They have just finished Quiet Time at Juliet's, during which Dean tried to get Owen to nap in the air-conditioned cool of her kids' upstairs bedroom. After an hour of listening to the other three down in the living room bicker about whose Parcheesi turn it is, Juliet ended the game, and they were all treated to her reading-aloud voice. She impressed Dean with her Roald Dahl regional accents and nonsense words in *The BFG*, while Owen flopped like a breathless fish in the twin bed beside him.

"So?" Dean counters. He has given up on getting Owen to sleep, sitting on a barstool in her kitchen.

Juliet coaxes a peachy mango from its thready green and gold skin.

"You're leaving us, I can't believe it. What about Luc?"

Dean kisses Owen's sweaty temple; he holds him captive on his lap so he can't play Godzilla to their Monopoly game. He lowers his voice. "Tony says he's making noises that he wants to stay forever, never go back to reality."

"Would you let him?" she asks, serving a boat of mango and salted watermelon to Owen, who crams it in with loud slurping, Juliet gently smoothing his curls out of the way of the juice.

"I hope he'll come with us. I'm planning to tempt him with the little bottles of vodka from the flight attendant's cart." Dean whistles, simulates ringing a mini-bottle like a bell.

"Or, you all could stay... " Juliet stops, slipping the rest of the mango into a Tupperware for dinner. She looks up at the clock; it's almost five. "We should probably get going on our runs, unless we want to feed the mosquitos."

They struggle through uninspired runs. The heat index on the Brookstone thermometer at Juliet's cottage says 98. She is back in less than twenty minutes, her cheeks a mottled magenta. He barely makes it to the restaurant at Kai Bo before he turns back. At the end of his run, he doesn't find them at the cottages but across the street at Rum Point beach, where the smoke of the tiki torches and lit punks keep the mosquitoes at bay.

The sunset paints the water peach and rose. Juliet's back is to him, a silhouette of curves. Dean has the craziest impulse: to run and grab her around the waist and drag her into the ocean. He imagines her snaking her arms around his neck like they have always done this, as though their kids don't exist, tilting her face up to his. He swallows; it has been too long.

Juliet, still in her running clothes, splashes in the bathwater-warm ocean with the children. She fake screams and throws her arms over her head when Owen chases her into the shallows. Dean watches from the bar as she scoops a dripping Owen into her arms before they cross the empty sandy road. He notices she looks for him, down the long lane to Kaibo and his heart lurches—she is waiting for him to come home. It reminds him of a thousand nights at the window over the kitchen sink in Saline, the percolating of the last coffee pot of the day, his hands in the soapy, grease-scummed water from dinner's dishes, the chatter of the TV in the room behind him. It reminds him of watching for Amélie's square Volvo headlights to crest the hill and turn into their driveway, waiting like a housewife. He shakes the image, wondering how, in the course of fourteen years, he let things become so unbalanced?

"Hey," Tony calls from inside The Wreck. "Come in and have a cold one."

The only other customer is a man next to Tony with snow-white hair and the ruddy cheeks of a hard drinker, sipping at a sweating tumbler.

"What can I getcha?" Leo asks.

"Anything that's cold. We're out of everything, and I can't face the drive back to Red Rabbit."

"Haven't seen much of you the past few days," Tony says.

"Yeah, the littles keep me busy."

"And what have you two got going on over there? Fucking Queen's botanical gardens? You always were a sucker for a woman with dirt under her fingernails, I guess."

Dean ignores Tony and orders a beer from Leo. There is so much unfinished business here, but Dean isn't sure he's up for it tonight.

"Heading out this week, eh?"

"Tickets are for the Friday, the 2:20 to Charlotte."

"What about Luc?" Leo asks.

"I'm hoping he'll come with us. I've got to get his life together, GED. I think it'd be best for him."

"I disagree." Tony stares straight ahead.

A few months with his kid, and suddenly he's an authority? After everything that happened on his watch?

"Leave him here with me. What he needs is hard work!"

"And you'll look after him like you did last time?" Dean says, and he sees on Tony's face it lands exactly how he intended.

Leo tries for lightness, "Hey, you can't take Romeo now. That hair! Those abs! All the girls and half the chaperones from the Washington trip are propositioning him."

Leo and Tony share the lucky-young-bastard look of men past their prime.

The white-haired man from down the bar lifts his glass in appreciation and calls out a hearty, "Amen."

"We should all be so lucky," Tony says. "This is Alistair, from Northside, but everyone calls him Doc. He comes here to cure what ails him after patching up the war-torn and mentally unstable all week."

Confused, Dean takes his sweating Corona from Leo, gives Alistair a polite smile.

"He's a shrink, like you. Runs a private practice for all the degenerates out this way. Carries the secrets of the masses up there," Tony taps his temple. "Don't you, Doc?"

"Oh," Dean says, not surprised that Tony lacks a grasp of the nuances of mental health professionals. "You're a braver soul than I am then. I'm in academia, tenure track."

"Good on ya," the man says, nodding and sipping. His accent is hard to place; Australian, South African or UK, Dean cannot tell.

"I wanted you two to meet. I think you'd have a lot to talk about," Tony says, but the problem with introductions like that is they are both suddenly reduced to half-smiles and nods, followed by pensive stares into their drinks.

"Private practice on an island, must be interesting," Dean tries.

"Private practice." Tony is too loud, drunk, Dean realizes. He tilts his head to the side dramatically. "Private practice? Say, didn't you once enjoy being in private practice, Dean? What ever happened with that?"

Of course it was Amélie, and Luc. She wanted to teach in multiple disciplines of the arts, as an adjunct professor, but they needed health benefits. It was her idea that Dean leave the counseling center he loved, Amélie who got him the interview in the psych department. For the first few years, he still talked about converting their garage, setting up his shingle on the lawn and listening to people as the sun streamed through the lone, paned window. But then she got sick, and the department head mentioned tenure, and they needed his benefits more than ever.

"Other things were more important," Dean says.

Tony orders another beer. "I thought I warned you, about the Wealthy Widow."

"You're really on a roll tonight. I thought it was Happy Hour, not Bust Your Buddy's Balls." Dean signals to Leo for the check. He wants to go home—Juliet will be worried, and they don't have much time together left.

"She's good, then?"

Dean wants to hit him. "Nothing's happening," he says evenly. Smug, know-it-all, exaggerator—the qualities he hadn't liked in his roommate at nineteen are still there at forty-one, magnified.

"I never did get there," Tony laughs, missing his mouth with the neck of his beer bottle. It runs down into the curled silver hair on his chest. "Not for lack of trying, but I never got to this one first."

"Can I have the check?" Dean asks Leo again.

"But I have it on good authority," Tony slurs, "that you would trust, that someone else was."

Leo slides a bill to Dean that says, instead of numbers, *I been here since 2pm. IGNORE.*

Dean stands up. "It doesn't matter. I'm leaving." Let Tony figure out if he's talking about right then, or Friday, or both.

"In that case. Leo," Tony waves the bartender over. "Bottle of Cuervo for my roomie here. On me."

Beside him, Tony starts whistling. He's always been unusually good at it, and Dean recognizes the popular country ballad that Leo plays at least three times an afternoon: "Tequila Makes her Clothes Fall Off."

Walking back to the cottages, he thinks he knows why Tony would be trying to warn him off Juliet: To a chronically-single, commitment-phobic, forty-something career dive master, a widow with two kids looks like baggage. To a widower with three of his own, it's more like a future.

CHAPTER 21

Dean

At Juliet's, she is laying out an early dinner. Her face breaks into a smile when she sees him coming through the screen door.

"I was starting to worry! Dinner's ready: cold food only. Cucumber salad, cold chicken and mango smoothies," she tells him. He likes that she worried. If only he were more like Luc, if it came naturally to him to be unavailable. But these are not really the luxuries of a single father of three. Hard-to-get would last all of about four minutes, until he needed someone to distract Owen while he pried a dock splinter from his heel.

She bumps gently past him in the tiny kitchen to reach for the glasses. His hand palms her hip to move her to the side, as if they are a long-married couple with a carefully choreographed dance routine for their galley kitchen. But they aren't, and Dean's hand buzzes where he touched her. He wants to do it again.

After dinner, despite Simon's wails of protest, Dean puts on a full-length G-rated Disney DVD. They wash the dishes to the cloying opening music of *Snow White*. He comes up with two more excuses to touch her, a hand on her hip and waist, thrilling each time.

"I hate this cra-ap!" Simon tries once more as the previews play.

Juliet swipes her sponge over the counter and turns off the overhead light. In the dark and cool of the air-conditioned kitchen, he can feel the day's heat coming off her body. She is only inches away from him, her hands twisting and wrenching the ice cube tray, the frozen water crackling as it pops and gives, tumbling to the counter.

"It's like what I was saying before, about the kids." She circles back to one of their regular topics: single parenting, a safe one. The very tips of her nipples brush his biceps as she leans around him to put the tray back. The glass of water is so slippery in his sweat-slick hand that he nearly drops it. She chatters on, and he almost wishes he had taken up Tony's offer for the bottle of Cuervo, for himself.

"I mean, doing this alone might not be ideal, but if you do your best, it can turn out okay. Look at Disney. Name one Disney movie where they haven't killed off a parent."

"Or replaced them with a wicked stepmother," Dean adds. He fills a glass of water for her. "Let's take these outside," he suggests, grabbing them each slices of lime.

They leave the kids to their movie, and he notices that where it used to be Simon in his sacred corner spot of the couch with Sonny sagging against him, Holly and Owen banished to the far end, now their four are all mixed up, their slack, sun-browned limbs tangled.

In the sweltering but starlit privacy of outdoors, he and Juliet wedge themselves into the woven hammock strung between the two squat palm trees.

"I asked the guy at Vigoro—these are called Bismarck palms. I always thought of them as Hollywood backlot scene-setting trees. Whether we're in *The English Patient* or *The Birdcage* is up for debate."

He likes that she laughs at this.

"Or what was that Tom Hanks movie," he continues, "with the shipwreck, and the volleyball? *Castaway*?"

"I love that you're interested in names of trees," Juliet says. The hammock forces them together, plastering their sides and pinning their shoulders against each other. Her hair brushes his cheek. Dean swallows.

"Trees, birds, you name it. This morning, I learned that the female West Indian Woodpeckers are into polyandry, that a single female can raise two broods with two different males at the same time. I am," Dean sighs, "officially an old bird nerd."

"I have a confession to make," Juliet laughs. "Yesterday, Professor, I used your reading glasses to read the back of the jalapeno seed packet, and it made everything so much easier!"

"I wish I'd seen that, you in my reading glasses."

They swing gently, facing out toward the North Sound and a rising moon. After a moment, Juliet sighs.

"What does that mean?"

"Nothing. It means, I'm happy."

"Me too."

This is, in large part, due to the fact that he has decided he will kiss her tonight. Soon, but not just yet. The feeling of her arm and warm thigh pressed against his, all of this so close to him; it is enough right now.

"I wish you weren't leaving. The kids will miss yours; it will be so lonely."

The kids.

"You look out at this," he gestures to the swollen moon reflected on the inky water of the inlet. "Tomorrow will be another perfect day. It's almost like waking up to two feet of snow, a broken furnace and a car that won't start, commuting in the dark with Owen wearing pajamas under his snowsuit because I couldn't get it together to get him to the daycare dressed by 7:25 for the 8:00 Psych 111 lecture... You forget those days are coming, that they even exist."

"It's like we live in another reality here. I can't thank Holly enough for frying my laptop. I've been fantasizing..." she stops.

"First, confessing, now, fantasizing? Tell me more," he says, clearing his throat. "I am a trained psychologist, you know."

"Not that," she laughs. "About the farmhouse, and things that are happening back home..." She trails off. "I've been thinking more about here. About giving it all up. Let my siblings squabble over everything there and just... staying."

"Here? For good?"

"Why not?" He can hear the smile in her voice. "You don't get many chances in life to start over, to completely change your reality. Why not now?"

A thousand reasons scramble across his mind like roaches on the tile floor of the cottage's utility closet: the fixed, unfavorable exchange rate to the US dollar, gas running nearly five dollars a gallon, the endless holiday attitude—where else would he order a margarita with lunch—the stifling summer, the high cost of living, the isolation, the mosquitoes, the lack of inherent, honored and indigenous culture, the thirty percent import duty on all goods, the expatriate headache, work permits, limited access to conveniences, the fact that everything closes on a Sunday, that a greasy burger and fry lunch for the family at Rum Point sets him back a hundred and twenty dollars—

She interrupts his thoughts, perfectly reading his silence. "It's remote, which isn't necessarily a bad thing. And it can be inconvenient, but that's part of the charm."

"What about the cost of living—seven bucks a gallon for milk!"

Juliet is quiet, and then she says, "Money isn't really my first concern anymore. Jack had a very good insurance policy."

A feeling washes over him, not resentment exactly, but acknowledgment of different paths, the same way he felt when other fathers, those who picked careers in litigation or plastic surgery, dropped their kids off outside Luc and Holly's school in hundred-thousand-dollar cars. It is like walking to the gate in Detroit International to board a flight for a psych conference in Iowa and reading the destinations at other gates where he might rather go: Martinique, Baton Rouge, London. It is simply an acknowledgment of a road not taken—he hasn't let it bother him much, until now.

"I'm finding I'm really happy here," Juliet says softly and Dean feels panic, worse than when she mentioned sharing email addresses and photos, when he had a flash forward of them drifting back to their separate cities. What if Juliet stays in their idyllic life here, tending to their vegetables and reading aloud and pointing out squirrelfish and needlefish and brittle stars at the reef? Can he really leave all of this? Her?

"There are other ways to change your life, without moving," he says, and he feels the catch in his breath when he exhales.

"What do you mean?"

"Every time you fall in love with someone, you reinvent yourself. That's the chance of every new relationship; it's why some people never settle down. Think about it: we both married in our twenties, when we were still formulating who we wanted to be, our grown-up selves. Doing this alongside someone else, it can't help but shape you."

Dean is thinking about Amélie, the first time they met again for lunch at Sodexho, six years after Africa.

"I need to see you," she'd said. Five words, and the years of returned letters evaporated. He let her pick the restaurant, a mediocre vegetarian place, and got there first, pacing for twenty minutes. He remembers when she bent over the backseat of her Volvo, her peasant skirt dusting the curb, seeing her ankles, those beautiful slim appendages he'd kissed under the African sky, poking out underneath. Dean had assumed she was getting her cello out, rather than leave it to be stolen. Instead, Amélie had emerged with the hand of three-year-old Luc clutched in hers, a sly smile on her thin lips. Everything in Dean had shifted, whole tectonic plates of personality as in twelve seconds he evaluated and decided that the package would be worth playing for, and he held out his hand for Luc to shake.

"Who would you be now," he asks Juliet, "if not for Jack?"

"Softer." Her answer is one word, spoken so quietly he can barely hear it.

"Softer?" he asks. How would he have been different if he hadn't been so hell-bent on proving himself as an adjunct father, on finding a well of patience and nurturing and fanning it out for Amélie like a peacock's opalescent display?

"Yes, softer. With Jack in sales, he had to develop this tough outer shell, a cynical, hard, prickly side to him. And then when we took bad hits, when things didn't meet their projections, when people he considered friends stole deals from him, it added another layer. He wore it home, and in self-defense, I grew one of my own. Without Jack," she says again, "I might have been softer. I might have been less defensive, when things happened with my family. Who knows? I might have even been," she laughs without bitterness, "an optimist."

Now or never, Dean turns his head and kisses her.

The kiss is perfect. Soft, tentative, questioning. Is this how we work best? It seems to say, or this? More gentle than hungry at first.

Later, when he thinks back on this, it will bother him that the impetus for their first kiss might seem to be her revelation of Jack's life insurance policy. Not that he worries she believes that this is what attracted him to her, but taken out of context, if one were reading this night in the stage direction and dialog of a script, there were more romantic words that could have been hanging in the air as their heads first tilted toward each other.

Like she can read his mind, she sighs into him and changes the script, whispering between kisses, "It's not…just…the kids…who don't want you to leave…"

It continues, their kiss, and Juliet braces one bare foot against the sand below the hammock to turn her whole body to him. Where his mouth is tangy with lime, hers is ice water cool, and it's not long before her hand is sliding up his thigh with purpose.

He responds, one hand palming the rise of her hip, his fingertips searching, sliding under the thin fabric of her T-shirt at her waist, and then they both move at just the wrong moment, and the balance is tipped, and the flimsy hammock dumps them both to the hard, gritty sand below.

They both laugh, but it is easier here, on the ground.

This may work better, he thinks.

"Are you alright?"

"Are you kidding?" he whispers back, both of his hands on her waist, pulling her on top of him—he wishes she would give him all her weight, sink into him.

"Mmm," he says as the kiss deepens, the delicious heat and anticipation of what is to come creating an urgency.

"Ow." She breaks the kiss. "Shit, ow, ow, ow, ow!" She scrambles off, hands smacking at her bare legs. "Fire ants, ow! Look out, they're everywhere!"

There are colonies of them in the brush around the cottage beach. Owen had gotten bitten the first week, nasty welts that itched for days.

"Come on, the water." He grabs Juliet's hand and drags her toward the shallow beach. They wade in, Juliet still slapping at her legs.

"I'm sorry." He laughs, glancing back at her cottage over their shoulders for the blue glow, the flickering of the movie. "C'mere."

Sitting in the shallow, waist-deep water, he pulls her back to his lap, and they kiss again, but she is distracted.

"What?" he whispers.

"Nothing, just…I'm thinking of the things Luc was talking about at dinner the other night."

Luc had said how at dawn when he drives the boat out to the main channel of the North Sound, it is like a shark super-highway, that all the large predators come inside the barrier reef at night to feed head back, cutting through the main channel to cruise the deeper waters of the North Wall for the day.

"I'm just wondering, with us rolling around, making little splashes, what kind of signals we might be sending to hungry sea creatures?"

But he wants to keep kissing her, so he tries again.

"Who says we're going to be rolling around?" He laughs as she presses into him. His arms clamp around her waist.

Let them come, he thinks, feeling like he could fend off a Great White with his bare hands.

"I mean, aren't we?" she whispers, her lips against his ear.

He scoots, holding her on his lap, backwards out of the water to the sandy shoreline, where they lie back, covering their wetness with a coating of the fine, gritty sand, like blintzes in sugar.

"Hmm," he says after a few minutes of trying to get it right—her on top, or underneath, with him propped on his elbows. How does it work best? "Is it… Does this usually look more romantic in movies?"

She laughs. "Can we possibly be too old to make out on the beach?"

"Maybe the pool shower?" They consider it briefly; a cold, sputtering, aggressive jet with a hand-painted sign instructing residents to rinse off their sand and suntan oil before using the pool.

"We're probably pushing our luck outside anyway. We just washed off all our bug spray." He knows she is also thinking of the movie, about the children and how long they have been out here.

"We could go to my place," Dean says half-heartedly, but they both know neither will be comfortable there with the children alone two doors down, and Luc coming home any second.

They sigh, standing up and dusting the worst of the sand off them.

"A bed," Dean says ruefully, "a bed, in a temperate setting with a lock on the door. Highly underrated."

"The movie is probably almost over anyway," she says. They make reluctant progress back toward her cottage, her hand now folded securely in his. He likes this, hopes he can count on this from now on, that she will let him hold her hand. The truth: long before Amélie had gotten sick, they had stopped holding hands.

They open the screen door, and check the movie's progress; ironically, the prince is bent on one knee over the glass coffin, about to touch his coral lips to Snow White's.

"We have a few minutes," she whispers, and allows him to pull her into a shadowy corner of her screen porch, under the vibrating hum of the window unit, presses her body up against his, and lets him kiss her dizzy. He notices his arms are doing the work of holding her up; this is what he wanted.

"I've got you," he whispers, his lips on her throat.

When she moans, a soft little animal noise, it reminds him of Tony's first words about her: "She's a bit of a fox." He thinks of Tony's drunken, knowing wink when Leo offered him the tequila bottle, as though he put all this together. Dean pulls back.

Don't overthink this. Just go with it.

But then the movie ends, and Owen calls for him.

Inside, Juliet's cottage is icebox-cold and too bright, and they have to explain themselves in the fluorescent light of the hallway, dripping wet and sandy as the kids yawn and stretch and kvetch during the credits.

"What happened?" Simon scowls as Juliet tugs at her clinging, wet clothes.

"We were taking a walk, and I fell in the water, on the dock," Juliet lies. "Dean fell in trying to save me."

"You were gone a long time." Holly's eyes narrow, and he gets one of those glimpses of future Holly – how much she will look like Amélie.

"Did the barracuda get you?" Sonny yawns, her bare foot brushing against Holly's shin.

"Come on," Juliet says, pulling Dean down the hall, "I'll get you a towel."

He follows her to the utility closet, conscious suddenly of the eyes on his back, his feet on the tile, of where this is going, and he hates his hesitation, but it is different now, inside, with the children.

How would he be different, Dean thinks again, if he wasn't a father of three?

Juliet pulls him quickly into the dark, sliding the bi-fold door closed behind them.

"Shh," she cups his cheeks in her cold, damp hands, these kisses so much hungrier, more desperate than the first in the hammock. "What's wrong?" she whispers, between each one.

"Nothing," he tries. In the cold air, her sea-wet body is shivering and she presses into him, the softness of her bellybutton right at his cock. He's so hard it hurts. But…

"Dad?" It's Holly, yelling. "Dad? Where are you? We're ready to go. O's practically asleep."

"I not!"

Dean pulls back from Juliet, a shaky sigh.

"Before," Juliet's whispered breath is hot against his ear, making every hair on his arms stand up, "whenever this happened, Jack would say, 'I swear to god, these kids have a Hard Dick Alarm.'"

"Dad?" It's Holly.

He cups Juliet's shoulders. They feel perfect under his hands.

"Mom?" Sonny chimes in.

"Okay!" Dean calls back. He slides his hands down her arms, but he doesn't want to let go of her hands. "I'm sorry," he sighs. Maybe, he thinks, they should stop now.

For good.

She tilts her forehead so that it rests against his chin. He lets his lips linger on her scalp.

"Dad, I said we're ready to go!"

"It's probably better that we stop," Dean says into the air by her neck, just below her left ear where, a minute ago, he was laying urgent kisses. He slides a hand behind him to open the closet door. He heaves another shaky sigh. "With us leaving, it's not fair, to any of us."

Juliet blinks; the light in the hallway is painfully bright.

"I have three plane tickets for the day after tomorrow. I have a conference in Ypsilanti and Owen's swim lessons—"

"You could change plane tickets. If you wanted to."

"If it were just us…" Dean turns before they get to the living room, shaking his head. Flecks of sand fall from his hair to his shoulders and she dusts them off with her fingertips, her breasts grazing him. He has to look away from her face tilted up to his, her lips kissed pink and hungry.

"But it isn't just us," she finishes the sentence for him.

CHAPTER 22

Dean

To: **Juliet B. Wilde <jbwilde@gmail.com>**
From: **Lear Burke <ljb@hotmail.com>**
Date: **July 1, 2007**
Subject: **FWD: Meridian Life Insurance**

J-
Sorry. Doing everything I can.
—L
ps Ease up on the credit card.

To: **Lear Burke <ljb@hotmail.com>**
From: **Barbara Fletcher <b.fletcher@meridian.com>**
Date: **June 30, 2007 3:48:57 PM EDT**
Subject: **RE: #2597502364 update**

Dear Mr. Burke:

Thank you for your request for a status update regarding the case of our insurance claimant, Mr. Jack Wilde, as executor of his estate and on behalf of the beneficiary, Juliet Burke Wilde. I am sorry that this is not resolving itself and can only say it appears that this will take some time. The number of days required to resolve or settle on a life insurance claim is a "best guess" and it is against company policy to make those estimates in writing.

Meridian has currently retained an outside firm to investigate the records and police reports regarding the auto accident of Mr. Wilde on the night of December 1, 2006. With incomplete physical evidence and without the certified report of a state medical examiner, the status of this investigation remains OPEN and PENDING. We cannot make payment on this policy at this time.

We will of course keep you up to date on the process of the investigation and its findings.

Sincerely,

Barbara Fletcher

Senior Benefits Administrator

Meridian Life and Casualty

To: **Juliet B. Wilde <jbwilde@gmail.com>**
From: **Daily Inspirations**
Date: **July 1, 2007**

Our most basic instinct is not for survival but for family. Most of us would give our own life for the survival of a family member, yet we lead our daily life too often as if we take our family for granted. ~ ***Paul Pearshall***

The night after their kiss-cut-short, Dean does not sleep. Instead, he rattles around the stifling cottage, and reads the emails from Juliet's Gmail account, which she always leaves right in the Trash folder on the desktop of his computer.

He re-reads these communications from the United States, littered in with her deleted emails—twenty percent offers from Old Navy, reminders about the next selection for the Bucks County Classics Only Book Club, and requests for things to be deducted from the rent from her house sitter. What does the insurance agent mean—incomplete physical evidence?

On the morning of their last full day on the island, he gets up for coffee with Luc. They watch the bananaquit dipping in and out of her nest.

"You're sure you won't go back?" Dean tries again and Luc sighs. "There's a chance you could get your GED this summer, think about college."

"Dad…" Luc's voice is heavy with warning.

"It's hard for me to imagine leaving all this, too." Dean doesn't add that Luc isn't the only issue.

"I got a phone call yesterday, from Bridget." Luc changes the subject.

"And?"

"She's been fitted. She's starting PT. She sounds okay."

"Do you miss her?"

"Me and Bridge weren't like that."

"Like what?"

Luc shrugs. "Like the others."

"You mean, you cared for Bridget?"

"We were friends, Dad, for months. Roommates! I'm smarter than that. That night, we just kissed. Once." Luc sighs. "First time, last time, probably a mistake, I don't know. It doesn't matter now."

"But you miss her."

"She was different. Funny. I wanted to be with her all the time. I wanted to tell her everything, like, my whole life story, even the bad parts. And she listened. I didn't want to kiss her, because I didn't want to ruin everything."

"That's not how it's supposed to be, Luc. I hope you know that."

"I don't really want to talk about this, girls, women, with you."

"Why not?" Dean sips his coffee.

"Because you loved my mom—"

"Of course I did! I still do," Dean interrupts, but he is looking out at the inlet where the imprints of him and Juliet the night before mark the sand in the shallows, remembering how the curves of her body fit into his. He wonders how they're going to get through the next thirty-six hours without him wanting, needing, to do that again.

"And she gave you crumbs."

A line of sweat breaks out between Dean's shoulder blades.

"What?"

"Mom gave you crumbs. Other women," he glances meaningfully down the beach to where Juliet is setting out breakfast, "give you crumbs. And no offense, but I'm not really interested in that. I want, like, salad, appetizer, dinner and dessert."

"Who is to say I don't want that too!" Dean explodes and Luc stands up, putting his sunglasses on.

"I wasn't drunk the night of the accident." Luc carries his mug back to the kitchen. "But everyone else out here was."

"What are you trying to say?" Dean panics. Is this what Tony was talking about? Had Luc and Juliet been together that night?

"I'm sorry I made a mess and you had to come clean it up. I'm glad you came, it was nice to see everyone but…"

"But?" Dean asks, his heart thumping.

"But I'm staying here. You guys should go home. I don't want you to get hurt, or any more bad things to happen to our family, Dad."

As soon as Luc leaves for work, Dean hurries Holly and Owen through breakfast, and leaves a note that says "Sightseeing" taped to their sliding door, drives his two as fast as he can away from Cayman Kai, before Juliet can call them to breakfast, for a day full of questions he might not be ready to hear the answers to, for the ache of being near her all day and not touching her.

"We can't leave the Cayman Islands without having a true tourist day! We need to get souvenirs for Aunt Amy, and your field hockey friends."

But Owen is crabby and Holly keeps pointing out things Simon and Sonny would like. When they stop at a gift shop on the harbor waterfront, Dean tries to get Holly to pick out something for his sister, but she keeps coming up with shell necklaces she thinks would be pretty for Juliet.

For lunch, they do the rooftop water slide and swim-up bar at Margaritaville, but even though he tries to be fun, gamely following Owen up the wet stairs and sliding down with him on his lap no less than fifty times, and even though Holly doesn't say it, he knows it would be more fun if the rest of them were there too.

At night, instead of facing the questions or worse, trying to go through the motions of their last regular running date and dinner, Dean takes Holly and Owen to the Lone Star Bar and Grill on the West Side. With slow service, they manage to kill almost four hours. The sky is full of stars when they pull into the parking lot behind the cottages, and though all of their eyes drift to Juliet's golden window, Dean puts his foot down.

"It's late, everyone in for bed."

Dean watches his fan blades spin, Owen's sweaty head on his biceps.

He tells himself, over and over, that he's done what he came here to do—make sure his son doesn't end up in some foreign jail, that he's doing reasonably well in Tony's care—and now it's time to go home.

So why do the suitcases he's lined up in the front hall look so ominous?

Why, when he gets out of bed in the middle of the night to search airline change fee policies, does he find Luc on his laptop, hurrying to close windows? And when he checks, Luc has emptied the Trash folder, and all of Juliet's old emails are gone.

"I hate to ask, on your last day, but I need a favor." It is Juliet, outside his screen porch, backlit by the early morning sun. "Like, a neighborly favor."

Awkwardness sits between them, formal, like garden statues in the hedges.

Luc has left for work after brusque goodbyes and sleepy, weepy hugs from Owen.

"When you go to the airport, could I follow you into town today? I need to do our Immigration extension, and I have to stop by Andy's—I'm trading in the clown car for something bigger."

He remembers her suggestion, before, about them splitting a euro van.

"I have another lumber order and…" she trails off. "Then, we could drop you all at the airport."

"I do have to return my car before noon." Dean nods, aching at the distance between them.

"Great. The kids wanted to see yours off. I told them we could have lunch upstairs at the Hungry Horse, watch your plane from the observation deck."

The way they talk, it's logistics—officers planning something tactical.

"Alright, we'll be ready by ten."

They drive separately to Andy's Autos, Holly and Owen silent in the back, dressed in their clothes for the plane, Holly's expression unreadable behind Amélie's glasses, but her mouth a wistful pinning of her mother's thin lips. Inside, while Dean settles up his bill, Juliet rents a dented Daihatsu van with vinyl-covered jump seats that can be flipped up and down. Simon and Holly roll their luggage out to it on the cart.

"Did you all have a nice day, yesterday, sightseeing?"

"Yes, yes. We had to pick up souvenirs, for friends back home. Errands. Last day of vacation type things."

Juliet nods, sliding her credit card across the counter.

"We missed, we *will miss*, you." She doesn't look at him while she says this.

By instinct, Dean walks to the left front door, and finds himself in the van's passenger seat.

"We can switch," he says. A true European, Amélie scorned the constant American use of cars, and though she had her trusty Volvo for getting back and forth to the university, she hated to drive.

"No, it's fine," Juliet says lightly. "I don't mind at all."

They are careful with each other; polite. This is the kind of conversation they will have today. If they have to wait long in line at Immigration, they'll be reduced to comments about the weather. Looking over, he remembers how perfectly the mound of one breast nestled into his cupped palm, the thrill of touching her, the taste of her cool mouth.

As she shifts, Dean realizes he's glad she is driving so she has to watch the road and doesn't notice how many times he glances sideways at her. That skin peeking out from the hem of her shorts is as soft as it looks, he knows now from sliding his hand over her thigh, like freshly opened frosting. Her sinewy arm works the giant rusted gearshift, the runner's muscles in her legs popping as she alternates between the gas and clutch.

"What?" She turns to him at the four way stop sign by the farmer's market. A skinny, chestnut horse with a rope around its neck drags a cinderblock as it snuffles through bushy sprays of spiky grass in the vacant lot.

"Nothing. I, I didn't know you could drive a stick shift," he mumbles. It's not just her hands—everything about her is capable. "On the wrong side of the road, the wrong side of the car."

"My older brother Lear taught me to shift when I was eleven, riding shotgun to school. He'd work the clutch and call out the gears. This, it's kind of nostalgic for me, shifting with my left."

Her knuckles form ridges like a mountain range, as she palms the head of the gear shaft, her thin platinum wedding band winking in the sun streaming through the salt-speckled windshield.

It's better this way, he thinks, noting the twenty inches that separate their bare arms. She still wears her ring. They have four vulnerable children cackling over Scooby and Shaggy on Si's iPod in the backseat and at the resort, there is Luc. The whole reason he was here. Of course, Dean was right to put an end to things.

As if she can read his mind, she says, "I told Luc, even after you go, he's not to make himself a stranger, come by. Remember, I make the best mac and cheese on the island."

Dean eyes her carefully.

"Though without my laptop, I guess, a little less of a draw. But I hope he'll still come by sometimes, for dinner."

"Your laptop?" What was she talking about?

"Never mind. I thought, I told him, he should tell you. I thought he'd told you." She waves her hand, her expression impossible to read, eyes on the road as she parks the van expertly in a narrow space. "It doesn't matter now."

The rusted parking brake screams when she jerks it, hard, into position.

"Okay, Wildes," she calls in her cruise director voice as they pile out under the canopy of a bright orange flame tree in the Immigration lot. "We'll get our passports stamped and then we've got to get these guys to the airport, and then we're going to stop, on the way home, for some groceries."

At the mention of all this, and the food, Dean wants to cook things for her, cool yogurt sauces and exotic spices to complement the heat of summer, chilled soups and crisp, fresh salads, ice cold bottles of Chardonnay. Afterward, a flash, he wants to lay her naked body out on white sheets and eat mango and kiwi off her honey-colored abdomen, alone.

But ... he's leaving.

"And then we'll head back to Rum Point. We'll be back in time for...what's next on the agenda, kids?"

"Sandcastle creations," Sonny says, mentally ticking through a list in her head.

"Right. We'll be back in time for sandcastle creations." Juliet is filling the silence, as though the other night, as though the reasons he drove to another part of the island to hide from her, never happened. She bends down to pick up fallen blooms from the flame tree among the empty Ting bottles at the edge of the parking lot, pinching them into tiny bouquets and handing them to Holly and Sonny.

God, Dean thinks watching her bend over, the fabric of her shorts pulled tight, why does he always have to be so honorable?

Juliet tucks a last bloom off the flame tree behind her ear. Seeing him watching, she offers him a sad, crooked smile. His breath catches, and then Sonny needs help with her sandal buckle—she sticks her sandy foot between them, all urgency and entitlement, and Owen grabs Dean's forearm, twisting the skin like a fox burn, and demands to be picked up.

He wants things to be uncomplicated! Just for a moment, for half an hour, he wants to go back in time, and for all of their children to disappear.

CHAPTER 23

Dean

In line for Juliet's Immigration renewals, the kids camp out at their feet, Simon holding the iPod, their four heads—his blondes, her brunettes—touching as they watch the rest of the movie. A tidal wave could break over George Town Harbor and they wouldn't notice.

"So," Juliet says meaningfully to Dean, and he is relieved she has initiated it. His stomach clenches and relaxes. "Let's just get this over with. The other night..."

"I'm sorry," he begins. He looks her directly in the eye for the first time all day; the hairs on his arms prickle. "I..." He starts and stops. "You'd think," he tries to joke, "that a trained psychologist would be better at this."

Dean is ready with his argument, carefully constructed, about what's best for the children, stability, the psychological effects of trauma and loss. Whatever happened, her tequila night, with Luc, before he got here, is irrelevant, since he is leaving, which is definitely the right thing, even if it means ignoring—

"I mean, I get it," Juliet says. "You're a good man. You're thoughtful and caring. And I know, the other night," she catches her bottom lip between her teeth and holds it there while she is thinking. He loves when she does this. "You're right. It was the right thing. It's one of my favorite things about you: You always do the right thing."

Not always, Dean thinks, and he remembers the stunned honk of the swans as they circled Ford Lake last October, after what he did, and then flew off into a sky like an oil painting.

They inch forward in the line, one person in front of each of them.

"I don't think it's really for me to say, but since you're leaving, it doesn't matter, but I already knew I wanted to know you, because of Luc, before you got here. Before we ever even met."

Dean feels this like a punch in his hollow stomach.

"I don't need to hear the details," he growls, wishing they had just gone straight to the airport, taken a cab from Andy's, the lone captain of the ship.

"He loves you, very much. He didn't want to hurt you. I don't even know why I'm telling you now," Juliet's cheeks flush, "with you in your airplane clothes, leaving, but the way Luc talked about you, before I even met you, I was fascinated by—"

Dean's blood is running like lava, despite the blasts of cold air coming from vents in the ceiling like a vaporized waterfall.

"That's enough," he says, through gritted teeth. "I don't want, I can't, hear any more!"

"But after the laptop incident, we never found him."

"What? Who?"

"And yesterday, when you and the littles were gone, Luc came by. He told me it doesn't matter to him anymore. My ruined computer, the lost progress we'd made."

"What are you talking about?"

"Next!" the woman behind the partition calls to Juliet.

He grabs for her arm. None of this is making sense. "Wait, what are you talking about? You and Luc, before?"

Juliet is frowning, those lines he'd studied, the lines he loved on her face, that he wanted to see when they were old and gray. Juliet pinches her lips together.

"Luc was using my laptop, I was helping him, to try and locate his biological father, Robert."

All the blood drains from Dean's burning face.

"That's it? That's what you're talking about? Before? You and Luc?"

"Yes, what did you think? Oh, god," Juliet snorts. "Not that?! Luc is a child! A little boy who lost his mother, trying to figure out where he belongs in the world, in his family, with her gone. He didn't have a laptop, and we met when I was plugged into Leo's ethernet one day at the bar, and… "

"Next!" The woman yells louder, as sour-looking and sagging as any government employee and though the air conditioning has even the ever-sweaty Owen complaining he is cold, the woman fans herself irritably with a stack of forms.

"I'm sorry; this was all before I knew you. I-I was only trying to help." Juliet turns away from Dean. "Hi," she says cheerfully. "I'm here for the summer with my children, and when we arrived, the airport only stamped our passports for thirty days. They said we'd need to come here for an extension."

Relief courses through Dean like an electric current.

In the line in front of him, there is a man with an Australian accent asking for six months extension. The worker behind the glass giggles and stamps it, asking if he will be bringing more Maori dolls for her daughter.

"I always do, m'dear!"

While Juliet's woman flips through and scowls at her three passports, in the line on the other side of Dean, a Jamaican with an expired work permit gets a two-month extension. And then the girl in front of him signals, and there is an open space in front of Dean, beside Juliet.

"Next?"

"Oh, I'm just..." Dean feels his pocket, the three stiff, navy booklets.

And then he steps forward, and passes them across the counter. "Extension, please."

He glances to the right. Juliet's worker flips Sonnet's passport closed, unstamped.

"You have no work permit or proof of income." She pushes the stack back to Juliet.

"Wait. What do you mean?" Juliet does not pick them up. "I have plenty of money, back in the States."

"For what date?" The girl in front of him asks Dean. His heart thuds. *This doesn't mean anything*, he tells himself.

"Um, August? End of August."

It's just the summer. A vacation. He'd be home in time for Orientation.

"August 21?"

Dean nods.

Beside him, the woman glares pointedly over Juliet's shoulder for the next person in line.

"Why would I need a work permit? I'm not trying to *move* down here—I'm trying to have a summer vacation with my kids! You know, relax, umbrella drinks and conch fritters, no worries?" Juliet looks to Dean for confirmation. In front of him, the rubber stamp is working its way through his stack—Dean, Holly, Owen. He is having trouble breathing. It doesn't mean anything—seven weeks. Except, he could spend more time with Luc. Isn't that why he came, in the first place? It's time Luc knows the truth.

"Wait, what are you doing?" Juliet hisses at him, her eyes wide.

"Here you are, sir!" Dean takes his stamped passports and stuffs them back into his pocket with sweaty hands. He can feel Juliet staring at his flaming face. It doesn't change anything. He could still get on the plane, in two hours. It just means, all of his options are open.

"Next!" the woman in front of Juliet drones, smirking like a bullfrog.

"Wait, what?" Juliet pushes her passports back under the window. "You're not renewing them? What do I have to do, leave the island in two days?" Her voice rises to a shrill panic. "But we're already here." Juliet gestures to her children in line and their heads snap up from the iPod. "Our plane tickets aren't until the end of August!"

"Then you are welcome to buy three tickets on our national airline, Cayman Airways and return to your home country."

"What? What do I do then, fly up to Miami and turn around and come back so I can get another thirty days?" She waves an arm at Dean as if to say, *he just got three passports stamped, no questions asked!*

"Whatever you do when you clear Immigration at the airport is up to them. Next!"

"No, this is completely arbitrary!" Juliet sputters, looking to the giggly girl who stamped Dean's passport, and the two before him. "What's the problem? You think I'm going to draw on your social services? Need medical care? I'm healthy! I have insurance. I am an economic stimulus to your island! All I do here is spend money—on gas and groceries and plants and rentals! Look, I just," Juliet digs in her pocket for the slip, "I just rented a van for five hundred dollars a week!"

"Next," the woman sighs, giving Juliet's three passports an extra little push in her direction. Juliet places both hands on the counter.

"No, I don't think you understand..." It is the same cool tone she used in the Rum Point bar to complain about her lack of Internet access, the day he first met her.

"Next!"

Juliet smacks her palms, making the navy booklets jump.

"My dead husband had a five million dollar life insurance policy!" Her voice bounces off the high ceilings and tile floor. Silence.

The girl at the adjacent counter hiccups, and the guard by the door glances up. Between them, Simon lets out a whoop and grabs the pocket of Juliet's shorts.

"Whoa! Wait, Mom, what? We have five *million* dollars? Can I get the Lego Star Wars Clone Turbo Tank? And a pogo stick? And a dirt bike?"

Dean imagines Amélie's snarky little smile and comment here, "So she was not kidding the other night when she said money was not her first concern anymore."

But then he thinks of the deleted email he has seen——"incomplete physical evidence?"

"If that is the case," the Immigration officer says deliberately, "I will need you to bring verification tomorrow. Otherwise, you have to leave the island in two days' time."

Juliet sighs, her shoulders rounding as she scoops their passports up.

"You must come back in person with documentation from your bank that you can support yourself and your children while on island. We close at noon."

"Can my brother just fax it here?" But Dean knows from his secret reading of her email that there is no insurance money yet. Juliet pushes her hair back into a ponytail; her children hang off her legs. Her expression is unreadable.

Five million dollars.

"Our fax machine is bro-ken."

Juliet jams her passports in her purse. "You're telling me you have one fax machine in the entire office of Immigration? And it's broken?"

"Since February. Next!"

⌒

Back in the van, Juliet slams the passenger door and slouches in the seat, kicking off her flip-flops and resting her bare feet up on the dashboard. With her arms around her waist, she reminds Dean of Luc.

"It's so unfair, and arbitrary! It's true! All I'm going to do is spend money here! This is so ridiculous!"

He waits for her to say something about the money. *Five million dollars.* He scrambles to do the math in his head—what must the monthly payments on that have been?

"And you? What's that?" She looks at the stamped navy booklets he tucks in the cup holder. "No questions asked?"

Dean shrugs, sheepish. "I guess I look like a nice guy."

"Ever honorable," she says wryly. "So now what?" She lowers her voice, "Are you going to stay?"

"What?" Simon yells from the backseat where they are finishing the movie on his iPod.

"Nothing!"

"It's just an extension." Dean grinds the van's gear as he struggles to find reverse.

Juliet's laugh is an incredulous yelp. "Isn't the irony a little thick here? You have an extension, and you're leaving, and I can't get one, but I can't go home?" Juliet opens a bottle of water and glugs from it. "Maybe it's a sign. Maybe *I* should just go!"

"What?" Simon yells again from the back.

"Please don't," Dean says softly as he turns the van left on the road at the harbor and the sea opens up in front of them in all its sun-sparkling majesty. "I'm not ready to..." He falters and stops.

"What?" Now it is Juliet asking. Her voice has a hopeful upswing.

"Nothing." Dean swallows, and accidentally turns on the windshield wipers instead of the turn indicator—they shriek as they scrape across the dry, salt-sticky glass.

What am I doing, he wonders, as they face the ocean, and instead of turning right, toward the airport, he turns left, to Rum Point.

CHAPTER 24

Juliet

You steal a glance at the man turning down South Church Street, one hand on the wheel, the other stabbing the shifter into gear, anxiety hunching his shoulders. You want to reach over and put a hand on his, tell him it's okay, tell him today, in Immigration, extending his stay, that he surprised you. You like that. It reminds you a little of the best parts of Jack.

The first time you met Jack, you were in the airport just before Christmas, your senior year of college. You were crying at the baggage claim—your luggage had been stolen, you worried you had failed an important exam, you hadn't seen your family since summer—and Jack, handsome Jack, stopped to ask if you were okay.

You told him about the stolen luggage, about the exam, even about the ugly ending of your last relationship, the recent ex-boyfriend who showed shades of scary possessiveness, who once choked you breathless in your sleep and blamed it on night terrors.

"Let me take you away from all this," Jack had smiled, standing up and hefting his backpack to his shoulders.

You stood up with him—you were the exact same height—and noticed his brown eyes had an actual sparkle. The baggage claim was nearly empty and an instrumental version of "I'll Be Home for Christmas" played over the speakers.

"Come with me," he'd said, sliding his ticket out of the envelope to show the destination: New Zealand. "I have a job with a luxury developer there—I just sold out a project for them in South Africa—have you ever been shark diving? Come on, I'll buy you a ticket, first class. Are you brave enough to bungee jump?"

You had paused, but not for very long.

Jack took you by the shoulders, the first of a thousand, of a hundred thousand times he would touch you in the coming years, and turned your body to the long windows outside baggage claim at Philadelphia International, where taxis belched out exhaust and SEPTA buses hissed as they pulled away from the curb. Policemen without a hint of holiday spirit blew hysterically on their whistles and gleefully ticketed cars that weren't actively loading. Beyond all of this: winter drizzle, yellowed grass peppered with litter and the faint skyline of the city.

"Who wants to go out there? Come with me! It's summertime Down Under. We'll dive the Great Barrier Reef, hike the Tongariro Crossing, go white water rafting. If I get this job, the money's ridiculous. We'll live like kings and queens."

"But," you looked at the empty baggage carousel, the lost luggage claim ticket crumpled in your hand. You thought, too briefly, about Lear coming to pick you up and drive you to a family dinner at Lam's Chinese with all of your siblings. You thought about your last semester of college. "But, I don't have any clothes," you faltered, blushing at his suggestive grin, his eyes traveling your body.

"Have you heard of Baku?"

You shook your head.

"They're the premium, the most famously expensive bikinis in Australia. I'll buy you one in every color."

And though you had known him all of twenty minutes, you called Lear from the payphone by the carousel and followed Jack Wilde up the escalator to the international terminal; he proposed before you touched down in Auckland.

"It just doesn't seem responsible, to stay here all summer," Dean says beside you. He sounds like he is trying to talk himself into a decision he doesn't want to make, but you are driving away from the airport.

"Then why did you have her stamp your passports?"

"I don't know." Dean laughs. "It felt good. Different! What were we saying, the other night? About reinventing ourselves? I'm about as far from spontaneous as you can get. But it felt good."

Percy always said you were a sucker for impulsive men.

"Your husband's crazy!" Percy had screamed into the dry, winter air. You were at Lear and Jenna's lake house for a long weekend when a record-breaking snow fell, with your sister Percy and her husband, Sonny just a baby. You were drinking mulled wine around their big stone fireplace when Jack proposed midnight skitching, hauling the little boys, Simon and your nephews, out of bed in their pajamas and stuffing them into snowsuits so he could pull them around the frozen fields on sleds behind Percy's Jeep. Lear seethed in the red chair by the fire, made no move to join in. By this point, he and Jack were barely civil.

"We used to do this all the time when I was a kid! Come on, Si! This will be epic!" Jack boomed, slapping an Eagles hat over Simon's curls. They had been drinking, Blake and Jack, but not much; you weren't worried until you stood at the window with your sister and she grabbed your arm.

"He's crazy!" You and Percy and Jenna watched from the house with the babies while Jack skidded and turned, too fast, spinning the Jeep and whipping the sled behind it like a horse trying to shake a rider. One of the twins broke lose, and Jack had to jerk the wheel left to miss him.

"Goddamit, he's going to kill someone!" Jenna slammed the door and screamed at Jack to stop. Her twins weren't ready to quit, red-cheeked and exhilarated.

"Uncle Jack is awesome!"

But little Si stumbled into the house, white, tears frozen on his chapped face. He broke down in your arms.

"That's the problem with Jack," Percy said as you comforted Simon. Outside, you could hear the thud of Jack and Blake stomping the snow from their boots on the porch. "It's impossible to tell if he's crazy-fun, or crazy-dangerous."

"No," Lear said coldly. "The problem is, Jack doesn't know the difference."

Dean is still talking about his work conference, and the swim lessons at the YMCA. "I'm not even sure I can afford a summer here."

"There's the garden," you say. "What about our plants? The peppers and the Sweet One Hundreds? I saw some blossoms on the aubergine today. And we could ride along and fish when Darvin goes out... Caribbean homesteading, on a shoestring!"

You know that back at The Wreck, they call you the Wealthy Widow.

They don't know anything.

Five million dollars—you had been stunned when Lear first told you, the week after the funeral. Just like in a movie, he had to help you sit down. You didn't know what was more shocking—the amount of the policy, or that Jack had drawn up a will that named Lear as executor. You think of this morning's email, the one Lear forwarded from Meridian. Everything has changed, and nothing has changed. All these years later, you're still waiting for Jack's promises, the big money, for things to pay out.

"This next project is going to be the pinnacle, the huge money."

"When we get the investors lined up and this strip mall up and running, it'll put the kids through college."

"Do you know what our percentage of seventeen million looks like, Jules? Because that's what they're projecting."

"Marty says laundromats, high-end laundromats with wireless, are where it's at."

"Once the returns on this start coming in, we'll be in the big time, Jules."

"It's only money; we'll make more it!"

You always hated the last one, Jack's stock phrase when a deal wasn't going well or when, in a boon, he did something grand and rash—drove home in a brand-new Mercedes-Benz or took you all downtown to Bookbinders for lobster dinners. Finances were in constant, dramatic flux. Liquid money was never a given. One month, he would berate you for buying groceries at Whole Foods instead of Bottom Dollar. Another, he'd tell you to have an architect start drawings of the addition, sleeping porches you dreamed of adding to the farmhouse for the cousins. But then you'd go to the pharmacy for Sonny's ear drops and find the credit cards were maxed, have to raid Si's piggy bank for the co-pay. Two weeks later, you'd overhear Jack and Marty, sitting up late at your grandmother's kitchen table, poring over catalogs for corporate jets.

⌒⟶

"So what does this mean, you staying?" you ask Dean. He is, after all, the second man you have kissed since Jack who has walked away.

"I can't leave Luc, right now. Not after what you just told me. I need to talk to him, about his biological father."

"You're staying for Luc, then. Nothing more?"

He slows down as a pack of dogs lunges out of the bush, snarling and yipping at the tires of the van.

"Potcakes!" your kids scream out the van window as you pass, Dean accelerating to leave them behind, sniffing and panting.

Dean sighs. "I don't know what I'm doing. I need to sort things out with my son."

"How did you do it?" you ask.

"Do what?"

"Love someone who has already loved someone else."

Dean swallows.

"We were all in Africa together, a college service semester, me and Amélie and Robert. They were together, until he got sick—dengue fever. He had to fly home early. Amélie and I had two months..." Dean's voice goes soft with memory. "Afterward, she went back to him. But when she got pregnant with Luc, he panicked, and broke it off. Three years later, when Amélie decided Luc needed a father, she knew exactly where to find me."

"Isn't it funny how different, but how similar our stories are? Jack loved the kids, but his way of showing love was more through working, providing. He worked long hours, and even when he was home, it was this—" You mime frowning at a phone screen. "Last year, we bought the kids a trampoline for Easter; it took Jack all day Sunday to get it put together. Monday morning, Easter Monday, the kids had off of school, and Si was begging Jack to come bounce with him. Jack said, 'Who do you think earns the money so that you can have nice things like a trampoline?' Jack didn't come from much, and he was always trying to create an appreciation for expensive gifts. But they don't get that. All little kids want is for their daddy to take off his tie and bounce with them."

Beside you, Dean opens his mouth to speak and closes it again.

"What?" you protest. "I'm trying to pay you a compliment here! I've been watching you, this month. *You* would bounce on the trampoline—you'd probably do backflips."

"Let's not do this," he says.

"Do what?"

"I imagine people do this, second time around, if they start dating, trotting out the faults in the old marriage, but with us, the kids, with them dead, it's different."

"What do you mean?"

"I don't want to speak badly of the ones who came before," he says carefully, looking in the rearview mirror. "Not when they gave us this."

"You're telling me you extended your passports," you say, a blush heating your cheeks, "and you're staying, but only for Luc."

Dean exhales. You know what he is going to say, you could write it for him.

"It's not you..." There, yes, he says it with just the right amount of chivalry and regret, and you fill in the rest for him.

"It's me." You say in unison. He has the good grace to laugh.

"It's complicated."

It's okay. You have come to expect disappointment; a side-effect of tragedy. What you told Dean in the hammock is true; you might have been a softer, more positive person if all of these things hadn't been heaped, one steaming serving of misfortune after another, onto your plate. Lear says it's your fault—who gets on a plane with the charming stranger they meet in the airport? Who marries him two weeks later, spends years packing and moving, chasing the deal? Who has children with a man who is admittedly indifferent about them, a man who spends his weekend not at their soccer games, but in Atlantic City—"I'm only taking five grand, Jules. We can afford to lose five grand, but it wouldn't hurt us to double it."

Maybe what happened at Immigration is a sign—you should go home. If only you could be sure it was safe.

CHAPTER 25

Dean

At dinner that night, Sonnet and Owen sit in the two chairs between them. Dean touches Juliet's hand once accidentally in the passing of the water pitcher. At least, he thinks, the children are benefiting from this strangeness; they are getting an unprecedented amount of adult attention as Dean and Juliet avoid eye contact, feign rapt interest in their recaps of favorite cartoons and Simon's plans to catch a blenny fish in the tide pools with his bare hands.

"I can't believe you're not leaving!" Simon says, beaming.

"I can't believe you might have to!" Holly says.

"Just for the day, right, Mom? Then we're coming right back?"

Instead of answering, Juliet asks Dean if she can go over to his place to email her brother about the Immigration disaster. She uses the words, "May I?" He looks down at her plate—she hasn't touched the food.

"Be my guest," he says.

But when she leaves, it is like the stretching of a rubber band. Her absence creates a painful feeling in Dean's chest, a crippling tightness. Without her, he looks at the room, dinner is just sustenance, putting calories in a body. Without her, the dishes are a chore. Dean drops the ketchup-smeared plates into her sink, just high enough so they clatter nicely but don't break. Weeks, months, years of this, Dean alone in the kitchen back in Saline stretch before him. He struggles to breathe evenly, to find the argument that made not being with her seem like a good idea.

When Leo shows up with sparklers and offers to take the kids down to the beach, it is all Dean can do to walk, briskly, not running, to his cottage, and to her.

Juliet looks up from his computer and her hand flutters automatically up to close the screen. "Where are the kids?"

"Leo brought over some sparklers."

Dean sits on the couch opposite her. He folds his hands between his knees, then jumps to his feet and takes long strides around the living room as though he is measuring something with his pacing. He doesn't know where to start.

"I'm going to buy a phone card, call my brother tomorrow. But I think..." Juliet pulls her straight brown hair into a ponytail and then lets it fall through her fingers. "I'm going to have to book plane tickets in the morning, and go home."

"What?" Dean's voice catches. He makes a tent with his hands over the bridge of his nose, rubs circles at his temples. *No.*

"It's just better, with the Immigration thing, and some things going on back home I should deal with..." But she doesn't finish, and he cannot tell her that he has been snooping, reading her deleted emails like an older sister's diary.

"I was thinking about it. I have a plan: We'll go back to town tomorrow, and you'll get in the Immigration line with that older guy, the one with the pictures of his grandkids on the glass, and you'll do your sob story, throw around some money."

"Play the part of the Wealthy Widow?" Her lips have a twitchy little lilt.

"Whatever it takes. You're right, it is completely arbitrary, these Immigration extensions. And if that doesn't work, so you fly up to Miami for the day, go buy Simon the Lego Star Wars Turbo Tank, get a massage, whatever. But come right back, we'll finish the summer. It will be good for the kids."

Juliet stands up. She looks past the porch to the beach and the children.

"Look how happy they are. You can't leave yet."

"What you said in the car today—I don't want anyone to get hurt," Juliet says softly.

He follows her gaze. Outside he can see the reflections of the kids' sparklers in the pool water. Holly and Simon have theirs down on the beach making big swooping circles with their arms, writing their names in the darkness.

"What about me?" Dean reaches across the space between them and grabs her hand. This, this feels like the right thing.

"You're one of the people I'm thinking of."

He kisses her, hard and desperate, surprising her so that their teeth clink before she catches up. He pulls away.

"I'm sorry, about the other night. I panicked. And then today, I realized, enough hiding behind Luc, old relationships, I'm not ready to let this go…" he whispers in her ear, about to finish his urgent sentiment, to finish what he couldn't say in the van. His hands are on her waist, her arms looping around his neck when the cottage door opens with a bang: Luc.

They drop their embrace; take two startled steps back.

"Not necessary," Luc says. "Holly told me about the passports. Awesome."

He is pushing past when Dean grabs his arm. Now or never.

"Juliet told me about you two, working on the internet search. Before I got here."

Luc drops his backpack.

"Your father, Robert's name, is Anthony Robert Russell. The reason you and Juliet were having trouble finding him is your mom was the only one who called him Robert. Everyone else, including me, including you, has always called him Tony."

Dean waits for this to register on Luc's face, and beyond his, Juliet's.

"Before he was the love of your mother's life, he was my roommate. Anything else you want to know," Dean gestures to their couch, the angelfish pillows, and Luc sinks into it, his head in his hands. "I'm here."

"I'm going to go, check on the littles," Juliet says, and though their fingers hook briefly before she pulls away, Dean lets her go.

This is more important.

CHAPTER 26

Juliet

In the darkness, you go to bed. Before, you made sure Holly and Owen got home, waving to Dean and Luc through the screen door. At home, tucking in and kissing your son and daughter in their twin beds, sniffing their scalps and realizing that it has been days, maybe a week since you actually washed their hair with shampoo, relying on the saline and chlorine of the ocean and pool to simulate clean.

At last, alone, you undress and slip between the sheets, their cottony cool a caress. You hope that if nothing else, sleep will come and quiet the questions, the monkey-chatter of worry. Live in the now, not for Jack's promised futures and payouts. Now, you are here, in a place many people only dream of, with two healthy children. You wish for what you have to be enough. You wish you had found the courage to tell Dean everything, but maybe if you leave tomorrow, it doesn't matter—

The bedroom door opens. In the light from the hall bathroom, there is a shape looming in the doorway—the familiar silhouette of a man. He crosses the bedroom in three bold strides, a flash of something red in hand.

"Look what I found in the owner's closet," he whispers. It is the blinking light of a baby monitor, and as he turns up the volume, your room is filled with the soothing whoosh of a noisy ceiling fan clacking away, two doors down.

"What if they wake up?"

"I'll hear them." He puts the monitor on your nightstand.

"What about Luc?"

"He's fine. We talked. It's all good."

"Does Tony know?"

"Of course. It was his idea, last winter, that I send Luc here. Said it would be good for him. He was supposed to tell him right away. Typical Tony, never able to initiate the conversation. Luc," Dean laughs softly, "is more man than his own biological father. He's headed to the Wreck to talk to him now."

"But what about...?"

He closes your bedroom door softly behind him, shutting out the yellow light of the hall.

"I changed our plane tickets: August twenty-first."

We could have the summer then, you think. Because in the faint red glow of the monitor, you see him lift the shirt over his head.

"I realized, tonight, I'm not ready to lose you," Dean finishes the sentence at last. "Not when I just found you."

He crosses the room to your bed, to lift you up, fold you into his warm arms, pressing his mouth to yours, to finish what you started.

CHAPTER 27

DEAN

The trouble is, as he slips her tank top strap off one shoulder and leaves behind it a trail of light kisses, Dean should not be thinking of his dead wife. His fingertips trace Juliet's skin, still warm from the day's sun, and he cannot believe that her deft hands are flicking at his belt, the zipper of his shorts singing before he shucks them off.

Dark——her cottage, her bedroom, the air conditioner humming on high, the baby monitor crackling, an anxious check over his shoulder, his lips grazing Juliet's neck—how can she taste so familiar and so foreign at the same time? Remembering, before this, how long it has been since he touched a woman's skin. Other than the accidental brushing of fingertips with the horse-toothed bank teller back home or the awkward dry cheek peck at the end of that lone date with Erica from the English department, it has been months. And since he has wtouched one with intent? Years.

The last time with Amélie: like so many things with her, they hadn't known it was the last as it was happening. Thinking that this was just another battle. They had won before, breast and lung, lymph and uterus, but before it hadn't been in her brain, what Dr. J. called the human cockpit. Kissing her that afternoon, Amélie's skin tasted like metal, because of the chemicals, like licking cool bars of iron. It was early summer, when they were still trying to fight the good fight, when her temples still held the marks from where the steel halo had been screwed to her skull—gamma knife attempts to irradiate the tumors that were popping up in her brain like weeds after a summer rain.

"I wish I'd married a Trekkie," Amélie had said as she let Dean strip the clothes off her. "Then I would know for sure you were turned on by this."

She shed her underwear and tank top with the indifference of their sugar maple dropping leaves in fall and stood before him with the posture of the long married, though her body was becoming more foreign every day. The pounds winnowed away, and new bones appearing, straining painfully at the skin. Bald, purple sickle-shaped scars where there once had been breasts, her olive skin so gray it was almost irides-cent green in the late afternoon light. Her arms a watercolor of purple, magenta and yellow-green splotches, bruising from IVs and blood draws.

He'd paid Holly a dollar to sit in the pack-and-play crib and watch "Dora the Explorer" with Owen, for this: For Amélie to lie before him in the same resigned way that she offered her arm to the nurses to jab in hopeless search for a vein. Dean lay down carefully beside his dying wife, an attempt to cement their connection, to remind them of better times, to keep her here on earth.

If only it hadn't felt so much like mercy on her part.

But he shouldn't be thinking of this now! Not when there is a real woman who smells faintly of bug spray and fabric softener from the sheets, whose healthy, lightly-freckled breasts are just inches from his face, her fingers skittering across his bare shoulder blades like ghost crabs at sunrise.

A thought hits him then, startles him so that he stops everything.

"What?" Juliet whispers, warm and breathy in his ear.

If these are his thoughts, the final time that his wife laid beneath him and let him try with desperate urgency to commit the ritual of life, then what is Juliet think-ing, when the man who came before him died suddenly? Healthy. Younger. Athletic. Charming. Driven. Wealthy. Successful, by all accounts.

"What?" she whispers again, urging him on, her fingers in his hair, pulling his head back down.

"Nothing."

He wonders if they will always be there, all four of them, whenever they come together in this white-walled bedroom.

And then, when her lips find his, she tastes like coconut water and mint, and as he drinks her in, he stops caring.

INTERLUDE

Cayman Islands Hospital – August 19, 2007

O n Grand Cayman, with a hurricane approaching, it can be difficult to find
what you're looking for at sunrise on a Sunday. There is no shopping on
God's day; no drugstores, no grocery stores, and the gas station with mini
marts may be open, but only for emergency fuel. In the few without plywood hastily
screwed over the windows, the hot machines for jerk chicken patties glow empty.

Juliet and Dean know this because they stopped at two of the Essos on the
forty-five minute drive from Rum Point to George Town, Dean running in to ask,
while Juliet waits in the van, searching the battleship-gray dawn sky for signs of the
coming storm.

"But we're so hungry," Simon calls from the backseat.

"Literally starving!" Holly chimes.

But instead of turning back toward the rental cottages, Dean drives too fast down
Hospital Road. His mantra from the summer sits in the front seat between them like
a family pet: *We cannot afford more tragedy.* If they were speaking to each other, Juliet
would ask him to slow down with more than just her eyes.

Dean downshifts to turn the van into the palm-lined parking lot at Cayman
Islands Hospital. He has mastered so many things—the left-hand manual transmis-
sion shifting, the delicate integration of their families, the perfectly-timed crescendo
of mutual climax—over the course of the summer. Overhead, the wind whips the
olive-colored fronds like the swirling skirts of a flamenco dancer: the precipitating edge
of a hurricane, recently upgraded from a category four to a five as it churns toward
the small island. Sometime in the coming hours, it is expected to either make a direct
hit or pass mercifully to the south. The first drops of rain smatter the van's windshield.

"Why are we here?" Holly pops her head up from where she and Simon are bent over the shared iPod.

"I told you I'm fine." Juliet's arms clamp defensively across her stomach. It's the first they have spoken directly in hours.

Dean opens the rusted side door of their shared rental van, dubbed the Brave Little Toaster, and their five children climb out. Instinctively, Juliet reaches to help Owen with his car seat buckles, but Dean is there ahead, scooping his son out. Two days ago, the way the families blended over the summer, Juliet might have been the one to carry Owen's solid weight, chubby legs dangling down, square toddler feet slapping her thighs.

"Why are we at the hospital? Who's sick?" Sonnet asks, sliding her fingers easily into her mother's hand.

"Nobody," Juliet replies, because it's true.

"Is this because of the hurricane?"

Dean whirls around.

"Everything's fine! Juliet just needs a check-up." It's the first time in weeks he has used the long version of her name. Over the course of the summer, it had become shorter and shorter, Julie, occasionally a wry "Mrs. Brady," and in the days leading up to what happened last night, simply J.

"We'll try to be quick," Dean adds more softly; but the shift in tone is perhaps because he doesn't want to upset the children.

Inside, at the admission desk, the receptionist eyes Juliet's matted, wet hair, the marks on her face. She looks to Dean, the children between them still wearing pajamas.

"May I have the patient's name?"

"Juliet Wilde," she answers, as everyone else settles into plastic waiting room chairs. Before, she loved Jack's last name. It fit the reckless, driven and hungry way he lived, the life of travel and endless adventure they shared before Simon was born. Now, it catches in her throat.

"You're tourists, no?" Juliet and Dean share a look. After three months on the island, they don't feel like it's a fair characterization. "Even with all these little chickadees," the receptionist clucks, "you couldn't get on one of the emergency Cayman Airways flights yesterday?"

In the empty waiting room, Juliet and Dean sit down, miserable bookends for the four younger children rushed from their beds, only after Dean had wrapped Juliet in enough of his clothes to stop her shaking. Owen sags sleepily into his father, his bare feet on Holly's lap, then Simon, their heads touching over the coveted iPod and leaning against Juliet, a yawning Sonnet. Luc has gone down the hall to see if the Pink Hibiscus is open for anything that could pass as breakfast; it is barely seven.

Dean meets Juliet's eyes, briefly, over the children's heads, his face as neutral a canvas as the wave-washed sandscape of Rum Point beach first thing that morning. He has a strong brow bone that arches slightly down, just above the outside corners of his eyes. It makes him look empathetic, or sometimes sad, even when he is not.

There has been plenty to be sad about.

The nurse comes out in flamingo-pink scrubs, beautiful against her smooth skin and halo of white hair. She has a bosom that swells like a pigeon's, so soft and pillowy that Juliet has a childlike urge to lie her head there, confessing everything.

"Mrs. Wilde?" the nurse asks.

Dean makes no move to stand. Juliet wonders if this is significant or simply practical, that someone needs to watch over their children?

"What's the trouble, dear?" In the exam room, the nurse's voice, her lilting West Indian accent is so soothing, Juliet isn't sure where to begin. *Back on December first, when you heard your husband's scream before the signal was cut off by the icy Atlantic? Or later, when you had given Sonnet's chickens away, when your brother showed up one night with tickets and threw the suitcases down from the attic, insisting you and the children fly to Cayman Kai the next morning for "a change of scenery?"*

Was the trouble that lone hazy Saturday at the beginning of June when the Barefoot Man sang about a lonely yellow bird and the golden tequila flowed? Or had it only begun later, after Dean and his children arrived?

Juliet opens her mouth to answer the nurse's question and stops. Thirty-seven years old, close enough to forty that book club friends back in Pennsylvania are navigating the challenges of early menopause, stale marriages and irascible teenagers.

Juliet drops her face into her palms, unable to speak.

"Alrighty, dear," the nurse croons. Overhead, the first waves of rain from the hurricane beat down in steady rhythm. "Lord, spare us, your humble servants," she murmurs. "Trusting as we do in your grace. Amen." Juliet imagines she sings in a church on Sundays, in a large-print floral dress, mouth thrown wide open, broad hands clapping in perfect time to the hallelujahs.

Juliet assumes her preferred position, the way she held herself last winter, after what happened to Jack: Shoulders hunched, spine rounded, arms clamped tightly, solely responsible for keeping all her tender insides from spilling out.

"Alrighty. I'm going to take your vitals, and then have Dr. Childer come in, but I need a little information first. What brings you here today?"

Juliet knows she is supposed to talk about last night, the marks around her mouth, the bruise forming on her cheek, the circles on her wrists and the gurgling gulps of seawater making it impossible, even now, to draw a deep breath. She sees the nurse's kind eyes, taking this all in.

"Pregnant," she blurts.

The nurse does not blink.

"I think I might be pregnant."

BOOK TWO

July-August

CHAPTER 28

Dean

Dean can't help but congratulate himself—first the baby monitor, and then his second brilliant idea worked. After their first breathless, sleepless night together, Dean had brewed a pot of iced coffee. He loaded everyone into their shared van, the Brave Little Toaster, they decide to call it, and drove to Immigration. Juliet told her sob story to the grandfatherly man and got her passports stamped until the end of August, and with an extra twinkling of his rheumy eyes, a blessing of, "God's grace be with you all."

Their second night together, Dean feels like the old man's words might have done some good, sprinkled some cosmic fairy dust on them. As soon as Owen is asleep, Dean sets the baby monitor and sprints through the dark to Juliet's, scaring the night-white geckoes out of his path. His appetite for her is like a hollow-flanked bear stumbling out of hibernation in March, empty stomach roaring.

Once, when Amélie was still alive, Dean resolved to give up coffee—splitting, brutal headaches that faded to a dull pulse, followed by stumbling through flat, colorless days. He lasted a week, until a student came in to argue a grade, bearing a Starbucks bribe. One sip, and Dean's senses were singing back to life. His drive home, the ruby of the brake lights was so beautiful, his heartbeat so jaunty, tiny Owen's hug so tight—he felt euphoric, present in his body again.

"I don't know what I was thinking?" he laughed in the faculty lounge the next morning. He went right back to his three-cup-a-day habit, senses restored.

This is what it is like with Juliet now—Dean turns to kiss the ankle braced on his shoulder, slides his hands possessively up the smoothness of her inner thighs, the red glow of the monitor on her face. How did he go so long without this, he marvels, when he sucks her bottom lip between his? He buries his face in the damp hair that clings to her neck, drinking in the smell of her, the taste. She flips him over, and lowers herself, inch by sweet inch, the splay of her hands on his chest, kneading like a cat. Nothing else matters, not food, not sleep, not even children. Luc will be waiting to have coffee with him in three hours, Owen and Holly will need him all day, and it doesn't matter.

"You," he gasps, clutching at her waist, "are everything."

Until afterward.

"The important thing is we keep this in perspective." She still straddles him in the darkness, the monitor's red light blinking, his breath coming back. "This can be therapeutic," she whispers, bending forward, her tongue flicking at his earlobe, her lips dragging across his cheek. "Like running. It's good for us, a form of therapy."

"I am a trained psychologist, you know." Dean's heart rate is settling back down.

"Oh, I know," she laughs, slipping off him. "But we have to remember this is just for now."

Dean exhales. There is truth in this. He has calculated it already on Google maps—it is a ten hour drive from Saline to Bucks County, hardly a weekend trip. It is July; the thick of the summer, but like the milk that travels to the island on cargo ships, this relationship has an expiration date: August 21.

Which is why, afterward, she gently shakes his shoulder, to make sure he doesn't fall asleep with one arm tucked under her head and the other at her waist, her cheek on his forearm, her breath tickling the hairs at his wrist. It is why she tugs him inside the cottage's utility closet when they are meant to be doing the dishes, and takes him in her mouth, but he is not allowed to hold her hand when they follow the children in the blistering sunshine to look for hermit crabs in the slippery tide pools.

"Stop." She slaps him away. "We can't send our children the message that people are replaceable. My children have the right to grieve their father."

"Of course they do."

"I just wish," Juliet blurts, "that they'd start to show some of the signs!"

Sonny *does* grieve, Dean points out, does speak longingly, but it is about Marshmallow, a half-feral cat she had tried to tame by leaving cans of tuna open on the front porch of the farmhouse last year.

Whenever the local cats weave under the picnic tables at Rum Point begging French fries and battered fish, Sonny talks about how Marshmallow was almost their pet, before she had been run over by one of the construction trucks for Jack's development.

Sonnet collects pieces of shells and coral and sea glass. She unfurls her palm and holds them up for Dean.

"These are for Marshmallow's Garden," she calls, skipping ahead.

"Marshmallow's Garden," Juliet explains, "is a spot under a dogwood tree back home where Jack pretended to bury the body."

"Pretended?"

"It was November, the ground was frozen solid. He tied her in a garbage bag and put her out for Friday pickup. But he told Sonny she was buried under the dogwood."

The psychologist in Dean files this away: *lies to children*.

"Last spring, I went to the nursery to start a memorial garden for Jack. I put in a flowering cherry tree, and Sonny picked out twelve flats of cheddar pinks for Marshmallow's grave, you know, like we each had our own losses to grieve, our own gardens to decorate," Juliet switches to a whisper as Sonny runs back to them. "I think she might be having trouble processing."

"When we go home, I'm going to make a path to Marshmallow's grave," Sonnet tells Dean, her beach bag bulging with broken coral, shells and smooth, opaque sea glass. "Won't that be pretty? So when you walk out to visit her, it will be like walking on the beach, and when it rains, all the glass will sparkle."

"How about we use some for Daddy's garden?" Juliet suggests. "With the cherry tree?"

"But Daddy's not dead! These are for Marshmallow." Sonny slips her hand inside Dean's and looks out at the ocean, murmuring, "Marshmallow loved the sea so."

"Figure that one out, Professor."

Still, Dean can't help reaching for Juliet when they all arrive at her cottage for breakfast, as though he hasn't slipped through this same sliding glass door with the baby monitor in the dark hours before dawn.

"These sugar ants are everywhere!" Juliet moves out of his reach for a piece of paper towel to crush them.

Dean lays a hand on her hip and when he crouches down to reach under the sink for the counter spray, he lays two quick kisses on her bare thigh, just above the birthmark on her right knee before he stands up. "Here, try this. O likes to squirt them."

He wraps his arms around her, the oldest bar trick in the book—*let me show you how to line up that pool shot, little lady*—and puts his hands over hers on the nozzle of the spray bottle. At the breakfast table, the four children pay them no attention. The dynamics of their relationships have found a comfortable balance, filled with ever-shifting triangles and alliances, occasional bickering: they treat each other like siblings.

"Then as soon as they stop wriggling, you just wipe up the whole mess up with a paper towel." He drops his arms, steps back. Where her body had fit perfectly into the curve of his with its warmth and softness, he is now cold in the sputters of her constant air conditioner.

"When we lived in Africa, everything was full of bugs. You'd open a pack of crackers or pasta, and you'd have to set it out in the sun and let them crawl out before you could eat."

"'We' means Amélie?" she asks, her back to him.

"Yes."

"Your French-dancer-cellist-literature-translating wife?"

"Yes…" Dean says slowly.

He had noticed it yesterday, when he clicked on HISTORY, that someone has been using his laptop to search the web for **Amélie Alder, bio and images**. His first thought was that it had been Luc. There's an old interview with the University radio station Amélie had done to promote an upcoming recital. Last winter, they all huddled around his laptop, just to hear her voice as she talked easily about *jetés* and ensembles. It had irritated Dean a little, the way the interviewer was clearly getting off on her accent, kept asking her to say something again, in French and har-har-haring lasciviously. Still, it had been nice, hearing her professional voice—witty, intelligent, flirty—even if it was different from how she sounded at home.

But this recent internet search for Amélie had been sandwiched between Juliet's obsessive checking of her Gmail account, followed by a Google search for "estate law and creditors in Pennsylvania."

"I mean, I'm trying to figure out, should we talk about them?" Juliet continues. "Is that how we do it? Because here's where it gets complicated for me. How do we get to know each other? How do we share our stories, when so much involves the one that came before? How do we honor the past for the sake of our children, without hurting each other?"

"It is what it is," he says simply. "We're not nineteen-year-old virgins. I don't know what else to say."

"So we just, what, live with these ghosts? There are so many things I haven't told you..."

Dean thinks of the swans, the day Amélie died, his own secrets. He thinks about last October, how Amélie's stroke-garbled voice screamed another man's name, the slap of her wet spit in his face. *J'ai craive Robert!*

There are things he hasn't told her either.

"We have the rest of the summer," Dean says, reaching for Juliet, burying his face in her freshly-washed hair and placing a kiss on her nape, watching the goose-bumps rise on her arm, both of their eyes drifting to the breakfast table. Simon looks up, and she ducks out of his arms, carrying a bowl of cut up bananas and papaya to the children.

"Right. We'll just take it at face value."

"Take what at face value?" Si asks, eyes narrow.

When Owen scampers past with an open pint of Juliet's raspberries, grabbing great fistfuls and shoveling them in, she catches him by the hand.

"Wait, honey, share some of those with Si. They're the only fruit he eats," she adds, to Dean.

"You should try the ones we grow at home. When we get back," Simon asks his mother, "will it be time for the Autumn Bliss?"

"Maybe," Juliet says, a strange melancholy in her voice. Dean puts the plate of apples between Holly and Sonnet on the coffee table. Owen scrambles down from the counter, following the food like a seagull. Dean knows what is expected here; now he's meant to talk about raspberries in Michigan, tell them about the raspberry festival at the Sandhill Crane Vineyards. They have been doing this, like ambassadors of their home states, each making a veiled case for a future.

Today, Dean doesn't lob back. He lets the ball drop.

"I'm sorry," Juliet says when they pass. For the rest of the summer, she is careful to buy so many pints of raspberries that they go ignored, grow mold in the fridge.

CHAPTER 29

Juliet

To: **Juliet B. Wilde <jbwilde@gmail.com>**
From: **Laurie Munsch <laurieluvslavender@aol.com>**
Date: **July 15, 2007**
Subject: **This and that**

Hi Juliet!

I just wanted to run some things by you that have come up recently:

1. *the dishwasher stopped working and it flooded the kitchen. I called a repair guy but he hasn't come. I'll just deduct it from my rent?*
2. *speaking of flooding, we had a proper summer thunderstorm last week, and the tarp blew off the back half of the kitchen. Some old wooden table got rained on and it split down the middle. It looked pretty junky anyway. I tried to put it out for trash pick-up but they wouldn't take it so I had to call for large pick-up—it was $50. I deducted that from my rent.*
3. *when are the construction guys coming back to finish the roof? I thought you said it would be done by June?*
4. *your brother came by with the rock salt and the water is back to normal, but the tub and toilet is still orange so I bought some CLR ($14.72) and deducted it from my rent*

5. *last week something really creepy happened: I woke up to these noises and there was a guy in your office! He said his name was Marty and he had a key! He said he was picking up some papers? I hope that was okay.*

6. *I know you said no pets but after that, I've been getting a little freaked out. Your house makes lots of weird noises and I kept feeling like someone was creeping around at night so I got a dog. He's part Rotty, part shepherd, a rescue dog and he's mostly housebroken. I think he's just adjusting.*

7. *Yesterday, your car got towed. You should let me know when things like this are going to happen because the guys banging on the door really scared me. When I called your brother, he said it was for monthly service, but the papers the tow guy left said repossession? Is everything okay?*

8. *Also, the cable is not working*

9. *The place I had lined up for when you get home kind of fell through so I'm hoping it will work out for me to stay on for a few weeks/months? I could pay half-rent, or I could help you out with the kids or whatever?*

10. *You're still coming back at the end of August, right?*

Hope you're great! Be sunny! Laurie

* * *

To:	**Juliet B. Wilde <jbwilde@gmail.com>**
From:	**Lear Burke <ljb@hotmail.com>**
Date:	**July 15, 2007**
Subject:	**Business**

J—

I don't know if you saw, Compass was in the news? Here's the link:
http://www.nj.com/news/index.ssf/2007/07/Compass-tristate_consulting_scam_projects_stalled_investors_furious_remaining_partners_AWOL?.html

I haven't heard back from our mutual friend Marty – still leaving messages. Trying to touch base. Have you heard from him?

Nothing new from Meridian.

I paid your AmEx. Noticed your payments to Andy's Autos just went up? Did you not get my message from July 1 re: ease up on the cc?

Cars: there was some trouble with yours—we can talk about it when you call.

I hope you are having a great vacation—rest and relaxation, and the kids are good? Try to take a break from sunbathing—pick up a phone card and call me from a payphone. If you don't, I may just have to show up and crash your pool party.

Love, L

*Delete the contents of this email and erase it from your hard drive

You close Dean's computer, slide back between the covers of the bed. Today, at the pool, he held a towel over Owen's head to create a protective shade over him while he slept, and he told you the way to go forward is not to look back. Today, Sonny called him Dad-dean when she wanted him to watch her handstands. Focus on the future, he said. How are you supposed to do that, you wonder, when the past is breathing, hot, predatory puffs on the back of your neck?

You love how peaceful he looks now, breathing softly, the lines of his brow smooth. While he sleeps, you kiss the whole length of it. You lift one of his sleep-heavy arms and wriggle under it, press your cheek against his heart, reveling in the weight of his arm over you, the way he sighs and curls his hand, tucks it all the way around you. Before you fall asleep, you reach to the nightstand and slide down the volume on the monitor. You turn off the alarm that he sets for three. Shaken by everything you read today, you need to sleep all night in the shelter of Dean's arms.

CHAPTER 30

DEAN

Dean hears Owen's wails from two doors down, running in the still dawn. Luc meets him at the screen door, bouncing Owen on his hip like a much younger baby.

"Where were you? Here!"

Dean takes Owen into his arms.

"Shh," he says, cupping Owen's head against his shoulder. The alarm never went off, the monitor had been turned down. Buffered by the white noise of her air conditioner, Juliet's naked body tucked to his chest, Dean overslept.

"He woke up Holly too." Is he wrong, or is Luc enjoying this?

"Shh, it's too early, buddy..." Owen settles into Dean, the slack, give that means he will go back to sleep.

"I'd like to know when I am expected to be babysitting. You were gone all night!"

Dean doesn't answer. He holds a finger to his lips, walking in a circle until all the tension seeps out of Owen, and he is asleep.

"I made coffee. Sort of," Luc says, bringing Dean a lukewarm mug. "It tastes like shit."

They sit on the screen porch chairs, and Dean takes a sip. "Yeah, that's pretty bad. Sorry; my alarm didn't go off."

The irony that this was Luc's excuse for skipping school in the weeks after Amélie's death sits between them, silently acknowledged.

In the shutters, their bananaquit is frozen, terrified with them so close, but afraid to leave her post. Dean scoots his chair farther away from her, closer to Luc.

"Hear anything new from Bridget?"

"Not recently."

Dean thinks of Juliet's brother emails. "You could buy a phone card, call her yourself."

"I don't know. Tony says I should let her go. He's right; she's literally on the other side of the world."

"Location is only a rule in real estate."

"Tony doesn't like Juliet either."

Dean rubs Owen's sleeping back, sips the weak, too-sweet coffee, deciding how much he will say.

"He calls her the Train Wreck. He thinks you're making a mistake."

"Well, I don't know that I'd make Tony my romantic role model."

"Why not?" Luc asks, defensive.

"He was engaged once. You were little, five, maybe six? His fiancée thought Tony should be in your life. They asked us to come, to the wedding—Barrett wanted you to be the ringbearer."

"Why don't I remember any of this?"

"Like I said, you were little, and the wedding never happened."

"Why not?"

"Tony asked me to come to Chicago, for the bachelor party. Your mom thought it might be a good idea, that we could start mending fences."

"So what happened?"

"The night of Tony's bachelor party, it was meant to be low key, just a bunch of us hanging out at a hotel downtown, drinking. Tony brings out a tape."

Dean glances down, makes sure Owen is still asleep on his chest.

"A sex tape."

Luc expression is disappointed, knowing, *'ugh, prude-y old dad, can't handle porn.'* As though Dean wasn't just kissing the most intimate parts of Juliet a few hours ago. He continues. "A sex tape of Barrett. And him."

Luc's eyes pop.

"Of his future wife? He showed you guys? That's messed up!"

Dean nods.

"Did you watch it?"

"Long enough to realize who it was and figure out it had been filmed without her knowledge. You could see the corner of the towel he'd put the camera under."

"Jesus. Then what?"

"I left. From the one time I met her, I respected Barrett a lot. She'd worked as a model, putting herself through law school. She was smart, funny, beautiful, the real deal." Dean pauses; actually, Juliet reminds him of her. "And while I had my reservations about Tony in your life, with Barrett, I think it would have been okay. Healthy."

"So then what happened?"

"Amélie got suspicious—why was I home from a bachelor weekend at ten o'clock? I told her about the video."

"Holy shee-it."

"I probably shouldn't have, in hindsight. She got upset."

For a moment, they are both silent, and then burst into laughter at the understatement—Amélie never just got upset. She raged, threw things, cursed in French; afterward, their geriatric beagle wouldn't come out from under Holly's bed for days.

"But then of course," their laughter chokes out into a chuckle, "she told Barrett. The week Tony should have been starting his life with this incredible woman, he was on a plane down here, one way ticket."

"Wow," Luc whistles.

"Yep. Barrett wrote us a letter, after, thanking us. Remember those Red Wings pajamas you loved? She sent them. Last I heard, she was a DA in Arizona. It was a long time before I heard from Tony again, really, not until after..." He doesn't have to finish the sentence. In their family, there is only one dividing temporal line, one meaning to the words 'Before' and 'After.'

Out past the inlet, a cruise ship makes steady progress along the horizon toward George Town. They are not allowed to open their casinos in the harbor, so they arrive at sunrise, and leave at dusk—Dean sees them on both directions of his passing between the cottages.

"Listen, Luc, everyone makes mistakes. Maybe I shouldn't have told you that, how Tony ended up here, but I want you to take Tony's advice on women with a whole shaker of salt. Maybe a guy who walks out on his pregnant girlfriend, who takes eighteen years to step up to the plate where his son is involved, who has so little self-confidence that he—"

Luc jumps up, looking at his watch, ending the conversation. "I've got to get going."

"Right. Hey, I need you to babysit tonight," Dean says.

"Her kids too?"

"Yes."

Luc leaves his empty mug on the glass table. "We might be going out. Tony said he'd drive us to Royal Palms."

"We won't be late."

"Fine." Luc threads his ear buds up through his collar.

"And get yourself a phone card. Call Bridget, see how she's doing."

"Yeah, I might do that." Luc pauses in the screen doorway. "If Tony doesn't like someone, he has his reasons." He looks like he might say more. "There are some things, from that night in June."

"Would this be the night you weren't drunk, but say you can't remember?"

Luc doesn't answer.

"That was all before I got here," Dean says. He thinks of his advice to Juliet—the only thing they can do is look forward.

It rains, even in paradise, a welcome respite from the heat. This storm comes with heavy curls of billowing clouds, different from the usual shower that spits down while the sun continues to shine, as though the Department of Tourism controls the weather, conscientious that guests on one-week vacations don't have time for the inconvenience of clouds.

Dean carries Owen inside, his shoulder aching under the weight of his sleeping son. In the ultraviolet storm light, the oversized reef fish throw pillows leer at him. He turns their faces to the back of the living room couch. In the corner there is a hulking, squat black boom box. Raised in the land of iPods, Owen has been fascinated by this all summer, curiously poking at the buttons of this antiquated monstrosity, opening and closing the CD door and whispering, "Magic."

Dean puts in a disc he brought from home: Del McCoury, the skilled, picking father-son bluegrass band. Tossing the fish pillows aside, Dean sinks into the couch with Owen cradled in his arms. In the darkening living room, he listens as the rain pounds down on the inlet and pool, a shushing, percussion to the strings. It feels good to sit, letting music and memory wash over him like rain.

The last time things were good with Amélie was the first time he saw Del McCoury in concert, three summers ago. He insisted that they all drive from Michigan to the Gray Fox Music Festival in upstate New York, despite the fact that Owen was barely two months old and Amélie had just finished her first round of postnatal chemo/radiation and in her own weary words, '*il a débuté mon cul*'—it had kicked her ass.

It was Dean's idea, his dream of a road trip with the whole family to camp on the grounds of the music festival, to see Del and his sons Rob and Ronnie pick and croon on stage together. He promised they could leave as soon he heard the song "Get Down on Your Knees and Pray," because that is how he felt that first summer after Owen was born, as though he would do anything, dance with religion, barter, plead, for another lucky break in Amélie's health. And for an encore, if they felt like doing, "My Love Will Not Change," or perhaps "Love is a Long Road," he would close his eyes and he'd try not to embarrass Luc and Holly, but he might sing along.

Years earlier, Dean and Amélie had fought over whether Del's ballad, "Unequal Love" had a place in their wedding reception playlist; she was uncomfortable with the truth the lyrics told, a man who loves a woman who's already had her heart broken by the man who came before him. Like so many arguments, Amélie had won. On the nights when he waited for her to come home, his hands in the spaghetti-sauced sink water, looking out the kitchen window, he blasted it on the CD player, on repeat.

The long drive east for the Gray Fox set the tone for the weekend; fussy baby, Luc and Holly taking turns holding bottles over Owen's car seat like a guinea pig's water feeder, Amélie with her floral-cased foam pillow that went everywhere, recently released from a weekend in the hospital due to a skin infection at her port site. She had simply endured the eleven-hour drive, her cheek pinning the pillow against the passenger side window. She pinched her eyes closed, refusing to acknowledge his suggestion, every hundred miles or so, that she might like to sip from the six-pack of warm ginger ale he had left at her feet.

And when they got there, driving through the pewter clouds, it had rained and rained and rained, their borrowed tent leaking, Holly's white sandals literally sucked off her feet and disappearing into the mud on the walk from their campsite to the amphitheater. Poor Owen in the baby Bjorn didn't understand the import of this moment, batting at Dean's garbage-bag-attempt of a poncho over them both, the rain slicking his wispy newborn hair down the dome of his forehead. Dean remembers the horrified looks of other women, mothers, at the festival; first, that he would bring a tiny baby out in this weather, and second, that he'd put a bag over its head. As if Dean wasn't constantly checking, making sure Owen was okay in there, that the garbage bag stayed tented over him like an inky, dripping canopy.

Amélie hadn't spoken to Dean since the rest stop in Ohio, sulking first in their car, then on the puddled floor of the tent, leaving Dean to make the trek to the amphitheater alone with Owen in the baby carrier and the other two sloshing and bickering behind him like disgruntled ducklings.

"This weather's for the mallards," Dean told them. "For the red-crested Pochards. For the Muscovies and Northern Pintails." Trying to get them to chime in and play along. He knew wood ducks were Holly's favorites. Nothing.

Somehow, two hours later, as Del and his boys took center stage and the summer rain came down in car wash waves, Amélie found the four of them in the crowd, shifting their feet constantly so they didn't get sucked into the quagmire.

"I'm sorry," she had said to Dean, and she surprised him by slipping her fingers into his, her wig stinking of wet dog. "I'm here." With a jerk she had snatched off her false hair, and they had all laughed while the rain ran in rivers down her smooth head, Amélie blinking maniacally because she had no eyebrows or lashes to stop the water from flooding her beautiful chocolate eyes. Meanwhile, the music, those sweet close harmonies of bluegrass, the truest strumming of mandolin strings, washed over them all.

Her presence, her hand in his, the calloused knobs of her cellist fingertips, all of this a rare gift, a tightly kernelled seed Dean had clutched like a November field mouse, squirreled away for a future that would never be.

I'm here.

Dean cannot move. He sits in the island rain with Owen's sweaty cheek on his bare chest, the softness, the rise and fall of their shared breath, and he thinks about Juliet, and Amélie.

There is still grief.

I'm here. It is what he should have said to Luc when he first arrived, shoulders clutched under his hands. It is what he should have said to Amélie as he sat beside the hospital bed when she took her last breaths.

But he did not.

He pictures Juliet yesterday afternoon deftly cutting Owen's hot dog into wheels and then for safety, in half again, though he hasn't done that in months. And last night, when he tripped on the pool deck, Owen went to Juliet first, scrambling up into her arms to have his wounds fussed over and kissed. Dean had tried to hold back a smile at the curious way Owen patted at the softness of her breasts, looking up at her like *'what the heck are these?'* He muttered, "Pillows," before settling back against them.

I'm here, Amélie had said simply that rainy night in upstate New York. Three years ago.

And now Juliet is here, easily assimilating Owen, all of them, into her circle of care. It is startling to realize how taken he is by the easing of what he hadn't ever let himself think was a burden. Being his children's everything has been his reality. It wasn't until Juliet started to do some of it for him, unbuckling Owen's car seat clips, unstacking the dishwasher, entertaining Holly with weaving embroidery thread bracelets, that he realized how much he missed partnership.

—

Dean doesn't want to be alone anymore. He wants to be with Juliet, out, honest. He wants to kiss her hard in public, in front of Luc and Tony and Leo, everyone! When he wakes up with her tucked in his arms, he wants it to be intentional, more than a missed alarm.

Juliet is here, two doors down. Dean jumps to his feet, and stops.

But how noble would Juliet think you were if she knew the truth? If she knew about October, when he was running gasping laps around Ford Lake in his khakis and dress shoes, drawing stares from the real joggers, throwing stones and screaming at the swans?

If you are an honorable man, if you loved Amélie so much, how could you do what you did?

CHAPTER 31

Juliet

The rain stops in time for you to run. You ask to go first, early, long before
sunset. More than ever, after today's inspiration, you need it.

To:	**Juliet B. Wilde <jbwilde@gmail.com>**
From:	**Daily Inspirations**
Date:	**July 20, 2007**

*All changes, even the most longed for, have their melancholy; for what we leave behind is a part
of ourselves; we must die to one life before we can enter another.* – ***Anatole France***

After your run, it is Dean's turn. You walk the children across the street for
Shirley Temples, and to play on the wide white beach. Simon and Holly race ahead
for the hammocks. They remind you of you and Lear, when you were little. Sonny's
hand is tucked in yours, Owen's comforting weight settles on your hip. His mosquito
bites have healed to a pale shade of rose. You kiss his sweet, sweaty temple; you always
wanted a big family.

When you cross the street, you glance at the sea grape jungle. Sonny hasn't
mentioned seeing Jack. Now, it is all about Dad-dean. She yanks on your arm, asks
again how much longer until he comes back from his run. Down by the water, Darvin

is beaching the catamaran and Luc carries new tanks to the Whaler for the last dive of the day. Sonny drops your hand, dashes to join her brother and Holly. She calls over her shoulder, like you're her waitress, instructions to bring their drinks to the beach.

Inside, the bar is mostly empty, just Tony and Leo.

"Well if it isn't the Wealthy Widow and my buddy's little spiderling."

"What can I getcha?" Leo's expression is apologetic.

"You know," Tony's eyes slide over your body—you should have put on a shirt. "The last time I saw you like this, all hot and sweaty, you had even less clothes on." His smile is not warm.

You ignore him and order four Shirley Temples, and a diet Coke.

"Where's Dean?" Leo asks, passing a saucer of maraschino cherries across the bar for Owen.

"Running."

"Yeah, I notice my buddy's looking good. Got him on the jazzercise program, eh? Prefer 'em slim and trim?" Tony pats his own furred waist.

When you put your credit card on the bar for Leo, it makes a harsh clicking sound.

Tony sips off his Red Stripe, wipes where the bottle is making a wet circle on the bar. He looks straight at Leo when he talks. "You know, it's funny. Ebanks was by last night. They finally finished processing the DNA off the truck, got the results from Miami. Turns out Dusty was wrong; it wasn't a dog he hit."

"Is that right?" Leo asks over his shoulder.

"Yep. Human. Male."

"Really?" It is clear from his tone that Leo is interested, but only in the way that they enjoy gossip out here at the quiet end of the island. Unlike the rest of them, Leo has no ongoing concern about the details of that dark night in June.

You shift Owen to your other hip.

"Sorry." Leo looks uncomfortable, your AmEx in his hand. He extends it across the bar. "Might be our reader, or the strip, but this isn't going through."

"Oh." You take it back, your face on fire. It is time to stop hiding, to follow your brother's instructions, buy that phone card, run to the pay phone at the Esso. Call Lear. "I have another one, or some cash, back at the cottage."

"No worries; tomorrow's fine."

"Yeah." Tony's laughs. "We all know where you live."

CHAPTER 32

Dean

Back at the cottage, Juliet's hand flies up to close Dean's computer when he comes in from his run.

"You don't need to do that," he says, sifting a hand through his sweat-soaked hair.

"Do what?" Juliet flushes. His laptop pings, another email. Juliet's eyes dart from Dean to the screen.

"Shut the screen. Don't let me stop you. I won't read over your shoulder."

She laughs hollowly and tilts the laptop screen in his direction.

"It's just my daily inspiration. Luther Vandross."

To: **Juliet B. Wilde <jbwilde@gmail.com>**
From: **Daily Inspirations**
Date: **July 20, 2007**

A room is a still a room
Even when there's nothin' there but gloom
But a room is not a house
And a house is not a home
—LUTHER VANDROSS

When she has finished reading, she deletes it to his Trash.

"Isn't that sort of a strange quote for your brother to send?" Dean asks.

"I don't think these are coming from my brother anymore."

"What do you think it is?"

Instead of answering, Juliet says, "There's a lot we still don't know about each other, and I think that might be more appropriate. I mean, if we were back in the States, if we were just starting to date, if we'd known each other, what, five weeks, because your friend from work had seen me at the gym and suggested we go out for dinner or something, we'd be at a much different place." She adds, "I probably wouldn't have even introduced you to my kids yet."

Dean tries to steer things back on course. "I guess there aren't many circumstances where you get to see your potential partner in the equivalent of her underwear on a first date. I'll never forget you out there, doing a pirouette, making your electronic offering to the Internet gods."

He glances to where their kids are working on a puzzle of kittens tangled in yarn.

"This island, the kids, the cottages, sharing your computer and the van and everything," Juliet pulls her hair into a ponytail, "maybe it makes things feel farther along than they are. Or than they should be."

Something catches, a panicky hiccup under his sternum when she says this. Next she's going to start backpedaling, suggest they "take a break."

Dean stands up and pretends that he is interested in the fruit bowl on the kitchen counter, an attempt to put physical distance between them.

"The funny thing is," he says, "I was actually thinking, on my run, about asking you out." *Of telling you I want your partnership, that I want to think beyond the summer, even.*

"What?" Juliet looks up, startled.

"Tonight. A date. I asked Luc to babysit. I thought we deserved some time with just you and me. Like a real couple," he checks the living room to make sure Simon isn't eavesdropping. "Like one with no kids."

"Actually," she says, a smile wrinkling the corners of her eyes, "that sounds lovely. And I do have somewhere I'd like to go."

⌒‿➚

When they have showered and dressed and kissed the kids, they drive, Dean at the wheel, to the West Side of the island.

"We shouldn't stay out too long. I imagine Luc's got better things to do," Juliet says. He glances over, her wet hair twisted back off her perfect neck, thinking he already wants to be back home, alone, in her bedroom at the top of the stairs.

"He owes me dinner and maybe a little moonlight make-out on the beach." Dean reaches over for her thigh, still hard to believe they get to do this.

"Didn't we try that once, and find it a little overrated?" She grins, her teeth white in the dash lights.

"I'm so old I can't remember. We should probably try it again."

"Mmm. How do you think Luc's handling things?"

Dean sighs. "Okay? I think it would be good for him to spend more time with the family." What he does not say: That it is likely because of Juliet and her kids that Luc keeps his distance, circling the outskirts of their cluster like a gangly, ruff-necked wolf. "There are some parts of Luc that are very reminiscent of his biological father. Sometimes he defends Tony, sometimes I see a glimmer of hope that he might not grow up to be a lonely, philandering beach bum."

"Does he ever talk about the girl, from the accident? Bridget?"

"Some. I think he liked her, more than he lets on."

"Did you know, when you first got here, that Luc was telling the truth, not being able to remember what happened?"

"No," Dean admits. "I wasn't sure. He didn't used to be able to lie to me. He had this twitchy lip that gave him away."

"Simon told me it wasn't Luc who was driving."

Dean doesn't answer right away. How would a nine-year-old boy know what happened in the middle of the night? "You believe him?"

"Of course. I should have told you, earlier. Simon doesn't, he cannot lie to me—"

"Whereas Sonny pulls them off with the ease of a wizened Russian gypsy," Dean interrupts.

What does any of this matter now? What happened in June is over.

Juliet continues, "I can put my thumb on Si's soul."

"But, how would he know?"

"I told you. Si is incapable of lying to me. I know his heart. Those first weeks of life, when they left his chest cavity open after the operation, covered in the medical equivalent of Saran-wrap, to prevent swelling. I sat over him and watched his tiny heart beating. It was this big," Juliet holds up her finger and thumb, "smaller than a fig."

They drive through the bustle of downtown, with its traffic lights, and on to West Bay Road where a trickle of tourists are walking to the beachfront bars.

"I've gotten so used to the quiet of our part of the island," Juliet remarks as they pass a restaurant where a red, double decker UK bus serves as the outdoor bar, pop music blaring. Dean is relieved when she doesn't suggest this as their date location.

"Island fever. Tony told me when he came up to Detroit for our reunion, he had a panic attack in the Comfort Suites. It was his first time off island, his first time even putting on real shoes in eighteen months."

"Can we stop here?"

He is surprised when she gestures to a shopping center with a grocery, liquor and jewelry store. He had assumed she would pick a restaurant for their date. Honestly, he was looking forward to something special, *mahi mahi* fish tacos with fried plantains and mango salsa, maybe. Dean has heard locals talk about a small, open-air restaurant tucked back in breezy Morgan's Harbor with a sticky toffee pudding so famous there is a marl road in West Bay named after it. He'd like to feed it to her, and then kiss her brown-sugar-sweet mouth.

"You want to pick up something and take it back?" he asks as they get out in the parking lot off Seven Mile Beach. Surrounded by strangers, he reaches for her hand, still moved by how novel this is. She squeezes back; the tiniest of gestures instigates heart-fluttering consequence.

They grab two carts, the handle of his still so hot from the day's sun that it burns his palms.

Juliet picks up a bunch of greens, mutters over the price.

"Worse than Whole Wallet, right?"

"What?"

"Whole Foods, the grocery store, in the States. We called it Whole Wallet."

"Ha," Juliet laughs. "Jack called it Whole Paycheck; I wasn't usually allowed to shop there."

But, weren't they well-off? *Controlling? Stingy?* Dean files this away.

"Our garden will be ready soon. With the sun here, I bet we could sun-dry the tomatoes, preserve them in olive oil and some of your rosemary. They'll keep longer that way."

It is late July, but with plane tickets and departure dates looming, they don't really need to worry about preservatives or shelf-life.

Instead, he tells her about a recipe he used to make, a sauce with sautéed sun-dried tomatoes, chorizo and goat cheese simmered in red wine that he spooned over wide pasta noodles.

"That sounds amazing. I bet kale would be good in that, something green and hardy to give it texture. I miss kale; I doubt we could grow it here."

"Amélie used to put kale in her smoothies," Dean says. "After she was first diagnosed. She'd be picking green flecks out of her teeth. She'd come home from rehearsal in a snit, 'You didn't tell me I went to work with the entire salad bar stuck in my teeth!'"

"My grandmother, the one whose house we inherited, used to grow huge bushy rows of it all fall, right next to the Shasta daisies in her front garden bed. She'd go out and grab armloads of it and tear it up and roast it in the oven with olive oil and salt—we ate it like potato chips when we were kids."

They are carefully trading memories. Progress.

"Darvin says callaloo's the local green. It might work, or spinach," Dean continues, stopping to inspect a tower of green plantains.

"Are we doing this right?" Juliet's cart jangles as she strides ahead through the produce section, throwing clusters of local, tiny apple bananas into her cart so hard they fall from their bunches. "With the stories? Amélie and her smoothies?" Juliet trails off and then adds, "Do you ever feel like they're here, all the time? Like they're watching us? Like there are four of us trying to have a relationship?"

"Are we?" Dean stops dead in front of a stack of papaya.

"Are we what?" She picks one up, presses it gently with her thumb, and then puts it carefully in her cart.

"Trying to build something?" It feels like waiting, heart in throat, for the carefully folded note to come back in fifth grade: *Do you like me, circle YES, NO or MAYBE.*

"Because earlier, you said let's just take the summer at face value," Dean says carefully. "A relationship, that's different."

"What, we've known each other five and a half, six weeks? Made love twenty times?"

"Actually," Dean says, "it's twenty-three. Because remember the shower, the day before yesterday and there was the utility closet on Thursday…"

She blushes, smiling as she picks up a large breadfruit. She murmurs something about wondering how on earth to cook it.

"Was she beautiful?" Juliet asks quietly. "Because in the pictures, on the Internet…"

"What does it matter?"

"To a woman, it matters."

Dean takes the breadfruit from her and places it in the cart, sucking in a deep breath before he says, "Of course. You've seen my children. Their mother was stunning. So are you."

Juliet pushes past him. She picks up two pints of raspberries, imported from the States. They are small, maroon, expensive.

"How it stacks up is this: Amélie gave me three incredible children who are the epicenter of my universe. For most of my adult life, she had a vice grip on my heart that she twisted or loosened at her leisure. But she is dead. And you are here, with me." He grabs for her. "You are bringing me back to life. Cutting up my kid's hot dog so he doesn't choke. French braiding Holly's hair. Forgiving Luc's adolescent behavior, giving him space to figure out who he is, who he wants to be. And slowly, you're making me believe that I might get another shot at happiness. And it might even be better than before. "Juliet," he stops, before confessing it all. He takes a deep breath. "I'm falling in love with you. I want to be with you all the time. I want to buy you things, more than—" He looks into their cart. "I want to buy you more than weird tropical fruit and toothpaste. I want us to be together, building to something more—"

"It's more complicated than that…"

"Of course it is! We have five children. So if this is something casual, we need to slam it in reverse right now. We gave up the luxury of casual a long time ago. Are we…are we building to something bigger?"

Juliet's face is pained and she looks down, saying softly, "I mean, aren't we?"

"Okay!" A grin splits his face, his heart, wide open. Okay! He grabs everything out of her cart and throws it into his. "Then let's start with one goddamn shopping cart!"

"Okay," she says, and he can see from the winking of the freckles at the corner of her eyes she is smiling too.

"Okay. And put away your fantastic plastic. I'm buying tonight."

"Okay. Thank you very much, Professor."

They push the cart together in silence, a happy jingling, like proud parents at the head of their first baby's pram, with smiles as wide as Seven Mile Beach stretching their cheeks.

CHAPTER 33

Dean

"Should we head back?" Dean asks, closing the back of the van with the groceries inside. He takes her hand in his again, squeezes it. Anything is possible! He can't wait for the kids to go to bed, to be alone with her again. To plan their future!

"Actually, I was thinking of window shopping." She tugs him away from Foster's Food Fair—he would follow her anywhere—across the parking lot to the Kirk Freeport jewelry store.

Inside, everything sparkles in the golden light, unnaturally bright after the purple darkness falling outside. The saleswoman is petite with a long narrow face that in repose reminds him of Munch's *The Scream*, but is slightly better when she smiles. She nods to their clutched hands and asks in a meaningful singsong if they are ring shopping.

"Oh, no," Juliet says. "Just browsing."

"On your honeymoon?"

Juliet shakes her head, nudging gently against him to move Dean out of her hard-sell range.

"Something special then?"

"Actually," Juliet stops, "we're looking for something local."

"Then you want black coral." The saleswoman is ahead of them, opening a case of what looks like twisted, ebony sticks, wrapped in silver or crusted with diamonds.

The price tags are staggering, Dean notes, remembering that these are listed in the local currency, CI dollars, that everything gets multiplied by a fixed $1.25 when converting to US.

"Mmm," Juliet makes a negative noise, and keeps walking.

"Ahh, you are looking for something very unique then. You are discerning customers with good taste, perhaps the rare conch pearl, then? Only one in ten thousand Caribbean queen conchs makes a pearl, each one of them unique, in color and shape, with an incredible flame…"

For the first time since the saleswoman accosted them, Dean feels Juliet's insistent pull on his hand stop. She pauses and leans in over the glass display, enchanted by the creamy pearls in shades of peach, pink and ivory. When the saleswoman twists a large ring in her tiny, monkey-like fingers, Dean sees the pearl's iridescent flame and depth.

"These are beautiful," Juliet says. "May I see the necklace in the back?"

It's an ornate piece; maybe thirty of the smaller, seed-shaped peachy conch pearls tangled in a delicate, sparkling web of platinum and diamonds.

"May I?" the saleswoman asks but she is already lifting up Juliet's hair, fastening it around her neck, producing a hand mirror so they can both admire the way the pearls nestle along her sun-kissed collarbones, the biggest pearl and its mottled flame settling in the hollow of her throat.

"That's perfect for your coloring," the saleswoman gushes, adding meaningfully, "It's Mikimoto. Not everyone can pull off such an intricate design."

"It's a lovely piece," Juliet says, lifting her hair and turning so Dean can take it off.

"Because of the extreme scarcity of the conch pearl, these hold their value in a way other jewelry doesn't."

It had looked incredible on her. But the woman's fingers are reluctantly unlocking the case when Juliet interrupts. "I'll take it."

Dean is stunned; they don't even know how much it costs.

"Excellent!" the saleswoman chirps, clearly commissioned, definitely doubting that at almost eight o'clock on a slow Thursday night in the off season she might make such a sale.

Juliet flicks through her wallet, shifts the usual platinum AmEx aside, and passes the woman a Visa.

Though it has nothing to do with him, Dean feels sick to the point where he has to swallow some nausea saliva when Juliet's credit card beeps through: $78,000 USD.

He notices Juliet's hands shake as she reaches for the yellow slip and the leather-wrapped box, shaking her head at the offer to wear the necklace home. She tucks the bag into her purse, which is a battered canvas beach bag with her initials embroidered in the middle of the yellowing sunscreen stains on the side.

⌒➞

"Do you want to stop somewhere for dinner? Or a drink?" Dean breaks their silence, turning the Brave Little Toaster instinctively left out of the shopping center, in the direction of Rum Point. Honestly, he doesn't. He wants to get back to the intimacy of the cottages and the comfortable chaos of their children. *Maybe that's the only place they work*, he thinks, like a summer camp romance. He tries to picture Juliet in Saline, her lovely beach body covered in sweaters and jeans. Would she fit in? Would she chat it up with Burt's wife at the EMU football game? Would she and his older sister bond in the kitchen crimping piecrusts for Thanksgiving dinner?

He imagines pulling up to the house with Juliet in the front seat of the Honda, pictures all the things that he backburnered while Amélie was dying, like the cardboard square and duct tape that still cover the pane of the kitchen door that Luc broke, the crabgrass sprouting like Albert Einstein's hair in the narrow front lawn.

"Mmm," Juliet makes a neutral noise, says she isn't very hungry. Her gaze drifts out the open window of the van as Seven Mile Beach whizzes by in the dark.

"They feed the tarpon kitchen scraps out at The Wharf restaurant about now, if you want to stop." He'd read about it in the tourist magazine on the airplane, with photos of the impressive silver fins stirring up the water off the dock of the restaurant. He also remembered that the prices next to the menu items had been enough to assure him that chances were slim he'd be taking a party of four there to eat. But it's just the two of them, and he wants tonight to be more special, less surreal. Less profess our love for each other in the grocery store, stop at a jewelry store and watch Juliet drop his annual salary on a glittery necklace, then drive in curious silence. At the very least, they could have a piña colada together.

"We should probably head back, get the groceries in the fridge, let Luc go out," she says.

"Are you okay?" he asks. He is trying hard not to put too much import in every single thing she says, based on the evening's strange twist.

Back in Michigan, their wealthiest friends were Will and Sherry Sanders, a neurosurgeon and his advertising exec wife; friends only in that they knew each other because Holly had befriended their daughter, an anorexic, stoop-shouldered girl on her field hockey team. For several years, Dean and Amélie and the kids had been invited to their Christmas party. It was in the rich part of Saline, a hulking brick mansion behind an electric iron gate where all the adults drank too much and the kids watched movies in their home theater, complete with a famously-stocked sundae bar and popcorn machine. Amélie loved to make snide remarks over her spiked eggnog about the Sanders' professionally decorated sixteen-foot Christmas tree and white-shirted catering staff, about the excess of everything. She always cheered "Ah, *vive la vie de boheme!*" when Dean pulled the Honda back into their rutted driveway, the sparse, Charlie Brown Christmas tree twinkling in the front window. Sometimes, depending on how much she'd had to drink, Amélie would break into an aria from the Italian opera—the one artistic form where she did not shine.

Maybe, Dean thinks, Sherry Sanders owns a necklace worth eighty thousand dollars. Maybe she displays it over her orange-tan fake breasts at the holiday party, but she is the only woman Dean knows personally who might. He reaches across the van with his shifting hand to put a palm on Juliet's knee. Okay, so now he knows two women like that.

"Everything okay?" he asks again.

"Sorry, just thinking." She gives him a watered-down version of her smile before turning her face to the black window. The rattle of the diesel engine fills the space where conversation should be.

The truth: not only has the island living, their side-by-side cottages, accelerated the intimacy and pace of the relationship, but it has also been a curious equalizer. Whereas before he might not have even gone on a second date with a woman who pulled up in—what must she drive at home, he doesn't even know! A Lexus SUV? An Escalade?—What if she had worn an eighty thousand dollar necklace to their first dinner at King Wok?

All these stories she has told might be those of the privileged and understated. The grandparents' "farmhouse" must be a colloquial term for an estate. But what about the first story that charmed him, her growing asparagus on rooftop apartments and windowsills in her younger years? What about the lone, slim wedding band on her left ring finger?

"I'm fine," Juliet says finally as they pass Pedro's Castle, driving away from civilization and streetlights, her voice scratchy from the half hour of silence. "Just, thinking about things. The past…"

When she reaches across the space between them to lay her hand over his on the gearshift, it means everything.

CHAPTER 34

Dean

A t Juliet's, Luc is playing the part of the teenage babysitter perfectly, slouched on the couch, TV on too loud, Life game pieces scattered and bowls with Lucky Charms disintegrating in wasteful depths of milk on the coffee table. Owen barrels into Dean's arms as Luc waves off Juliet's offer of money.

He calls out a casual "Later!" as he pulls Juliet's door closed behind him, Tony's truck idling in the parking lot.

Dean watches Juliet take the box with the eighty thousand dollar necklace from her beach bag and tuck it into the small cabinet above the microwave, nestling it between two of the owner's yellowed cookbooks.

He wonders what else she is hiding.

"Okay," Juliet singsongs to the roomful of children in a tone that hints of good-bye and goodnight.

"We should have a family sleepover tonight!" Dean blurts.

Holly and Simon and Sonny cheer.

"You're not supposed to ask in front of the parents." The ripple of a frown passes over Juliet's face.

"Yeah, we can bring our mattresses out here! You promised we could watch a movie later," Simon hounds.

"We are the parents," he reminds her, startled at his boldness. He refuses to let an inanimate object, a piece of jewelry, intimidate him. So she has money! He rewinds to the part of the night where they agreed to build to a future.

Juliet shrugs and lets the kids haul the light, foam mattresses off the twin beds and ride them down the stairs into the living room, shaking her head over the parade of pillows and blankets thrown from the upstairs landing.

Upstairs, when Dean closes the bedroom door behind them, there is that crease by her eyebrows.

"You shouldn't have asked me right in front of them. Out to dinner, and then a 'group sleepover?' Isn't that a little obvious?" Juliet is trying to talk as Dean slides his hands under the hem of her sundress, kissing her. "What about Holly? What about Luc?"

"I appreciate your concern for my children." His mouth against her throat, Dean's hands guide her by her hips toward the bed. "But we agreed to give this a go, right?"

She nods against his neck, her fingers at the gaping waist of his khakis.

"So really, right now?" He places her hand over him. "What about *me*?"

It has been several weeks since their first desperate attempts on the beach, and they are moving into the realm of familiar. The curiosities are disappearing, and with them, the comparatives and questions: *Did she do this? Did she know this made your breath come fast?* Sometimes, they fumble; Dean takes it as an excellent sign that these moments are easily laughed off. Now it is simply the two of them, their physical bodies, sometimes gritty from dried saltwater and sand or slick from sweat, often bridging the gap of grief and an unknown future, coming together on top of her artificially cooled sheets.

Dean's hands cup her face like something sacred, and when he enters her, his mouth finds hers. But suddenly, instead of the release of the building orgasm, Juliet exhales, a shattered gasp. A keening sound comes out of her mouth. Dean cannot mistake it for a moan of pleasure.

"What's wrong?" He stops.

"Nothing," she says, her voice a choked, raw whisper. She gulps down a sob.

"Shh." When Dean places his hands over her bare shoulders he feels like a sculptor caressing wet clay, smoothing, shaping, rebuilding it again. "I'm here."

I'm here.

"I'm sorry," she whispers in the dark as they separate, those critical inches that break their intimate connection. But he doesn't let her go farther, holds her close anyway.

"I'm processing things, I guess. At really inappropriate times. I'm sorry."

"Don't be." Dean pulls her to his chest. "Remember I am a—"

"Trained professional," she finishes the sentence for him, and he is relieved to hear lightness in her voice. "Once, the first time I went to the dry cleaners, afterward… Jack's clothes came around on the metal trolley and it was like, seeing them, like he had walked in the door two months after his death. I threw up, ran out—I couldn't help it— I left eleven pressed shirts and my breakfast behind."

Dean kisses her salty, damp eyelids. "Totally normal."

"And then, later, Memorial Day," she continues, "these people from the beach at Belmar called me to say they had found my husband's lost driver's license and Costco card in the sand while they were collecting mussels. I could hear in their voices this hope that they had called quickly enough, that Jack would be so relieved at not having the hassle of a trip to the DMV that there might be some reward money." She laughs, a bitter tinkling, like a wind chime made of tin forks.

"Shh," Dean whispers into the wispy hairs by her temple that form tiny curls in the humidity. He may not be able to buy her diamond-crusted necklaces, but he can hold her, and he can listen. It is the cornerstone of all he has ever wanted to be—a good partner, a good father, a good listener.

"Sometimes, this is where it gets really twisted, when I can't sleep, I start picturing him, how he might look now, his physical body, I mean. I picture his skin all waxy and bloated and fish-pocked, his eyes gone cloudy. Wherever he is, the bottom of the Atlantic, or is he just bones now, washing up on the coast in Maine? Where would he be now? I worry, sometimes, when we're at the beach, even here. He could be anywhere."

Incomplete physical evidence, Dean thinks. Jack wasn't cremated. He drowned, his body lost at sea.

"Isn't that awful? I mean, what is wrong with me?" she moans. Dean can feel every bit of her rigid, holding tight to her own elbows. He kisses the hollows beneath her cheeks, waiting for the moment to pass.

"It's just grief," he tells her. "It will get better. We all have our demons." He remembers the swans at Ford Lake, startled into flight, how he threw stones after them—he hit one, blood spurting and scarlet against the white, while Amélie gasped her last, alone.

"I feel like, all the time," Juliet says, "I'm waiting for the other shoe to drop. And I actually want it to happen. I want it to be over. I want the rest of Jack to wash ashore."

Now or never, Dean thinks.

"I have to tell you something I never told anyone."

"Okay," Juliet sniffs.

"Amélie didn't die of cancer. I killed her."

"You what?" Juliet sits up, and Dean worries if he keeps going, she will leap out of bed, and never come back, but he can't stop now.

"There's this secret society, for the desperate and hopeless. Mischief night, before Halloween, Dr J, her oncologist, approached me. I thought," his voice catches, "he had something new. An eleventh hour plan, a new study, a drug trial. I was ready for anything. I was ready, rainforests of South America, vines and snakes, Owen strapped in the backpack, while I trekked around for some magical, curative herb. I would have done it. I would have done anything."

"What was it?"

"Angel of morphine." Dr. J was not offering him hope, but instead the *Tom and Jerry* of gifts; a neatly wrapped package with a ticking bomb, a lit stick of dynamite inside. "A mixture of Roxanol and Ativan, to keep her comfortable. One of the side effects is depressed respiration."

Dean remembers he hadn't thought he would cry that day; he was just stopping by on his way back from the university before picking up Owen and Holly at Mrs. Sanderson's, planning to sit with Amélie for an hour and, if she opened her eyes, he'd tell her the funny thing Holly said at breakfast, show her the picture on his phone of Owen in his penguin costume at the day care Halloween party. Now, since the stroke, if her pain was well managed, she might laugh. He hated her new laugh; garish and shrill, a donkey's bray.

"We'd been with this doctor for nine years—I changed both kids' diapers on the floor of his office during consultations. He let her try everything, Goji berries and acupuncture, he got her into three clinical trials. I asked him if there was another way, another chance, and it was like the code, of this secret society, he shook his head at me and said there's nothing more they could do."

⌣⟶

The day before, Dr. J had walked in on Dean and Amélie in a rare moment of lucidity,

Amélie's eyes had flown open and she'd lunged at him, fought him off, insisted that she go to the bathroom herself, lurching and flailing the short distance from the bed to the toilet, her IV pole clutched in her hand like a skeletal sailor holding desperately to the mast of a ship in a final storm.

"Robert," she'd screamed at Dean, her sour spit flecking his face. *"Je veux voir Robert!"* After the stroke stripped away the layers of lies they had built to construct a marriage, Amélie stopped pretending that it was Dean she wanted by her side as she breathed her last. *"Je désire Robert! J'ai craive Robert…"*

Amélie had collapsed, howling in pain, clawing at her head with the hand that still worked, while Dean and Dr. J lifted her gently, light as laundry, to the bed, and together they fixed the restraints to her wrists.

⌒

"At the end, she was calling for Luc's father. Shoving me away, screaming that she wanted Robert. Dr. J warned me her body would keep fighting, her spirit strong, because she had so much to live for. The kids, I mean. But how do you tell someone who has done nothing but fight for the past nine years that it's okay, necessary, to give up?" Dean sobs, turning his head away from Juliet.

"So I did it." He glances down at his bare torso. He has never felt so naked, the truth hanging in the night air. "Dr. J said it was for her dignity, for my memories. But let's not pretend it was not because she was asking for Luc's father."

"Of course not," Juliet murmurs.

"But, everything I did, all those years, stripped to nothing. None of it mattered to her."

When he looks down at Juliet, there are sympathetic tears shining in her eyes. She understands.

"I did it because of the ghosts."

"Ghosts?"

"And the skeletons. The stupid cardboard goggle-eyed ghosts and grinning skeletons the nurses plastered all over the walls for Halloween. They were staring at me while her doctor was giving me directions to Kevorkianland. Not very tactful for a hospice floor, if you think about it. I didn't want it to drag on, for the ghosts to become turkeys or elves and Santas, or goddamn Easter bunnies! I didn't want to have to force the kids there on Christmas morning, to this version of their mother. They didn't want to go anymore, especially Luc. She didn't sound right; she didn't look or smell like I wanted any of them to remember her. So, I did it. I told him yes. I killed her," Dean exhales a broken breath; the first time he has ever told anyone. "Because even though she loved someone else, in spite of everything, I still loved her."

Is this the first time, Dean wonders, *that he has talked about his love for Amélie in the past tense? Has the spell been broken?*

Juliet takes his face in her beautiful, capable hands and wipes away the stinging tears from under his eyes with the smooth pads of her thumbs. He has seen her do this to Sonnet and Owen, when a wave splashes and they come shrieking and squinting. He catches her wrists and holds them, bringing them to his lips. He is spent, his body wrung out from the telling.

"I had to lie to the kids, tell them it happened suddenly."

"How?" Luc had wailed, throwing himself against Dean's chest, shirt still soaked from running around Ford Lake, his shoes wet from where he had waded in the water to tend to the swan he hit, her wing bloody and broken, while across the city, his wife breathed her last, alone.

"But I just saw her!" Luc sobbed and Holly behind him, "I didn't get to say goodbye."

"Shh," Juliet manipulates him easily, murmuring soothing, motherly sounds. When she pulls his head down to hers, and wraps her arms around his neck, she whispers in his ear the sweetest words of all, "You did the right thing."

Dean takes a deep, shuddering breath. He has done it, shattered the vestiges of the marriage that came before her, scattered them like the wooden pieces of a Jenga tower.

"Did I really?" he whispers, a strangled gasp.

"You spared her an even uglier end. It was the ultimate mercy."

Dean heaves a shaky sigh; it is over. He has told her everything, and she is still here. Hope bubbles up through the grief.

"What do we do now? How do we write the happy ending to this love story, with all these," she smiles, as she waves her hands in the air above their bed, "obstacles?"

He wonders what she means? It can't be their children.

Money, the thing that always follows 'CHILDREN' in his mental list of worries, would be less of one, with Juliet's husband's life insurance...

"All love stories have obstacles," Dean says slowly. He is glad they are using the word "love" to talk about their story—it makes his stomach buzz and his head feel curiously unattached to his body. "True love means choosing to overcome them."

"Or ignore them," Juliet whispers, and though she continues their kiss, her words hang in the air between them, playing over and over in his head.

Dean waits until her breathing is quiet before he slips out of bed, pulling on his boxer shorts and offering to check on the kids.

"Two down, two to go," Dean reports. "Owen and Sonny are snoring like a pair of lumberjacks."

They hear Holly's knowing singsong as she calls up the stairs coyly, "Good ni-ight, you guys!"

Juliet follows him into the bathroom and picks up her toothbrush, scrubbing her teeth vigorously, as though a clean mouth will wash away what happened earlier. When she spits, the sink is tinged with pink.

"You're bleeding."

It had happened with Amélie, Dean remembers, when she was pregnant with Owen.

"Sensitive gums," she shrugs. "It sounds like Holly is onto us."

"My daughter's no dummy." Dean keeps his back to her while he uses the toilet. "I think she had us figured out a week ago. Shoot, my toothbrush is at home."

"Here," she offers him hers, rinsed, still dripping.

"But that's yours."

"Jack completely silenced a family dinner once, by telling everyone we didn't even own separate toothbrushes. When Percy freaked out, Jack said, 'What's the point of separate toothbrushes, when I'd put my lips on any part of her body?' My brother gagged and left the table." Juliet puts her toothbrush on the edge of the sink. "You can use it or don't, it doesn't matter to me."

"I guess he had a point." Dean picks up her toothbrush, mumbling about boundaries through the foam.

"Isn't it incredible," he remarks as he peels back the sheets, "that we both ended up here? I mean, my connection is obvious: Tony. But isn't it interesting that you didn't end up in Cancun or Bermuda or Belize? That we found each other?"

"If I'm learning anything this summer," Juliet says, "it is that everything happens for a reason. Even when you're completely unaware."

Dean hopes she means, because she has met him, that they are here, overcoming the obstacles to their love story.

"My brother picked it," she continues. "Lear and his wife came here on their honeymoon; they said it was perfect. Jack made him the executor of his estate, put him in charge of all the finances for me and the kids, which was funny, because when Jack was alive, he and Lear didn't get along."

"They didn't? That wasn't a red flag for you, when you were dating? That your brother didn't like the guy you were with?"

"Well, by the time they met, we were married. We dated less than a month. When we were younger, they used to get along. We all used to be close. Lear even lived with us in Aspen for a few months."

"What happened?"

"Typical stuff, things you should never mix: family, business, real estate. For nine years," she alters her voice for dramatic irony, "the sharp knife of money came between us."

"How is it now? With you and your brother?" He thinks of the curious signature to all of Lear's emails in the trash folder—delete the contents of this email and remove from your hard drive.

"Enh," Juliet laughs a little. "We're getting there. I emailed him the other day; I told him trust grows slowly, like a fungus. I'm going to call him." She swallows. "Soon."

"You said, when we first met, that your family insisted you come here. This was Lear?"

"Yes. One day, at the end of May, school wasn't even out yet, Lear showed up at the farmhouse. He had three plane tickets to the Cayman Islands for the next morning, a printout on the cottages. He said he was worried about me, that we needed a change of scenery. Anyway, here we are."

I'm here.

"It's perfect here," Dean says, tucking her into his arms, folding his own hands over hers. "Maybe we should never leave," he whispers into her neck. He is grateful; the squall that blew through the room seems to have passed and the air is clear.

But when he wakes up, she is gone. He pads to the top of the landing where he can see Juliet down in the kitchen, filling a glass of water. The velvet-lined box is open on the counter, the necklace lit by the square of moonlight from the window.

His laptop is sitting at the top of the staircase where the kids left it after playing Snood, the only video game his antiquated computer has. The truth? He has been waiting for a moment alone with it, thought of running home to check it ever since the bizarre trip to the jewelry store with the furtive, mind-darting of an online porn addict. Quietly, he opens it and clicks on the Trash folder, scanning Juliet's deleted emails, two new ones, from this morning, since he last checked.

"Mom?" Downstairs, Simon's whisper startles them both. "Is Dean upstairs, in your room?"

Clutching the computer, he backs toward the bedroom, waiting for the file to load. Dean swallows, the plastic of the laptop slippery in his hands, the fan of its motor whirring to life like an ancient crop duster. It if weren't for the constant rattle of her air conditioner, he's sure she would be able to hear it downstairs.

The first deleted email is from that morning, Juliet's brother:

To:	**Juliet B. Wilde <jbwilde@gmail.com>**
From:	**Lear Burke <ljb@hotmail.com>**
Date:	**July 21, 2007**
Subject:	**Diamonds are a girl's best friend!**

J—

I hope you're having such a nice time with umbrella drinks on the beach that you can't call me? Let me know you received this. Buy a phone card and call me—not from the cottage phone. It could cost... a fortune! Haha.

Maybe you've been seduced by island living and you're off house hunting for a casa by the sea? Let me know if you are finding anything promising in real estate, ASAP?

When Jenna and I honeymooned in Grand Cayman, she saw some beautiful black coral jewelry. You should check it out at Kirk Freeport—an investment via Visa in a special souvenir, plus diversification of your portfolio! Two birds, one stone—you know the rest.

Love, L

ps I've done some banking transfers—use V debit card for souvenirs and all expenses until further notice

*Delete the contents of this email and erase it from your hard drive

When Juliet bought the necklace, she was merely following e-mailed instructions?

While Dean scans the chunk of text again, trying to make sense, Juliet answers her son, downstairs.

"Yes," she says. "Dean is in my room."

"It's okay," Simon says. "I like him. Way better than the other guy."

"Who?" Holly's whisper joins the conversation and Dean's heart pounds.

The glass slips from Juliet's hand and shatters on the tile floor, startling Simon and Holly.

The next email loads.

To: **Juliet B. Wilde <jbwilde@gmail.com>**
From: **Daily Inspirations**
Date: **July 21, 2007**

If you cannot get rid of the family skeleton, you may as well make it dance. —**George Bernard Shaw**

CHAPTER 35

Juliet

You are driving on a dark, empty road, together. Jack is at the wheel, his sharp profile silhouetted against the watery gray of the night sky in the window, like a bird of prey. You round a turn and the swath of your headlights falls on the usual scene: Jack's silver Mercedes crumpled like it is made of nothing but kitchen foil.

You realize you are dreaming again, that it will play out as it always does. It doesn't mean you can stop it.

"Someone needs help," Jack says. In the dream, it is his voice that touches you, the familiar sameness of it, though you wonder about the sentiment. Jack's circle of goodwill did not spread beyond himself and you, and the children. He never understood how you could cry for strangers on the evening news; he begrudged your donations to charity.

"Donate to the cause of the Wilde foundation! Leave the money where it belongs!"

So you wonder if, in real life, he wouldn't have just called 911 on the cell phone as he drove past the accident?

But in the dream, Jack signals like he will pull off to the shoulder. Instead of the brakes he hits the gas, the engine roaring as the bridge approaches. You remember what Percy said, that it was impossible to tell if Jack was crazy-funny, or crazy-dangerous. When your tires meet the ice, the car slides like a throw rug on a polished wood floor. Then you are alone, sailing through the frigid winter air. You notice that the stars above in the obsidian sky are beautiful, and you think of your children, how they won't be orphans, before you hit the water.

You see Jack standing above you on the bridge.

"Jack!" You scream his name, once, twice, three times. When you go under, you gasp, gulping mouthfuls of icy, brackish water.

He is smiling as he watches you drown.

CHAPTER 36

Dean

Nobody seems surprised when Dean and Juliet come down the stairs together in the morning, Owen's hand in hers. Sometime before dawn, he had appeared beside their bed and Juliet lifted the sheet and nestled him between them.

"Here's the story," Dean sings, "of a lovely lady, who was living with two very lovely kids…" Now that they're out, he thinks, she can't mind him grabbing her ass occasionally in the kitchen.

Juliet is all business, picking up mattresses, shaking off popcorn kernels and sweeping them up with a fierce hissing of the broom bristles. She directs the children, calling out morning chores.

"Don't put the mattresses away," Simon and Sonny wail. "We want a slumber party every night!"

Holly asks Juliet what's wrong.

"Bad dream," she says. She looks surprised that the nightmare's lingering sour flavor is evident on her face, but Dean has seen it since she woke him and Owen with her screams. There are still two pinched lines between her dark eyebrows. In later years, these will be some of her deeper wrinkles, and he has a pang of hoping to see them then, when her face is etched with the hash marks of a long, complicated, beautiful life.

Juliet scrapes the scrambled eggs onto their plates. They are tinged with brown on the bottom, the pan too hot, and he knows Simon won't touch them. Sure enough, she serves them to the other three while cracking the last two eggs to make another batch for Simon. Behind her, he quietly makes the coffee.

"That's terrible," Holly says, squirting a smiley face of ketchup on top of her eggs. "I had a really nice dream. Mom came." Heads jerk up all around the table. "I was dressing Owen to go outside, at home, and he was as big as he is now, but as floppy as a baby, and as soon as I'd get one arm or leg in in his snowsuit, another came out."

Simon is watching Holly carefully. Juliet has told him that he never dreams about his father, that this worries him. He stabs at his new eggs with his fork.

"Mom appeared in the doorway," Holly says, "and I thought she was going to take over, or help me, but she just stood there and said what a good job I was doing."

Nobody is eating, everyone waiting, forks in hand, as Holly continues. "Then, you know, dreams are funny. She told me how the music in heaven is so incredible. And then there was this guy with her. He had dark, curly hair and he was cute, really handsome, and Mom said, 'We're spending a lot of time together, getting to know each other.'"

Dean casts a quick look over his shoulder, to gauge Juliet's reaction, wondering if they will be able to joke about this later: *So there's dating in Holly's version of the afterlife? Wow!*

"She said his name was Michel—" There is a clatter. Dean looks down; he has dropped the lid to the coffee pot in the sink. Holly continues, looking around the table at her audience, "Which I thought was funny, because that's a girl's name. Then she said she loved me, and she had to go." Holly's voice is wistful as she picks up her fork. "It was good to see her, but a little sad. And a little weird."

In the fierce late morning sun, Simon and Dean work with a skeleton of a toolbox and old broken screens they found in the back of the storage closet, cutting them to create tented frames to stand over Juliet's trays. Juliet brings her cutting board out to the pool deck. The girls and Owen are in charge of picking. They carry the bounty and Juliet slices the Camparis and Beefsteaks and Romas thinly.

"Amélie had a brother," Dean is finally able to tell her, in a moment alone. "She rarely talked about him, and her parents never did. His name was Michel; he died of pneumonia when she was four."

Juliet doesn't answer right away.

"Are you hearing what I'm saying? Holly never knew about Michel."

"Yes, I mean, that's crazy." She looks down at the ruby tomatoes, pinning their soft flesh with her hand as she cuts. "You want to talk about the other world right now? You think the spirits of our dead spouses are using dreams as a medium to connect with us?"

"What was your dream?" Dean asks. "Last night?"

"I dreamt that the kids and I would have to stay here on this island forever." When she lies, he notices her voice goes as flat as the North Sound.

"That's a bad dream?" Dean asks. "Look around." He points with his gaze at the chickens they have been watching all summer, the mama and her three dust-colored babies scratching in the disc-shaped mahogany-colored leaves of the sea grape bushes. Across the street, the colorful White Beaches flags flap in a gust of wind. "We're in paradise."

"Look," Holly points as a butterfly flits over the drying screen and touches down briefly. "Owen, look, it's Mom!"

"Hi, Mom!"

From the other side of the pool deck, Dean sees Simon throw Juliet an eyebrows-up, nostrils-flared *what-the-heck?* look.

She and Dean carry over the second frame.

"Did you teach her that, about the afterlife, reincarnation?" Her voice is hushed, the way one parent might surreptitiously ask another at a holiday party if all kids still believe in Santa.

"Holly came up with that one on her own." Dean makes no attempt to keep his voice down.

"It's another one of the ways my mom comes to me," Holly says. "Butterflies, and my dreams."

Juliet waits until they are far out of the children's earshot to ask him, "Do you dream about her?"

"Amélie? Only in the past tense. I dream about Africa, or when the kids were babies. I dream memories, nothing new."

"That must be nice," Juliet murmurs. "I had this theology professor in college who said it was impossible to dream your own death—that if you dream you die, your heart will actually stop." Juliet says. "But in my dreams, it's never Jack who is drowning; it's me."

"Do you believe in it? Heaven?" Dean asks. By the pool, the children have abandoned picking tomatoes and are turning the hose on each other, Simon fanning out a spray with his thumb while Owen and the girls run shrieking in the sparkling prism of its spray.

"My mother-in-law is a believer. She tells the kids about their dad up in the clouds with wings, looking down on them from the bosom of Mary. Serves it up with her lumpy rice pudding."

Juliet adds that Jack's Catholic school days, being physically abused by nuns, are why they never went to church, why his mother is the children's only avenue to religion.

"But what about you?" Dean asks. "What do *you* believe?"

Juliet shrugs and sighs. "I have a hard enough time with the realities of this world to worry about another one."

Across the pool deck, Owen is chasing the butterfly that is rising up over the jacaranda on the wind and Holly is calling, "I love you, I love you, goodbye!"

"Do you believe?" Juliet asks him.

"I believe," Dean says carefully, his shoulders flexing as he bends to pick up the final screen frame, "that there's no harm in anyone believing."

"I worry, about ghosts. Earlier this summer, Sonny was seeing Jack's spirit everywhere, in the sea grape bushes, outside the windows, floating up high in the corners of the house. She said he watched over her in her sleep. It scared me."

"I think it's normal, developmentally appropriate. Death is a pretty massive concept for kids, especially as young as Sonny."

"Sometimes, it was like she was seeing more than one spirit. She got into bed with me the other night, after you'd left. And out of nowhere, she opened her eyes and said, 'Whatever those things are, I want them out of here!' She was staring up at the ceiling. I couldn't see anything. I asked her 'what things, sweetheart?' She said, 'Those little glowing things, like lightning bugs, right there.' My heart was pounding."

"I think," Dean says, "you might be putting too much stock in the paranormal. She's just a little girl." He remembers their conversation from the drive, her irrational belief that Simon knew the truth about the night of the accident. "Children have big imaginations. And there are other explanations. They might have just been floaters."

"Floaters?"

"Shadows on the retina, vitreous debris? You know, when you open your eyes, in the dark? They're common."

"Oh," Juliet gives a self-conscious laugh. "You're probably right. I was afraid it might be him, Jack, and Amélie. Like they're here, with us. Watching us."

"Yoo-hoo!" It is Hazel, the realtor, dressed in a tight black skirt and peep-toe pumps, her pedicure polish the same color as the tomatoes Juliet is slicing.

"Are you ready, m'dear?" she asks, eying Juliet's shorts and tank top, the drips of tomato juice and golden seeds stuck to her bare feet.

"Oh, yes! Just a second." She turns to Dean. "You wouldn't mind keeping the kids for a bit, would you, while I go out to lunch?"

"Out to lunch? We just bought three hundred dollars of groceries last night."

"Yes, with Hazel. Just for fun, a lady lunch, for a little bit."

"Oh, okay." Dean takes stock of the children, assuming full parental duty. "Enjoy."

He reminds himself not to be resentful, that this is more partnership than he has ever had. But he has to push Luc's word—*crumbs*—out of his mind as he watches her go.

CHAPTER 37

Juliet

Hazel keeps her car air conditioner at full blast, though she rolls down the windows to exhale her cigarette smoke and gesture to a potential house as they pass.

"This would be a whole lot easier if you told me your price range," she says as you pass through Bodden Town. Hazel points out a hulking, Italian-style villa with gates and pillars, tells you that the owner had it built secretly, an exact replica of his mansion in Las Vegas. "He had to drive his wife by it three times before she even recognized it. That one," she points to another oceanfront palace, "twelve million, but it's been on the market for six years. They're open to offers."

"Can you stop here?" you ask, pointing to the gas station.

Inside, you buy a phone card, a grapefruit soda and a jerk chicken meat patty, the extent of your ladies lunch. You tell Hazel you'll just be a minute and step into a phone booth, a magnifying glass for the sun.

"Lear," you say when his secretary puts him through. "It's me. Enough cloak and dagger. What's going on?"

"Finally," he says, drawing the word out peevishly, but there is relief, too. "You're okay, you and the kids?"

You take a long swig from the syrupy-sweet, bubbly soda.

"My laptop got fried. I'm having to check things on a friend's. But I got the message, bought a freaking eighty thousand dollar necklace, but the AmEx got denied for my bar tab. What's going on?"

"I'm going to call you back, just let me get—"

"What? What is this? You need to switch phones again? What's going on?"

"We need to be really careful here. Have you found a house?"

"No, I'm out looking right now. My realtor's in the car. I have a house—why do I need to buy a house in the Cayman Islands?"

Back in Bucks County, Jack and Marty's vision, Poet's Promise, is in its final phase. The long spring after his funeral, bulldozers woke you and the kids, turning up the blackberry bushes at the bottom of the hill, noisily ripping them from the earth in the shade of the silver maples, clearing the roads for Phase Three, the last of the seventy-two luxury homes. Shipments of vinyl siding and Palladian windows arrived on flatbeds for the huge house frames on the newly-tarred streets criss-crossing your grandfather's cornfields, matching the scars on Simon's chest. The streets were named after all the famous poets you had loved in college; Longfellow, Whitman and Blake. Now they represent rifts in your family, painful dinners and barbed remarks.

"How's the Wilde Hotel coming, Jules?" Lear seemed to enjoy watching you squirm.

"You know renovations, always a work in progress," you'd been forced to admit.

Before, when family came to visit, you spent days preparing, trying to hide the evidence of your financial worries. You took down the tin foil Jack put up over the windows to keep the utility bill low in the poorly insulated old house. You'd carefully weed between the pavers of the original cobblestone driveway, laid by your grandfather's two hands forty years earlier.

"Nothing says the ruins of Great Gatsby like dandelions in the cobbles," you told Simon and Sonny, bribing them to finger-weed with promises of a trip to Rita's Water Ice after dinner.

"Listen, Jules," Lear says. "Marty's gone. He maxed out the line of credit with First Union and all of the Compass accounts are empty, the projects are falling apart, creditors, investors, construction equipment just sitting there, even behind the farmhouse, at Phase Three. It's a mess. I never trusted that shithead. I had a feeling this was coming."

"What?" you say, but you are both relieved—it's just a business thing—and not surprised; you never trusted Jack's partner either.

"Jules, this is really bad."

"What do you mean?" You think of Jack's life insurance policy. What does it matter what happens to Compass? When Meridian pays out, there will be more than enough for you and the kids.

"Jules: You're the other principle in Compass."

"What?" Sweat breaks out on your cheeks. "Lear, what? How could I be?"

"I told Jenna you didn't know! It's why we picked the Cayman Islands. I knew something like this might happen, but I didn't want you to worry."

"What?" you stammer, reduced to repeating yourself, meaningless queries. "Lear, what?"

"I found the paperwork when things started to unravel. It was back when you were signing a bunch of documents for the subdivision. The articles of incorporation are dated the same as the Poet's Promise stuff."

"What? That was almost ten years ago!! Simon was a baby! He was still at CHOP. His little heart, you could see it beating in his chest, and Lear, you know I was exhausted, I didn't know what I was signing!" You touch your forehead to the scratched plastic of the phone booth—it burns your skin. "Oh my god. Why would Jack do that?"

"I don't know. Maybe he wanted you to be involved later, when the kids were older, to make you feel like you had some ownership of things, since it all started with Nana's land? Or maybe for tax reasons. But he was writing off everything. Nana's house, your cars, everything's in the name of the company. And it's all double-mort-gaged."

"But what does this have to do with the emails?"

"What emails? Jules, listen. Right now, with Jack dead and Marty gone, you're left holding the bag. Everything you have is at risk."

"What are you saying?"

"I'm trying to come up with a way to get whatever money you have left out of the country and keep the farmhouse in the family."

The jerk spices of the meat patty burn when they slide up your throat.

"And I'm saying, right now, when the lawsuits start, you're better off staying in the Cayman Islands. If you understand."

"For how long?"

"Until I get this sorted out. If you come back now, you'll be subpoenaed. You could be arrested. You have to think of the kids. You're all they have now."

There is nothing to say, seconds ticking by in silence.

"Sorry, Jules. This could take a while. Hang in there. Besides," Lear adds, "there are worse places to be stranded, right?"

CHAPTER 38

Dean

The days pass, and turn into weeks. In the heat of mid-August, departure dates looming, the flavor of their relationship becomes sweet and condensed, but a little wobbly, like flan.

"We'll focus on the now," they tell each other daily, sharing little kisses as they top off their coffee. "Not worry about the end of the summer; it will sort itself out. Enjoy the time we have together."

They pull out the mattresses for family sleepover in Juliet's living room each night and climb the stairs to Juliet's bed where their bodies meet under the rusted blades of the ceiling fan. The oblivion is blissful, a place where words become gasps and the softest exhalations, where a hand sliding worshipfully down the arch of a hip says it all.

It is only afterward when they can't help but jab at the hornet's nest of the future. Dean points this out to her, that their heads get in the way of what their bodies understand to be magic.

"You see how we fit," Dean says. "How easy this is?" He lightly massages her bare neck and shoulders with the tips of his fingers.

"Maybe long distance is the best option," Juliet whispers as she rests her head on the warm planes of Dean's chest.

"Long distance between Michigan and Pennsylvania?" Dean twirls a strand of her hair around his finger. "Not drivable."

"It's a short flight."

"Hmm. Spoken like someone whose husband had a very large insurance policy," Dean says, and Juliet moves quickly off him, stung.

"I found a house tonight on the Internet," Dean continues in a tone of studied lightness. "Between Saline and Ann Arbor."

"What do you mean?" she asks.

"It's the perfect Brady Bunch house. Big, sort of modern-vintage split level. Six bedrooms."

"I like old houses, farmhouses. Stone. Something with character and history."

"I'm not that handy," Dean says. "And during the school year, between teaching and the kids' sports and plays, I'm so busy I can hardly change the light bulbs."

"We're tied to Philly forever," she says. "For Si's doctors. He goes to CHOP for follow-ups with Dr. Canfield every year. It's just a check-up, an EKG and a milkshake, but complications can develop. They've been monitoring him since he was a baby."

"There are doctors, even hospitals in Michigan."

In the quiet, Dean stretches his arm out so that it is under her head, pulls her back to his chest. Can she feel his heart beating?

"Tenure track is a big deal," he says finally. "At my stage in the game, professors don't just walk away from that."

"What about long distance between Michigan and Rum Point?" Juliet is staring at the ceiling. "The kids and I might just stay here."

"For how long? At some point, J, the vacation has to end. You have to go back to reality. What about the kids' school?"

"Obviously I'd make changes. I could enroll them or homeschool. And it wouldn't be as expensive, since there would only be the three of us."

"Well, I guess you've never had to think about money before; why start now?" Dean says, surprised at how quickly they have learned how to fight, to poke sharply at the other's tender skin.

Juliet rolls away from him.

"J, I'm sorry," Dean says, pushing himself up onto his elbow. "That wasn't fair. I interpreted your comment about it only being the three of you to mean that we, me and the kids are some kind of burden, that there's something inequitable in our distribution."

"Of course not!" she sputters. "Hasn't this summer's motto been one of 'it all comes out in the wash?' I get lunch, you buy gas, we use my shower but keep the milk gallons in your fridge? I don't keep spreadsheets, I don't think that way about money!" She adds, "I don't want to have to, ever."

"Actually, the only motto I've heard is 'It's only money—we'll make more of it.' How is that going to work here?"

She doesn't answer.

"Money aside, you're an expat. You can't live here without a work permit. You'd be at the mercy of that grouchy Immigration officer. You'd have to leave the island every thirty to sixty days."

"It sounds like you've looked into this," she says, and it's true. Dean has secrets of his own.

"Staying here is not practical," he says.

The bedroom is cast in the glow of the low hanging moon outside, framed by the plantation shutters of her windows, silence crackling between them. He tries again.

"I'm hurt by how easy it seems for you to imagine the end of things. Forgive me."

"Arguing with a psychologist is so strange." She rolls toward him and puts an open hand on his chest. "'I' statements. Feelings. Quick, sincere apologies. And for the record, it's not easy to picture the end of August," Juliet adds softly. "Let's just focus on the time we have."

"For the kids," they agree.

The next day, when Dean is washing up from lunch, alone, they lose power at Juliet's. Not that she is there to notice when the constant din of her air conditioner falls silent.

"I could take the kids," she'd offered, when she was leaving with Hazel. While she didn't say it, Dean imagines they are going to look at houses. But Simon and Sonny protested and Dean insisted her two made his life easier, not harder.

Late afternoon, Dean takes all four across the street to the resort beach, Shirley Temples for the girls and Owen, and, though he knows Juliet might not approve, a Coke for Simon.

"Power's out at the cottages," Dean tells Leo and Tony and Doc, the trio seated at the bar. Above them, the fan blades spin and the stereo is playing Willie Nelson's Greatest Hits. Dean checks on the children outside the open doorway and sinks into a stool next to Tony, orders himself a cold Heineken.

"Hazel says all the cottage owners are too cheap to go in on a generator," Leo tells them, wiping out a blender. "And you know CUC is in no hurry to come out here on the weekend. Get ready for a hot night."

Dean is still back on the mention of Hazel, because by extension, since Juliet is with her now, it is almost like they are talking about Juliet: That's how bad he has it.

"Hot night," Tony scoffs as Sonny runs in and deposits her empty drink cup in Dean's lap. "Looks to me like you're babysitting again."

"Well, half of them are mine." Dean throws out Sonny's cup and sips at his beer.

"Kids! That's how they get you," Doc laughs at the other end of the bar.

"For a guy whose tests I cheated off in Chem 112, you're not that smart," Tony says. "I'm trying to look out for you here. She's not everything you think she is."

"What's that supposed to mean?" Dean asks, noticing how uncomfortable Leo looks. Dean spins on his barstool to glance out the open door to where the children are swinging each other dangerously high, trying to flip the hammock.

"Geraldine," Doc is saying to nobody in particular, his eyes trained on the sepia photos of pirate ships dashed on the rocks behind the bar, sketches of the original Wreck bar, "wants to leave Northside and go back to England. Wants to go back to her sister and the rain and the damp and the cold. Says she's tired of driving twenty miles for her biscuits and PG Tips. Doesn't want to worry, wait around for another storm like Ivan to blow us away. Won't shaddup about it. I try to show her our million-dollar view, tell her my patients would be sunk without me—"

Tony turns his stool so that his back is to Doc, lifts his sunglasses up on his head. He has permanent raccoon eyes underneath. His original skin, the sallow-pale Dean knew him with as a freshman from Chicago, is only left in ovals around his eyes; the rest of his face cured to the leathery orange-brown of expensive boots.

Tony runs a hand down his face. "You're a good guy, Dean. Way better than I am. I can't watch it happen again. Can't watch another woman con you into raising her kid. Juliet's a train wreck, and I know because I've been there."

"You're saying," Dean says carefully, "that you know what she's going through, because you've been a train wreck yourself? Believe me, I know."

I have cleaned up the debris.

"She was out of her gourd the night of the accident. Her kid was running around, out in the fucking street, at one in the morning—could have been killed!"

Dean stands up from the bar and finishes the last swill at the bottom of his beer, warm and yeasty in the late afternoon heat. Tony has always been an exaggerator, ever since he's known him. Telling his mother they creamed the other team in soccer when it had gone into overtime, lying to their French professor that he couldn't take the exam because his sister was in the hospital, when Dean knew she had a cold, if that.

"It happens, even to good parents. Hell, once last year, I left the house in a fog and drove halfway to the university before I realized I'd left Owen at home in front of *PBS kids.*"

"Let her go, man. Luc and I've been talking. We don't want you to be taken advantage of again."

But what Tony doesn't know, what he'll never realize, is that raising Luc was not a burden—it was an honor.

"Juliet makes me happy."

And she makes me realize how much Amélie never loved me, because she was in love with you.

"Kids!" he barks, turning his back on Tony and the bar, "Let's go see if the power's back on."

But when they get to Juliet's it's not—the air is heavy inside, stinking of mildew, the windows closed, no fans to move it. Dean sends the kids to collect candles and flash-lights and open windows while he pulls the most expensive and easily spoiled food from the darkness of her fridge—chicken breasts, heavy cream, bacon and eggs. Using the gas of her cooktop, he'll make chicken Cordon Bleu before sunset steals the last of the light from the dim kitchen.

Where is she? He shakes the pan too hard across the flames, so that the meat spits flecks of grease, burning his wrist. He can't shed the irritation of his conversation with Tony.

Tony and Luc come by with coolers full of ice from the bar to rescue any other perishables from the refrigerator.

"You know, you should talk to Doc," Tony says. "He's ready to check out, looking for someone to take over his practice out here."

Dean can feel Luc watching, waiting for his answer.

"What's so important back in Saline anyway?" Luc says and he remembers his strangled confession the day they went to the hospital, about not being sure if he could ever go home.

"I'm tenure track at EMU," Dean says to Tony, just like he told Juliet. "At my age, you don't walk away from that."

"I told you he wouldn't listen." Luc drops the heavy cooler with a clatter.

Dean watches them walk away, their identical rangy gaits and red surf shorts. They look more like brothers than a father and a son, while Dean is stuck, cooking dinner and caring for the kids in her sweltering kitchen.

Where is she?

Annoyance is simmering with the roux.

It is sunset. In the living room, the children have disassembled the couch and mattresses to make a fort, spreading the woven blankets for a roof.

"Okay, now, Holly," Sonny bosses, her five-year-old hip jutting out at a sharp angle, "you're the mom and Si's the dad, and I'm the baby and O's the cat."

"I'm not playing. House is a girl game, and it's stupid," Simon says, picking up his book. "I don't want to be the dad."

"You have to," Sonny quips. "Every house needs a mom and a dad."

"Well, actually, not really." Holly, ever diplomatic.

"Yes, it does!"

"Lots of people don't have a mom and a dad. We can play just the three of us, since Si's being a pill. Come on," Holly takes Sonnet by the arm, lifting the blanket corner of their house fort in invitation.

Dean stands, the bag of frozen spinach dripping in the heat of his hands as this unfolds. He checks the window, wishes that Juliet were here, witnessing this important moment with him.

"NO!" Sonnet stands her ground. "Simon, you have to be the dad!"

Simon has curled up with *Harry Potter* in his sacred corner spot where the two couches intersect.

"Holl's right," he mumbles without looking up. "You don't need a dad."

"Yes, I do!"

"Hey," Dean calls from the kitchen, recognizing from the timbre of Sonnet's voice that tears are imminent. "Why doesn't O be the dad?"

"No! He's Marshmallow, because his hair is mostly white."

"I be da Dad!" Owen chimes, scrambling up off all fours and thrusting out his barrel chest.

"You're the cat!" Sonny shoves him by the shoulder to his knees again and her voice breaks when she wails, "I want a cat *and* a dad!"

Dean is there in two steps, scooping her up. This is how Juliet finds them: Sonnet sobbing in Dean's arms, the spinach bleeding green juice on the counter, Owen wailing, Simon pouting and the living room destroyed.

"Whoa," Juliet says, looping her fingers through the straps of her heels and placing them on the stairs. "What's going on here?"

Dean wishes he didn't have to wait to be alone with her, to analyze what the scene he just witnessed means about each of their children's grief processes, to confront her about leaving him to go house hunting for a future without him, but for now, there is dinner to get through. Sonnet transfers easily to Juliet, who pours herself a large glass of white wine with her free hand and sinks into a kitchen stool to watch Dean finish the sauce.

"Did you have a nice time?" Dean asks, words tight in his throat, speaking in code for the sake of the kids. "At lunch?"

Juliet doesn't answer right away, one hand smoothing Sonnet's curls, the other sipping off her wine. She has an air of elsewhere around her, like the smell of frost that swirls around guests when they first arrive for Thanksgiving dinner.

"I couldn't find anything I liked on the menu," she sighs. Her shoulders round in a defeated posture he's not used to seeing on her. "I feel like, I don't know what I want to eat, like I'm not hungry at all."

"You should have stayed with us!" Sonnet lifts her head from her mother's shoulder. "We had banana pancakes and watermelon smoothies."

"I wish I had, sweets."

They eat by candlelight—the food too rich and heavy in the heat—and then let the kids tear around the house playing flashlight freeze tag while Dean and Juliet shuttle the dishes and piles of uneaten, wasted food into the kitchen sink, no washing up tonight. The roaches from the utility room will migrate to the kitchen.

"Sorry, I was late. No run," Juliet says, her tone an apology.

"When the power comes back on, I want to show you: I bookmarked a few well-reviewed heart specialists at Detroit Medical."

"This is crazy," Juliet says, crushing sugar ants on the kitchen counter with her thumb. "We've known each other, what, nine weeks?"

"Some people get engaged after a few days." Dean tries out Leo's eyebrow arch, but the effect might be lost in the dark.

"I wouldn't hold that up as one of my more brilliant life choices."

"I also found a split-level, on a full acre in Ypsilanti. The interior is pretty dated, but there's room out back, for chickens."

"I don't even know if you're neat!"

"Neat? Like, groovy, baby?"

"No, like tidy!"

Dean laughs. Now that she's home, and they're sparring, his mood is swirling around her cottage's vaulted ceiling. "I'm wiping down your counter right now, lady."

"I picked up some glow sticks today. I'll get them out tonight. We should let the kids do a quick pool dip before bed, cool them off, if the power doesn't come back."

"See, you're worried about compatible housekeeping," he says, "but I already know what I need to know. Your capability, your thoughtfulness, are ninety-eight percent of what attracts me to you."

"What's the other two percent? Unknown?"

"Oh, no." Dean slides up behind her purposefully, puts his hands around her waist. "That's been established," he whispers into her ear. The candles flicker, all twelve from the cottage hurricane kit, where Simon has lit them on the table like a séance.

When she doesn't answer, he continues.

"I mean, really, what are you going to do? Go back to Pennsylvania and start dating? Join match-dot-com? Weed through all the dysfunctionals and never-married-living-in-their-mom's-basement? Or stay here, like Tony, and prey on unsuspecting tourists?"

"Of course not." She tilts her head the tiniest bit to the left to give him access to kiss behind her ear.

"Want to hear something funny?" Dean says, surprised that he is bringing it up, anxious to dismiss it, to spit it out and get rid of the sour pooling in him since the conversation in the bar. "Tony tried to warn me off you tonight."

Outside the slatted windows, the rustling palm fronds cast weak shadows in the light of a waxing moon.

"Don't worry; I defended you, told him you're my girl."

"He's very protective of you." The way she says it sounds like she's trying to find something nice to say about a hideous painting. "I don't get the feeling he likes me much."

"But I do." Dean loves that when he turns her around and she tilts her face up to kiss him in the dark, she tastes of the heartiness of bacon, like something that could sustain him over a long winter. It washes away the day's bitterness.

CHAPTER 39

Juliet

You are a veteran of trying to find the fun in a power outage. Three times in the year before Jack died, the PECO utility truck bumped up the driveway back home.

The first time, you were blindsided.

"Some bad news," the bald man said as he swung down from his truck, surprisingly agile for his age, an apologetic smile tugging his jowls. He waggled his fingers at Sonnet, her skinny arm wrapped around your thigh. "I'm going to have to shut your power off."

He handed you a paper, while you formed the words, "For how long?" thinking, they must be doing work on the main road, or that this was something to do with Phase Two of the Compass project.

And then you read the top of the paper: YOUR GAS/ELECTRICITY HAS BEEN SHUT OFF BECAUSE YOU DID NOT PAY YOUR BILL. You swallowed your question.

When he was gone, you instinctively picked up the kitchen phone—dead. You took your cell phone out of the eerily silent house and called Jack on his project in Atlantic City. He did not answer right away.

When he called back, you sobbed what had happened.

"Wait, where are you?" you asked, because the jangling in the background was suspicious.

"AC," he said. "I only brought two grand. We can afford it to lose it, but it wouldn't hurt to double it."

It took them three days to turn the power back on. Without electricity, the farmhouse well did not pump water. You scooped muddy water from the shallow pond to flush the toilets. You took the kids out for every meal on your credit card until they were begging you to just stay home and cook simple food—eggs and pancakes, pasta.

It was the same kind-eyed PECO man who came back to turn the power on. You met him in the driveway, with the speech you had prepared about an electronic payment error.

The second time, it was a sweltering July morning. This time, it took five days. Embarrassed, you hid behind the tin foil curtains in the front room and waited until the PECO man was gone to turn on the fans and run loads of mildewed laundry.

The last time, it was the middle of November, the month before Jack died. Jack was traveling, a work conference in sunny Florida, he said. You burned fires and slept in the living room at night. "Camping" you called it and bought marshmallows and Hershey's chocolates. Jack assured you that the bill was paid, an accounting error at the Compass office. He said there should be room on one of the cards, that you should take the kids to a hotel.

You were loading everyone into the car to drive to the hotel, four-thirty and already dark outside, when the PECO man arrived to turn it back on. You wanted to kiss him on his papery lips. Jack's story of "moving funds around" and "Marty's fault" tasted as fake as the cheese in Cheetos, but you opened your mouth to tell it anyway.

The gentleman held up one square hand to stop you. He laid it on your shoulder as Sonny and Si raced past you back toward the house, windows glowing golden, their loaded backpacks slapping against their backs with whoops of joy.

"I knew your grandfather. I worked for him here on this farm one summer, when I was fifteen. You come from good, hardworking people."

You nodded, hot tears slipping from your eyes to your wind-cold cheeks.

"'This too shall pass,'" he said, and got back in his van without another word.

CHAPTER 40

Dean

They fall asleep, finally, all the children, Sonny and Owen under the lightest draped sheet in the middle of Juliet's bed after three times through *The Very Hungry Caterpillar.*

Dean puts a finger to his lips and takes Juliet by the hand. They feel their way down the stairs in the dark, leaving behind the baby monitor loaded with batteries and switched on. They sneak past Simon and Holly in the stifling living room, to the expansive sky and briny smell of the outdoors.

They laugh like teenagers, Juliet remarking on the gloriousness of the stars here, with even the pathway lights out.

"Isn't that Pegasus?"

Dean doesn't look up. He pulls her along urgently, hands clutched in the blackness.

"I think, at my place, we can just change the channels on the monitors."

They feel their way through his living room, trying not to bang their shins on the rattan furniture.

"It's right here, by my bed."

There is a heart-stopping rustle, the unmistakable sound of fabric sliding across skin. Instinctively, Dean gropes the wall for the light switch, which does nothing.

Juliet squeezes his hand, tugs him back to the doorway.

"Dean," she hisses. They are not alone in the room. "Someone's here!"

"Shit. Dad."

"Who?" It's a girl's voice.

"You're in *my* bed?" Dean roars. The line he read to Luc a thousand times, the papa bear's growl: Someone's sleeping in my bed! He can hear scrambling, bare feet hitting the floor. Without the sense of sight, smell is heightened. The coconut tang of Malibu fills the room.

"I'm going to go." Juliet drops his hand.

"Me too," gulps the other voice. There is the sound of clothes, the tinkle of jewelry being collected off the floor. Something clinks, glass to tile, and liquid glug-glug-glugs.

"Shit, I spelled it!" There is a girl's giggle. "*Spilled* it!"

"No." Dean grabs for Juliet—not tonight. "NO. Luc is going to go."

"What? Dad, you can't kick me out of my own place!"

"My place! I pay for this! You," Dean wills his voice to be calm, steady and serious, his hand holding Juliet's so she can't slip away from him, "young lady, whoever you are, you need to go home."

There is the rustle of fabric, the sound of a snap closing.

"And you, Luc," Dean continues, swallowing his fury and frustration, directing his words in his son's direction. "First, you are going to escort this young woman home, and then you are going to take your jammies and your toothbrush, and you're going to sleep on the couch with the rest of the children over at Juliet's."

There is a crash of flesh, a press of soft breasts and jutting chin, as the girl bumps into Dean at the doorway.

"Sorry," she giggles. She smells like teen deodorant and sex. Juliet tugs him out of the way.

"Unbelievable," Luc mutters.

"What are you thinking?" Dean blurts. "What about Bridget?"

"Who's Bridget?" the girl asks from the doorway.

"Nobody," Luc says. "This is such bullshit."

"You're right." The blood pounds in Dean's throat, making his vocal cords throb. "This is absolute bullshit! Bridget is not nobody, but if this is how you want to go through life with women, go ahead! I am done caring."

"I'm going to go," Juliet says again. He grips her fingers, her left hand. That's when he notices: Juliet is not wearing her ring anymore.

"No! You're staying."

"*I'm* going," Luc huffs.

"Wait!" Dean continues. "Walk this young lady home, and tomorrow, you're going to feed everyone breakfast, and you'll get their gear off the porch, and you're going to take them all with you out on the morning boat trip to Stingrays. Make sure they wear life preservers and sunscreen and tell Tony he can settle up with me later."

"Dad—"

"I'm still not done! Juliet and I don't want to see any of you, unless maybe someone is bleeding from the eyes or unconscious, until at least lunchtime tomorrow. We want, we deserve, to be alone. Is that clear?"

"This is ridiculous," Luc hisses in the darkness, but there is the sound of him picking up jeans, the belt buckle clinking against the tile floor, a resignation in his voice when he mumbles to the girl, "Come on."

When they are gone, Dean heaves a deep sigh. He drops Juliet's hand to run his through his hair—it sits heavy on his head in the heat. *Enough*, he thinks. If his son wants to follow in Tony's footsteps, let him. But there are lines he can hold.

"Well," Juliet says, the threads of a cheeky smile in her voice.

"Yeah, I give it twenty minutes, an hour at the most, until someone shows up here."

She clears her throat in the darkness, like she is going to say something.

"What?" he asks.

"Nothing."

Dean is delighted to hear the distinct sound of a bra unclasping.

"Just, you did it again. You surprised me, that's all. I assumed you would want to tend to Luc…." she trails off.

"Luc loves Bridget, and he's making terrible choices. Tony choices. And I can't stop him." Dean sighs. "But it can't always be all about them," he is reaching for her in the darkness, guiding her toward his bed, "if there's going to be a future for us."

Though she doesn't answer that directly, her hands are sliding up his bare chest. In the darkness, she whispers, "Anyway, Professor, I'm still waiting for *my* orders."

CHAPTER 41

Dean

Amazingly, another one of his ideas works. They are left alone. Sometime before dawn, the power comes back on, Dean's fan blades spinning the air around them, cooling them enough to sleep at last. There is a new element to this night, a shift. Juliet is relaxed and soft, a receptive vessel. When Dean enters her, the word forms in his throat: *mine.*

It is even better in the morning light, so that he can see Juliet underneath him, her arms thrown over her head, her fists, those capable hands, twisting the sheets.

"I could get used to this," she sighs, the woman who normally revs at 1000 rpm, who is usually up pulling weeds from their garden at sunrise, is content to lounge in bed, lazily running her fingers up and down his arms wrapped around her.

"Me too."

"Remember," she says, her voice dreamy, "what you said, Professor, how there is no competition in grief? How neither of us have had it worse? How all we can do is go forward?"

Dean doesn't remember all of what he has said, but he likes that she remembers, that sometimes she calls him Professor.

"That's what this is," he says, pulling away enough to see each other's faces. "This," he gestures to the space between them. "*This* is our lollipop for everything we've both been through. And we're here, and the kids. Going forward. That's something."

Juliet nods and she whispers, "I'm realizing, maybe the great tragedy is not the loss of our first loves. Maybe the great tragedy would be letting this get away from us."

There are no words to describe the hope that soars inside him at her saying this, that threatens to break open his cracking heart. It is noon before they put on clothes, sip coffee among the angelfish pillows on Dean's couch, admitting to each other that they actually miss the children. It might be, Dean thinks as he hooks his fingers through hers, the happiest day of his life.

Until they come back, Owen and Sonny's faces smeared with peanut butter and jelly. Beyond them, Simon and Luc, and it is obvious from their body language that something is seriously wrong.

"How was the boat trip?" Dean asks, reaching to help Owen climb onto the couch between them, holding his sticky hands out of the way. The girls are laughing, running to rinse off at the poolside shower, chattering about the silky feel of the stingrays. Out the doorway, Simon is sulking on the screen porch, curled into a chair, his skin is the color of the sand.

"Fine. I've got to go. Back to work."

"What happened?"

"That kid," Luc begins, and stops, jerking his head at Simon. "That fucking kid."

"What?" Juliet puts her coffee cup down, sits up straight.

Luc stands awkwardly, like he is not sure what to do with his hands, his gaze is fixed on a spot on the wall between them. He reaches to close the sliding door behind him. "Something happened, Dad."

Juliet opens her mouth, closes it, tries again. "I just want to say—"

"Out on the water today," Luc cuts her off with a look. "I took the kids out to Stingrays, like you said, to the sandbar. It was crowded; there were six cruise ships in George Town, all kinds of charters, Red Sail had both cattle boats loaded up. I could barely drop my anchor without hitting a tourist. When we got there, Si and Holly jumped in with the bait. But O got sunscreen in his eyes, so it took me a few minutes.

"Then I hear Holly yelling. When I look up, this guy, he looked like a fucking pirate, beard, scars, wild eyes, he's got Simon, under the chest. He's dragging him across the sandbar. Simon freezes. Completely limp. White as a freaking ghost, just letting this creeper snatch him, drag him away!"

"Oh my god." Beside him, Juliet covers her mouth with both hands.

"I yelled at the guy, and he dropped him. Just dropped him in the water. He put up both hands, smiling like the Joker, batshit crazy. He laughed, like, 'Hey, just messing around, no harm, no foul.' When he dropped him, Simon went under like a stone, and he didn't come back up. It was like he was in shock or something. I had to jump in, and haul him up, drag him back to the boat. When I looked up, the guy was in his dinghy, and he'd pulled anchor. He had this little Zodiac, a rubber inflatable with a forty on it. He took off to the south, toward Harbor House. Gone."

"That was it?" Dean asks. "But, what did he want?"

"I don't know. I don't know if it was a joke, or if he was crazy, or what."

"What did he look like?" Juliet's voice is shrill.

"What? Like a pirate, I told you. What was I supposed to do, radio the Interceptor?" Luc holds his hand up to his ear like a telephone. "'Um, so my tour boat kid was almost kidnapped by Blackbeard?' I told you, he had a forty horsepower maxed out, cutting a serious wake. He was gone."

"You should have called us, right away!"

"Called you how?"

Dean agrees, "You could have radioed to Tony."

"Why?" Luc's voice breaks, and he tilts his face up to the ceiling, sniffs hard. "So you guys could yell at me? I get it, I screwed up again. I wasn't looking, for five freaking seconds, I wasn't looking, and this happened! What if I hadn't gotten to him? Or what if the guy didn't let him go? I'm thinking," he gestures to the two of them, Dean's arm behind her along the back of the couch. "I'm thinking, how many more chances am I going to get? How many times am I going to get to fuck up, before you walk away, before you pick the Brady Bunch over me?"

Juliet jumps up and pushes past Luc, out the sliding door, to Simon.

When Dean stands, Luc backs away. Dean grabs him by the shoulders, clutches them under his bare hands.

"All of them," Dean says.

"What?" Luc sniffs.

"You're my son. You get all the chances. You can make all the mistakes in the world, and I'll still be here."

Luc pulls out from under his grip, wiping his knuckles under his nose. He glances over his shoulder at Juliet and Simon. "I've got to get back to work." Two points of color burn in Simon's blanched face as he stares blankly into space.

"I can't believe it..." Juliet comes back in, yanking open Dean's laptop. "I'm emailing Lear."

"Your brother? For what? He's here, safe. It sounds like it was a fluke," Dean says. "Sounds like nothing, a crazy person. Nothing happened. I mean, unless you have enemies, someone who wants to snatch your kids?" He is thinking of money, of every action movie where wealthy kids are held for ransom.

"No." She shakes her head. She opens the computer and it pings, a new email.

"What does it matter? It's over. Si's here. He looks shaken, but okay."

Dean reads over her shoulder as the newest email loads, another one of her daily inspirations.

To:	Juliet B. Wilde <jbwilde@gmail.com>
From:	Daily Inspirations
Date:	August 16, 2007

It becomes more and more difficult, but in fighting the difficulties the inmost strength of the heart is developed. —**Vincent van Gogh**

She snaps the computer closed.

"Where are you going?"

"I'm taking Si back to my cottage," she says. Over her shoulder, she adds, "Lock your doors."

CHAPTER 42

Dean

Luc shows up at Juliet's just before sunset. He turns on her TV because there is more news—the buzzing threat of a tropical storm building out over the Lesser Antilles. The Cayman Islands are three tiny dots in the broad swath of its projected path. The children demand definitions of words like "trajectory" and "barometric" as they track the storm.

"I hope you'll stay for dinner?" Juliet asks Luc, and Dean is filled with gratitude. Owen insists on sitting on Juliet's lap to make room for Luc. Holly and Sonny are recounting how they were chased by Halloween, the large, orange dominant male iguana they've been feeding in the bush just before sunset, and though Si is quieter than usual, he smiles at parts of the story.

"Si, you're not eating?" Juliet fusses over him, offers to make mac and cheese, or get raspberries out of the fridge.

"What's wrong, buddy, you don't like my gazpacho?" Dean teases. None of the children are interested in the cold soup he blended with their bounty of vegetables.

"So what are we watching tonight?" Luc asks, and Dean can't believe he might be staying.

"Hazel let me into one of the other cottages for new DVDs. I have *Mary Poppins*, *Sound of Music*, or *Nanny McPhee*?" Juliet offers.

"No!" Simon howls. "I want *X-Men!* Or *The Fifth Element!* I want to watch *Memento!*"

"No," Dean, Juliet and Luc say together.

"You let him watch *Memento*?" Luc looks at Juliet.

"Of course not. What's wrong with *Nanny McPhee*?"

"That one is like us, all the kids. Except the stepmother in that is so disturbing-looking," Holly laughs.

While they argue about movie options, Juliet and Dean get up to clear the table. She says, "I'm sorry I freaked out earlier. I suppose I come with a little more baggage than a magic carpet bag."

Dean insists, "I love everything that comes with you." He means the kids, their comfortable mayhem.

"I tried to talk to Si, about what happened on the Sound. He's like a mollusk, shut tight."

"Maybe we let it go, for now?" Dean suggests. "He'll talk about it when he's ready."

"Maybe." She passes him a plate and their hands brush.

As the kids clear the table, Dean thinks this is the kind of family dinner he always imagined, loud and silly, lots of bantering.

"Is this what it was like, for you, growing up, with all your siblings? There's Lear, then you, then Bella, then … "

"Right, Bella, then Serena, and Percy's the baby."

"And Percy is Persephone, the one whose wedding you missed when Si had the seizure?"

"Yes," Juliet smiles. "You remember everything."

"When it's important, I remember."

Later, at the sound of the water running upstairs in her bathroom, Dean's stomach does a happy jump—the shower usually signifies good things for them. It means a door with a locking handle and the sound of water to muffle them. He looks down at Juliet's living room, thrilled to see Luc stretched out on the couch, Owen sprawled against him, the opening credits of a Disney movie playing.

But when he taps Juliet's bathroom door once and pushes it open, he finds her sitting on the tub floor in the classic pose of the bereft, knees pulled up, arms hugging them, her eyes as red and swollen as crushed raspberries.

Dean fingers the towels on the rack, choosing the softest one to hold open for her.

"Come here," he says, and folds her up in his downy wings, shushing as he guides her, towel-wrapped, to the bedroom. "Luc put on a movie," Dean tells her. "Simon was asleep before the barracuda ate the mom in *Nemo.*"

He hopes she hears this for what it is — love language, act of service, their families blending. "What's wrong?"

He sits on her bed, pulling Juliet to his lap, where she tips her head to his shoulder and rests it there. As much as he is touched all day, as many times as Owen does this, he wants to bottle the feeling. He likes Juliet leaning into him.

"I don't even know where to start. What happened with Si, today, or maybe I'm just grieving again? Hormones, or something."

Tonight, he wants to tell her what he has been thinking about, a possibility for their future, presented unintentionally by Tony, of all people. It's a long shot but—

"Do you ever want more children?" Her question interrupts his thoughts, falling out of nowhere into the bedroom like a hand grenade.

"Are you kidding?" His incredulous laugh comes out sharper than he meant. "I think we've got plenty going on with the ones we've got."

"Jack and I used to argue about it. I always wanted another, a sister for Sonny anyway. I can't imagine life without my sisters, or Lear. They say that a woman will always wonder if they are done, until they've had as many as their family of origin. And I'm one of six."

"Who's 'they'?" Dean asks. "It might have been different, if Amélie hadn't gotten sick. Ever since, I've been the mom and the dad," he says. "But try mixing that with keeping up with classes, politics at the university. We're not meant to be mothers. Studies have shown men are not bred for multitasking."

"You do an amazing job. Your parenting is one of your most attractive features," she says, running her fingertips down his cheek.

"Anyway, you're on the Pill." He has seen it on her bathroom counter, seen her taking it. "Right?" he prompts.

"Yes," she says, with the strangest inflection.

"What does that mean?"

"It means, yes—I started taking it again, this summer."

When, exactly, and why?

"I'm forty-two this year," Dean says. "I've already done the dessert baby thing." He remembers that night with Amélie so clearly, his argument that there was no better way to celebrate her remission.

"I'm sure all my eggs were chemically-cooked anyway," Amélie had snorted, running a hand over her smooth scalp. He had prepared bacon-wrapped scallops for dinner, pouring generously until they had split a bottle of Chateaux Margaux. In bed, there was Amélie's rare laughter when he chucked her sponge out the bedroom window.

"Why not? Celebrate life with life!" she had agreed.

Afterward, Dean had to go back outside with a flashlight to retrieve the birth control from their shaggy, dew-damp lawn so the kids or dog didn't find it. Four months later: the ultrasound where they found the uterus spots. Five months after that: Owen.

They sit in silence. Juliet sighs and Dean watches as she pushes purposefully off his lap and crosses to the dresser. She drops her towel and he is sad to see her dress. Disappointing; the sight of clothes covering this woman he adores.

"Anyway, you're sure you don't want any more kids?" She keeps her back to him. He can tell by the resolute way that she snaps her bra closed that this is an opportunity officially missed.

"Absolutely not."

When they get into bed, it is without the passion of the night before, more like a long-married couple. This is okay too, Dean thinks, the right atmosphere to introduce the secret plan he has been quietly putting together, what he was going to tell her, before he found her crying in the shower. But when he checks, Juliet is sleeping so peacefully he doesn't have the heart to wake her.

CHAPTER 43

Dean

Saturday, it is still brilliantly sunny, and they are playing in the sand while around them, storm rumors swirl at the resort. Everything is tinged with anxiety about the coming hurricane, and the nostalgia of the summer's end. It has been upgraded to a Category Three and given a name. The locals whisper the moniker of its predecessor: Ivan, 2004's Category Five hurricane that flooded the flat island and left a wake of devastation.

"I thought I was the big deal." Dean laughs as they dig deep trenches in the fine sand for their castle over at Rum Point. Because this storm, after the inconsequential Chantal in the Northern Atlantic three weeks earlier, is ironically named Hurricane Dean. "Who's this Ivan guy? I could probably kick his butt."

"You think it's funny," Tony calls from where he and Luc are hauling the rental catamaran up the beach. "You tourists don't have any idea."

"I hardly think after weathering a summer here we still deserve to be called tourists." Juliet piles sand high on the walls that protect the castle from the surf. They have been working on it all afternoon—a lumpy replica of Notre Dame. "Uh-uh," she reminds Owen for the tenth time, redirecting him to his own castle. "Remember the rule: you can only wreck it if you make it."

"You haven't weathered anything yet. And we'll find out just how local you are when you run and stand in line at the airport, begging to get off the island. He's your ticket," Tony points to Owen, stomping on Sonny's princess castle. "But it'll cost you."

Dean squints out at the Sound where the day couldn't be more perfect. Sparkling sunshine dances on the water and there's a hint of a breeze today.

"It's hard to believe bad weather is coming."

"Moving slower than they thought," Leo chimes in, coming out of the empty bar to perch on a picnic table. He shoos the ching-chings and tabby cats away. "Weather channel is saying Dean'll hit Jamaica by tonight, maybe."

"You guys should get out of here," Tony says again. "You're leaving anyway— what's a few days off your vacation?"

Tony does not understand that they are in final days, that every hour with Juliet has its own bittersweet flavor, tucked away like reserves of sugar and honey and lemon barley in the back of the pantry. Tony doesn't know about Dean's meeting with Doc later—that he has a plan.

"You don't understand." Tony shakes his head. "After Ivan, there were roofing tiles embedded five inches deep in the telephone poles. These storms are no joke. When you live on an island, you have to respect nature."

"And there's no higher ground, no topography here," Leo adds. "During Ivan, the sea touched over Seven Mile Beach. Highest point on this island will be the roof of Tony's truck."

"You should leave while you can," Tony says. "Over a hundred miles an hour, the wind screams like a woman."

Juliet stands up and dusts the sand off her thighs.

"You said the tickets will be expensive?" Dean asks.

"They added extra flights with Ivan, but the tickets were over two grand each." Dean whistles.

"I'll be back," Juliet says, and every adult male watches her go.

"Don't you ever wonder where she's going all the time, man?" Tony jibes as they both watch Juliet's back, her lean legs flexing as she jogs across the street toward the cottages. "Odd time for a jog."

"I assume," Dean says carefully, "that she is going to the bathroom."

"We do have restrooms here, behind the bar." Tony won't let it go.

Dean gets to his feet and moves away from the sandcastles and Simon's acute hearing, annoyed to have to stand up for her to Tony again. Tony and Luc are de-rigging the main sail of the big catamaran and rolling it: an automatic, practiced routine and even though there's plenty going on, Dean likes seeing his son so comfortable here, so accomplished at something he has no idea about and never taught him. Luc's months here have not been for nothing.

"What are you going to do next week, anyway? Take her and the kids back to Michigan with you? Introduce her to your sister? 'What kind of souvenir is this? I thought you were bringing me rum cake!'" Tony singsongs.

"You can't stand to see me happy, is that it?"

"She's another Amélie, man," Tony has the grace to glance at Luc when he says this. "Looking for a baby daddy."

Out over the ocean, three frigate birds swoop low, their wing tips touching the water.

"All I'm saying is, if I were the guy in charge of naming Atlantic storm systems," Tony continues, "I'd have picked 'Juliet'."

Back at her cottage with the kids, Dean is vindicated to hear her reply when he calls up the stairs—she is in the bathroom, just like he said! But on the kitchen counter, Dean finds his computer open, and evidence of a flurry of emails that have pinged in the last few minutes. With a guilty look up the stairs, he sits down at the counter to read them:

To: **Juliet B. Wilde <jbwilde@gmail.com>**
From: **Daily Inspirations**
Date: **August 18, 2007**

Life's a voyage that's homeward bound. —***Herman Melville***

To: **Juliet B. Wilde <jbwilde@gmail.com>**
From: **Daily Inspirations**
Date: **August 18, 2007**

What's the good of a home if you are never in it? —***George and Weedon Grossmith***

To: **Juliet B. Wilde <jbwilde@gmail.com>**
From: **Daily Inspirations**
Date: **August 18, 2007**

A man travels the world over in search of what he needs and returns home to find it. —**George Moore**

To: Juliet B. Wilde <jbwilde@gmail.com>
From: Daily Inspirations
Date: August 18, 2007

"Home" is any four walls that enclose the right person. —**Helen Rowland**

To: **Juliet B. Wilde <jbwilde@gmail.com>**
From: **Daily Inspirations**
Date: **August 18, 2007**

Not going home is already like death. —**E. Catherine Toble**

Dean wipes the sweat from his forehead and jumps, startled by a pounding on the front door of the cottage. Through the slats of the blinds, he sees the red and yellow of the DHL van idling in the parking lot. He opens the door and signs for the fat envelope addressed to Juliet Burke Wilde, handling it as if it contains anthrax.

Upstairs, the toilet flushes. He hears her retching, the flush of the toilet again. The computer pings, another email has come through, and Dean lays the thick envelope on the counter, crosses slowly to the screen, where the new email is already waiting for her.

To: **Juliet B. Wilde <jbwilde@gmail.com>**
From: **Daily Inspirations**
Date: **August 18, 2007**

Your body must become familiar with its death - in all its possible forms and degrees - as a self-evident, imminent, and emotionally neutral step on the way towards the goal you have found worthy of your life. —**Dag Hammarskjold**

"What's that?" Juliet asks, coming down the stairs. Despite a summer in the sun, she is as blanched as the inside of an almond. She grips the railing, using the tips of her fingers to touch the corners of her mouth.

"You got a package. DHL. Do you feel alright?"

Sonny and Owen run inside and push past them both in a scramble for the refrigerator. Juliet has to reach for the counter to steady herself from the wind of their wake. She picks up the envelope and tears the perforation, walking away from him as she does, her shoulders forming a privacy wall for the papers.

"I'll run first, tonight, if that's okay," she tells Dean. Outside the window, the yellow van with red letters turns around in their parking lot and heads back to town.

"You're not going to tell me what that is?" he asks, nodding to the envelope. "What's so important that the document van has to come hunt you down on the tip of the edge of nowhere? On a Saturday, with a hurricane coming?"

Juliet shakes her head. "Nothing interesting." She bends down to tie her shoe.

"You don't look like you should go running. Are you okay?"

"I'm fine." Juliet sits down at his computer; he hears the frantic finger tapping and zipping of files being sent to the trash—the deleting of her barrage of inspirational emails.

"What do you think we should do about the storm?" Dean changes the subject. "It's sounding pretty serious."

"I'm not feeling up for making any major decisions right now," Juliet says.

"We're running out of time. I certainly don't have a spare eight grand, so I guess we're staying."

There is a long silence from Juliet. Dean is surprised—angry—that she is not offering to help. What have her kids been chiming all summer—it's only money?

Juliet pushes past him up abruptly, before he can say anything. "I can't think about any of this right now. I need to run."

CHAPTER 44

Juliet

You run, away, from the computer and the document that renders you homeless, and the man from whom you have kept too many secrets. You run, knowing with certainty that what is coming for you is less predictable and more dangerous than a swirling wall of weather and wind. Your shaking legs take you not on the long road, but a short, guilty dash across the sandy street to the slat wall shack. He is waiting for you. Before you can tell Dean about what happened, before you can do anything else, you have a question only Tony can answer.

The sight of his goatee brings back the flash from the tequila night, the roughness of silver-flecked stubble burning already sun-scorched cheeks. You were reminded of it for days afterward, the sharp sting of your lips whenever you sipped orange juice.

You stand in front of him like a knock-kneed sorority girl on a Sunday morning, forced to play CLUE to put together the pieces of the dark spaces in that night at the beginning of June when the Barefoot Man sang not to worry about a thing.

You are alone, the two of you, in the rentals shack, where several months ago you let him press you against the splintered outside wall and kiss your mouth raw. The air in here smells like sun-rotted rubber, spoiled sunscreen and O-ring grease. You are conscious of Luc filling tanks in the room just behind the slatted white doors, grateful for the muffle of the intermittent compressor. What does it matter, now?

Outside in the final strains of late-afternoon sun, the wind rustles the palm fronds, a sound like restless gossips. You look over your shoulder to the sea.

"It will do this, on and off, as the storm gets closer. Just like Ivan. It will get louder, and then right before, late tonight, or tomorrow morning maybe, it will go quiet," Tony says. "Dead quiet."

"The calm before the storm."

He locks the drawer of the cash register. "What do you want?"

"I have to ask you something," you say. "About that night, in June, when I was…" You trail off. In the back room, the compressor rumbles and sputters before it cuts out.

"When you were out of your fucking mind?"

"Did we?" you finally whisper, eyes on your toes.

"Oh, you wanted me to." He laughs, enjoying this. "But no. We definitely did not."

"You're sure?" you whisper, conscious of Luc in the next room.

"You were blind-staggering-slurring drunk. I'm not that much of an asshole. And I was the one who brought your kid back home, so you're welcome."

"What?" Your head snaps up.

"Exactly," he snorts. "End of the night, I'm getting ready to go home, but I can't find my truck, or Luc or Dusty or any of them. And then I find them, a hundred yards down the road, wrecked, and your kid out running around in the middle of the street. Nearly got killed."

You know exactly why: Sonny's ghost.

"Thank you," you say, meaning for rescuing your daughter.

"For what? For not fucking you when you practically begged me to? You're resistible; trust me," he snorts.

Luc comes out of the back room then, the necks of two full oxygen tanks hooked through his thumb and fingers.

"That's not exactly how it went," he says, and Tony gives him a hard look.

"What do you know? You're on record that you can't remember anything!"

Luc opens his mouth like he might say something, but he grits his teeth together, looking from you to Tony. Then, like he thinks better of it, he tucks his chin to his chest, head down, not looking at either of you. Everything about him reminds you so much of Dean your chest hurts.

"I was the one who stepped in." Luc's voice is so low you have to lean in. "So don't make it out like you were being so honorable." He raises his head to Tony, a challenge in his eyes. "I was the one who told you she'd had too much to drink, and it wasn't a good idea."

"So now your memory is miraculously returned?" Tony is bright red.

Luc hitches the tanks to his shoulders, turning to go.

"I remember everything about that night," he says as he leaves.

"Wait, Luc!" You go to follow him, but Tony grabs your arm, hard.

"Hey! Let Dean go. Let him go back to his life. He and the kids have been through enough."

"I am not a bad person! You're making a lot of judgments about me based on one tequila night."

"That's all it takes."

"But nothing happened! Yes, I drank too much, and Sonny was outside without me, but nothing happened, with her, or thank goodness, with me and you!"

"Nothing happened? I think there's a girl without half a leg in New Zealand, and a guy sitting in a jail cell in Canada who'd beg to differ!"

"The accident wasn't my fault!" Your throat throbs like the coming of the flu, still burning from the bile you heaved up earlier. "It was the anniversary of my husband's death. I had an off night."

"A mother doesn't get to have an off night."

"You, of all people, are seriously going to tell me about what good parenting looks like? I don't know why you hate me so much, but I love Dean. I want to be with him."

"Dean's biggest flaw is he falls hard for the wrong women."

"I said I love him!" you protest. "I made a mistake, that night, but I love Dean." The fact that you're screaming it to Tony, before you've even told Dean, makes you realize you need to run home.

"We have a name out here for women like you," Tony says. "Call 'em Train Wrecks. They show up with their baggage, running away from lives they've screwed up, and go on to fuck up plenty more on island, if they don't wash up dead at Head of Barkers. I'm not going to let my buddy get mowed down."

You push off the counter, back toward the open door of the dive shack. You got the answer you wanted—it is time to leave, to go tell Dean everything. "Are you threatening me?" you whisper.

Tony laughs. "I don't have to. Women like you, secrets and lies, happens all the time. Given enough rope, you'll hang yourself."

CHAPTER 45

Dean

here is she? Dean turns off the air conditioner and opens the windows of Juliet's cottage where outside the wind is crackling through the palms. On the Weather Channel, somber broadcasters deliver the news that Hurricane Dean has been upgraded to a Category Four, headed straight for Jamaica. His laptop is open where he was searching for flights off the island. Just as Tony predicted, the prices are astronomical and there is a banner at the top of the Weather Channel stating commercial airlines cannot fly once the winds surpass thirty-five miles an hour.

Dean wonders what it must have been like for the islanders in the early years, like the one documented in one of the cottage's coffee table books. The Storm of '32 blindsided locals and claimed over a hundred lives. Is it better, he wonders, to watch with agonizing accuracy as the approaching storm is tracked, to see the televised devastation, until the power goes out?

Where is she? Dean paces, checking the darkening evening sky. He has an appointment, with Doc. He was hoping to surprise her, invite her out for a sunset drive, show her their future.

The yellow envelope from DHL sits on the kitchen counter, already open. He shakes it just the tiniest bit, so the papers shimmy to the edge. Scanning the top, he reads only,

TRANSFER OF PROPERTY AT 429 Furlong Road

"I said, don't touch them!" On the floor, Simon is not sharing his Legos with

Owen. Dean drops the envelope back to the counter.

"You've got to be the bigger kid here," he snaps at Simon, more sharply than he might if Juliet were in the room. He slips the papers back into the envelope. "You know he's just a little guy," he adds, more softly. *She's selling her house?*

"But these are mine!" Simon contests, his face flushing fuchsia.

Dean looks to Holly for help but she is deep into a *Warriors* book, a pillow pressed over her lap.

"My stomach hurts." Juliet vomiting, now Holly? There might be a virus going around.

"Why can't O go get his own toys from his own house?" Simon yells.

What is he thinking, Dean wonders, imagining they could merge all this? Maybe they should all just go home. Everything would be simpler, familiar. He knows how to be a single dad, and though it won't be the same, not after this summer of partnership, of passion and comfortable chaos, at least it will be less complicated.

Fine, he thinks. Except the idea of never seeing Juliet again makes his throat throb like the time he mis-swallowed an apple quarter.

"Where have you been?" Simon yells as Juliet walks in. "I'm starving!" His back is still to Owen, forming a hulking, protective wall around his Lego creation.

"Sorry," she says blandly, "I'll get out some fruit."

"I already had fruit! I want dinner!"

"How was your run?" Dean asks, when he means to say, *why are you selling your house?* But then she will know he's been peeking at her private papers, the same way he obsessively reads her deleted emails.

The laptop pings, a new email. She makes no move to hide it from him. They read it together:

To:	**Juliet B. Wilde <jbwilde@gmail.com>**
From:	**Daily Inspirations**
Date:	**August 18, 2007**

Watch therefore, for you know neither the day nor the hour in which the Son of Man is coming
—**Matthew 25:13**

"Can't you unsubscribe from this?" he asks.

"You don't think I've tried?" Her hands shake, and her eyes slide from the computer to the envelope on the counter. "You should probably get going on your run," she tells him. "I don't think we have much time left."

It is impossible to run at sunset along an island beach, Dean thinks, and not feel nostalgic, noticing the bittersweet in the beauty. That the day is ending, that a storm threatens everything, that there are people who are no longer here to experience this, that Luc is poised between two mentors like young Luke Skywalker, mourning a girl who has lost her leg, that Holly and Owen have no mother, that everything here is coming to an end just when it feels like the beginning. Dean sucks the heavy, humid air into his chest.

Maybe the great tragedy would be letting this get away from us.

He grabs for this, the recent words of Juliet's that he clutches whenever Tuesday looms too large. Tonight, he will put into place the last part of his plan, his last-ditch effort at his version of a solution. Soon, he will be able to show, to tell, Juliet everything.

It is dusk when he jogs home and finds Luc waiting on the sand road outside White Beaches.

"Hey," Dean calls. "I've got a quick errand to run with Juliet, but you want to come by, have some dinner? I'm making clean-out-the-fridge-for-the-hurricane-hash."

"Tony needs me to help him with the hurricane shutters at the hotel."

"Okay, come by after?"

"Dad," Luc gulps, looks away. "I have to tell you something. It's important. About Juliet."

"What about her?" Sweat drips off Dean's slack hands, hanging down by his sides. He squares his shoulders. He feels every pound on his frame, lighter by twenty than back in June, but he is paralyzed. His feet find roots in the sand.

"And Tony. And that night. Things happened."

Dean stares at Luc's face, the beautiful, bronzed angles of the boy who looks so much like his dead mother. Luc tilts his head so his bangs fall low, obscuring his eyes. He continues, the dam broken, words coming rapid fire.

"Before you got here, Juliet was drunk—I saw her and Tony on the dance floor, and behind the compressor shack, kissing. She was out of her mind, letting her kid run out in the road in the middle of the night. That night, Dusty nearly ran Sonny over."

"I thought you didn't remember that night."

"You don't believe me, fine, but I was the one looking out for her, who had to tell Tony that it would be wrong on his part."

"Are you finished?" The sweat on Dean's body has dried and chilled.

Luc juts out Amélie's stubborn French peasant jaw. "Juliet might not be what you think she is."

"You don't say things like that," Dean hisses, swallowing his fury, "about the woman I love."

"Okay," Luc turns to go. "But after I told Tony off, later, when he was halfway down the road chasing after Juliet's kid, I see another guy at her cottage, wrapped in a blanket."

Sonny's ghost. Why Simon knew Luc wasn't the driver.

"And for the record, the reason I wasn't drunk that night? I'd decided I was finally going to kiss Bridget, and I wanted to remember every single second of it."

"Where is he?" Dean bursts into the bar and finds only Leo, boxing up the glasses in the dimly lit, empty bar. The twang of Willie Nelson's guitars fills the air.

"Whoa, Hurricane Dean arrives early," Leo tries to laugh. "Hey, Doc called here earlier, looking for you. Said he was waiting for you, something out at his house?"

"Where is Tony?" Dean's teeth are gritted, the nerves in his jaw throb.

"He's gone to Cox, for more lumber."

"Is it true? Did the whole goddamn island lose their mind that night in June?"

And it's obvious that like every good bartender, Leo knows more than he says. He just shakes his head, one sad smile.

"Dean!" It is Doc and his wife, coming into the bar in traveling clothes. "Geraldine and I are off to the airport, see if we can get on one of the flights out. Sorry you never got out to Northside this evening. I'd show you the gardens first; they'd sell her on the place immediately."

"A lot of things…" Dean starts and stops. "A lot has changed since we first talked about this."

Luckily, Doc assumes he means the coming of the hurricane.

Doc's wife, the one who wants to go back to England to live closer to her sister, is wearing a rose print-dress. Her eyes drift to the Weather Channel on the TV over Leo's head at the bar.

"After Ivan," she says in her thick Scottish accent, "it took seventy-one days to get power back on out our way. We were the last district to be served. You can't imagine the coconut rats. Flushed out of the bush. Bigger than a cat. Our dogs, Sugar and Wilton, killing three or four of 'em a night under the house. We'd hear a growl," Doc's wife chuckles, staring at the TV, "and then the most terrible SNAP! of their necks! We left the carcasses out, bait—they'll eat one another, you know."

"Mmhmm," Dean says. Doc had never mentioned dogs—does he plan to take those with him?

"Probably best you didn't bring her by, with it all boarded up. House isn't that big, but right on the ocean. The million-dollar view, that's something." Doc is tugging on his wife's arm. "We've got a plane to catch."

"United States newspapers got it wrong." She is still talking as Doc moves her to the bar doorway. "Reported hundreds dead, floating in the streets of Bodden Town. And they were, but they weren't the recently dead." Doc's wife cackles and the whites of her eyes glow blue in the light of the TV. "It was the graves. Ivan washed all the corpses into the streets. A storm so powerful," she widens her eyes at Dean, the loose skin under her jaw wobbling, "it raised the dead."

When Dean runs back across the street to Juliet's, the hairs on his arms are still standing straight up.

CHAPTER 46

DEAN

"I was starting to worry." Juliet smiles when he comes in through the screen door, stepping around the children piled on the mattresses watching the opening credits of *Babe*. "I saved you a plate, in the fridge." She startles at the noise when he slams the cottage's front door. "What's wrong?"

What Luc said, about Juliet and Tony—it happened before, before they even met. Does that negate everything he and Juliet made, their garden and their memories, this summer? Two and a half months ago is ancient history—dinosaurs and cavemen—prehistoric, in the story of Juliet and Dean. He thinks of the other man, Sonny's ghost. He has to ask.

"Is there something you wanted to tell me, Juliet?" He hits on every syllable and consonant of her name. His voice doesn't sound like anybody he knows.

"Here." She hands him a glass of water, breaks out ice cubes from the tray to add to it, but he notices her hand is shaking when he takes it from her. She turns her back to him in the close kitchen and opens the freezer to return the ice cube tray.

"Okay, yes," she says softly. "I think I might be pregnant."

Breath rushes out of his lungs, like he has been kicked in the chest. She keeps her back to him. His eyes blur, a pounding pulse in his ears. Everything he envisioned is falling apart.

Juliet might not be everything you think she is.

He turns to the living room, grabbing for his laptop, eyes sweeping around the room for anything else he can't leave behind. "Owen, Holl, let's go! No movie! We're leaving! We're going home!"

Outside, the wind is whistling, an eerie singsong. By tomorrow night, this could all be underwater. The birds are silent; there is only the occasional high-pitched screech of the rats scuttling in the sea grapes. In the parking lot, Darvin is knocking coconuts out of the tree with a long pole and stuffing them in garbage bags so they won't become projectiles in the coming wind.

"I want da moooooovie!" Owen's screams reverberate up off the water.

"But I don't feel good," Holly whines. "What do you mean, we're going home? Like, Michigan-home?"

"Home?" Owen stops, mid-wail, his eyes twin Cheerios of surprise.

"Dean!" Leo is jogging toward them, lit by the only streetlight in the White Beaches parking lot, where Tony parked when they arrived, where Dean first saw Juliet and her children cross in her broad-brimmed hat, where the police cars conducted their interviews, where Dean and Juliet and the littles crossed more than a hundred times over the course of the summer on their Camp Sunshine schedule.

"I'm glad I found you," Leo huffs from running across the street, wiping his wire glasses on the hem of his hibiscus print shirt. "Luc left with Doc and Geraldine, and a backpack full of stuff. He took his passport."

Dean gets the key to the Brave Little Toaster and drives, Owen and Holly quiet in the back. The road back is a narrow, twisted finger. On the right side of him there is nothing but the dark gnarl of sea grape, the hulking casuarinas. On the left, the van's dim headlights illuminate the shallow, reef-protected beach spotted with driftwood dried in the shapes of tortured arboreal skeletons. The anger inside him has melted to a leaded heaviness so severe that just lifting his left leg to press the clutch feels like an enormous effort. There are few cars out on the roads and everywhere, the boarding up of stores and homes.

Dean's mind can't stop turning over tonight's revelations, washing over them like wave grit on sea glass—*Juliet, Tony, Sonny's ghost, a baby.*

At the airport exit, he downshifts and glides to a stop. Everything is dark, the parking lots empty, the interior black. Only yellow emergency lights flicker outside the glass terminal doors. Two local teenage boys are using a power drill to cover the gift shop windows in heavy sheets of plywood, spray-painted with the words:

CLOSED FOR DEAN

"Mon, what a gwan?" They laugh to each other, and at Dean. "What you doin' out dis night? You no know they cancel the flights, no planes fly no more? You no know Ivan's big brother comin?"

Why is he immune to the contagious, breathless panic that is spreading throughout the island as the barometer drops? But in its place there is nothing—a blindsided numbness. Juliet, Tony, Sonny's ghost, a baby. And now, Luc gone—everything's crumbling.

In the dark, he stumbles to engage the clutch and that's when he sees Luc, wearing jeans and Adidas—real, traveling American clothes, hunched on the curb at Departures, his backpack stuffed and wrapped over both shoulders. Once, Amélie forgot to pick up nine-year-old Luc from soccer practice. When they interrupted Dean at a departmental meeting at the university, he was thrilled to have a reason to leave. He found Luc on the edge of an empty green field, tapping a soccer ball apathetically between his arches, with the same affectedly-disinterested, lost expression.

"Hey, need a ride, kid?" Dean says out the window.

Without a word, Luc gets in the passenger seat, stuffing his pack at his feet. He slouches, putting his size ten sneakers up on the dashboard.

Already, he feels lighter—all three of his children in one place, even if it is a dented rental van traveling on a deserted island road with the mother of all hurricanes coming.

"Where were you going to go?" He thinks of home, the house in Saline, Luc's bedroom the exact same mess he left it in nine months earlier, a signed David Beckham jersey and zombie movie posters on the walls.

"Honestly?"

Dean downshifts to turn left, away from the hospital, to drive the bypass.

"Yes, honestly. Where?"

"Auckland. Bridge called."

"Is that right?" He can't keep the smile off his face. "How's she doing?"

"You mean her leg? She says it's funny. All people want to talk about now is her leg, but she thinks it's, like, the least interesting thing about her."

"I suppose it's just the most different. It's human nature to focus on the differences."

"I guess. She's getting fitted for a cheetah."

"A cheetah?"

"A prosthetic for running."

"Really?"

"Yeah," Luc chuckles. "When she lived here, Dad, she was the, like, the laziest. Always faking girl problems so she could sleep in or get out of the last trip of the day. Making me carry her tanks to the Pure Air cart. She loved her fish and chips and beer, loved to have what she called a 'proper lie in' on her day off. Now, this happens, and she wants to start running?" Luc looks out the window. "Thought I might go there. Help her out, with her training and stuff. But they grounded the planes."

At the corner, under the streetlight, there is a man opening a pipe gate on three emaciated horses, slapping them on the rumps and chasing them out into the street. Yesterday, Darvin explained that this is the best anyone can do for their animals in a hurricane, turn them loose and let them find their own shelter, hope to recover them after.

They drive back to Rum Point, Owen and Holly asleep in the rearview, her cheek pressed against the side of his car seat. Dean turns up the radio for the weather.

"Dean is a dangerous force to be reckoned with," the newscaster intones. "Winds up to 165 miles are being recorded and it is expected to grow in size and intensity throughout the course of the night. While there is still hope that it could turn, Dean is currently predicted to make landfall in the Cayman Islands either early Sunday morning or afternoon with catastrophic consequences. There is a small craft warning in effect from nine am tomorrow. All residents are advised to make disaster hurricane preparations."

Luc turns to him. "The other night, when the power was out, I wasn't mad that you showed up. I was kind of relieved, looking for a way out, with that chick. I always am, afterward."

"With the right girl," Dean says, "you don't want to disappear after. You want to tuck her to your chest and breathe in her hair and..." *so* much more.

"Is that how you knew Mom was the one?"

He thinks of Africa, of the first time with Amélie, the spice of her mouth, and the feel of cradling her skull as he knit his fingers in her curly hair. "Your mom was the first time I felt that way."

Luc nods. "With Bridge, I don't know. We never got to that part. She's just who I always wanted to talk to. I told her everything. She knew I was looking for Robert, that Juliet was helping me. She said it might help me find closure, to understand why he didn't want me, or whatever. I told her, on the phone, the other night, about Tony being my biological father."

"What did she say?"

"I believe her exact words were, 'that wanker!'" Luc laughs. "She said thank god the apple fell far from that tree, that it rolled all the way down the hill."

They pull into the parking lot at the cottages.

"What about her?" Luc jerks his head up to Juliet's window, where her bedroom light is the only one on, a glow of invitation. It feels like a shard of metal under Dean's sternum when he thinks of the nights on the other side of that window at the top of Juliet's stairs, the sliver of light where the door didn't quite meet the floor mingling with the monitor's red glow to illuminate Juliet in bed with him. Afterward, toward morning, the golden sun as the door yawned open to reveal their bed-headed children stumbling sleepily in, Sonny or Owen. He remembers Juliet lifting the blankets to welcome them into the fold. "Is it like that with her?"

"Yes," Dean says simply. *It was.*

They make no move to get out.

"I'm sorry, okay, Dad?" Like his mother, who would throw dramatic fits and then follow Dean around the house and wheedle forgiveness out of him, Luc can't let it go. "I don't want to see you like this again. Tony's right."

"Tony?" Dean bristles, incredulous. "After all this, you're still taking his words as wisdom?"

"Not at all. But he's right, about before, that Mom didn't appreciate you enough," Luc mumbles.

"What?" Dean leans forward.

"Mom took you for granted," Luc repeats, adding, "Now you're back like you were. You're making the Face." Luc swipes at his nose with his knuckles.

"Luc's right: You're making the Face," Holly chimes in. Dean wonders how long she has been awake.

"I want things to be better, Dad. For you. And if that means with Juliet," he jerks his head up to Juliet's window, "then I want that for you, too. The whole buffet—Golden Corral, Cracker Barrel, soup and salad, crab legs and cheesecake."

Dean lets his chin fall to his chest; his head feels too heavy to even nod. He doesn't know what to think now.

CHAPTER 47

Juliet

You sit at the foot of the children's bed, cupping one of your daughter's bare heels in your palm. Before, you used to touch them all the time, used to pull them to your lap as they passed, ruffle their hair as they ate their oatmeal, kiss the napes of their necks when they were bent over sticker books or the strawberry plants in your courtyard pots. But after Jack died, physical gestures felt impossible. Just when they needed you most, you imploded, spent whole rain-filled days in Jack's thick wool ski sweaters, your shoulders hunched, arms wrapped around your waist like a hunger victim, paralyzed.

It is only since coming here, to the island, that touch feels like less of a conscious effort. It is because of Dean, you know, the example of the generosity of his body, the way that he gives endlessly, genuinely, of himself.

Dean makes love look easy.

Now, he is gone. You heard his children's wails, heard the van start, and then Hazel came by with the hurricane shutter keys.

Hazel pressed the hard metal into your palm. "You'll want to wait to close the shutters until it's imminent—it gets stifling with them shut, when the power goes out. Remember, you won't have the fans even."

"Okay." You nodded like a green cadet, receiving instructions for the battle.

"It looks like Dean and the kids are making a go of it?"

"What?" You startled.

"I was by his place a moment ago. All dark. Last I heard, the line at Cayman Airways counter was all the way down the street, but they were shutting down soon. With the wee ones, he might've got a flight?"

He left you and your children to face the storm alone? You placed a hand just below your bellybutton, stunned.

"Smart one, that," she'd said. "After Ivan, they found my dining set a hundred yards down the road, tangled up in the tennis net at Cocoplum, and back in my condo, at Mariners, anything that wasn't matchsticks and rubbish was gone. Looted."

Alone, but not, you think, looking down at Simon and Sonnet. You are the lone captain of this ship; Dean's maybe-baby is the whisper of a surprise stowaway. You kiss your sleeping son's forehead, tinged with salt, lift your daughter's thick hair off her neck. You close their bedroom windows against the barometric pressure.

In your bedroom, you turn on the rattling air conditioner, its noise a strange, familiar comfort. You can do this, you think, digging deep for the reserves. You undress to nothing but underwear, and slide between the sheets. Just when you wonder if you should lock the screen porch door, you hear the unmistakable *shh* of it sliding open.

You roll to your side, away from the bedroom door. Let the Professor be greeted with your bare back in the glow of the baby monitor, the clear body language of hurt. A trained psychologist should have no trouble figuring that one out.

Only when the bedroom door opens, you wait, feeling his eyes on the vulnerable space between your bare shoulder blades, long seconds measured by the slow, insistent dripping of water into the full bathtub.

You roll over. A familiar silhouette is framed by light leaking from the hallway. He crosses the room and cups a hand tightly over your mouth to muffle your scream.

CHAPTER 48

DEAN

"I'm bleeding."

Dean looks up from the laptop in his cottage, where he is reading the newest email to Juliet, before she has even opened it. What does it matter now?

To: **Juliet B. Wilde <jbwilde@gmail.com>**
From: **Lear Burke <ljb@hotmail.com>**
Date: **August 18, 2007**
Subject: **HURRICANE DEAN**

J—

Jenna and I are watching the weather channel. Please tell me you got on one of the flights today? Nothing is worth risking lives over. We'll figure everything out when you get on US soil. There are always options. We'll get the very best lawyer. Come home; Dean looks deadly.

-L

"You're what?"

"I'm bleeding."

It is his daughter, the one he held first, second only to Amélie's obstetrician. Standing in his doorway, half of Holly's lanky body is lit by the glow of the lamp of his nightstand. Beside him in the bed, Owen is asleep under the fan.

"Where, sweetheart?" he asks, imagining stubbed toes or scraped knees, remembering how carefully he dusted the asphalt cinders from her skinned elbows when she learned to ride a two-wheeler.

And then he realizes what she means.

Dean sits up in bed.

"Can you take me to Juliet's, please?"

He hates that he needs her help with this, but why shouldn't Holly want a woman now? When they go back to Michigan, these are the things he will need to be able to handle on his own, single father. But not tonight. Not for the first time.

So he pulls shorts on over his boxers, a T-shirt over his head. Eleven-thirty, she's probably asleep. He could let himself in. He knows where the supplies and Tylenol are in her downstairs bathroom. He knows she leaves the light on at the top of the stairs for the kids.

If Juliet is awake, or if he is caught with the box of supplies in his hands, he imagines making a joke of it, saying to her, "Isn't the irony a little thick here?"

He already misses laughing with her the most.

CHAPTER 49

Juliet

You don't struggle; he will take his hand from your mouth. You don't think that he could ever mean any of you harm.

He is here—that you are not as surprised as you should be registers somewhere, because you knew. After sixteen years, there is something tenable that hums between you that has never been severed, despite the things you buried.

Your eyes skitter over the familiar parts of his face while you wait, breathing the scents of gasoline and rubbing alcohol on the skin of his hands, still smothering your silent scream. There are old cuts, scabbed over on his jaw, and a new one that should have had stitches along his brow bone. He has the smudge of a bruise under his eye socket. Though he had always been fit, never missed a six am workout, he is now the harrowing skinny of hunger.

"You look terrible!" you tell him when he takes his hand from your mouth, his white teeth glowing in the light of the hall landing you leave on for your children.

You sit up, pulling the sheet to your chest, as though modesty matters with him. You would know his smell anywhere, blindfolded and spun around three times, you would be able to find him. There is a spiciness to his sweat, the unmistakable hint of garlic—as though generations of little boys doted on at a Nonna's knee, dipping fresh bread into the *aglio e olio*, has been laced into his very DNA.

"I knew it!" you hiss. "I knew you couldn't be dead! They all said I needed to get over it, but I couldn't believe..." you trail off.

"I came back for you!"

When Jack sits down on the bed, his slight weight barely shifts the mattress at all. How small and vulnerable he seems. Like Simon. Part of you wants to open your white sheet like wings and engulf him, protect him. Hide him.

"I couldn't let you down again, Jules. I knew we were going to lose everything, the farmhouse, everything, and your family…."

"Jack," you marvel, adding, "I knew it. Not consciously, but—"

A flash of your dream comes then: Jack standing on the Belmar bridge, watching, while below you gulp salty, icy ocean water, him smiling from above while you drown.

"God, it's so good to see you, to be close to you again. Hi, Jules," he says, his eyes darting to the doorway and you think, is he going to kiss you now?

You move back, the slightest of inches, wondering why that feels so wrong?

"How did you find us?"

"Please," Jack scoffs. "I found you here the first week you arrived. I kissed you, in your sleep."

"What? When?" You grip the sheet tighter.

"Your credit card, our credit card—it's all so easy! You call the automated line, get a list of the recent charges. I was in the area anyway. Working. Moving items, shall we say, from one location to another."

"Wait, you were here? In the cottage? In June?"

"June first. Six months since I had seen you! You looked so good to me." Jack's eyes sparkle in the light from the hallway. "But I knew I couldn't tell you yet. So, I kissed you while you slept."

You realize then, that Jack did more than kiss you that night in June.

"That was going to be my first quote, the next day, but I didn't want to be too obvious. 'The only thing worth stealing,'" Jack quotes, "'are kisses from sleeping children.' And beautiful naked wives," he adds.

Sticking out of his pocket is your old copy of Bartlett's *Familiar Quotations*; you recognize a tea stain and your dog-earring from college term papers.

"You're the Daily Inspirations," you say, but, of course, you knew that too.

Jack. Here. Eyes twinkling, bright—too bright—in your bed. All those years, months of wishing for the chance for things to get better, a second chance with your children's father. Possibly the father of all of them. And here he is.

His mouth stretches wide over his white teeth. You reach up to trace the raised scar, ugly and unstitched, along his brow bone, stopping before you run your fingers along the black bristles of his jaw.

"You grew a beard," you say. It's the most obvious, most superficial, of the differences.

"Not exactly by choice, but I think it works." He cocks his head to one side, mugs for you.

It's still Jack, you think.

"I wanted to tell you that it was never meant to go down this way. Marty disappearing with the money, sonofabitch, leaving you holding the bag, him gone with the wind. Motherfucker! Don't worry, I made him pay. And I never would have left if I'd known somehow it would all come down on you, Jules. But if I'd stayed, we'd have been years in court against him, drowning in legal fees."

"Odd choice of words," you say, thinking of his death, of your dream, gasping breathlessness, and shaking in this very bed with Dean's arms wrapped around you, whispering '*Shh*, it was only a dream.'

"I had to do what I had to do, to get our money."

"What are you saying, Jack?"

"All the investor money. I took back from Marty what was rightfully ours! He'd drained everything from Compass, stealing from us, everything we built, Jules... I trusted him!" Jack sounds exactly like a wronged Simon, fighting righteous tears. "Now it's ours again. There's a house, a giant hacienda, in Cayos Cochinos, practically a private island, overlooking the ocean. It's perfect. Nobody will ever find us."

"What, where?"

"Near Roatan, off the coast of Honduras. I have a boat tied up in the mangroves. With the Compass money, and the insurance money, we'll be set for life. Remember, before, how well we traveled? I've still got our old kayak. Remember when we lived in Tahoe, how we loved to go paddling? Remember that time at Emerald Bay?"

You know what he is talking about: beaching your boat and peeling your neoprene kayak skirts and then your clothes off in the cove, but leaving shoes on against the shells and stones. How Jack pressed you against the trunk of a cedar tree, its bark leaving deep imprints on your bare back when he entered you.

"Remember, before," he nods his head toward the bedroom across the hall where the children are sleeping. "Before Si, how well we traveled together?"

What you remember is that you had agreed on twenty standard moving boxes, what fit along with your queen-sized mattress into the minimum size U-Haul, so that anything acquired in a new city meant you shed something else. Books were easy to leave on a practical level; their weight made them a first tier cut. But you have always regretted abandoning your college volumes of Whitman and Emerson in Park City.

"I've got two passports—" Jack grins.

"Two?" you interrupt. Were you really considering this?

"Four passports, fine, I'll get four. Maybe too much time, maybe just another challenge." He cocks his head, then beams. "Okay, fine, four."

Five.

"Sure, why not? More complicated. I guess we could take the kids!" Jack twitches, grimacing anxiously.

"You're putting me in a complicated position," you say. He is the father of your children.

"Not really." Jack smiles—his smile as winning as ever. You think of him calling from his marketing jobs all those years. "Hi, this is Jack Wilde, and I'm calling from the base of the slopes of Eagle Mountain where we have thirty-six inches of fresh powder and we're developing a luxury, partial ownership opportunity that I just know you'll want to hear more about…"

"We'll go, tonight." Now, you're sure, from the way he's leaning in, that he's going to kiss you. "We can do it, Jules, but we have to go tonight. We'll get out of here before Dean can catch us."

You think of Dean, who stands beside you in the kitchen, hand outstretched for the next dripping plate, loading the dishwasher, both of you easily, gratefully dancing the partnered rhythm of daily life.

Dean, who cups your jaw in the palms of his hands when he kisses you, like your very face is precious to him.

Dean, who left you, who jerked his own children away from you tonight as though you are dangerous, as though you are Tony's train wreck.

Dean, who was clear he does not want more children, but whose newly formed life might be unfurling and swimming in your maternal sea.

Or is it Jack's?

"You know about Dean?" you ask. How long has he been lurking in the tangled bushes outside, slipping in and kissing you in your sleep?

"Yeah, it's going to be great fun."

"Fun?"

"I hear he'll be a Cat Five by tomorrow. We're going to outrun him—adventure of a lifetime. Timed it just right. His wake is going to cover our tracks."

This is Jack, Simon and Sonny's father. A house on a private island, where nobody would ever find you. You think of the necklace, above the microwave, take a quick mother's inventory of three sets of clothes, shoes, the contents of the medicine cabinet, the hurricane supplies of food.

Downstairs, the sliding door opens. Jack jumps up, backing into the shadows.

"Juliet?" Holly's voice drifts up the stairs. "Are you home?"

CHAPTER 50

Dean

It could be any night, the solar lights glowing along the path to Juliet's, moths circling them, lizards skittering up the cottage walls, land crabs rustling in the leaves. It could be them coming together for dinner, or movie night, or Dean sneaking over with the monitors set, but it's not. Tonight, it is cooler, the tree frogs are silent and there is a steady wind, the palm fronds rattling overhead. Dean keeps a hand on Holly's shoulder. He stops.

"Are you sure you don't want to just go back and have some tea?"

"I have my period, Dad, not the flu."

"Right. Okay." Dean pushes through the tangle of potted plants Juliet must have moved to the safety of the screened porch. It smells loamy and earthy, like the inside of a greenhouse. Dean is careful not to break the tomato's fragile stems.

He files this away, plans what they might talk about, if they end up alone, the vegetables, the hurricane supplies lined up in her front hall. He'll say what Darvin told him, about how you'll likely lose some of the vegetable plants in the raised beds to salt burn, but this is where it gets complicated. In his head, Dean is tripping over the right pronouns—is there a *we* anymore?

"Juliet?" Holly calls up the stairs. "Are you home?"

Juliet comes down the staircase wrapped in nothing but the sheet from her bed—a goddess in a Roman toga. Her head turns, glancing up to the top of the stairs where her children are sleeping. Dean notices her hands clutching the sheet closed, her knuckles smooth, showing the pale flesh that is usually hidden in the creases of summer brown.

"You're still here?" Her voice is a ragged whisper. The curve of her bare neck is achingly vulnerable in the lone light from the top of the stairs, the shadows falling on the folds of her sheet like an ancient statue. Dean's palms itch, aching to touch her. The ambivalence, the weighted exhaustion of earlier is gone, and every sense is razor-sharp, buzzing with the anxiety of the unknown, hissing like the palm fronds outside.

"Holly needed--" he clears his throat, starts again. "Holly needs you. She needs some supplies, from the bathroom."

"Oh, honey, okay." Juliet nods in understanding, reaches past Dean to draw Holly to her own side. "Come with me."

"Thank you. In the future, I've got to be able to handle this sort of thing, but—" Holly leaning into Juliet, the way her hand cups his daughter's shoulder like a protective epaulet, stops the words in his throat. Never mind what he wanted for himself; he'd wanted this, so badly, for them.

CHAPTER 51

JULIET

You come out of the downstairs bathroom, closing the door behind you.

You whisper fiercely, "I thought you left us!"

"Left you?"

"Hazel came by, with the keys for our hurricane shutters. She said you were gone, your place locked up, the van…. I thought, after what I said, you left us." You look down at your bare feet.

"I went to the airport, to get Luc. He tried to get on a flight, to see Bridget, but the planes are grounded." Dean shakes his head. "It's a little unclear to me why we're all still here, why we didn't just use credit cards and fly back today, but, no, I would never leave you and the kids to face this alone."

Of course he wouldn't. This is Dean.

"I guess we'll see what's left of any of this, after the storm," you say. "I don't think we have any idea what's about to hit."

"What about, what you said before?" The way his eyes travel your body, you know he is talking about the baby.

"What does it matter?" You take one step back, toward the stairs. "You told me you never wanted more children!"

"Have you met me?" Dean wails, loud enough to wake the kids. Loud enough for Jack to hear. "Have you not seen me upend my entire life for someone who is technically another man's son?" Dean rakes his hands through his hair. Now his voice is dangerously quiet. "Do you want to know, what it was, that made me think I was in love with you?"

You swipe at a tear running down your cheek, because he is speaking in the past tense, just when you most want it to be the present.

"I have to tell you, if it was the money, I'm not who you think I am. I'm not the Wealthy Widow—"

"I don't care about money!" he explodes, then drops his voice again. "If you must know, it was your hands."

"My hands?" You clutch at the sheet.

"Your beautiful, strong, capable hands. The way they seemed to take care of everyone, of your kids, my kids, of the gardens, of me. They made me believe, in something, I'd never had the luxury of having before."

"But you don't believe," you swallow, "that you could have it anymore?"

I choose you! I am, I want to be the woman you see in me! I want the Brady Bunch house and the messy blending of our families and doing dishes, together, late into the night—

But you can't say any of this, not with Jack upstairs.

"I don't know what to believe, Juliet." And when you don't answer, Dean continues, "Luc told me, tonight, he saw another man in your cottage, the night of the accident."

You feel your face go as white as the sheet, more conscious than ever of your nakedness beneath it, of your dead husband listening, waiting, at the top of the stairs.

"I-I don't know what he saw. Probably Sonny's ghost."

"No!" Dean shakes his head, quietly furious. "No more lies, no more hiding behind childish stories."

"That's all I can say," you sob. "I don't want you to be involved in this, in my life, any more than you already accidentally are." You feel him take this like a blow. "Dean," you swallow, "you should go."

The bathroom door opens—Holly.

"All good, sweetheart?" Dean looks up, his eyes red, his expression a closed door.

"Can I stay here, tonight, in Sonny's bed?"

"Not tonight," you and Dean say in unison.

"Your dad needs to take you home, because of the storm."

Dean looks affectedly past you, pretending to be intent on the Weather Channel. It has been on for two days straight, volume low. It is now flashing early images of Dean's destruction, flattened banana crops in Saint Lucia.

"Jamaica prepares for total devastation—low lying areas have been evacuated, and curfews are in place to prevent looting," the plum-lipped newscaster reports.

"It's so weird. It doesn't seem that bad outside," Holly says. "It's hard to believe a hurricane is coming."

When you open the sliding door, the wind has gone curiously quiet and still.

"The calm before the storm," Dean says, and he leaves, just like you told him to.

When they are gone, you run back up the stairs, trying not to trip on the hem of the sheet. At first you think, hope, Jack has left, or maybe he was never there at all? But then you find him, in the shadows of the landing outside the children's bedroom.

"They sleep in their own beds now?" Jack's expression is incredulous. There's an alarming heat coming off him, as though he has sucked up the day's sun like an ancient baking stone, a smoldering fever. You shift away, slightly.

"Shh." You put a finger to your lips, lay your hand over his burning forearm to stop him from opening their door. Under his skin, you feel a sickly vibrating, like the back rattle of Simon's lungs when he had viral pneumonia, the body's alarm system: something is wrong.

"God, I wanted to blow my fucking brains out, Jules, and I would have, before I let you down again—" Jack breaks off. "How'd you get them to stop sleeping in our bed?"

You cannot tell him that it is because of Dean and Holly and Owen, that their summer of sleepovers downstairs, the comforting space Dean took up in your bed, made the transition easy.

"A lot has changed," you begin.

"But I couldn't do it. Couldn't kill myself and leave you with nothing, not when I'd pumped all those premiums into our insurance. That's another shit ton of cash coming our way. I had to be careful, plan ahead. First, I got our old kayak. Then I had to get supplies. I bought everything with cash—the wetsuit, my backpack and kit, the bottles of water, the rubbing alcohol, those little hand warmers we used to slip inside our gloves when we were skiing, remember? And the guidebook," he slips it out of his pocket, a mold-speckled, paperback edition of *How To Vanish*—it's swollen like bath toys, dehydrated sponges that puff up in the shapes of ocean animals in the tub.

"I called that stealing sonofabitch at the office and told him I was out in the field, but I didn't say where, because I knew I needed plenty of time before they found my car, knew that my boat wouldn't be leaving until four for five in the morning."

"Jack," you say, but he keeps going. *He can't wake them*, you think.

"It took me all day to get it set up—new hair-do, cut it short-short-short, so I leave less follicles around, less of a trace, in case anyone starts looking for me, but of course, nobody is! Amazing! But you can't get cocky, that's the number one mistake. Do you like it?" He touches his shorn hair, doesn't pause for an answer. "And then you'll love this one, Jules: I ate three double quarter pounders with cheese at McDonalds. When have you ever seen me eat at McDonalds? Never! But I knew I needed high calorie/high fat while I could. Then I tied the kayak up under the bridge out in Belmar, and swam back, in the dark, fucking freezing. And then I got in the car with the heater on high and warmed up—Jesus, the Atlantic is a cold-hearted bitch in winter—and I was thinking how I'd be like this forever, alone. Cold. Ha! But you go south, you don't get cold."

He looks like he's going to move again. His head jerks, eyes tracking down the stairs, where Dean and Holly have gone.

"I drove around, working up my nerve. And then I called you, and I wanted to tell you everything, in case it didn't work, in case I didn't make it, tell you how sorry I was, but I couldn't say any of that, in case it *did* work. And then of course, there's the kids, I wanted to…"

Suddenly, Jack springs forward. When he moves, his left leg lingers and hitches slightly behind, like Sonny trying to keep up with her big brother. You hadn't noticed it in your bedroom, but in the stairwell light, the open wounds on Jack's face look worse, and there is still the heat, the stomach-souring electric energy humming under his skin.

"Jack, don't." You put yourself between him and the children's bedroom door.

"I knew I got one shot at death, now or never, but then we were fighting, about the fucking chickens, and I knew I couldn't tell you the truth, so I just stepped on it. Figured if I died, I'd be dead, but if I didn't, you'd be okay. You and the kids would get the money and the house and I'd be free. Scariest, craziest fucking stunt of my life—I wasn't expecting the ice, that was a wrinkle, but I made it. Broke my goddamn leg, but I made it. I made it, babe."

Fast, he reaches around you, and cracks open their door. The landing light falls on them, sleeping like brittle stars flung from the sky on top of their sheets. They are both in Simon's twin bed, limbs tangled, Sonnet's mouth gaping like a goldfish.

You remember Simon's hand, the week after the funeral, swollen and swirling purple and blue, from slamming it so hard in his closet doors that they bounced free from their hinges, how back home the doors are still hanging loose, how you explained to the doctor at the ER that he did this because his father had just died, and Simon had not been able to cry.

"I just wanted to cry," he had whimpered, a leaky Ziploc bag of ice over his ballooning hand, his face tilted against the side window of your car as you drove on sleet-slick streets home from the hospital.

You think of Sonny's big brown eyes, and you remember how the two of them took in the funeral from the rosy protection of her Hello Kitty umbrella, a splash of red in a sea of black overcoats and dismal drizzle.

"I dream about him." Jack does his best to whisper, though he's never been very good at it. The shaft of light from the hallway casts his shadow across their sheets, putting Jack's black, looming shape in bed next to Simon. "All the time. I dream of slitting his fucking throat, and then making him beg while the blood bubbles and runs and pools—"

"What?" You startle, until you realize he's not talking about Simon.

"Last I heard, he's in Dubai, son-of-a-bitch, living like a sultan," Jack says, too loud. Standing in front of your beautiful children, Jack talking about Marty, work, money. Some things never change. "I'll find him. Ruin him. With pain."

"Shh!" If Simon wakes, this will all be over. With Sonnet, you are already planning how you will explain it away as a dream. You wonder suddenly if it isn't, your fingers drifting up to your own face. What was it Helen from book club said? If you can find your hands in your dream, it's the beginning of being able to control them? You'd like to take the wheel of this one.

"I've got a Zodiac at the dock. There's a boat leaving before dawn, from Morgan's Harbor," Jack says, more softly but no less urgent. "Cuba first, and then the Bay Islands, or Nicaragua will be a good place to come ashore. I'm making my way to him. He'll suffer. We'll get the money that's coming to us."

"But I thought…" *you already had the money?*

He pauses now, and his eyes slide around the house, searching.

"So…. I heard you, downstairs. Where's the other money, the insurance money, really?"

"What money?" you laugh. "There's nothing! Lear says Meridian's not going to pay out without a body. The credit cards are all maxed…"

"Nothing?" Jack's face falls, the overt disappointment of the little boy whose bucket, stick, string and carrot failed to capture a wild rabbit. You realize it is the only reason he came.

When you reach around him, for the handle of the children's door, you see the knife.

"I've had an epiphany," Jack whispers, waggling his eyebrows. He flashes the six-inch paring knife from the kitchen that you use to coax thready mango from its skin.

For the first time, you are a little afraid.

"I'll cut off my hand, toss it out to sea. Some degenerate can find it in Daytona. They'd pay out then, if someone found my hand, my real fingerprints. Maybe just a finger, a little one. What do you think?"

Simon shifts in his sleep, rolls toward Sonnet and drapes his arm across her ribcage.

Earlier today, Sonny asked Dean about their mama bird, the bananaquit they had watched all summer, which had laid three eggs smaller than the tip of Dean's thumb in the nest in the accordion of his hurricane shutters. "Dad-dean, who will take care of her, if the storm comes?"

Dean had assured your daughter that the bird and her babies would be safe.

You wonder how far away Dean is—is he lingering out in the night, listening for bird song, his head thrown back to drink in the stars like he sometimes does on the walk between your cottages?

"Or there's you," Jack says, and you know what he means—the million dollar policy he took out on you. He spins the knife in his hands.

Will Dean hear you scream his name with your windows closed?

You take half a step back, the hem of the sheet shh-ing against the floor.

"I'm joking," Jack says. "I want to wake them up." He lunges for their room.

"No!" you hiss.

"I've been watching them. All summer. Did they tell you? I followed them out to the Sound that day, with the boat. Jules, I came here to give you the chance, the choice. So our kids don't grow up without their father. Remember? You never wanted to raise damaged children. Here I am."

Two doors down, Dean is tucking Owen in the crook of his arm where you used to lie. He's angry—rightfully so. You should have told him, at the beginning—the secrets you kept from Dean piled up, like unpaid bills you are ticking through. Now, you want to scream out everything, you want him to shelter you from the storm. But you sent him home.

Jack takes a step toward you, his fingers close around your wrist, hard.

"You made that choice for both of us," you tell Jack, shaking your arm free. "Nine months ago."

"Okay," he says. "I deserve that, fair enough."

"Jack," and you can feel the weight fall out of the air between you, as though the humidity has been halved—the way the K catches in your throat.

"Is it him?"

"Who?"

"Downstairs, Mr. Neighborly-Neighbor? Is that why?"

Yes.

"No, Jack. It's you."

He lays a hand over his heart.

"Because it's a little hard to stomach, that I'm losing out to a guy like that."

"I'm pregnant," you say, and watch as he takes two more steps back, away, exactly like you knew he would. "Maybe yours, maybe his."

His eyes slide to the staircase. The knife spins in his hand.

"What are you going to do, Jules, go back home? ''America,'" he closes his eyes, like Simon being tested on a spelling word, "'America is a hurricane, and the only people who do not hear the sound are those fortunate if not incredibly stupid and smug White Protestants who live in the center, in the serene eye of the big wind.' It's Mailer," he smiles, opening his eyes and patting the pocket where the paperback bulges.

"I know," you tell him. "But you have to be dead to us, Jack," you say softly. "And this time you have to stay dead."

He laughs, bowing jauntily before he whispers, "'To die... will be an awfully big adventure.'"

You aren't expecting it when he grabs you, and this time, he covers your scream for real.

CHAPTER 52

Dean

Dean sits on his screened porch, listening, waiting for the wind to pick back up. He is worrying about the power of the coming storm, and the cruel nature of the universe, an exacting balance to everything: the gift of Owen meant the loss of Amélie, and in the face of a lost future with Juliet, cells might be dividing, a heart the size of a pinprick might be beating.

"Dad?" It's Luc, in the eerie emergency light from the pathway. He's been over at the resort with Leo and Darvin and Tony, putting up sheets of plywood on the staff apartments down the beach. Luc yanks open the screen door and catches his breath.

"Tony said to tell you, there's a private plane out at the airport! The tower's closed, nobody's technically allowed to fly, but he knows a pilot! He says if we want to go, meet him there in forty-five minutes. But we have to go, right now. This is our only chance to get out. We have to trust him. If Tony's leaving, Dad, this is going to be bad."

Dean stands up. "What do we need?"

"He said come to the gate by the runway, just passports, no bags. He told me to bring this," Luc holds up large, green handled wire cutters. "To get in the gate, by the runway, but we have to go now."

Dean glances toward Juliet's cottage but Luc shakes his head.

"It's a Cessna, six seats: pilot, Tony, you, me, Holly and O."

Could he leave her? Dean wonders.

"If you're worried about Juliet, she's already going."

"What?"

"I already saw her, out at the dock."

"When?"

"A few minutes ago. With some guy. Headed for a boat, tied up. She's leaving too."

"Where were the kids?"

"What kids?"

"Her kids! Simon and Sonny!"

"I don't know, I didn't see them—just Juliet, wearing a long white dress," Luc winces, "holding hands with some guy."

"Stay here! With Holly and O!" And Dean runs for her cottage, to make sure her kids are safe.

CHAPTER 53

Juliet

Though you and Jack are the exact same height, he has always been stronger. He pulls you down the dock, your wrist clamped in his hand, half-dragging you. The dock is old and weathered—all summer, you had to remind the kids to wear water shoes when they run it, because of splinters. Now, they enter your feet like tiny knives. If Jack hadn't duct-taped your mouth back in the utility room at the cottage, you would scream.

At the end of the dock, he throws you in the bottom of a boat and leaps in after you. You breathe hard through your nostrils, a panicky tightness in your chest with your mouth taped closed. Fast, Jack's knee is jammed in your midsection, pinning you down while he goes to work with the rope.

"Hate to have to do this," he says, wrenching your arm, and tying your wrist to one of the inflatable boat's ropes. His breath is rushed, fetid, souring the air between you. The knife, which he uses to sever the extra rope, is tossed to the bottom of the raft. He hums to himself while he works.

You make a noise against the duct tape, so he will take it off.

When he rips it, much of the skin around your mouth goes with it.

The dock at White Beaches is over two hundred feet long. You know this because Holly and Simon calculated it, walking the length in their Crocs, and doing the math. Past that, it is a long way up the beach to The Wreck, not that it matters. There is nobody there; the bar's hurricane shutters fastened like eyes sewn closed.

There's nobody to hear you.

"Jack," you gasp, drinking in the humid air, the skin around your mouth on fire, "think! If you kill me, and you're supposed to be dead, how are you expecting to collect any insurance money?"

He pauses.

"Leave me here, Jack." You know it means nothing to him, to point out that your children will be orphans.

"But I can't, now you've seen me."

"It could all be a dream! I won't tell anyone. This is nothing but a bad dream."

The sheet is pooling around you, falling open to reveal nothing but underwear, your bare chest vulnerable to the open night sky. Any minute, the mosquitoes will find you and feast. There will be nothing you can do to defend yourself with both of your wrists tied to alternate corners of the raft.

"It's funny, you don't *look* pregnant." Jack tilts his head. "You always used to get this vein, right here…" He runs his finger between your breasts.

"Jack, back in the cottage, above the microwave, there's a conch pearl necklace. It's worth eighty thousand dollars. Take the necklace, leave me and—"

"You know what?" he interrupts, standing up. "You want to take the kids? We could take the kids. My first choice would be Sonny. She's always been my favorite. Simon's a little whiner. But Sonny, cute as a button, looks just like me. I was going to take her. Before, I had her coming with me that night, after she nearly walked in on us! I wrapped up, in the blanket, told her I was a ghost! But then," Jack's face goes dark, "those fucking idiots nearly ran her over! Plowed into me! Did this!" He points to the jagged scar on his head.

He stops untying the lines from the dock cleats, loops them back in a fast figure eight.

"You're right. Everyone, your family, thought you were too good, too smart for me, but you're not the only smart one. I'll go get the kids. Or at least Simon. I never told you, did I? It was one of the first things I did when he was born blue, a fifty thousand dollar policy. Just in case he didn't make it through the surgery. Who says that wasn't smart?" He ties off the dock line and squints up at the sky where the clouds are moving on fast-forward.

"Leave us, please, we'll only slow you down. You never wanted to be tied down."

"No, you're right! Brilliant! I'll go get the kids! A family adventure! We never did do Disney."

Before he leaps out of the boat, he bends low and slaps the duct tape back over the burning skin around your mouth, pushing it so hard your lips mash into your teeth. You taste blood.

CHAPTER 54

Dean

Dean lets himself into her cottage through the screen porch, sliding the door back. It's dark inside, only one light on up at the landing, her bedroom door open, Simon and Sonny's door closed.

The living room flickers blue from her TV, the Weather Channel, images of roofless homes and floating cars in Jamaica. The ticker reads: **The Cayman Islands are upgraded from Hurricane Warning to Hurricane Watch, the final stage before impact.**

"We're predicting early bands of rain, followed by wind and surge, to reach the sister islands first and then Grand Cayman by early to mid-morning. Sometime in the coming night, the final course will be known. A slow moving, double-walled Category Five, forecasters are hoping for a turn, like Hurricane Mitch in 1998, which passed 180 miles to the south, sparing the Cayman Islands from a direct hit."

"Juliet?" he calls.

"Well, what the fuck are you doing here again?"

Dean spins—there's a man in her kitchen. He's small, maybe 5'8", and thin, but muscles cord his forearms, where he is rifling through the cupboard above the microwave. At first, Dean thinks it's an early looter, but then he sees, if he looks past the scars, the beard and the general grime, the same sparkle from Sonny's eyes, Simon's long chin and narrow shoulders.

"Where's Juliet?"

Between the Caribbean cookbook and the wall, Jack locates the Kirk Freeport box.

"My wife? Waiting in my boat, with the money. Probably halfway through our first bottle of champagne." Jack opens the jewelry box and yanks the necklace from its black velvet display, slipping it easily into the pocket of his camo cargo pants.

"What are you doing here?"

"Um, picking up my kids? We're going to outrun the storm. We're meeting a boat, in Cuba. I have connections everywhere, Nicaragua, Roatan, Dubai. There's a house, in the Carpathian mountains, remote, ski-in, ski-out all winter long. Guarded by black bears. Nobody will ever find us."

"Juliet knew about all this? She knew you weren't dead?"

Juliet might not be everything you think she is.

"How rude of you to underestimate her. Just because she's beautiful doesn't mean she has no brains. But then, it takes a pretty simple guy to think that she'd choose you, when she could have … me." Jack moves toward the stairs, the bedroom, where Dean imagines Simon and Sonnet are sleeping. The clock on the microwave says it's after midnight.

"Dad!" It's Luc, pounding on the front door of Juliet's cottage. "Dad, we have to go!"

"Smart boy. You take what's yours, I'll take what's mine. The necklace is mine. Upstairs? Those are mine. The baby inside her, also mine. What was it she said, earlier? We'll see what's left, after the storm?"

How many more signs do you need? Dean berates himself as he runs out to the parking lot. *Everyone tried to warn you! How could you be so blinded by love, so stupid? Save what you have left!*

But Luc is standing beside their van, looking like he's been slapped.

"Dad, she's dead."

"Who?"

"The Brave Little Toaster! I went to start her up, so you could go get the littles. She won't turn over, nothing."

"But I just picked you up at the airport a few hours ago." When Dean walks around the side, he sees the gas door hanging ajar, a loop of cut garden hose dangling out like intestines. "Dead, or out of gas?"

Luc reaches inside the driver's seat and pops the hood.

Something is not right, about Jack and Juliet, but Dean can't think straight now. *Save what you have left!*

Why did Jack say, what's upstairs is mine? Juliet is in the boat, but Simon and Sonnet are in the cottage, in their beds?

"Oh, shit, Dad. Shit."

Juliet would not leave her children.

"What is it?" Dean comes around the front and sees, from the lone light of the parking lot, what Luc means.

"Someone stole the battery."

"Luc," Dean's heart thuds in his ears, "are all the work boats already moved to the yacht club?"

CHAPTER 55

Juliet

Y ou have time, alone under the cloudy sky, your arms tied out to either corner of the raft, not so different from Jack's mother's beloved crucifixes, to make some peace with what will come next. Tears run down your cheeks; they burn like hot wax on a candlestick. You marvel at the speed of the night-silver clouds traveling across the dark sky, so that the quarter moon and sprinkling of stars are only visible in small windows. You wait for it, a glimpse of light in the dark beyond, the comforting glow of the ever-present orb, a gift. Each time you spy the moon, you get to make a small moon prayer:

—let Jack change his mind, decide not to bring your children

—let the way he kills you be drowning, the deep blue water, not the knife by your feet

—let you be unconscious, not struggling, when the liquid floods your lungs, or when the sharks find your body

—let Dean realize your children have been left behind, don't let them face the hurricane alone, banging on the outside of Dean's closed shutters, mistaken for projectiles in the storm

You won't be greedy. You don't ask for him to come back tonight, one more time—why would he, after you pushed him away?—to the bedroom at the top of the stairs. You don't waste a moon wish on him seeing your bed, the missing sheet, the tangle of covers, and realizing you need help. No, that's too much.

—let him raise them, after you're gone, take them home to the split-level in Ypsilanti, the one you saw in his search history, with the awful globe lights and sculptured arborvitae

—let Luc coach Simon's Little League

—let Holly go with Sonny to pick out a prom dress

Then Jack comes back, half-running down the dock, a hitch in his gait like a three-legged dog.

See, you think, when you see he is alone.

One of your prayers is already being answered.

CHAPTER 56

Dean

When a storm comes from the Southeast, as most Atlantic hurricanes bearing down on the Cayman Islands do, mariners have to make decisions. Will their boats be safest tied to the floating docks in the yacht club, or is it better to run them up into the gnarled knots of the mangroves, and secure them to the largest trunks and roots in the brackish, inland forest? Like the farmers who release their animals, locals know that sometimes the island itself is the best way to protect what matters.

"We moved everything else to the yacht club this morning," Luc calls over his shoulder as they run, "but Tony says he always likes to keep one boat on this side, just in case the road gets washed out or anything. He's friends with a guy, who has an empty bush lot in Cayman Kai, lets him run the Whaler up into the mangroves there."

They have sprinted most of the way, along Dean's old running path, to a wild lot filled with sea grape and mangrove, Dean gasping out what he knows as they go, about Juliet and Jack. He's glad that because of his runs, he can keep up with his son, grateful for the moments when the clouds move off the moon, and they can see what they're doing when they reach the boat.

"Tell me what to do, how can I help?" Dean cries, pushing through the twisted bush.

"Go up to the bow, and when I tell you, push as hard as you can!"

Luc works fast, untying, dropping the motors and starting the engine. He turns on the running lights so Dean can see to step on the twisted roots like curly balance beams, bracing himself against the front of the boat.

"Okay, push her off, Dad!" Luc puts the boat in reverse. The stench of smoke and silt fills the air as Dean shoves off, then throws himself over the bow.

"But how will we find them in the dark?" Dean asks as they make their way out of the shallows, heading for the open Sound.

"There's a lot of cloud cover, but there should be some dive lights, a flashlight, in the center bench. See if any of those work?"

Dean finds two large flashlights, and he hands one to Luc, who is driving, focused, eyes squinting.

"You said his boat was fast, when you saw him out at Stingrays?"

Luc nods, leaning into the motion as they accelerate in the deeper water, the throttle maxed. "I wouldn't call it a boat. It's an inflatable, a glorified dinghy. He's got a forty, but we've got twin 250s." Luc yells over the engine, clapping his hand on Dean's shoulder. "If it's a matter of speed, we can easily catch him, Dad!"

"Really?" It's a new phenomenon, having to ask Luc for information, reassurance. Dean scans the dark ocean flying by on either side of them, their flashlights catching on flecks of spray.

"He said Cuba?" Luc yells. "And when I saw the boat, it was tied up at the main dock, so, "Luc checks the illuminated compass on the dash, "we know he'll be headed north. Question is, will he go out the break in the reef up by Rum Point, or head for Main Channel?"

"But you said we can get there before them, faster?" Dean leans into the speed beside his son, sea spray in their faces. He has the larger flashlight, shining out on the black water all around. Beside them, silver flying fish break the surface, singing along in the boat's arching wake. "If we get there first, we can rescue her?"

"Yeah, only... " Luc doesn't say more. He swivels his head, eying the vastness of open water in front of them.

"Only what? He said he was planning to outrun the storm. To meet a boat in Cuba. So which way would he go?"

"Dad," Luc says carefully, "he's not going to make it all the way to Cuba, if he's in the inflatable I saw, with a forty horsepower. Not even with all the gas from the van."

"So what are you saying? Maybe another boat is picking them up here? Where would they go for that?"

Luc's eyes are trained straight ahead, on the red and green channel markers, distant points of destination. Is it Dean's imagination, or are they slowing down?

"Or," Luc says, like he is speaking to Owen, "maybe the plan is, just not to be found. As far as the rest of the world knows, the guy's already dead." Luc lets up on the throttle, slowly, and the boat settles, coming off its plane. Dean and Luc shift their weight to adjust. Luc turns to him, "He's got nothing left to lose, Dad."

"Then why are you stopping?"

Up ahead, Dean sees the channel markers that define the edges of the barrier reef. Beyond that, the North Wall forms some of the most dramatic deep dive sites in the Caribbean. The underwater cliff is six thousand feet, straight down.

"We have to keep going!"

"Dad," Luc begins, their engine idling, their boat tossed lightly on the small waves inside the reef. "If we knew exactly where they were going, maybe, but—" Luc stops. "If they were even going where he said."

"Use your radio, call the police boat!"

"And say what? It's the night before a hurricane, there's no moon to speak of and we have no idea where they're headed."

"We can't stop looking! Do you understand? Si and Sonny were upstairs! Juliet would not go to the boat and leave her children behind, not for five minutes! Not by choice!"

For a moment their eyes meet, and Dean knows Luc is thinking of what both he and Tony have told him, about that night in June, with Sonny in the street.

"No, you know her, Luc! She would not leave her kids!"

"Okay, hang on, I have an idea." Luc flips the switch that cuts their engine completely, puts his finger to his lips. "Shh."

And then Dean hears it, distant, in the direction of the Rum Point markers, the whine and slap of a small craft, going for broke. Luc engages their engine and slams the boat into gear. "Let's go!"

"Juliet!" Dean runs up to the bow of the Whaler, his hands cupped around his mouth. "I'm here!"

CHAPTER 57

Juliet

Through the blur of salt spray in your eyes, you see lights ahead, out on the dark water, a red boat and a green boat. If your mouth were not taped, you could call to them. Beside you, Jack is crouched, driving the Zodiac as fast as he can, the rise and slap of the swells increasing as you get closer to the two colorful boats. Both of you are drenched from spray, shivering in the night air.

He looks every bit like Simon, back home, playing his cousin's Nintendo, controller in hand, intent on winning the game.

No, don't think of your children. Leave them where you left them under the wishing moon sky at the dock: *Luc coaching Si's winning baseball game, Dean and Owen cheering, Sonny twirling in front of Holly in a seafoam dress, her dark curls piled on top of her head.*

The red and green lights, you realize as you get closer, are not boats. They are lonely buoys, bobbing nuns, the channel markers. Luc has told you and Dean about them, about the natural cuts in the barrier reef that surrounds North Sound, protecting it from the deep blue of the vast Caribbean.

As soon as you pass the colorful Christmas lights, the waves are bigger—you ride up and down each one like the dragon train kiddie coaster at the fair. Up, and down, with a slap that jerks your wrists against their ropes. A wave breaks over the front of the dinghy and Jack curses, looking over his shoulder. He slows the engine. You strain against the ropes, try to turn your head, to see what he saw, but you can't.

Jack lunges for the knife in the bottom of the boat, and you're afraid you've pushed your luck, that only one of your moon wishes will come true. But instead of stabbing you, Jack starts mumbling.

"Dead weight. Can't overload the vessel. Small craft warning. This isn't how I wanted this to go." He saws at the ropes chafing your left wrist. He doesn't meet your eyes. "But if he wants you," he switches to the other arm, cutting it free, "he's going to have to find you!"

Jack yanks you to your feet and you both stumble, like a surf simulator, as your boat is tossed and pitched on another dark swell. Behind your boat, inside the breaking waves on the reef, past the channel markers, red and green, are the lights of a boat, with a figure on the prow. Your freed hands fly up to your mouth, ripping at the tape that silences you.

Stars explode in your eyes, the staggering whip of your head snapping on your neck, the stunning crack of Jack's hand—

Is this your third moon wish coming true? You blink to clear your vision as Jack grips your shoulders, steadying himself against the next wave.

"I do love you, I hope you understand," Jack is saying as, wrists pinned in his grip, he drags you, stumbling.

Above the sound of the wind, and the thrum of the coming boat, you hear the words, "I am here!"

You try to call back, but the tape smothers your voice. Searchlights from the approaching boat blind you—they're close enough that they have to cut their engine, or risk coming down on top of yours. You make out the second figure at the console, *a white knight, in a white polo.*

With the next wave, Jack shoves you toward the front of the Zodiac, the clouds shift, and the moon illuminates the knife in his hand. "I don't want to have to do this, but, you understand, it's only money…"

You push back against Jack, clutching for the knife, your fingers closing over the familiar, worn handle, but when he shoves, he's stronger, and you stumble, fall. The sting of the water slaps your naked back, knocking the breath from your lungs as you go under.

Breathe! You claw at the tape over your mouth as your head surfaces, so close your cheek scrapes up the canvas side of the Zodiac. The tape tears free and you gasp.

"Juliet!" the lights pass over your face.

"HERE!"

You realize you're still holding the knife, as the next wave lifts you, and then forces you under, sucking and choking, deep into your lungs.

You open your eyes to the sting of saltwater, desperate to find the surface, the watery green moonlight above. When you break, you inhale and scream, flashlights dancing on the water around you, before the next wave slams something crushingly heavy on top of you, plunging you back into the liquid blackness. A whale, a shark, you think, but underwater, too close, you hear the thrum of an engine surging to life, feel the current, a blender of bubbles on your face, inches away.

You push against the bottom of Jack's boat, forcing yourself down, deeper into the abyss, away from the churning water and spinning propellor. With a surge of adrenaline, you lash out with the only thing you have: the mango knife, slicing deep into the inflatable pontoon of the Zodiac.

We'll make more of it.

CHAPTER 58

Juliet

On Grand Cayman, with a hurricane approaching, it can be difficult to find what you're looking for at sunrise on a Sunday.

There is a knock on the exam room door at the hospital in George Town. You lift your head, expecting the doctor, or the kind-hearted nurse; the answer you have been waiting for.

But it's Dean. He closes it behind him, and for the first time since the boat, you are alone, together.

"Wind's pretty steady," he says. His beautiful brow furrows, arches like the curve of a boomerang. "We're, um, getting a lot of rain out there."

"Yes, I can hear it in here."

"Tony came by," he adds. "The pilot never showed last night. Luc and he took the kids home; I gave them the van. Said they'll take everyone to your place, since it has two stories. They'll wait for us, and then we'll close up the shutters, lock ourselves in. Hope for the best."

Nothing has changed. Though you're speaking, it's about the weather, storm planning, the children, practicalities. You look down at the marks on your wrists from the rope.

The night before, it was Dean's arms you clutched, who hauled you out of the deep water, wrapped you in the shirt off his back, crushed you to him, while over his shoulder, Jack's raft disappeared over a wave. Dean held you, silently, all the way back to Rum Point while you shook, your teeth chattering. At the dock, Luc had to pry your fingers open, to get the mango knife out.

"How are you?" There are several deep scratches on Dean's forearms, either the mangroves, or your own fingers, clawing up him, escaping the surging ocean.

"I'm okay." At the cottages, in his bedroom, Dean dressed you, like a child. Layers and layers of his summer clothes against your constant shaking. "How are *you* doing?"

"Physically," you touch your tender cheek, where Jack hit you. The raw skin around your mouth and lips still stings. "Okay. I told the nurse I was in a boating accident, that I fell in when we were moving boats, for the storm. I swallowed a lot of salt water. She said all my vitals look good."

"How about, mentally?" Dean asks, and you note that he does not joke, doesn't say anything about being a trained professional.

"Okay. Processing."

You remember the give of the raft, your knife leaving deep tracks, plunging into its underbelly.

"The kids are really fine?"

"Everyone's fine."

"Luc?"

Working with a headlamp, Luc had found a gas can in the compressor shack, a replacement battery for the Brave Little Toaster in a White Beaches truck. You shivered in the front seat, while Luc had carried Sonnet, half-asleep, and then Owen out to the van in the first light of dawn.

"He came back from the café with four Dairy Milk bars and three bags of chips. Breakfast of champions."

You nod.

"Si, of course, was thrilled."

You try to smile.

"Any other news?" Dean looks at your abdomen.

You shake your head.

Dean leans against the exam table.

There is a painting on the wall behind him, a landscape of a stream flowing through an icy, Northern forest, mossy rocks and mini waterfalls. You think of the irony—that the one over Simon's bed in the NICU you stared at for all those months was a poster of Cassatt's oil painting *Two Children at the Seashore*.

"Nobody is ever happy where they are—everyone is trying to escape to a different version of paradise."

"What?" Dean looks worried. "What are you talking about?"

"The painting, behind you. It looks like the mountains, the Poconos, back home. But, we're here."

"Juliet, are you okay?"

You hate that he is still using the full version of your name.

"No." You tuck your hands as hard as you can around you, your fingers curling behind the lower ribs of your back, holding everything inside. Your voice is hoarse when you confess, "I cut Jack's raft, with the knife."

"You what?"

"When I fell in, when I was trapped underneath it, I punctured it, stabbed it, as many times as I could." You look away. Who could love you now?

"He was trying to kill you!" Dean straightens, crosses the room to you. "You had every right to do that! He left you to drown! He was willing to orphan your children!"

"But, I killed him."

"No," Dean looks deep into your eyes. "How was it, you said it to me, that night? When I told you about Amélie? You called it the ultimate mercy. You 'spared him an even uglier end.'"

"Do you remember everything I say?"

"When it's important," Dean says earnestly, "I remember."

"You asked, earlier, if I had anything to tell you." Your voice is low, hoarse. "I have so many things to tell you, I don't know where to start."

"'Start at the beginning,'" Dean quotes Lewis Carroll—*Alice in Wonderland.* "'And when you come to the end, stop.'"

"I was trying to tell you, last night, if you were choosing me because of the money, and the necklace, I need to be clear: Jack's insurance may never pay out. I don't have millions of dollars." You sniff, gesturing down. "I am basically a gigantic liability."

"I know about the insurance," Dean confesses. "I've been reading your deleted emails. I owe you an apology. It was a terrible breach of trust. But why would you ever think money was what attracted me to you?"

"You really don't care about the money," but as you are saying it, you know it's true. This is Dean.

"God, no!" he roars. "I'm relieved; I'm glad there's no money! Honestly, I was starting to feel out of my league with you, like I wasn't sure what I had to offer you that you couldn't buy. I can't buy you eighty-thousand-dollar necklaces! I can't take you around the world."

"And all I wanted to do," you say, "was put down roots."

He reaches for you, to cup your face, but stops. He rubs his left shoulder with his right palm, his face twisted in pain, like trying to touch you hurts him.

"What's wrong?"

"I think I might have torn my rotator cuff, when I punched Tony."

"You what! When?"

"Just now." Dean's shoulders round down to match his brow bone, mumbling, "The kids didn't see, and I sort of missed. I think he's alright."

"Dean, why?"

"For what Luc said, that he had to stop Tony from taking advantage of you, for the way he's behaved all summer. All my life really. It felt good, or it would've, if I'd actually connected." Dean rubs his shoulder again. "Probably misplaced anger, directed at the wrong man. Storm stress, adrenaline overload, losing everything I've found. I, I don't know how to go forward, anymore."

"I'm sorry I brought more tragedy to your life."

"Julie," Dean stops. You clutch at this—he has dropped the T from your name. He squares his shoulders, and takes a deep breath. "This summer, after, what we have been through… It's more than a lot of couples weather in a lifetime. But, we're here."

Overhead, there is a clatter, followed by the insistent slap of a palm frond against the roof of the hospital.

"There's still the issue of the storm, and the future, the kids…." His voice is rueful, and he has to clear his throat more than once. "Five, six of them…" he sighs, and is that a smile dancing at the corner of his mouth? "Whatever. A half dozen. Why not?"

But you don't want him to choose you because he's Dean, because he's honorable.

"These hands." Dean reaches for them, murmuring, "What is it about hospitals that makes the hands of the women I love so cold?"

He cups his own over them and blows into the space, warming your chilled fingers. The fluorescent light bulbs hum, as loud as cicadas in a Bucks County summer and over them, the steady thrumming of the rain. You can feel your heartbeat pulsing in your cheeks. Is this the first time he has ever said he loves you, in the present?

Suddenly, the door flies open, and the nurse throws her arms in the air crying, "Wonderful news!"

Dean tilts his forehead to yours until they touch, forming a peak over your clutched hands. He closes his eyes, like he is bracing for a blow.

"We've scared Dean off—he's running!" You can see every one of the nurse's teeth, all the way back to her molars, in the broad expanse of her smile.

"What?"

"We'll get wind and plenty of weather, but the eye of the storm turned, going south. Just like Mitch! The Good Lord is sparing the Cayman Islands again."

Breath fills the tented space between your foreheads, relief floods and warms your hands, still clutched in his.

Behind the nurse, a redheaded doctor has a clipboard in her hand. She waits for the nurse to stand aside.

"This is the couple waiting for the labs?" she asks in a clipped, British accent. "I'm Dr. Childer, I have the results of your bloodwork."

Dean squeezes your hands, but his eyes are open, searching yours. There are no words for this moment. You study his face but can't read it.

"Everything, your panels, look remarkably normal, given what you've been through."

"Good," Dean murmurs, nodding.

"And on the pregnancy test, I don't know if it's champagne or tissues you'll be wanting," Dr. Childer says. "But it's negative."

"There's no baby?" Dean is still holding your hands in his.

It is impossible to read his voice: relief or regret?

"No baby," the doctor confirms.

"Now what?" you whisper.

POSTLUDE

December 24, 2007

Because Juliet and Dean have planted their kale on the north side of the house under a muslin shade cloth, it is thriving, thick, leafy and hardy, perfect for tonight's holiday dinner. It may not be a traditional Christmas eve, not the old Bucks County one with the extended Burke family crowding the banquet room at Lam's Chinese with eighteen Peking ducks, or Dean's sister Amy's with over-salted, over-thymed roast turkey and giblet gravy, but it is time for new traditions. Besides, they have to eat early tonight. They have plans.

Juliet cuts the ruffled edges of the kale into her wire basket. She'll sauté it with garlic from the kitchen garden, a little dash of wine, sausages and Dean's specialty, rosemary-sundried tomatoes, crumbling some of Holly's dairy goat's fresh *queso blanco* over the top.

Dean and Simon are experimenting in the raised beds along the back fence with Heritage raspberries, recently planted for the cooler winter weather after they chilled the canes in a paper bag at the bottom of their refrigerator for a month.

She has promised Lear and Jenna and their boys a berry cobbler, as good as their grandmother ever made, when they fly down to visit after New Year's. Throughout the fall, Lear has called with news from the States: Meridian has agreed to review the rebuttable proclamation of death case before the seven year time frame.

"It makes sense, Jules, when a body is lost at sea."

Marty was found in the UAE and extradited to the United States. Because of his testimony, the original incorporation documents that included Juliet were declared invalid and unenforceable.

"Jules, you can come home any time," Lear said.

"I am home," she told him, her gaze out the window: Doc's million-dollar view of the Caribbean.

Doc's private practice client list that was included in the sale price of the Northside house was exactly six people. But since then, there have been a steadily-growing stream of them stopping by. The word is out—the American Professor who strung the two hammocks under the coco trees at Doc's place is a good listener, and he'll take payment in everything from local honey to Stingray beer.

In the mornings, Juliet runs Wondertime, a home-based preschool where they do shell crafts and garden, bake bread and make homemade basil pesto plucked from between the delphinium and English phlox in Geraldine's old flowerbeds. Dean teaches two days a week at the College of the Cayman Islands. On the days when he drives the long commute to town, he shops for provisions at Hurley's, stopping for chicken feed and six of Frankie's fresh mango smoothies on his way home.

"Miss Julie and the Professor!" It is their neighbor, Miss Dahlia, whose granddaughter is one of the nine children enrolled in Wondertime, whose son sometimes sits beside Dean on the hammocks and talks, looking out over the sparkling sea.

"Merry Christmas eve," she calls as Miss Dahlia makes her way along the path in the towering sea grapes that border their properties. Miss Dahlia hands Juliet a cassava cake, wrapped in cloth and still warm, dense and heavy as a newborn baby in her arms.

The families sit across from each other on Sundays, when they attend the white-washed church out by the old Tortuga Club, Dean's idea, to give the children a space for gratitude, a ready-made community and a moral compass. He and Juliet have to bookend Owen to keep him from running out into the aisle, and they reach over his head to clutch hands when it is time to pray. There is plenty to be grateful for.

Sunday nights are becoming famous around Northside: Dean's crepes made with Sonny's eggs, Holly's banana pancakes and Simon's berries, a potluck breakfast for dinner. Last week, their little beachfront house bulged with thirty guests and a steady flow of children streaking sandy-footed in and out to the fire pit on the beach. Sugar and Wilton, the two potcakes Doc and Geraldine left behind, barked and joined in the chase. Even Uncle Tony and Uncle Leo stopped by.

"Miss Dahlia," Dean tells her, wiping the sweat from his forehead, "according to my boys, you told them we need to bring more wheelbarrows of white sand up from Old Man Bay to make the yard look like a snowfall?"

"Mmhmm!" she laughs. "Every Caymanian around Old Man Bay knows you back your yard on Christmas eve!"

"This place will make an old man of me!" He throws an arm around Juliet, but really, Dean has never felt better.

"And are you two lovebirds ready for the Christmas float tonight?" Miss Dahlia asks them.

The float is another Caymanian tradition, three flatbed trailers decorated with thatch roofs and Christmas lights in red, yellow, green and gold, carrying a living Nativity complete with real burros and chickens, the coveted roles of Mary and Joseph and Jesus, an angel choir and a sixteen piece, heavily-amplified band.

After dinner, they will join the island Christians who ride the slow-moving, three hour circuit from North Side all the way to West Bay, singing and clapping, serenading the balmy island night with a combination of calypso and Christmas carols.

Later, they have to set their alarms for a Skype with Luc and Bridget in Auckland, fifteen hours ahead, where they teach SCUBA diving and attend college. They are training for the Hawaii IronMan the following October—Dean and Juliet talk about leaving the kids with Miss Dahlia and meeting them there, cheering them on.

They talk about the ones that came before. Sonny swears she inherited her love of raw carrots from Amélie. Simon knows he gets his dark hair from his father, but it is Dean who shakes his shoulder and takes him out to the flats for bone fishing at sunrise. Holly thinks she might be a dancer, or a botanist, or a writer, or an artisan cheesemaker—it changes daily. Owen sleeps between them at night, horizontally, like the cross to an H, his head on Juliet's ribcage, his feet braced against Dean. He won't remember anything before his island life and family.

Juliet and Dean revel in the quiet and ritual, the sameness of their days in Northside, as predictable as the ever-sunny Cayman Islands forecast. Sometimes, it rains, a relief for their cistern and garden.

"Girls," Juliet calls to Sonny and Holly now, "run up to the College Fund and see if your ladies have any eggs for Dad-dean?"

Across North Side Road is the landlocked half of their acre lot, purchased from Doc with the funds from the sale of their homes in the States. Up here in the tangled overgrowth and scrubby grass, Sonny's chickens and Holly's three goats run loose. Dean has dubbed it the "Send Six Kids to College Fund." There are only five—there is no baby now, but they imagine, hope, whisper in the dark of their bedroom with the sea breezes, that there might be one more.

"Next year," Miss Dahlia says as if she can read their minds, "we're going to have your littlest chicky to play the baby Jesus in our Christmas float." She winks at Juliet and Dean. "I know what I know."

AUTHOR'S NOTE

This story began as an actual dream ten years ago—I was on book tour for CHOSEN, in a hotel room in Santa Monica with my three kids in one king bed. At book clubs throughout the tour, readers kept asking me to write 'a love story with a happy ending'. They mentioned that they liked Nicholas Sparks and I laughed and said I didn't know if I had that kind of story in me. That night, I dreamed Dean and Juliet, and the messy beautiful of their chaos and loss and love the second time around. I sat up and scribbled the whole thing down before my kids woke up. Maybe it was the sound of the ocean through my window, I don't know. I wanted to tell a story with island themes, and I have always loved Rum Point and the quieter side of Grand Cayman. I consider this both a tribute to my memories of simpler times on remote beaches, and to the people in my life who hope for a second chance at love.

If you want to continue the conversation, please check out the Book Club Discussion Questions section on my website. I am also happy to stop in with a glass of wine for a virtual visit!
www.chandrahoffman.com/for-book-clubs

If you loved this story and want to let others know, please consider posting a review on Goodreads, BookBub or wherever you purchased the novel.
www.goodreads.com/chandrahoffman
www.bookbub.com/profile/chandra-hoffman

I am hard at work on my next book. To stay up to date on my newest releases, please sign up for my newsletter.
www.chandrahoffman.com/subscribe

ACKNOWLEDGMENTS

My thanks...

To Romy and Asya, the architects and design artists of this carefully constructed novel.

To Jessica and Linda, my most trusted East and West Coast betas.

To Emily, whose keen eye catches everything.

To my ARC and street team, for reading and shouting out these stories from the rooftops.

To Hayden, Macrae and Piper, who keep asking what and how I'm doing, even when I forget to buy food.

To Jonathan, who continues to ride the ride with me.

Made in United States
Orlando, FL
11 September 2022

22296380R00163